GYPSY
BLOOD
MOON

GYPSY BLOOD MOON

ISBN 978-1-938842-78-8
Copyright © 2025 by Dan Watts

Published by Bardolf & Company
www.bardolfandcompany.com

Cover design by *shawcreativegroup.com*

To my wife Sherry

Your intelligence, patience, wisdom,
and empathy bring joy to everyone
around you.

Thank you for balancing
and completing my life.

GYPSY
BLOOD
MOON

Dan Watts

Bardolf & Company
Sarasota, Florida

PROLOGUE

CASTLE
OF VLAD DRACUL

WALLACHIA
1437 AD

"**O**h, Sweet Mary, Mother of Our Lord, deliver me of this child. Pray it be a daughter. A daughter!"

Within the confines of her stonewall bed chamber, Princess Vasilissa Dracul bit down hard on the leather strap between her teeth as the next round of labor contractions engulfed her. Cries of agony poured from the young princess' lips like those of a suffering spirit locked in the dungeons of Hell. Ioana, her loyal maidservant, held her hand and wiped the beads of sweat from her brow.

As the pain eased, Vasilissa lay back against the pillow but held on to Ioana's hand with a claw-like grip. "Not a son, not a son," she whispered, half-delirious. "You promised."

Cejorn, the trusted midwife of the Moldovian royal family, looked on, evaluating the princess' condition dispassionately. She could see nothing out of the ordinary. The delivery was going well, although the outcome might cost them all their lives. "Another push, my Lady, and soon it will be over," she encouraged.

She had arrived six months earlier when it became obvious that Vasilissa was with child and quickly understood why the princess wanted a girl. During her time at the castle, Cejorn had witnessed the cruel training Count Dracus imposed on his two sons—Prince

Micea, the son of his first wife, who died in childbirth, and young Vlad, the bastard child of his mistress, Câlt-Una. It was one thing to instruct young men in the art of warfare, but Dracus was determined his sons become sadistic killers who relished inflicting cruelty and pain on their victims. He beat them mercilessly when they didn't perform to his satisfaction. To teach them how he wanted captured Turks, their sworn enemies, executed, he had his sons practice on helpless farm animals—tethered goats, sheep, and pigs—gutting them to cause maximum pain before ending their misery by slashing their throats. The central castle court became an abattoir among the squealing and screaming of the tormented beasts, and the young butchers were steeped in blood.

No wonder Vasilissa wanted no child of hers to be part of that.

Little did her parents know what a cruel fate they bestowed on their daughter when they married her to Prince Dracus, a powerful nobleman. But Vasilissa was not one to bemoan her misfortune. She came from proud Viking warrior stock and wove a desperate plot. When she presented her plan to Ioana and Cejorn, swearing them to secrecy on their oath of loyalty to her and the House of Moldavia, they had agreed. Under no circumstances would they let Dracus have another male heir.

When the next spasms racked her body, Vasilissa squeezed Ioana's hand so hard that it turned white. "NO, NO, the pain. I cannot do this!" she yelped. "O Merciful Father, God of all that is holy, deliver me."

Cejorn noted with grim satisfaction that the baby's head was crowning. She glanced at the side table where her midwife's basket lay. In it was the tiny, cold corpse of a baby that had been stillborn a week earlier to a young peasant woman. Cejorn had attended the delivery, paid the mother for her silence, then buried the dead child in the snow until her lady's time came.

Another contraction wracked Vasilissa as she started to nod off, and she screamed. "Release this burden from me!" she pleaded desperately.

Cejorn whispered close to her ear, "You are doing fine, Dear One. Relief is drawing nigh. Now push!"

"Oh God, please!" Another ear-splitting scream issued from Vasilissa's lips as her body seized at the pressure of delivery.

The baby slipped from the womb into Cejorn's hands—a boy! Anguish seized her heart, but she didn't have time to give in to her feelings.

Ioana's eyes filled with tears and she whispered to the exhausted Vasilissa, "You have born a beautiful son, my Lady."

Vasilissa's face was a disarray of conflicting emotions—pride, joy, and dread. Then a stoic determination came over her, just as another contraction distorted her expression and the afterbirth started to burst forth. Quickly, before the baby's first cry, Cejorn filled his mouth with dry gauze. She cut and tied the umbilical cord and swaddled his arms and legs tightly. While she presented his sweet face to her mistress, she nodded to Ioana. Vasilissa kissed his rosy lips and drew the sign of a cross in blood upon his forehead.

"I shed but a single tear for my little prince, knowing I will have a lifetime to mourn his loss," she said faintly.

She affixed a gold brooch to the swaddling cloth, her token of love from his birth mother. It had been crafted by a Gypsy smith and embossed with the symbol of Vlad Dracul and the Order of the Dragon—a serpent biting its tail. A lock of Vasilissa's golden hair was wrapped tightly inside.

With jaw clenched in resolve, Cejorn took the corpse of the baby girl wrapped in clean linen from Ioana. She placed it beside Vasilissa and took the boy from her, holding him up for his mother to see one last time. His muffled cries were no louder than a mewling kitten's. Then, Cejorn handed him to Ioana who wrapped him in the cloth bloodied from his birth and placed him in the midwife basket under the afterbirth.

The maidservant hesitated for a moment until Vasilissa said, "Go. Save him. Time is of the essence. I will give this poor child here a Christian burial and ask forgiveness from the Lord for what we have done."

Ioana curtsied and hurried out of the chamber. On the other side of the thick oak door, the other maids and attendants were waiting with worried expressions. When Ioana sadly shook her head, some of them burst into tears and started to wail. She didn't notice an older servant giving her a searching look as she hastened into the torch-lit passageway.

As Ioana rounded the corner, she spotted Lord Dracus marching toward her followed by his entourage of guards. Their long swords clanked by their sides, and the metal scabbards flickered, catching the light of the wall torches as they approached. The heavy scent of smoke and coal oil from the lamps they carried assaulted her senses and her heart beat so loudly she worried the others could hear it. Holding the basket close to her gown, she kneeled submissively, avoiding Dracus' eyes. Her voice shook—she hoped he would take her fear as grief. "Most humble regrets, Sire. Precious heavenly princess, she was born not of this world. Sweet angel, she rests tonight in our Lord and Savior's arms. Her mother fares well. She was brave but quietly weeps as she mourns next to her baby. I will attend to her as soon as I dispose of these filthy rags through the sewer gates."

Dracus looked at the trembling maidservant with dark, piercing eyes and sneered. He cared little about the loss of a baby girl or the grief of his young Norse wife. He gestured to his guards and said with a deep, raspy voice, "Let us go from here and give the princess time to rest in peace. Cejorn and my servants can attend to her grief."

Ioana rose, curtsied, and waited for them to pass. She closed her eyes briefly, thanking the Lord for protecting her. Then she proceeded swiftly through the castle's lower labyrinthine corridors until she came to a small oak door. She put the basket down, removed the wooden crossbeam that barred it, and turned the key in the large metal lock.

When Ioana pried the door open, a cold breeze blew in from outside, chilling her. The flickering light from a wall torch shone on the snow-covered ground. She called softly into the darkness, but there was no reply. As her eyes adjusted, she could see the forest across the meadow. She called again, a little louder. Still nothing. She started to panic, not knowing what to do, when she heard a soft female voice, "Here." To Ioana, it was like a sound from Heaven, and relief swept over her.

A dark figure emerged from a small alcove in the castle walls. It was a young Gypsy woman bundled in a woolen cape with a colorful, knitted shawl peeking out from under her hood. Ioana picked up the swaddled child, wrapped in bloody cloth, and thrust him into the stranger's arms. "Take care of this precious gem. His mother loves him too much for his soul to remain among these heathens."

The Gypsy girl nodded once and left. Ioana watched her walk carefully down the embankment and across the white field, her leather boots crunching the crusted snow underfoot until she reached the safety of the woods and merged with the shadows of the night.

Ioana shut the door, replaced the wooden crossbeam, and headed to the sewer gates where she tossed the bloody rags and remnants of the afterbirth. No one saw her. She shivered with cold but was glad that everything was going as planned. Her mistress would be pleased despite her suffering.

* * *

Later that night, however, things took a dangerous turn. When the older servant thought she heard a muffled baby cry, she had peeked through the keyhole. After mulling it over, she went to Lord Dracus and shared her suspicions that she had witnessed the birth of a baby boy. His paranoia roused—he was susceptible to plots and conspiracies—he marched to his wife's room and confronted her. His wrath was terrifying. He threatened to throw her and her

"Viking" accomplices into the dungeon and torture the truth out of them. He had his soldiers search the castle and its surroundings by torchlight. They came upon the footsteps in the snow, leading to and from the castle, but the wind had blown hard enough that it was impossible to determine when they had been made.

Dracus continued to rage in impotent fury, convinced he had been deceived and deprived of a rightful heir. Vasilissa and Cejorn, in turn, denied all accusations. Their vigorous, unwavering disavowals gave strength to Ioana when she threatened to falter under the Count's relentless onslaught. Fortunately, the other maidservants swore that they had seen and heard nothing.

For three days, Vassilisa, Cejorn, and Ioana were confined to the princess' chambers under heavy guard, in peril of their lives, amid renewed threats of torture and execution. Meanwhile, mayhem struck the Kingdom of Wallachia. Soldiers continued to scour the castle and its environs for any sign of an infant boy, but despite their intense search, they could find no evidence to confirm the older servant's story.

At some point, Cejorn decided enough was enough. She sent a secret message to Vasilissa's father about what was happening and met Dracus' ire with steely anger of her own. How dare he even imagine a mother would scheme to get rid of her firstborn child, delivered in agonizing pain? What kind of a man was he to add to the anguish Vasilissa felt at losing her baby girl?

When envoys from the King of Moldovia arrived, relating his extreme displeasure of the treatment of his daughter, Vlad had to give up his obsessive pursuit and publicly exonerate Vasilissa, even though he was not convinced that she'd told him the truth.

Seething, he exercised his sadistic cravings by punishing the older servant for insolence and spreading false rumors. He had her broken on the wheel, cut off her head, and mounted it on a pike high above the castle gate.

Chapter 1

IN THE ER
Tarpon Springs, Florida
Present time

Jonathan Curtis lay face down across the bed exactly as he had fallen asleep the night before. He wore only his boxer shorts, and his darkly tanned, muscular frame reflected the early morning light. Yesterday's late-night carousing with his best friend, Jimmy Pappas, had gotten the better of him.

When his alarm clock blared, he groaned and, flailing with his arm, knocked it off the bedside table. He squinted at the digital display on the floor: 6:45 a.m.

Jonathan sat bolt upright—he had only fifteen minutes to get to the hospital! A pain stabbed behind his forehead and his neck felt stiff from lying in the same spot all night. The warm shower water helped loosen it. After a quick shave, he threw on some blue scrubs, grabbed a white lab coat, and rushed out the front door.

Fortunately, it was a short jaunt by motorcycle from his two-bedroom, golf course apartment down the street to Tarpon Memorial Hospital. He was only five minutes late and his dark curly hair still glistened wet when he reported for ER duty.

He was happy to see all the exam rooms open and the stretchers empty. The way he felt this morning, he hoped it would be a normal day in the small-town emergency room: children with coughs and snotty noses; teenagers with cuts and scrapes; perhaps an adult suffering a heart attack or stroke. Jonathan could cope with any of that, even with a hangover.

There was only one patient, an old, disheveled-looking, shrimp fisherman, who stood swaying by the check-out counter. Jonathan remembered treating him before. He had one arm in a sling and multiple facial contusions—no doubt another early morning bar fight down at the Sponge Docks.

Valerie Hawkins, the head nurse, was processing his final discharge instructions. A slightly overweight, middle-aged blonde, she wore her hair brushed back and plastered down with cheap hair spray. Without looking up from her paperwork she said, "I see you're late again, Dr. Curtis."

Jonathan sighed inwardly. It was going to be another one of those days. "I'll be in the cafeteria," he muttered.

"I'll page you if I need you."

Irritated, he gave a polite nod. Thankfully, the other nurses were too busy with morning reports and hadn't taken notice of their exchange. Most of them did their jobs and followed the doctors' orders without fail. All except Hawkins, as she preferred to be called. With her stern demeanor and stiff, high-topped, nurse's cap, she moved around the ER like a wildcat on the prowl. She was known to eat young inexperienced doctors for lunch. At 28, Jonathan was the youngest physician on staff, and they had already had a few run-ins. He hoped they wouldn't have another one. He was not looking forward to doing battle with Hawkins today.

With his forehead throbbing again, Jonathan sauntered to the dispensary closet, grabbed two aspirin, tossed them into his mouth, and swallowed hard. Then he walked down the hallway to check on Dr. Clark, a surgical resident from Tampa General who had worked the ER night shift. Jonathan knocked on the door of the "sleep" room, cracked it open, and called out, "Come on, Sunshine, get up. More lives to save."

A labored grunt came from behind the door, followed by, "That you, Curtis. What time is it, anyway?"

"Quarter after seven, Clark. Get rolling. Surgical rounds with 'Dr. Buzzard' in an hour."

"Okay, yeah. Thanks, Man! I'll be out of here in ten minutes. Just let me get a quick shower and shave."

Jonathan smiled empathetically. He knew it was not unusual for moonlighting residents to get disoriented regarding the time or day. They often put in twenty-four to thirty-six hours at school, only to work another night shift or a full day to earn extra money.

No stranger to long hours, Jonathan had worked odd jobs in college and later on. At Duke, on a full academic scholarship, he filled in afternoons in the library and worked nights as a bartender. During medical school and residency, while other students studied every waking hour to make the grade, Jonathan spent his nights and weekends moonlighting. Although he felt tired and groggy throughout school, he still managed to stay at the top of his class. Now that he headed an Internal Medicine practice, he still worked part-time at the ER.

Not that his life was all work and no play. Since coming to Tarpon Springs, he had acquired several "toys," all used but in good shape: a 28-foot, open console fishing boat, a "Fat Boy" Harley Davidson motorcycle, and a 27-foot sailboat named *The Breezy Babe*.

The lights in the hallway to the cafeteria were flickering on when Jonathan turned the corner. As he reached for the main door, he could smell the aroma of freshly brewed coffee and almost taste the sweetness of oven-baked baklava. But before he could go inside, his cell phone vibrated. The letters "ER" glowed on the screen. "Call from dispatch. Come quickly."

Jonathan rushed to the ER, where a nurse handed him the emergency phone. It was patched through to a paramedic en route from Tarpon Lake in an ambulance with an ETA of less than six minutes. An eight-foot alligator had attacked a twelve-year-old boy during an early morning swim. Luckily, the boy's father had spotted the trouble and beat the alligator off with his fists. The paramedic reported that the boy was recovering from nearly drowning but had lost a great deal of blood. His right thigh had been mangled and lacerated as the alligator thrashed about. His vital signs were stable, an IV was running, and the bleeding was controlled with a pressure splint.

Jonathan alerted the staff, and Hawkins sprang into action. She ordered a nurse's aide to clear the emergency entrance, had another nurse ready a room for trauma treatment, and sent two large male orderlies outside to wait with Jonathan at the emergency entrance for the ambulance's arrival.

A Rescue Fire Truck pulled off the road, its sirens winding down. The gumball light atop continued to flash as it came to a stop. A uniformed paramedic jumped out and opened the two swinging rear doors. At the same time, a convoy of cars and trucks, which had followed the ambulance from the R.V. Park, arrived in the hospital parking lot.

As the paramedics unloaded the boy on a stretcher, a crowd of gawking spectators quickly assembled, including a few curious staff from the hospital. An overly enthusiastic female reporter from the local ABC television station elbowed her way through to get a few close shots and find eyewitnesses to interview.

The paramedic and two orderlies rolled the boy on a gurney through the onlookers, closely followed by Jonathan and the boy's panicked mother. An oxygen mask covered the youngster's face. He was caked with mud, and his hair and swim trunks were still wet.

While the medical team disappeared through the double doorway, a hospital security guard called to the crowd, "Everyone, go on home, now. The boy is in good hands."

People milled about for a while, then slowly dispersed. The news crew left, having gotten word that the boy's father was back at the lake gathering up a vigilante squad to hunt down and kill the "rogue" alligator. Nothing could be more exciting for the local 6 O'Clock News than a "blood and guts" story about a young boy, a mean-spirited alligator, and an angry mob of drunk rednecks.

When the orderlies and paramedics got to the examination cubicle, they lifted the boy onto the bed. He lay there cold, clammy and in shock as Jonathan carefully assessed the injury. He ordered a complete blood count, X-rays of the entire leg, and Doppler vascular studies to estimate the blood flow in the veins and arteries. He also called for a chest X-ray to rule out pneumonitis from lake water possibly remaining in the boy's lungs. While Hawkins quickly took another set of vital signs, he turned to the anxious mother sitting in a chair and asked her about her son's medical history. She answered with a jerky voice, interrupted by repeated sobs.

Within minutes, Radiology was on hand. Thankfully, the boy's lungs were clear, his leg not broken and the vasculature intact. Stat labs indicated that, while his hemoglobin levels were a little low, he would not require a blood transfusion.

Jonathan pulled the oxygen mask off the boy's face and smiled at him. Turning to his mother, he said, "He's going to be all right now, Ma'am."

The distraught woman gave a long, relieved moan.

Jonathan carefully removed the vacuum splint and pulled a spotlight overhead to examine the injuries more closely.

As the mother rose from her chair and looked, her eyes popped open. "My poor baby!" she gasped and immediately sat back down.

Jonathan caught the eyes of a nurse and indicated with his head for her to make sure she wasn't fainting, then turned his attention back to the boy's leg. Multiple deep, V-shaped lacerations extending through the fat layer exposed the muscles of the thigh and hamstrings. A small amount of blood still oozed from the deep gashes, with tissue and skin hanging from the leg like chunks of hamburger.

Jonathan administered a local anesthetic, cleaned the wound with a scrub brush and Betadine, and elevated the leg on a sterile field. "Give him a Tetanus shot," he ordered Nurse Hawkins. "Administer one unit of Cephalosporin and set up a suture tray with ten packs of 2-0 Dexon and fifteen packs of 3-0 Ethilon. Better call in a surgeon, we're going to need a lot of work here."

"I'll have the ward clerk call Dr. Miller," she said tight-lipped as she left.

Jonathan gave another comforting smile to the boy's mother, who sat wide-eyed and ash-faced in her chair. "He's going to need a lot of stitches, Ma'am, but it looks like there's no serious damage," he said. "He'll be sore for about a week, and we'll need to watch for infection, but he's a strapping young lad. I'm sure he'll recover just fine and have a proud scar to show off to his buddies."

His gentle, professional manner finally settled her nerves. "Oh, thank God. Thank you, Doctor." She sighed with a grateful smile.

Jonathan stepped outside the cubicle, concerned. He hoped Dr. Joe, as everyone called Dr. Miller, would be sober. When he first arrived in Tarpon Springs from the hills of Kentucky many years ago, Dr. Joe was the town's only surgeon and a well-loved, local fixture. Robust, gruff-talking, and always quick with a joke, he cultivated the flair of a "mountain man," driving a four-wheel drive Bronco with a back-mounted rack and a sawed-off 10-gauge shotgun.

Jonathan fondly remembered the night he went to Dr. Joe's house for an interview before his acceptance to the hospital staff—

the surgeon was as close to royalty at Tarpon Memorial as anyone, and no major decision was made without his endorsement. After they had gotten drunk together, Dr. Joe gave his approval. Jonathan liked him a great deal. Although Dr. Joe was past his prime, he was still a "crack" surgeon. Unfortunately, years of late-night drinking and carousing had taken its toll, and he wasn't always reliable in the morning.

* * *

When Hawkins returned from her coffee break 30 minutes later, she found the waiting room backed up and the ER suite bottle-necked at admissions. Two nurses loitered in the medicine room, laughing and exchanging gossip. The orderlies were not back from break, and Dr. Curtis was nowhere to be seen. The curtains to cubicles two and three were pulled shut.

She barked a sharp order, "Waiting room's backing up. Time to get busy."

The idle nurses snapped to attention like two marine grunts caught loafing.

"And, just where might I find Dr. Curtis?" Hawkins asked, sneering, "Off in one of the back rooms with the ward clerk?"

One of the nurses nodded toward cubicle two.

Hawkins pulled open the curtain with a scowl, her fist firmly pressed against her hip. She was surprised to see Jonathan, masked and gloved, suturing the boy's leg, with a nurse's aide assisting. He was working meticulously, placing in mattress sutures to minimize scarring. She could see that the skin was reapproximating nicely. However, careful stitching took time, which in Hawkin's book meant slow and inefficient work. She had an ER to run and had no use for a doctor frittering away valuable time.

Without a second thought, she lashed out at Jonathan, "What is going on here?"

The boy's mother looked up, surprised. The young aide sat frozen.

Jonathan turned to Hawkins with piercing eyes, a needle holder in one hand and forceps in the other.

Undaunted, Hawkins continued, "Waiting room's backing up, Doctor. Your staff's out there playing tiddlywinks. And, just where is Dr. Miller? I thought he was called in to suture this leg. This is Surgery's job, Dr. Curtis, not Internal Medicine. Are you a surgeon now, too?"

A barely contained growl issued from beneath Jonathan's mask. In a rare lapse of southern gentleman manner, he said in a voice dripping with sarcasm, "I'm so glad to see you back from your extended coffee break, Hawkins. If you're rested now, and your waiting room is backing up, you being the head nurse can take care of it! As for your surgeon, I put him in cubicle three to sleep it off. Why don't you do something useful, like taking the cigar out of his mouth before he blows something up in there!"

The nurse's aide gasped. Hawkins' back stiffened. Jonathan had never spoken to her like that before. She struck out like a venomous cobra. "I was working in this ER before you could tie your shoelaces, much less do surgery. I've seen tons of alligator bites just like this one and treated them myself without the help of some young whippersnapper just out of medical school."

Jonathan rose to his full height, pointed a trembling finger at her, and shouted, "Get out!"

For an instant, Hawkins seemed cowed, almost frightened. Then she rallied. "I'll bet this is a first for you, huh?" She waited and when Jonathan didn't say anything, added with a smirk, "I thought so."

After a moment of silence, she harrumphed and left the room, jerking the curtain closed behind her.

Jonathan's hands shook with a noticeable tremor. He took several deep breaths to calm his nerves. Smiling grimly, he nodded to the aide. "Let's get back to work."

For the next thirty minutes, he remained silent. Sweat beaded on his brow as he concentrated, shutting out the sounds of Hawkins storming around and shouting orders to the staff, and the banging and clanking of wheelchairs and stretchers being moved about in response.

Finally, the suturing was complete. Although the boy's leg looked like a tic-tac-toe board with over a hundred stitches, it was a beautiful job. Jonathan ordered the aide to wrap the leg in surgical dressing and admit the patient for observation overnight.

"Oh, and, one last order," Dr. Curtis said, smiling at the boy. "A prescription for plenty of ice cream."

It was the first moment of levity since Hawkins had thrown her tirade. The boy smiled back. His mother's eyes welled up with tears, grateful for the extra care.

* * *

For a while, the atmosphere around the ER remained tense. Hawkins stomped about in her heavy, white clogs, which seemed to make dents in the hard linoleum floor, while the rest of the staff walked around as if on eggshells. She and Jonathan ignored each other.

By early afternoon, everyone's nerves had settled, and Jonathan took a well-deserved lunch break.

The cafeteria was filled with nurses and doctors engaged in lively conversation. Jonathan was in no mood for small talk. He got himself a gyro sandwich and a cup of coffee and stepped outside into a small, open courtyard. Braving the humidity, he sat on a bench in the shade of a palm tree and tried to relax.

But halfway through eating his sandwich, his cell phone buzzed. It was a text from his fiancé. "Hey Babe, remember dinner at the club tonight. Cocktail attire. See you there. So excited. Love ya. Pricilla."

Jonathan experienced a moment of tunnel vision and broke into a cold sweat. With his hangover and the chaotic start to the morning, he had completely forgotten about the dinner party in his honor at the Palma Verde Country Club in Tampa. Priscilla's parents wanted to present their future son-in-law to their friends.

He quickly texted back, "Got it. Can't wait to see you. Love ya." Leaning back in his chair, he sighed with relief. Saved from a major blunder.

He still felt like he was living in a fairy tale, a poor boy from Tennessee winning the affection of the woman of his dreams and falling into the lap of luxury. Priscilla's parents were friends with all the politicians and dignitaries in Florida that mattered. Her family name graced a building in every hospital in the greater Tampa area.

And Pricilla? She was a gorgeous blonde who always looked well-groomed, like a chaste debutante. Yet her passion always surprised him. A red flush washed over his face as he recalled the first time they had sex. After several dates, following an intimate dinner out, they were at the door of her apartment. Jonathan had expected a good-night kiss, but before he knew it, she had pushed him inside and they were stripping off each other's clothes. They made love on the couch, on her bed, and again in the shower. With each encounter more passionate, Jonathan's breath had grown ragged and he had—

An urgent buzzing of his phone interrupted his reverie. It was a call from the ER. Jonathan punched the screen and heard Hawkins's urgent voice on speaker, "Dr. Curtis, we need you, now!"

Instantly, the hair on the back of Jonathan's neck bristled. He dumped the remains of his sandwich in the trash and rushed from the cafeteria. As he ran down the hallway, his imagination spun myriads of emergency scenarios. But when he turned the corner and pushed through the double doors of the ER, Hawkins greeted him with a smug, twisted Cheshire Cat grin. It stopped him in his tracks.

"Odd," was his first thought. Then he sputtered, "What's up? What's the emergency?"

Unperturbed, Hawkins reported on all she had accomplished in his absence: "A couple of sprains, fractures, and whatnots. I sent them all to Radiology. A sliver of metal in a boy's eye. Took care of that myself. He's got an eye patch and an appointment with his ophthalmologist in the morning. You can sign the chart when you've got the time." She paused dramatically, then continued. "It's the patient down in five. I'm at wit's end what to do about her. She says she's dying!"

"Dying?" Dr. Curtis gave a concerned look. "From what?"

"Mmm, that would require a medical diagnosis. I wouldn't have a clue about that, being only a lowly nurse and all." Hawkins handed him the patient's chart. "I've already drawn some routine labs. All I can tell you is that she says she's under the spell of a 'Devil's curse.'"

She waved her hand toward cubicle five and stomped off, leaving Jonathan looking after her in bewilderment. He scanned the reports and admitting complaint: A 37-year-old female, EKG-normal, vital signs-normal, "Devil's curse." He raised his eyebrow when he came to the name, Kizzy Lee. He'd never heard of a Kizzy before.

Jonathan took a deep breath and entered the cubicle. On the bed behind the curtain lay an olive-skinned woman in her forties.

When she saw him, her eyes flashed. She thrashed about on the stretcher and pleaded loudly, "Oh, Doctor, please help me! I'm dying!"

Her accent was heavy, perhaps Eastern European. Jonathan couldn't place it. She wore an excessive amount of make-up and was dressed in colorful attire. A long purple skirt and white, ruffled blouse, belted high, accentuated her buxom breasts. The fabric over her midriff was thin, exposing her belly button. Large gold earrings dangled from under her dark, shoulder-length hair, and an assortment of gold and silver bracelets and rings decorated her arms and fingers. A prominent, round, blue-and-white amulet hung from her neck.

Jonathan approached her with deliberate cheer. "Well, Kizzy, is that your name? I'm Dr. Curtis."

"Yes, Kizzy, that's my name, Doctor. Please, I'm sick."

"What kind of sick? It says on your chart, a curse."

She grasped Jonathan's coat, pulling him closer. "I'm dying, Doctor. Tsuri cursed me. That miserable bitch gave me the evil eye. I know it was her!"

As she talked, she sprayed spit all over. Jonathan tried to draw back, but she held on and sputtered, "I go outside. There's blood all over my steps. I find a broken mirror and a wig on the ground. I tried to wash off the blood with ammonia like Tatyana said. I had gobs of garlic and a raw egg Tatyana gave me. I drank chicken blood too, so much that I puked. Nothing washes it away. I can't eat. I can't sleep. There's buzzing in my ear. What am I to do? I've tried everything. Please help me!"

Jonathan disengaged her hands and said forcefully, "Kizzy, you need to calm down now. I need to examine you to see what's wrong. We will take care of you!"

That seemed to soothe her, allowing Jonathan to complete a thorough exam. There was nothing physically wrong as far as he could tell. He looked at the lab results again. They were all normal. Her symptoms fit no medical diagnosis he had encountered in his training. Maybe she was mentally deranged, suffering from paranoid schizophrenia—with delusions of people out to get her. Perhaps she had a psychotic break. He'd have to admit her to the psychiatric ward for observation and a proper diagnosis.

But first, he wanted to check with her family. He padded her arm reassuringly. "Everything will be okay, Kizzy. I'll be right back."

She nodded, trembling, making small mewling sounds.

In the waiting room, he saw three women who had to be her family. They were all about Kizzy's age, attractive, dark-featured, and dressed in the same elaborate fashion.

As soon as they saw him, they converged and surrounded him like a flock of cackling hens, gesturing wildly, shouting on top of one another: "How is our precious Kizzy? Tell us please, Doctor. How is she? Will she be all right? Oh, dear God, I'm so afraid for Kizzy."

They all spoke the same odd, guttural dialect, smelled of garlic, and worst of all, had the same disgusting habit as Kizzy of spitting as they talked.

The scene was almost comical and Jonathan had to keep himself from smiling. He placed a finger to his lips, then pleaded, "Ladies, ladies, please, shish! One at a time. I have been speaking to Kizzy just now and completed a thorough examination. She is going to be fine."

The three women looked at each other, perplexed. Then the tallest spoke up, "But that can't be. Kizzy is not fine, Doctor. She is dying, yes?"

"No, Kizzy is not dying. She is under some delusion she has been cursed, a Devil's curse, she calls it."

The woman with the darkest hair stepped forward. "Oh, Doctor, she is most certainly cursed. It is Tsuri, that devil dog. Kizzy ran over Tsuri's cat a year ago. It was an accident, but Tsuri never forgave her. Tsuri began giving Kizzy the evil eye. Her magic is strong. Tatyana says she is a white witch, the old bag. Everyone in the camp is afraid of her."

The dark-haired woman joined in, "Tatyana said not to come to the Gadjo, but Kizzy is dying. We have tried everything. Oh, please, can something be done?"

Taken aback, Jonathan's eyes widened. "Wait a minute, please. Let me get this straight. So, Kizzy is cursed by Tsuri, and Tatyana asked you not to see a doctor, right?"

They nodded in unison.

"Okay, so who is Tatyana?"

The dark-haired woman began, "Tatyana is a Magi, a prophet. For you, the Gadjo, a fortune teller."

The tall one picked up the thread, "Tatyana said not to come to the Gadjo. She said they would lock Kizzy in a padded room. But we can see you are kind. You would not lock Kizzy up. Maybe you have a pill or a shot, or maybe you can cut this Devil out of her."

The third woman chimed in, "We have done as Tatyana said. We soaked Kizzy in salt water, lit four candles at the corners of the tub, and poured the water onto the sand. Kizzy bought a blue Nazar to wear around her neck."

It occurred to Jonathan that the women were all involved in a Wiccan cult.

Just then, the ER entrance door burst open. A fiftyish woman with fierce eyes and long, curly, bleach-blonde hair swept in. She was dressed like Kizzy and the others but wore a brightly colored silk scarf over her head, and displayed twice the gold and silver jewelry on her arms and around her neck. She looked like a carnival fortune teller.

The three women turned toward the arrival. "Uh-Oh!" said the tallest. "That's Tatyana!" They lowered their heads, like children caught in a lie.

Tatyana scowled at them as she stomped past without a word.

Jonathan followed to run interference, but Tatyana moved swiftly as if she knew exactly where she was going. By the time he arrived at the cubicle, it was too late. Tatyana had her hand on Kizzy's forehead and shook a branch of herbs over her quaking body. She closed her eyes and started to murmur what sounded like a spell.

Jonathan could make out phrases: "Heavenly Father, Ruler of the Universe...bind all of Satan's evil...wicked demons...tormenting

Kizzy…divine healing tresses of righteousness…the planting of the Lord… all of Kizzy's cares… give her strength against the curse of Tsuri…" To his ears, it sounded similar to the prayers he had heard back home in his mother's small Pentecostal church in the Appalachian Mountains.

Tatyana's voice rose as she finished, "We thank You for answering her prayers and give You the glory, the honor, and praise. Amen."

Immediately, Kizzy's moaning and writhing ceased, and she sat up. Before Jonathan could say anything, the curtains burst open and Kizzy's friends arrived. Kizzy jumped off the stretcher with outstretched arms and they all hugged each other, laughing and crying with joy.

Tatyana, her forehead beaded with sweat, fixed her eyes on Jonathan. They were coal-black and piercing. A shiver ran down his back. He remained silent and thought, "Have I just witnessed my first exorcism?"

The tall woman patted his arm and kissed him on the cheek. "Oh, thank you, thank you! You and Tatyana broke Tsuri's curse."

Kizzy hugged him, pulled his hand to her lips, and smothered it with kisses.

The dark-haired woman kissed him too and said, "Your power is great. You were right in your foretelling, 'Kizzy is going to be just fine.' You are such a good doctor. Thank you."

Tatyana took a step forward, as if to get a better look at Jonathan, then turned away. As quickly as they had arrived, the five women left the ER, their voices chattering away.

Jonathan followed them in a daze as far as the waiting room and watched through the glass doors as the merry band walked to the parking lot.

Hawkins stood at the check-out counter with her hand on her hip, smirking. "Nice work, Doctor. You broke the Devil's Curse," she mocked. Then she turned to the ward clerk. "Okay, Clara, secure every magazine and small piece of furniture, lock all your doors, and hide your children inside. The Gypsies are back in town."

Chapter 2

THE PALMA VERDE COUNTRY CLUB
Tampa, Florida

As Jonathan turned onto the long, divided entrance drive to the guard gate of The Palma Verde Country Club, he felt increasingly anxious. He desperately wanted to make a good impression on Pricilla's parents and their friends.

Despite his momentary memory lapse about the evening's event, he had managed to pull it all together. He had knocked off early, calling on a colleague who owed him a favor to take the rest of his shift. After a quick shower and shave at home, he'd visited an exotic car dealership and rented a sporty Porsche for the night. Then, he made a detour to the Tampa Men's Warehouse and threw himself at the mercy of Cedric, the owner.

"Cocktail attire?" Jonathan asked when he burst through the door with a pleading look and only minutes to spare before closing time. Those were the words Priscilla's mother Muffy had uttered when requesting his attendance at a dinner party given in his honor. He hadn't a clue what to wear.

Fortunately, Cedric had plenty of cocktail attire in stock, but he stumped Jonathan when he asked, "What type of affair is it? Casual, formal, semi-formal, or festive?"

Jonathan hadn't a clue about that either. The last formal outfit he'd bought was for his high school prom. His mom helped him pick a polyester suit from the on-sale rack at a J.C. Penney's outlet store. But he wasn't about to call Priscilla for help, not after all the ribbing he'd gotten from her sorority sisters about being a hillbilly the time he'd arrived at a party on his Harley Davidson motorcycle.

Priscilla had been good-natured about it. "Don't worry, Honey," she had said. "We'll make a polished gentleman out of you yet."

It had been her suggestion to upgrade his wheels. "Rent a nice Town Car, like a Lincoln or Cadillac. It'll make a better first impression." He looked forward to her reaction when she saw him arrive in the Porsche.

Jonathan heaved a sigh of relief when he mentioned where the dinner was being held, and Cedric knew exactly what to recommend: a white linen dinner jacket with solid black pants; and for a splash of color, a powder blue, cuff-linked shirt and a pewter tie.

"Spiffy," Cedric commented as Jonathan admired himself in the full-length mirror. He felt confident that he would measure up.

However, after giving his name to the guard and being waved through the grand iron gates of The Palma Verde Country Club, he was not so sure. The place was beautiful and intimidating. The drive meandered through palatial grounds past spacious, manicured estates, where large Southern-style mansions stood like opulent megaliths. Thick Spanish moss, dangling high above the road from great canopied oaks, wafted lazily in the soft summer breeze.

Leading up to the clubhouse, the paved driveway circled a large water fountain rimmed with flowers before reaching a grand front entryway with a portico staircase.

As Jonathan gazed up at the lavish edifice with fluted columns, an almost nauseating fear gripped his stomach, but he tamped it down. It was time to present himself to high society. He fervently hoped he would pass muster.

Priscilla's parents were both from old Tampa stock. Brian Pennington Randolph III, her father, was a modern tycoon with aristocratic bearings. His great-grandfather had made a fortune in the shipping industry in the 1880s when the city underwent explosive growth, long before New York Yankee owner George Steinbrenner came to town. Priscilla's father carried on the family tradition fully aware of his exalted position in society. A fierce competitor, yet also a sporting gentleman, he was gregarious and never at a loss for words. As a philanthropist, he gave to hospitals, universities, and local charities. Jonathan had been surprised by how much he liked him, despite his generous support, both verbal and financial, for right-wing politics.

His wife Muffy was from old Tampa money, too. Her grand-father had fared well in the early South Florida banking industry. A shrewd investor, he had tripled his fortune in the 1920s Florida housing boom and had been savvy enough to get out before the market went belly up. Although his granddaughter gave back, too, maintaining a seat on the boards of many local non-profits, she had a love affair with the game of golf. Muffy had won the club's women's championship for the last five years. At the same time, she was on a quixotic quest for youth. Her girlish hairstyle and clothing were not becoming for a woman her age. Jonathan found it amusing but also knew that there was a sharp mind behind the coquettish getup.

As Jonathan got out of the car and handed his key to the con-cierge, a striking young woman appeared at the top of the portico staircase. She wore a plum colored lace cocktail dress that sharply contrasted with the golden tone of her suntanned body and the soft strands of her blond curls. Her eyes lit up when she saw him. A lovely princess, and his, if he measured up tonight.

Jonathan bounded up the stairs two at a time and halted before her.

"Wow, Handsome! Nice car!" she said.

Her voice instantly brought a smile to his face.

She let him air kiss her, then took his hands and pulled back, evaluating him with a coy expression. "I've never seen you so dressed up. So debonair. And Ray Bans. Just look at you! If you keep showing up like this, I'm going to have my hands full beating all the other women away."

A huge grin split his face. "You approve?"

"I approve."

Jonathan felt a tingle run down his back when he looked into her baby-blue eyes. He ran his fingers down the delicate features of her face, admiring her beauty. She kissed their tips. He leaned down and lightly caressed her lips.

Priscilla took Jonathan by the hand, "Come, Sugar, I'm anxious for you to meet some old friends of the family." She straightened his tie and led him inside. "Now remember, what I told you. These folks will decide on your membership to the club. Be on your best behavior."

Jonathan smiled. "Yes, I know. No discussing sex, religion, or serious politics, no matter where they take the conversation," he teased. "Laugh at the Congressman's jokes, no matter how lame, and keep my bleeding-heart liberal comments to a minimum."

With a look betraying how much it meant to her, Pricilla said lightly, "I'm glad you've done your homework."

A doorway of thick, Castilian wood marked the side entrance to a spacious courtyard. Shades of muted sunlight shining through the tall Cyprus trees dappled the poolside atrium. A cool summer breeze swirled about the patio and steel-roofed loggia. Jonathan found it a bit over-the-top and considered what it must have been like for Priscilla to take such opulent surroundings for granted growing up. He took a deep breath to keep his anxiety at bay and joined the party.

Brian Randolph was standing by the bar talking to a small group of guests. When he saw his future son-in-law, he waved his hand and called, "Jonathan, Son, come on over here." His deep Southern drawl carried over the patio.

Brian shook Jonathan's hand and motioned to his friends. They were all in their late fifties or early sixties and fashionably dressed. As they gathered, Jonathan felt like royalty at a receiving line being ushered from one guest to the next.

The first man he met exhibited a stiff, military posture. As Brian introduced him, "Jonathan, this is Colonel Frank Burdock," he nodded slightly. They shook hands. The Colonel's grip was firm and almost challenging.

Priscilla had warned Jonathan not to tangle with him. He was a decorated, full-bird, Air Force colonel, who had flown helicopter missions in Vietnam and F-16 Fighter jets in the Iraq and Afghanistan Wars. Jonathan needed to make a good impression on him because the Colonel was president of the Palma Verde Country Club and the chairman of the membership selection committee.

Next in line came a refined, proper-looking couple. "Jonathan, I'd like you to meet my dear friends, Congressman Riley and his wife," Brian said.

Karen Riley, a petite brunette, returned Jonathan's smile. "Please, call me Karen."

"Dr. Curtis," the Congressman said, "Muffy and Brian have told us so much about you. All good, of course, and now I have a face to go with the name."

"The pleasure's all mine, Congressman," Jonathan said gallantly.

Brian guided him to a stout, nearly bald man and a wispy woman. "Last but not least, let me introduce Dr. Ben Ferrari and his wife, Maria."

The man was shorter and more muscular than the others. Maria offered her bird-like hand, "Dr. Curtis."

Jonathan took it with a courteous nod.

Then Dr. Ferrari took his hand in his two paws and gave him a big grin. "Well, I want to congratulate the man who won the heart of our precious Priscilla," he said. "It's a pleasure to meet you, Doctor."

Brian said, "Dr. Ferrari is the founder and director of the largest, and I might also add, the most successful multi-specialty group in Tampa. I encourage you fellows to talk business at a later date, but not tonight." Nodding toward the bar with a wink, he continued smoothly, "Jonathan, may I get you a drink?"

Just then a high-pitched trill came from the back of the receiving line. Everyone's eyes turned toward the ravishing woman teetering toward Jonathan. Muffy Randolph was dressed in a hot pink cocktail gown with the swell of her breasts showing. She embraced him like a long-lost friend. Then she stood back and announced with a megawatt smile, "I think I'm going to have the most handsome son-in-law, not to mention the most brilliant."

After that exuberant greeting, the party returned to normal decibel levels. The conversation consisted of small talk, polite and entertaining, mostly regarding the weather, recent news events, the Tampa Bay Bucs, and Muffy's two favorite topics, her golf game and how the Florida Gators football team would fare this year. Jonathan was pleased that he could hold his own among the Randolphs' sophisticated friends. Soon he was on a first-name basis with everyone except Colonel Burdock who eyed him as if evaluating a fresh recruit.

Eventually, even they hit it off when they discovered that both their fathers had been pilots who died while serving in the military. Jonathan's father had been killed on maneuvers in the Air National Guard. The Colonel's father had been downed in a fighter plane in the Pacific Ocean near the end of World War II. He and Jonathan commiserated over growing up without a male role model. Colonel Burdock had been raised by a single mother, a German nurse her father met in San Francisco and married during the war.

Unfortunately, she was showing increasing signs of aging. She had intended to join them for dinner but, feeling poorly, had sent her regrets.

Dr. Ferrari was most impressed with Jonathan's scholastic record. "I've never before met a Phi Beta Kappa from Duke," he acknowledged, with a firm pat on the back.

Congressman Riley and his wife invited Jonathan and Priscilla on their boat for a cruise to the Islands—after the wedding, of course, for a second honeymoon. Priscilla was quick to point out that the "boat" Congressman Riley was referring to, was a 150-foot yacht with six staterooms and a crew of five. The cruise, most likely, would be to Aruba, Karen's favorite vacation spot.

Brian and Muffy's guests seemed enchanted by Jonathan. Priscilla beamed proudly over her fiancé's unexpected social graces. From all indications, it was a done deal.

As evening approached, the maître d' ushered the Randolf party into the clubhouse for dinner. Muffy had reserved a private room overlooking the palatial golf course with a view of the sun setting over the fairways. "Oohs" and "Aahs" accompanied the last splash of an orange glow above the horizon.

The gourmet entrees were served by waiters, neatly clad in white uniforms.

The dinner conversation was casual and soon turned to questions about how Jonathan and Priscilla met. Jonathan deferred to his bride, and she launched into the oft-told story like a seasoned entertainer. Her audience listened with polite attentiveness.

"It's a little embarrassing, and certainly not the 'love at first sight' you see in the movies," she said. "A sorority sister of mine invited me to an 'Oldies Night' at Hooters. After a few drinks, she began talking to a young man named Carl who told us about his friend, a good-looking doctor from Tennessee, and asked if he could bring him to the table. Jennifer winked my way. I rolled my eyes.

Shortly, Jonathan was sitting down across the table from me. Neither of us said much. He was attractive, but we didn't hit it off. Jennifer and Carl began dating, and I didn't give Jonathan another thought. About a month later, Jen called me and asked if I would like to go to a Merry-Makers party with her and Carl, a night cruise on the Bay. It sounded great but I didn't have a date. Jennifer said, 'What about Jonathan?' I asked 'Jonathan who?'"

Everyone at the table laughed.

Priscilla chuckled, too, then continued, "I found out later they were setting us both up. I thank them for it now. We started dating, our relationship grew, and"—she paused, looking up at Jonathan with her baby blues—"we fell in love."

The group responded approvingly.

A bright smile crossed Priscilla's face. "And here we are, going to be Doctor and Mrs. Curtis next June." She laid her head on Jonathan's shoulder, hugged his arm, and looked into his eyes, "My great big handsome prince."

There were sounds of admiration from the women as Priscilla flashed her engagement ring around the table.

Eager to turn to a more manly subject, Ben Ferrari said, "So, Jonathan, I understand you were raised in Tennessee. I would have thought you would have been a Volunteer; maybe played football for them. You're so athletic-looking." He chuckled. "From the looks of last year's records, U.T. could have used a man like you on their football team."

Muffy quickly joined the "Volunteer" bashing. "I seriously doubt Brian or I would have allowed such an 'interracial' marriage. Go Gators!"

Jonathan shook his head with a smile, "My mother discouraged me from contact sports, Ben. Said it was too rough. An academic ride to Duke seemed like my best choice...and, thank goodness for that."

He made a show of kissing Priscilla's hand and was rewarded with appreciative chuckles around the table.

Karen Riley piped up. "I watched a clip on the 'Four O'Clock News' this afternoon from Tarpon Springs. A twelve-year-old boy barely escaped being drowned by an alligator. Was that you, Jonathan, who took care of him in the ER?"

Jonathan nodded, "Yes."

"Oh, my, and how is the poor lad? I was so worried about him. His mother must be a mess."

Jonathan hesitated. He knew, no matter how curious non-medical individuals were, the blood and guts details disturbed them and did not make for good table conversation. He smiled and said, "The last time I saw the boy, he was resting comfortably in his room, watching cartoons and eating a big bowl of chocolate ice cream."

Karen relaxed. "Oh, thank God. I'm so glad to hear it. Is that what you do all day, Jonathan, take care of terrifying emergency cases like the doctors in television shows? It sounds so exciting. Tell us more."

Jonathan knew this to be a trap, too. Genuine accounts of snake bites, strokes, heart attacks, and broken bones bordered on horror stories for the faint of heart.

"No, Karen, it's not like TV at all. Most of my day consists of little kids with runny noses, rashes, coughs, and sneezing, and retirees who forgot to take their blood pressure medication."

Dr. Ferrari smiled and gave an approving nod.

Karen seemed disappointed. "Oh," she murmured.

Jonathan had an inspiration. "There was this one patient, however, this afternoon." He paused significantly, gazing around the table. "I had to break a Devil's curse to cure her."

Ben Ferrari's mouth dropped open. "What?"

Everyone's eyes were on him, so he launched into the story of Kizzy, her fellow Gypsies, and Tatanya, the fortune teller. When he finished, there was a momentary hush.

Then Karen said, "I heard the Gypsies are back in town and camping out at Tarpon Lake. I happened to find a flyer at my massage therapist's yesterday, announcing a Gypsy fortune teller. Maybe that was her."

Maria wrinkled her nose and said, "Oh my, Gypsies. One of my very dearest friends, Phyllis Rhoades, was scammed by them last year. She paid this man to build a concrete porch—half up front to purchase materials, and half later for labor. It sounded reasonable enough and at such a good price. But after paying the man $4,000 in cash, she never saw him again. When she inquired at the Better Business Bureau, she found out she was dealing with Gypsies and there was nothing that could be done about it. It wasn't the money she was so upset about. Lord knows that was only pocket change for her. It was the idea of being conned."

Muffy chimed in, "Yes, and she's not the only one. Some say they possess psychic powers—invoke curses, conjure spirits, and do all kinds of mystical things." She shivered. "Gives me the willies!"

"But, wouldn't it be fun to have your fortune told?" Karen said. "I mean, I don't believe in such things, but on a lark." She turned to Priscilla. "Surely you have questions. How many babies are you and Jonathan going to have? Boys? Girls? I think it would be a hoot!"

The Colonel interrupted, "I wouldn't be so flippant about that, Karen. Those fortune tellers are tricksters and con artists. To send these kids out there would be like sending a pair of bunny rabbits to a convention of wolves. Those hucksters come on easy, charging ten or fifteen dollars for the first session. Then Priscilla will discover she has a rare curse laid upon her, and it'll cost another $500 to make sure one of her children isn't born with a birth defect. Gypsies have been running scams for a thousand years. They haven't been known for generations as the 'niggers' of Europe for nothing. There is truth in the saying 'You play close to a tarpit, you'll soon get black and sticky.' I say, stay away as far away as possible from those voo-doo-worshipping hustlers."

Jonathan was shocked. He stared at the tablecloth, shocked, his ears burning. Growing up in the poor South, he had heard the n-word plenty of times in off-color jokes and racist remarks, but now found it deeply offensive. Yet, no one else at the table so much as blinked.

He felt heartened, however, when Karen said pointedly, "Well, Colonel, why don't you tell us what you're really thinking." However, then she chuckled, making light of it. "I was just trying to add some zest to the romance. I thought the kids might have some fun. Of course, everyone here knows it's a scam, with a little 'woo-woo' thrown in, but what's the harm in that?"

Colonel Burdock scowled, "Whores, beggars and thieves. Take my word for it, Karen. I've dealt with them before. They're a slip-pery lot of dark-skinned con artists, and I wouldn't trust any one of them as far as I could throw 'em."

Karen rolled her eyes.

Jonathan had enough. His elbow hit the table, rattling the glasses and silverware. But before he could explode with indigna-tion, Priscilla kneed him under the table. Her eyes widened. "No," she mouthed.

Her father, noticing, snickered. He'd received the "knee-un-der-the-table" treatment many times from Muffy. Like mother, like daughter. But it was time for him to step in and rescue his future son-in-law from committing an unpardonable social faux pas. He rose, raised his hand, and said, "This conversation is not meant for delicate ears. Why don't we retire to the Admiral's Club, grab a Scotch and a cigar, and leave the ladies to themselves to discuss wedding plans and such."

As Jonathan stood, he stiffened noticeably. His neck felt tight around the collar.

Priscilla gave him the "look" again and whispered, "Be nice, you promised."

Jonathan followed Brian and the other men into a dimly lit room whose walls were covered with thick wood paneling. The Admiral's Club was exclusive. Its exorbitant entry fees eliminated even most members of The Palma Verde Country Club, and women were not allowed. The comfortable smell of old pipe tobacco permeated the air. Well-worn, thick leather couches and armchairs sat among mahogany furniture pieces. It was a room secluded from unwelcome ears. Many a clandestine business deal had been struck here. There were no other guests in the room.

A black steward dressed in a red waiter's jacket bowed and said, "Your orders, Sirs? Mr. Randolph, Colonel, Congressman, Dr. Ferrari." He added a polite nod to Jonathan.

Shortly, their drinks arrived, and the five men settled into their seats.

Brian started things off. "I imagine that Colonel Burdock and the doctors would be natural adversaries. Doctors spend their whole lives learning how to save people while the Colonel studies the most efficient way to kill them. At the same time, our consummate politician, Congressman Riley, keeps one foot in each camp. Maybe we should hear from him first."

Congressman Riley leaned forward on both elbows. "Gentlemen, may I consider this a confidential exchange of ideology?"

There were affirmative nods all around.

"You understand, in public, I must maintain 'political correctness.' However, in all honesty, I'm with the Colonel. There are still too many free-loaders and liberals in Washington that couldn't wipe their asses with both hands. And, with all of them on the meal ticket these days, it will be hard to vote them out."

Brian chuckled, "Well said, Joe, and my sentiments entirely." He turned to Dr. Ferrari. "Ben, any comments you wish to add?"

Dr. Ferrari quickly lowered his eyes. "Hmmm", he murmured with a short hesitation, then said, "My medical oath demands that I treat everyone equally in my practice."

"At least those who can afford it and have insurance," the Congressman teased.

Ferrari smiled as if caught and said, "Well, of course. But when it comes to politics…"

Jonathan, trying his best to stay out of the conversation, sat with a clenched fist and a tight jaw.

Colonel Burdock, noting his disengagement, interrupted, "Let's hear what Doctor Curtis has to say on that subject. You've heard the comments from a dedicated public official, which, I might add, cannot be made openly in this 'Freedom of Speech' country of ours. Where do you stand on this matter? If we're going to welcome you into our club, we must be certain of your loyalty."

Jonathan took a deep breath. "I hope you're not questioning my loyalty to this country, Colonel?" he said. "Let me assure you, I stand for the American way. I pay my taxes like anyone else. I vote, I try to help others, and I'm a productive, law-abiding citizen."

The Colonel scoffed. "And, you think that's enough, Boy? Is it not clear to you there's a war going on? White Americans and our way of life are being threatened. We, the race that is responsible for most of humanity's great achievements, are under attack from all sides—darkies, kikes, A-rabs, Hispanics. So, I'm asking you. Whose side are you on?"

Jonathan bit the inside of his cheek. Priscilla had warned him that the Colonel had a problem with the "color" divide of politics in Washington—it's why he retired from the military and never attained a higher rank. But this was something else. The man was a dyed-in-the-wool white supremacist. It was a Catch-22. An honest answer would break Jonathan's promise to Priscilla and threaten his acceptance into the country club. He was on the spot, with all eyes on him and a question on the table, and he couldn't bring himself to lie outright.

Thankfully, Congressman Riley, uncomfortable with a friendly discussion turning into an inquisition, interfered. "Hold on now, Colonel. Let up on the young doctor. He is an intelligent young man, but he doesn't have your experience. Given time and seasoning, I'm sure he'll figure things out, even if he doesn't fully share your point of view yet."

The Colonel was about to answer but thought better of it. He gave a casual wave in acknowledgment that the subject was closed.

The rest of the evening went smoothly with Jonathan holding his own and ended in cordial parting among all the guests. But when Colonel Burdock shook Jonathan's hand, he looked at him with a penetrating stare before relenting and breaking into a crooked smile.

To Priscilla's questioning look when he came out of the Admiral's Club, Jonathan nodded confident that everything had gone well.

Relaxing, she kissed him passionately and whispered, "I'll see you tomorrow. Wish you could keep the Porsche."

Jonathan appreciated her sense of humor. It was one of the things he loved about her.

As he drove away on the tree-lined road, he hummed to himself. He wasn't worried about his prospects. He knew Priscilla's father would take care of things, even if he didn't quite pass muster with the Colonel. Still, he wondered: What have I got himself into?

Chapter 3

THE FORTUNE TELLER

It was late morning. Priscilla pulled her shiny, top-down, new Mercedes sports car to a rubber-squealing halt in front of Jonathan's condo. Wearing casual boating clothes—dockers, shorts, windbreaker covering polo shirt and cap—Jonathan joined her. He was surprised to see her in a dark blue-colored dress and a string of pearls.

"Hop in, Sugar. We're runnin' a little late," she called to him cheerfully. Jonathan got in the car and gave Priscilla a peck on the cheek as she pulled out onto the street.

Settling into the passenger seat, he asked, "Did you bring a change of clothes for the boat?"

"Change of plans, darling."

"What?"

"It's a surprise!"

Jonathan couldn't help but notice how beautiful his fiancé looked, her blonde, wavy hair blowing in all directions and her slender legs extending from her dress like two finely carved alabaster limbs.

A bright yellow flyer on the floorboard caught his attention, and he bent over to pick it up "Gypsy Fortune Teller," he read. "Take a mystical adventure. Find out what the future holds for you."

"Is this the surprise, Baby? I thought you were opposed to such witchcraft." Jonathan chuckled loudly over the wind whistling past his ears.

Priscilla gave a pout, "Oh, you found it. That's not fair. Now it's not a surprise."

Jonathan bent forward in his seat to talk under the shelter of the windshield. "Honey, I don't know if I approve of this. At best it's hocus-pocus and they'll try to con us."

"Oh, come on now, Mr. Fuddy-Duddy, relax," Priscilla chided. "Be a good sport. Why are you so serious these days? Let's have some fun."

"Honey, I don't know—"

"Please, Jonathan. Just for the day." She gave him her best coquettish pout.

Jonathan sighed and leaned back in his seat. "Okay, Sugar. Just for the day."

By the time they turned into the state park entrance at Lake Tarpon, Jonathan had made his peace with the idea. He was almost looking forward to it.

Driving under the canopied road, they could see a wide glistening lake surrounded by pines and cypress. The reflection of the sun from the ripples of water created a scintillating display of light among the leaves and branches of the trees. A soft breeze carried the scent of fresh pine growth from the forest.

Children in bathing suits ran around the camping area, laughing, throwing softballs, and tossing Frisbees. A few men were firing up charcoal and gas grills for an afternoon family cookout.

Priscilla's sparkling white Mercedes looked out of place among the older cars and campers parked among the trees. She drove until they reached a prominent marker nailed to a tree—Number 28.

"This is it," Priscilla said.

As they turned into the narrow gravel driveway, Jonathan felt like he had been transported into a fairytale. Tucked among the trees, tightly crowded in, were an assortment of caravans. Most looked a bit run-down. But set apart, nestled below tall pines was a Gypsy wagon right out of a time travel movie. Except for its modern undercarriage, it looked like it had materialized from a fantasy land. The sides were painted bright yellow and orange, with a curved roof, ornate gold scrolling under the eaves, and intricate wood-carved window frames. A cobalt blue door marked its entrance.

Off to one side under an Easy-Up Canopy stood a large, round, multi-colored table surrounded by four straight-back chairs. A curly-haired blond woman sat in one of them. as if she had been waiting for them. She rose just as the car halted. Jonathan instantly recognized the vivid colors of her garb and the multitude of gold and silver bobbles, bracelets, and necklaces. Tatyana!

As they got out of the car, a small, black-and-brown-spotted mutt barked and came running up to greet them, its tail wagging. He sniffed at Jonathan's shoes, then jumped up on Priscilla with both front paws and buried his nose in her crotch. Flustered, Priscilla quickly brushed him away.

The woman called out, motioning with her hand. "That's Mugs. He won't bite. Come on over here and have a seat."

Jonathan waved his hand in the air, "Hello, Tatyana."

Priscilla looked puzzled, "You know her?"

"Yesterday afternoon, the Gypsies in the ER Remember?"

Jonathan offered Tatyana his hand and smiled. "I don't believe we've been formally introduced, but I do remember Kizzy's curse."

"Oh, yes. "Tatyana chortled loudly. "We meet again. The Devil's curse Doctor." Her Slavic accent was thick and raspy.

"Please, just call me Dr. Curtis or Jonathan. This is my fiancée, Priscilla Randolph. Priscilla, Tatyana."

Priscilla extended her hand, but Tatyana gave her a scrutinizing gaze before shooting a glance at Jonathan. Then she bowed in an old-world curtsy.

A bit flustered, Pricilla inquired, "So, you're the fortune teller I called earlier?"

Tatyana instantly became an affable hostess. "Yes, yes. Please have a seat. We can talk around my table. Get comfortable. Get to know each other. Make yourselves at home. Would you like some coffee? I made some fresh only minutes ago."

Priscilla shook her head. "Not for me, thank you."

Jonathan nodded. "Sure, I'll have some."

While Tatyana went into her wagon and bustled about, Jonathan glanced with amusement at Priscilla and received a slap on the arm in return.

Within minutes, the heavy aroma of coffee filled the air, as Tatyana returned carrying two mugs filled with a thick brown liquid.

When Jonathan put the glass to his lips and took a swallow, his eyes bugged out, "Whoa!"

Tatyana winked, "Yes. Is brewed in Turkish fashion. Strong. Can wake up the spirits. Sometimes makes the Gadjo sick. Just sip. Is better."

Jonathan chuckled, "Wake up the spirits. I guess that's what we're here for. Right?"

"Yes," Tatyana nodded with a slight hesitation. "But first, I'd like to know what you two young people are looking for."

Jonathan looked questioningly at his fiancé. Priscilla explained, "Karen, a friend of my mom's, suggested we come here for a reading. Ask some questions about our future together. She thought it would be fun. I don't know if I believe in all this stuff. I mean, I don't want to conjure up some long-lost relative or anything like that." She gave a nervous titter.

Tatyana chuckled, then stared at Jonathan. "Okay, okay. I understand. And you, Doctor?"

For a moment, Jonathan's eyes locked on hers. Her dark gaze with pupils dilated seemed to burn right through him. He gulped and a chill ran down his back. After an awkward silence, he cleared his throat and said, "Sorry, strong coffee, I guess."

"Yes," Tatyana said. "Strong coffee, indeed." She nodded discerningly and continued, "Sounds like you got dragged here, Doctor. Like so many other men. It's not unusual. Women seem to be more open to this kind of experience. Relax. We won't go anywhere you don't want to go."

She turned to Priscilla. "Well then, you and I will have some fun, and I will answer questions about what the future holds. You can ask me anything you wish, and I will have to tell you the truth, but I make no promises or guarantees. I charge 60 dollars for a half-hour, and 100 dollars for an hour. So, what will it be?"

Jonathan smiled at the disclaimer, but Priscilla beamed. "I think an hour will do," she said, grasping Jonathan's hand. "Oh, isn't this exciting?"

"Come on, then," Tatyana rose and motioned to her trailer. "Follow me. I do my readings inside where I can concentrate."

They climbed the wooden steps. Just inside the cobalt blue doorway, Priscilla stopped with a gasp. "Oh my, it's so darling."

The little cabin was charming—wall-to-wall natural cedar paneling and a crowned arched ceiling. Dark burgundy drapes hung over the open windows, billowing in the breeze like a sail on a mild spring day. In the backroom, Jonathan saw a large king-sized bed, covered with a soft, gold comforter and oversized blue and burgundy pillows. A fat, white Persian cat curled up in the center, sleeping. It lifted its head, flicked its tail once, then settled back down.

The front room was minimally furnished, with a built-in, overstuffed couch to one side and a white, wooden dining table on the other. Four beautiful white chairs, painted with blue and yellow posies, were neatly pushed up around the table. A scented candle stood in the center, filling the room with a thick aroma of herbs and fresh flowers. There was no electric illumination, only flickering kerosene lanterns affixed to the side walls.

"It really is darling," Priscilla exclaimed.

"Thank you, Dear," Tatyana replied. "We Roma call our trailers 'Vardos.' I bought this one from a carnival that went bust several years ago. It reminded me so much of the home I grew up in."

Priscilla asked. "Where are you from, Tatyana?"

"All over, Dear. I am a true 'Traveler.' But I guess you could say I come from Romania. My family immigrated to America years ago, to escape the persecution of my people in Europe."

"But I don't see a sink, or stove, or bathroom. Where do you cook and…you know?" Priscilla questioned. "And no air-conditioner. It must get hot!"

Jonathan smiled to himself, knowing Priscilla's idea of "roughing it" was a cozy suite at a Five-star Ritz-Carlton in Miami's South Beach.

"I think you can see this Vardo is very basic," Tatyana said. "Some get pretty fancy these days, but this one was built in the early 1900s. So, it's cooled by air breezes, and we do our necessities outside." She pulled out one of the chairs and continued smoothly, "But, please have a seat, Dear. I think we will do palm readings today. That's always fun!"

Priscilla sat and eagerly laid her hand across the table, palm up.

As Tatyana joined her, she said matter-of-factly, "I get paid before my reading. And, remember, I make no promises or guarantees."

"Oh, yes, of course." Priscilla quickly pulled out a small wad of money from her skirt pocket. She stripped off a 100-dollar bill and handed it to Tatyana, who stuffed it in one of her pockets.

Jonathan caught her staring at the rest of the money with crafty eyes and appreciating the diamond-studded, gold Rolex sports watch on Priscilla's wrist and the two-karat engagement ring on her finger. They both glistened in the candlelight. He glanced suspiciously toward the front door.

As if reading his mind, Tatyana said, "Relax, Jonathan, not all Gypsies are thieves and pick-pockets. You'll be safe in my home."

She peered at Priscilla's hand and ventured, "I see you are a fun-loving young woman, Priscilla."

Priscilla, amused, answered like a good girl scout, "Yes, Ma'am."

Jonathan rolled his eyes.

Undeterred, Tatyana continued, "You come from an old, established Florida family, banking and shipping, I believe. Your mother dotes on you and worries too much for your liking. Your father is protective and knows how to take care of things."

Priscilla, captivated, leaned forward. "You are so right."

"You have a nice family," Tatyana said soothingly. "You want that for yourself, too. Yes? A nice family?"

Her face aglow, Priscilla gasped, "Oh, yes!"

Tatyana took Priscilla's right hand. She gazed into her eyes and gently palpated the soft areas of her palm. "Your fingers are long and flexible. You are emotional, looking for praise. You are a little anxious, sometimes impatient, and don't like stressful situations. The Venus mound under your thumb, this fleshy part tells me you are intuitive, sensual, and bound for love and vitality."

Priscilla was enthralled.

Jonathan rolled his eyes again although he had to admit the Gypsy woman was very good at her game.

Tatyana adjusted the candle to accentuate the shadows over the creases in Priscilla's palm. She moved a finger slowly along one of them and mused. "A long line here, Priscilla. It goes all the way around. You will have a long, active life."

"Oh, goody!" Priscilla purred.

"The heart line, mmm," Tatyana murmured, tracing another. "You will have a satisfying love life."

Priscilla turned to Jonathan smiling warmly and gestured for him to sit down. Reluctantly, he followed her prompt.

Tatyana went on as if she hadn't noticed. "I see travel to fun, exotic places like Europe, Asia, and the Caribbean."

Priscilla beamed, "Oh, yes!" She scooted forward in her chair.

"You will do that. Lots of it!" Tatyana eyed Priscilla's palm more closely. "I see a union with a man. A gorgeous man! I see a big, beautiful wedding. Your father and mother are crying tears of joy, watching as their little girl, dressed as a princess, walks down the aisle."

She surprised Jonathan with a sharp, cryptic side glance.

Without missing a beat, Tatyana sighed dramatically and continued. "Oh, my, Dear, it is a wonderful, sunny day. See here!" She pointed to some small creases. "Little divisions along your lifeline after the union." Her eyes widened.

"What? What does it mean?" Priscilla's breath quickened in anticipation.

"Children! I see lovely, towheaded, blue-eyed cherubs running, giggling, playing at your feet."

Priscilla squealed. "Oh, please tell me. How many?"

"At least two."

"Boys? Girls? What are they?"

"That would depend on your fate line. Let's see."

"Yes, please!"

Jonathan watched in disbelief as Tatyana flattened Priscilla's hand and examined it more closely. Priscilla looked on with rapt attention, hanging on Tatyana's every word. "A deep line here. Not everyone has a fate line, Dear. It means destiny controls you, but it's up to you to believe it or not."

Tatyana folded Priscilla's fingers into a fist and let go. Then she smiled warmly and said, "So, you have questions. Questions about your future, Dear?"

"Oh my, Tatyana," Priscilla gasped. "This reading is so much better than I imagined. But you never answered my one big question."

"You want a boy and a girl—in any order, but only two."

"Yes." Priscilla's expression changed from pleading to surprise.

"Remember Priscilla; I told you that was up to destiny. We fortunetellers have little to do with changing destiny. However, there are things we can do to tilt the odds in your favor."

"What do you mean?"

Tatyana put her finger to her lips and let out a sigh. "Oh, I don't know, Dear. I can't promise you anything, but my grandmother made special candles for the Gadjo in Europe. Many of her clients were royalty, kings and queens from many countries. One of her candles was particularly prized and sought after." She paused, squinting her eyes.

Priscilla was on the edge of her seat. "Yes?" She said anxiously and leaned forward.

"I still have two in a special wooden treasure box somewhere. Let me see if I can find them for you."

Tatyana left for her bedroom, and they could hear her moving things about on a shelf. Jonathan leaned back and shook his head. Priscilla kept her eyes intent on the doorway between the room.

When Tatyana returned, she was carrying an antique wooden box with a brass lock, holding it with both hands as if it contained a prized gold crown. She placed it on the table before Priscilla and opened it, revealing two slender, lavender candles lying on a purple velvet cloth.

"Here they are, the boy and girl candles," she announced with a broad, proud smile. "The most sought-after candles among royalty. As I said, I can't make promises, but every woman that lit one of these candles on their wedding night had a boy and a girl."

Priscilla sighed. "Oh, Tatyana. How much? Please, I must have one! May I hold them?" When Tatyana gave her a small nod, she took up one of the candles and carefully rolled it between her fingers.

Jonathan looked on, thoroughly disgusted. He was certain he had spotted a candle just like it on a trip to Target for some fishing tackle only two days ago.

"How much, Tatyana?" Priscilla asked, her eyes pleading.

The Gypsy looked at her like a kind grandmother. "How much? I don't know. I should just give you one. You make such a lovely couple." Closing her eyes, she mused out loud, "Queens paid thousands of gold coins to my grandmother for just a single one, and I have only two left." She tapped her chin and opened her eyes. "Three hundred dollars," she said, then hesitated. "No, on second thought, for you, $200. But, please don't tell anyone, especially my friends. Every one of them will be in here looking for a bargain."

Priscilla let out a shriek of joy. "Oh, thank you, Tatyana. But what should I carry it in and where should I keep it? I don't want to lose it or have it damaged. It's a whole year until our wedding."

"Let me see if I can find you a small bag," Tatyana said, all business now, and disappeared again to her bedroom. Within seconds, she returned carrying a small red Yankee Candle bag just large enough for one, possibly two candles.

Priscilla reached into her pocket, pulled back out the wad of bills, and peeled off two more one-hundred-dollar bills. She glowed with delight as if she had just made the deal of a lifetime.

"When you get home, Priscilla, place the candle on your bedside table. Be sure not to light it until your wedding night," Tatyana cautioned. "Oh, I'm so happy for you both!"

Jonathan couldn't help himself. He shook his head and grunted.

Tatyana turned to him and said amiably, "And you, Jonathan? You've been quiet until now. No questions?"

He was about to answer when Priscilla said, "Oh, Jonathan, please let it be. You're always so serious! I had fun. That's what we came here for, right?"

But Tatyana wouldn't let it rest, taunting, "No questions, doctor? No questions from the Devil's curse healer?"

"Oh, for God's sake," Jonathan exploded. "It's all just hocus-pocus nonsense. A candle to assure a boy and a girl. Fairytale predictions."

Priscilla pulled at his arm. "Jonathan, please just let it be."

"No, you got ripped off, Priscilla," he said mockingly. "Conned by this Gypsy, this self-proclaimed fortune teller. And she didn't even have to pick your pocket. You gladly shelled out 300 bucks for half an hour's work. That's way more than I earn as a doctor!"

With icy serenity, Tatyana said, "It is not trick or hocus-pocus. I have been doing this my whole life. I learned it from my mother and she from hers. I do not lie. I have foretold Priscilla's future, as I see it."

Jonathan's back stiffened. His eyes bore into Tatyana's, "Really?! Then tell me something about my future. Something I don't know about myself or never could have known."

Tatyana's triumphant look made clear she relished his provocation. "But I thought you didn't want any foretelling."

Jonathan snapped back, "Priscilla is naturally impressionable and drawn to words of affirmation. You just reinforced her preconceptions. You seem to be good at that. I'll give you that much. But I am a man of science. Let's see you try your magic with me."

For a moment it seemed that Tatyana grew in size and her voice resonated with authority. "You carry great anger, Doctor, and you're afraid to let it out fearing it will devour you. Since you insist, I give you this prediction: Your future is full of struggles and anguish if you continue along this path."

"But you didn't even read my palm or anything."

Tatyana lowered her voice, "I didn't need to, Dr. Curtis. It's written all over your face."

Jonathan struggled to recover his composure. His ego shaken, he counter-attacked. "Bullshit! Tell me something that isn't just far-fetched crap, something not so vague."

A smirk played about Tatyana's lips. "Well then, Dr. Curtis, I stand accused, and you stand on a threshold. I may be guilty of a bit of flimflam, but you are on dangerous ground, denying that a person cannot gain insight through prayer, meditation, dreams, or other spiritual means. Will you at least grant the possibility that there are other modes of perception than science recognizes for now?"

"Okay, dreams, prayer, the subconscious—yes, I give you that. But it doesn't make you any less of a charlatan."

Tatyana nodded to herself, gratified, and said, "Your fiancé wanted only to have some fun. That, we did. The readings from her palms were true. For most Gadjo, this is as far as we go. However, you asked me to tell you something you don't know about yourself. I say you already know it and are unable to admit it. So, we will go there." She squinted. "I see anger in your eyes. A rage, centuries old, that will soon be discovered."

As she continued to speak, she seemed to stare right through Jonathan. "You ask me to prove this. So, let me take you to what I call 'the realm beyond' and show you who you are. This higher reality is not a place one should go alone. We may catch only a glimpse or nothing at all. Either way, we must be thankful for that. On this path of surrender, there may come a moment asking you to leap. Be ready for it. Join me, if you wish. But above all, know we must surrender."

Her gaze returned to his eyes, as she asked for his commitment. "Do you have the courage to do that? Join me as we both surrender to a higher reality?"

Jonathan dismissed the flicker of fear that licked at his heart. He stared back crossly and gave a nod.

"Then, we will go. One warning I give to you. All you will witness in the realm—a spiritual manifestation of the transcendental—may change your perspective of the world you see now."

Priscilla squirmed in her seat. "Jonathan, please, we came here to have fun. I'm getting scared with all this heebie-jeebies stuff. Please, let's just leave."

Jonathan took a deep breath and his eyes narrowed. "No, Priscilla, I want to see for myself. I have accused Tatyana of being a sham, and she is asking for a chance to prove she is not. I should give her that." He turned to Tatyana and nodded again.

Tatyana looked at Priscilla. The young woman looked worried. To set her mind at ease, she said, "Nothing terrible will happen, and Jonathan will return to you shortly. Just watch and listen. You are the keeper of the memory of this moment."

Priscilla nodded, gratefully, although she didn't look like she understood the task the fortune teller had given her.

Turning her attention to Jonathan, Tatyana blew out the candle. It was getting dark outside. To Jonathan's eyes, the kerosene lamps turned low barely illuminated the room, giving it a mysterious atmosphere, like a secret cave or the hiding spot under the stairs in the home where he grew up.

"Are you ready?" Tatyana's voice sounded full-bodied and rich.

He must have nodded because she continued, "Jonathan, take hold of my hands and don't let go, no matter what happens. Remember, I will be with you." He felt her hands grasping his. They were surprisingly strong.

In a deep, guttural command, she instructed, "Close your eyes, Jonathan. Come with me now, as we leave this earthly world and invoke the imagery of folklore and dreams."

The last thing he saw was her head moving back and forth, and in and out, in a figure-eight pattern. Then her voice began to resonate with incantations in a language that sounded familiar but he didn't understand. As the vibrations deepened, pulsating tones emanated from the walls as if loudspeakers were hidden behind them. Tatyana's voice built to a rising and falling rhythm, moving through him like the wind. Although it seemed to come from farther away, it kept calling to him. His breath deepened and his head began rolling in figure eights, too. It felt as if conscious thought were separating from his body and rising over it, not like a dream, but a dream-like creation, more vivid than reality itself.

Then, her voice was close by again. "Jonathan, come with me."

He floated for a moment with outstretched arms and legs, weightless as if suspended in a salt ocean, released from the power of gravity. It was a warm, comfortable feeling, not scary at all. As earthly connections gave way, he began to move up through the firmament and into dark space, toward the edge of the cosmos. His body flew at the speed of light past the stars and galaxies, back in time.

A starburst exploded far away leaving a central, florescent blue dot amid the darkness. That speck generated shimmering green, red, gold, and silver spheres, like Christmas tree ornaments, dancing around him in rotating patterns. He felt giddy, much as he did when he was six years old, and let go of a balloon for the first time to watch it fly up into the clouds.

Mysteriously, the orbs began to coalesce into beautiful sights, sounds, and smells, which he recognized from his past—a burbling waterfall plummeting from a tall mountain, the fresh scent of rhododendron and mountain laurel, sunlight filtering through spruce trees high atop mountain ridges.

Jonathan looked around and found himself kneeling in a patch of green grass and dandelions, surrounded by a white picket fence. A single four-leaf clover caught his attention. He reached out to pluck it. "A lucky find. It will make a great addition to my clover chain," he thought.

Suddenly, he was in his childhood bed, and afraid. There was a scratch at the door. And then another. And another. A chill ran down his back, and he trembled. He knew what it was—a large, fierce wildcat with spots and stripes like a tiger, eyes glaring with golden fire, and sharp fangs dripping saliva hungrily. He scrambled out the window and up the morning glory lattice to the roof as the big cat burst through the door. He heard it growl behind him, its breath hot on his neck. Near the top, it lunged after him, swiping at him with razor-sharp claws. As he heaved himself onto the roof, the thin, wooden lattice gave way and the cat tumbled to the ground. He was safe for the moment, but he had painful, crimson stripes on his arm.

Once more he was whisked away, to a mountainous region on an exposed hillside. It seemed like dusk, but he realized the twilight was the result of dark thunderclouds hiding the sun. The surrounding sky was illuminated burgundy red. Lighting struck in the distance. Smoke rose from primitive structures in the valley below. He walked to the top of the barren hill. There were no trees or houses on the other side, but hundreds of men, women, and babies. Their naked bodies were impaled on sharp wooden stakes driven through their bodies, leaving their feet dangling helplessly. Those still alive were praying for death. Their anguished voices sounded like a cacophony of bleating sheep. They moaned and cried out for help, to release them, but there was nothing he could do to relieve their suffering. He was too late. The foul stench of rotting flesh filled his nostrils, and blood ran from the stakes, forming a river around his feet. He cried to the heavens, begging God to forgive him.

Strong fingers intertwined with his. They pulled him down through the cosmos, as fast as he'd ascended, until he sat again at Tatyana's table. His hands were shaking with uncontrollable tremors.

Tatyana's voice rang out with comforting clarity, "Jonathan, it's all right. You're back, back in my trailer. You are fine. You are safe!"

He heard Priscilla plead, "Jonathan, please, you're scaring me now. Please answer me."

Tears flowed from Jonathan's face. He choked as he wiped them with his shirttail. Seeing her frightened face, he started to apologize, "Priscilla, I'm sorry, I..." But he stopped mid-sentence and wheeled toward Tatyana. "Where was I? What does it mean?" Her eyes were like two hard, black marbles. "Was it a d-d-dream?"

he stammered. "It seemed so real. I was having such a wonderful trip and then a nightmare."

"No, Dear. Not a dream," she said soothingly. "It was a glimpse of a higher reality." Her eyes brightened. "You did as I instructed. You surrendered and took the leap."

"But, what does it mean? My nightmares. Please."

"I don't know, Jonathan. However, I believe the meadow with the clover leaf and the bloody hillside are messages from your past."

Jonathan muttered, "One I recognized from my childhood. The other was a hellish place I've never seen before." Startled, he called out, "Wait, you were there?"

Tatyana nodded slowly. "Yes, and I must tell you something, not to prove myself or win any argument. This was a gift to both of us, but it has come with great trouble. I want you to rest assured, though, that just as I was there with you just now, I will be with you when it comes."

Jonathan's eyes widened. He bent forward in his chair clutching his pants with his fingers.

Tatyana quickly rose and placed her hand on his shoulder. "Jonathan, I told you, I did not know what it all means, but the dream is both a memory and a premonition, very strong and very real." She paused, then added ominously, "So is the wildcat: very real, very dangerous, and very close by."

"Oh, oh." Jonathan moaned and buried his head in his hands.

Frantically, Priscilla grasped his arm. "Please, Jonathan, let's just get out of here!"

Jonathan got up as if in a trance and let her lead him from the trailer. She settled him in her Mercedes and drove off without looking back.

Tatyana gazed after them, a fearful expression on her face.

Chapter 4

BIG JACK

Jonathan woke the next morning feeling groggy, leaden, and confused like a giant boulder had sat on him all night. He looked at the clock on the nightstand and did a doubletake—had he really slept for twelve hours?! Then he realized that he was still fully dressed.

As he slowly sat up and peeled off his shirt, pants, shoes, and socks, he remembered the Gypsy fortune teller's comment: "Your future is full of struggles and anguish if you continue along this path." What did she mean by that? And the horrific scene of torture and execution he'd witnessed during his bizarre, out-of-body experience—what was that all about?

On the drive home, Priscilla had recovered her poise and tried to laugh it all off, but she kept casting worried glances at Jonathan. Although they'd made plans for dinner at a seafood restaurant, he was so exhausted that he begged off and asked her to take him back to his apartment. She was understanding but disappointed. Somehow, he'd made it inside and collapsed on the bed.

By the time he showered, ate breakfast, and downed several cups of coffee, he was feeling better. The short ride to his office on his Harley Davidson helped too. The wind rushing past his face always exhilarated him.

Jonathan pulled off the highway onto a shelled parking lot by a one-story grey stucco building and shut down the engine. His modest medical office had been someone's home in the late 1960s.

A sign in the window read "Dr. Jonathan Curtis, Internal Medicine." The waiting room was clean and comfortable, and decorated with eclectic second-hand furnishings.

Lynne Carrington, his receptionist and medical assistant, greeted him. She was a tall, young, pretty brunette, dedicated to her job and eager to see the practice thrive. As she handed him the morning schedule, she wrinkled her nose, dissatisfied that it was not full. A light schedule would have normally worried Jonathan too. He had bills to pay. But today he was happy to have more time to mend his wounded psyche.

Fortunately, the morning brought only a few new patient walk-ins and routine, easily solved complaints. His scheduled patients presented with minor problems. Mrs. Sakellarides, a sweet old lady but something of a worry wart, came in complaining of stomach pains. After repeated reassurances, she left happy that her "tummy issue" turned out to be a simple gastritis. Although still a young doctor, Jonathan knew that half his job was offering a sympathetic ear and encouragement.

Then Mrs. Pappas arrived. Her main symptoms were bloodshot eyes and persistent morning headaches, and she wanted pain medication to relieve them. She had researched her symptoms on the internet and concluded that she was suffering from a brain tumor.

While Jonathan checked her vitals, Lynne cracked open the door to the exam room. "Sorry to bother you, Dr. Curtis, but there is an urgent matter."

Jonathan turned to his patient, "Excuse me, Mrs. Pappas. It'll just take a minute."

He stepped into the hallway and asked, "What's up?"

"Nurse Hawkins is on the line. She sounded rattled."

Lynnee's observation surprised Jonathan. Hawkins had many faults, but getting rattled wasn't one of them. He went to his office and picked up the telephone.

"Hawkins here, Dr. Curtis," her voice rang out. "You'd better come over stat. We've got a patient with chest pain. We've run some tests, but he refuses to be treated by anyone but you. Insists you're his 'personal physician.'"

Jonathan rubbed his forehead, puzzled. "Who is he?"

"Patient's name is Jack Lee. Dr. Evans took a look at his EKG. Thinks it could be a heart attack."

"Jack Lee?" Jonathan scratched his head. "I don't have a patient by that name."

Hawkins clucked. "I didn't think so. Says he was referred by Kizzy and Bicca."

Jonathan sighed. "Gypsies again?! Is he stable?"

"Stable? Oh yes. He's convinced it's just a little gas. He's begging us to let him go, but I suggested he wait a few minutes until we get his 'personal doctor' to see him. So, you'd better high-tail over here before I need to call a mortician."

On the way to the examining room, Jonathan beckoned to Lynne to follow him. "Well, Mrs. Pappas," he said amiably, "I don't think it's anything serious. We'll do an MRI just to be sure, but I suggest you cut back a bit on your drinking." Before she could say anything, he pushed Lynne forward. "I'm sorry, but I've got to run. Emergency at the hospital. Lynne here will take care of the paperwork with you."

* * *

It took him less than 10 minutes to get to the ER where Hawkins was waiting for him at the nurse's station with the patient's chart. "Your next exorcism, Doctor Curtis," she said with a haughty smile.

Jonathan glanced around the busy corridor. All the exam rooms and curtained cubicles were occupied. He caught Dr. Evans, the on-call doctor, coming out of a cubicle with a harried look.

Waving the chart, he caught his attention. "What's going on, Chris?"

Dr. Evans came over, his eyebrows raised. "You missed all the excitement. The patient came in on the first ambulance followed by a red stretch Cadillac convertible with his 'friends'—two giant goons who refused to leave his side. They're both packing 38s, so I suggest you let them be." He gave a quick nod toward Cubicle One. "I put Big Jack in there, so he could be more closely monitored."

"Big Jack?" Jonathan asked, perplexed. "Who is this guy?"

"Why, he's the King of the Gypsies." Evans said it like everybody knew that. "He's a likable guy, but he scares the bejeezus out of me. Says he was playing a friendly game of pool at J-Wags, when he began to notice chest pain. He got a little dizzy and passed out on the floor. I put him on oxygen and drew some labs. He's not happy with any of this 'medical shit'—his words. You're gonna have your hands full with that one."

Jonathan nodded and prepared to leave, but Dr. Evans held him back. "That's not all. Shortly after Big Jack was admitted, three ambulances brought in five young men with multiple injuries— broken ribs, jaws, and fingers, one sprained elbow, and lacerations to the head and face. All of them suffered injuries from 'accidental falls.'" He grabbed Jonathan by the arm. "And get this, all from J-Wags."

"What?"

"That was my reaction." Dr. Evans said, smiling. "One of the paramedics told me the bar was a mess when the ambulance arrived: chairs and tables turned upside-down; pool balls, broken beer bottles, and cracked cue sticks littered everywhere. They found Big Jack out cold in the middle of the floor without a scratch on him. Lying all around him, the five skinheads were licking their wounds. Apparently, they belong to the same gang, because they all have identical dragon tattoos on their forearms."

"According to the bartender, they came in looking for trouble. When they noticed Big Jack sitting by himself sipping a beer, they started to taunt him, calling him all kinds of names. But they failed to notice his two bodyguards at the bar who went into action and cleaned their clocks. And not a scratch on either of them. I get the idea they're used to this kind of entertainment! If I were you, I'd watch my back."

Jonathan rolled his eyes. "Thanks a lot!" He took a deep breath, gave the chart a quick once-over, and pulled back the curtain.

A stout man in his late forties lay on the stretcher. His face was olive-colored, and he looked dejected. He had an IV in his arm, an oxygen cannula on his nose, and a heart monitor taped to his chest. His round belly stuck out between a white sleeveless muscle shirt and beltless Khaki trousers. Except for the gold jewelry around his neck and the diamond-studded Rolex on his wrist, someone could easily mistake him for a street bum.

Two tall, refrigerator-shaped men jerked to attention. Like their boss, they had dark features and sallow skin and were dressed alike: in two-piece, linen Panama suits, white T-shirts, and gold chain necklaces. They scrutinized Jonathan with critical eyes.

Jonathan ignored them and walked over to the patient. "Mr. Lee, I'm Dr. Curtis."

The man's worried expression instantly transformed into one of roguish charm. "Oh, thank you, Doctor. I'm so glad you're here," he gushed "Let me introduce my cousins, Pinky and Carl. We go way back. They're my trusted family and you can call me Big Jack." He gave Jonathan a megawatt smile. "And now that we're all friends, can you let me out of here?"

The two bodyguards eased up on their aggressive stance.

Jonathan put on his best, bed-side smile. "Mr. Lee, I'd like to do just that, but I'm concerned you may have had a heart attack."

"Oh, no. I'm sure it's just some gas." He looked up at Jonathan with the eyes of a naïve youngster. "There are some pills? Pills for the tummy like I've seen on T.V. The 'purple pill,' huh, Doc?"

Jonathan smiled, taking an immediate liking to this quirky character. "Mr. Lee, I sure hope you're right, but your EKG—this thing hooked up to your chest—indicates you might have something more serious," he admonished. "Right now, I'm waiting for the lab results. Then, we'll know for certain."

Big Jack winked. "I like you, Doctor. Can't we just strike some kinda deal? I could make it worth your while. You tell 'em I'm good to go, and I'll sign whatever paperwork you need."

Jonathan's lips crinkled in amusement. "Good try, Big Jack, but we'll wait a little longer for your tests. In the meantime, let's do a more thorough workup."

Big Jack sighed and sat back, accepting the inevitable. Pinky and Carl looked on impassively. Throughout the interview and exam, Big Jack kept Jonathan entertained. Between jokes and what sounded like tall tales, he told a familiar immigrant story. He was a first-generation American whose parents came from Slovakia. He'd grown up on the streets of New Jersey, a school drop-out in the fifth grade. His father was killed in a bar fight over a card game when Jack was twelve. His mother died from complications of diabetes shortly after. Except for a few scrapes and scratches from street scuffles that required medical attention, he had not seen a doctor.

His health choices were atrocious: fast food, pizza, hamburgers, eating on the go; having breakfast in second-rate diners after spending all night in bars and casinos. "I smoke a Cuban cigar daily, drink Turkish coffee 'til noon, Pabst beer 'til six, and whiskey 'til I drop," he bragged.

Listening to him, Jonathan thought it was a miracle he'd lasted this long. He shook his head and said, "Big Jack, you've been eating, drinking, and carousing like you think you'll live forever."

"Amen to that," Big Jack said.

But the physical exam revealed a host of problems: high blood pressure, abdominal obesity, poor circulation. His oily skin reeked of a toxic diet. When his lab work returned, the news got worse: sky-high cholesterol and triglycerides; abnormal liver profile, most likely caused by too much alcohol and junkfood; and abnormal cardiac enzymes.

Jonathan gave his patient a pat on the shoulder. "So far, there are no complications, but I want to run more tests. One of your major heart vessels has narrowed, the one they call the 'widow maker.' We may have to put in a stent to give you more good years. I'd like to keep you here in the hospital on a monitor for a few days."

Big Jack's face sagged like the air deflating from a balloon. "Am I gonna die, Doctor?" he asked like a fearful child. "I ain't scared of dyin' myself. Well, maybe a little, but I got a daughter to think about. I'm all she's got, so I'm worried for her."

Jonathan gave him a confident smile. "I'll make sure you stay around a little longer. With luck, you'll live long enough to see your grandchildren."

A look of relief replaced Big Jack's worried expression. "Thanks, Doc. I like the sound of that! Kizzy said you were all right."

Jonathan shook his head, chuckling, and turned to leave. "I'm going to write up some orders and get you a private room so you all can relax. I'll come back to check on you later."

But as he started to pull back the curtain, Pinky tapped him on the shoulder. He looked sternly at Jonathan and, with a quick head tilt toward the hallway, said, "Doc, outside. I need to go over some business with ya."

Looming over him with cold, beady eyes, he said, "Doc, you're a good man and everything. I can see that, but I got to make something clear."

Jonathan blinked. "Okay."

"We can't have Big Jack die, you understand. You gotta do whatever it takes. We'll pay for it. We ain't got no insurance or credit cards or things like that, but whatever it takes, do it!" Pinky leaned in further, "'Cause if he dies, you die."

Jonathan's eyes widened. "You've got to be kidding," he said and laughed nervously. "Of course, I will do my best, Pinky, but I can't promise anything. Big Jack's put a lot of miles on his body, but you can't just fix things by replacing parts like with cars."

Pinky frowned. "Well, I hope your best is good enough," he said. "We all like you, Doc. But we brought Big Jack in here alive, and we'll be taking him out alive. We don't, you die."

He turned with surprising grace and went back into the cubicle.

Jonathan drifted back to the nurse's desk, perplexed and bewildered. He had never dealt with someone like Pinky before. So much for the honor of being the personal doctor of a Gypsy King. As he wrote out orders, his sense of humor got the better of him. "That's one way to have a doctor put some serioius skin in the game," he mused.

He imagined Big Jack would not like the bland, low-salt, low-carb, low-fat diet he was prescribing. He'd have to monitor him carefully to make sure cutting off his alcohol didn't put him in withdrawal. Plus, Big Jack would get no coffee in the morning, which would give him a migraine headache.

When he presented the list to Hawkins, she scoffed and chided, "No insurance, no money. They'll run up a big bill, steal everything that's not nailed down, and probably slit your throat if anything happens to their precious king. I've heard a bunch of them are pulling their R.V.s into the parking lot out back. Word is, they intend to carry on an all-night vigil."

Jonathan turned on his heels, muttered a few curse words, and headed for his motorcycle to return to his clinic. He thought again about Pinky's threat and dismissed it. Little did he know that more danger was looming from another quarter.

* * *

Colonel Frank Burdock sat in the study of his plush, two-story townhouse, grumbling in exasperation. A slew of papers—faxes and e-mail printouts—covered his mahogany desk. He absentmindedly stroked the white Bichon Frise on his lap under its pink rhinestone collar and muttered, "Something's missing, Mazy."

The fluffy little pup, which lay curled up like a small stuffed animal, raised its head as he checked through the stack of papers on his desk again. A look of irritation crossed his face.

After the party, he performed a routine background check on the fiancé of Brian Randolph's daughter, and nothing untoward turned up. But the smug, young doctor had raised his hackles, and the Colonel had learned to trust the itching at the nape of his neck. Shortly after Jonathan and Priscilla left, he spoke to her parents about Dr. Curtis' pedigree.

"Father—English, mother—Irish," Brian Randolph assured him.

"His mother died years ago, leaving him with his only living relative, an aunt back in Tennessee," Muffy added.

"I have never seen a Brit or Irishman that dark-skinned," the Colonel said. "Perhaps he has some Melungeon or Cherokee Indian blood."

Randolph chuckled at the assertion. "With DNA tests these days, you can never be sure you haven't some wayward ancestors somewhere, but I am confident that Jonathan is well above board."

Burdock acquiesced, but as soon as he got home, he went into action and called on all his contacts in the military and intelligence services to get him any information on Dr. Curtis they could find.

It was an exercise in frustration. All of Jonathan's records were in order. There was one minor incident. He popped up in a police report in Durham, North Carolina. During a fight at a Duke fraternity party, Jonathan decked a couple of football players. However, all charges of assault were dropped when it became clear that they had provoked the fight, and the school authorities chalked it up to a combination of too much beer and testosterone-driven bravado.

The Colonel ran his fingers through his close-cropped hair and looked at his memorabilia-studded walls as if seeking help from his war exploits, mentors, and heroes. A tryptic of photographs hung among the host of medals and citations. One showed him and General Westmoreland dressed in battle fatigues, standing beside an Apache helicopter on a clearing in the dense jungles of Vietnam. In another, Burdock was in a flight jacket outside the hangers at MacDill Airforce Base next to General "Storming Norman" Schwarzkopf, the commander of the coalition forces during the first Gulf War. The centerpiece was him receiving a commendation from President Reagan after the invasion of Grenada.

The Colonel was about to go over the papers on his desk once more when Mazy raised her head. An instant later the FAX machine started up, its chugging disturbing the quiet in the room. By the time the beep sounded that the transmission was done, Burdock was waiting impatiently, with Mazy tucked under his arm, to retrieve the report.

He returned to his desk and spread out the three pages on the table. It was the response to his NSA inquiry. The Colonel's smile grew as he read the report. Sensing her owner's growing excitement, Mazy perked up in anticipation. When he finished, he chortled, sat back with a smug grin, and softly patted her back. "Just as I thought, Mazy. Something fishy going on."

* * *

When Jonathan returned to the hospital for afternoon rounds, campers and Gypsy wagons filled the parking lot and a small crowd had gathered in front of the entrance. As he made his way through the gauntlet, they pulled at his shirt and arms and called out, "Dr. Curtis, Dr. Curtis. Thank you, Doctor. You're here to see Big Jack? Is he okay?"

Inside the glass doors, a hospital security guard blocked the entrance, scowling. He nodded to Jonathan and let him pass.

When Jonathan got to the cardiac wing, the nurses at the desk gave him quizzical smiles. He glanced at the monitor marked LEE "Normal sinus rhythm; blood oxygen 98%. Perfect." Heading for Big Jack's room, he muttered wryly, "Not going to get my throat slit this afternoon."

His patient greeted him with a broad grin. "Dr. Curtis, I'm happy to see you again."

Big Jack was propped up in his hospital bed with an oxygen tube running to his nose. Playing cards and poker chips were spread across the covers. A male nurse's aide sat in a chair by his bedside. Jonathan recognized him. Gary Jackson was a big, muscular, black man in his early thirties, who looked as if he had been lifting weights his whole life.

Smiling, Jonathan said, "Hi, Big Jack. I hope they're treating you well here."

"Yeah, sure, treating me just fine. You play?"

"Yes, but not today." Realizing that the cousins weren't there, Jonathan asked, "Pinky and Carl step out?"

"The security guard wouldn't let 'em stay after visiting hours," Jack explained. "They didn't like it but were nice about it... Hey, you should have been here about an hour ago. The room was full. It's a Romani tradition. I'm some kind of royalty to them. The guard ran them off too."

"Not all the way, Big Jack. Your loyal subjects are all still out front. I got mauled by them on my way in just a minute ago. Isn't there something you can do about that?"

Big Jack shrugged his shoulders as if it didn't concern him.

Jonathan's eyes were drawn to a sparkle on Gary's wrist. It was the diamond-studded watch he had seen Big Jack wear earlier. A glance at his patient's empty arm confirmed the switch. His eyes narrowing, Jonathan said, "I'm surprised you're still here, Gary. I thought you'd be long gone by now."

"Doing private nursing duty after my shift, Doc," the burly nurse's aide said. "Big Jack hired me."

Jonathan raised an eyebrow, "Really?" He looked around the room and spotted a crumpled bag in the waste basket along with a super-sized drinking cup. Both items bore the familiar yellow arches logo. Turning to his patient, he said, "Did you enjoy your dinner, Big Jack? I thought your heart might benefit from more vegetables in your diet."

Big Jack assumed a poker face. "Oh yeah. Delightful, four stars!"

"Then, I gather the Big Mac was Gary's, right?"

"Sure, Doc. Of course. He had to eat, you know,"

As he took a stethoscope from his pocket, Jonathan noticed that the drawer on the bedside table was ajar. On a hunch, he pulled it out, revealing a bottle of Johnny Walker Black Label and two Presidente Cigars.

"I'm going to assume these are yours, too, Gary," he said, glancing hard at Big Jack. "Make sure they go home with you."

The color drained from Gary's face. He answered like a child caught in the act, "Right, Dr. Curtis."

After checking his patient's vitals, Jonathan said, "Your heart sounds good, Big Jack." Then he took a step back and continued, severely, "If I'm going to be your doctor, there's something we need to discuss. Pinky and I had an encounter earlier."

Big Jack looked chagrined. "Yeah. Pinky told me about cornering you in the hallway," he said guiltily. "Sorry about that. He's just scared for me, that's all. It's the only way he knows to get things done. I already told him that kind of strong-arming don't work here. He won't be bothering you, again. He likes you."

Jonathan grinned. "He's got an odd way of showing it. Thanks for understanding and calling off your guards."

"Sure, Doc."

"So can you do me a favor and send your followers home?"

Big Jack considered. "I don't know. They're just concerned about me being in the hospital all alone. They're suspicious of the Gadjo. It's their way of way of showing respect, you know, support. Nothin' menacing."

"I totally get it," Jonathan said. "You're a well-loved man and we're taking good care of you, right? Could you just let them know you're okay and ask them to go home?"

Scratching his head, Big Jack said, "I don't know if that would work. They don't have a home. We're a clan, a family that travels together. Right now, their home is in the hospital parking lot, close to me." A cunning expression crossed his face. He glanced at Jonathan and said, "You know, my daughter Aisha—everyone calls her Isha—she's a good kid. Her mother, my wife Maria, bless her soul, died shortly after she was born. Now, Isha's worried she's going to lose me, too. She came in here earlier acting like she was already attending my wake."

Jonathan waited, not sure where this was going.

Sighing, Big Jack continued, "You see, Doc, it's stressing me out. If I could just get her distracted somehow, I could get some rest and recover sooner. I know tomorrow she'll be fussing at me all day. Could you come up with something for her to do to take her mind off things? Could you do that for me? Take her mind off things."

"You mean me p-p-personally?" Jonathan sputtered. He started to pace. "I don't know, Big Jack, a young girl. I'm a single man, engaged to be married."

For a moment, Big Jack looked at him with a hangdog expression. Then he brightened. "Oh, don't worry about that. I'll send a friend with her. Besides, she won't be the least interested in you, believe me." Seeing Jonathan's eyebrows narrow, he quickly added, "No offense, Doc, but you're Gadjo and too reserved for the likes of her." He chuckled. "Besides, if I did hear of anything happening, I'd have to call on Pinky to handle it for me."

Jonathan thought quickly. He had planned to go out on his boat with Jimmy Pappas tomorrow anyway. Why not take a guest or two along? "And, if I do?" he ventured.

Big Jack beamed at him. "If you do this for me, I'll be forever grateful, and the parking lot will be cleared by morning. There won't be a Gypsy Vardo in sight."

"You promise?"

Nodding solemnly, Big Jack said, "I swear on my dear Maria's grave."

"All right then, have her meet me at the Tarpon Springs City Marina at 8 a.m. tomorrow morning."

Big Jack saluted him in acknowledgment.

Jonathan left the cardiac wing pleased he had struck a deal with Big Jack. In the hallway, his phone vibrated. The caller I.D. showed the Randolph residence. "Priscilla," he thought.

But when he answered the call, he heard her father's voice at the other end. "Jonathan. This is Brian Randolph."

Jonathan was taken aback. This was the first time Brian had called him directly. "Yes Sir, uh, Brian, this is Jonathan. Is Priscilla there?"

"Yes, Priscilla is here. I'm glad you answered so promptly. I need to see you as soon as possible. Something has just come to my attention, something we need to talk about. Can you meet me here at the house this afternoon?"

Jonathan frowned. "Sure Brian," he said. "Is Priscilla okay?"

"Priscilla is fine," Brian responded in a terse tone. "What time might I expect you? I'll call security to let them know you're coming."

"I can be there by five," Jonathan said, bewildered, and ended the call.

Chapter 5

THE RANDOLPH MANSION

For the second time in two days, Jonathan visited the Palma Verde Country Club. The phone call he'd received from Pricilla's father had been so troubling that he had hopped on his motorcycle and headed directly for the Randolph mansion. It was the only residence inside the gated grounds that had its own private security, a small guard house next to the tall iron entrance portal. The guard gave him a condescending look, but when Jonathan identified himself, he opened the heavy gates.

The Randolph residence was a huge, white-columned Southern mansion with a double portico overlooking an expansive oval lawn. Jonathan couldn't imagine what Brian Randolph had in mind—maybe some last-minute change to the wedding plans. But why had he sounded so aloof? And why had he given him no hint regarding what he wanted to discuss?

When he reached the front entrance, he parked his motorcycle alongside the curb and bounded up the steps.

He lifted the heavy brass knocker and rapped on the door. Immediately he heard footsteps approaching. William, the Randolph's butler, opened up.

With a detached glance and curt nod, he said, "Sir." He pointed down the long hallway and added, "Mr. Randolph is waiting in his study for you." Then he turned his back on Jonathan and walked away.

Watching William give him the cold shoulder treatment, Jonathan was again puzzled. In their previous encounters, they had always had friendly conversations, mostly about fishing. Only the week before, when Jonathan had complained about a wily snook taking runs over the sharp-edged oyster bed to snap his fishing line, William had laughed and said, "Must not have wanted himself to get caught."

"What is going on here?" Jonathan pondered as he passed the grand double staircase leading to the mezzanine. As he headed down the wide hallway, he became aware of his footsteps on the marble floor echoing from the walls. It was a desolate, hollow sound like walking alone in an empty cathedral.

The door to Priscilla's father's study was open.

Jonathan put on a smile to cover his nervousness and the bad feeling in his gut as he entered. With its tall, dark wooden wall cases filled with leather-bound books and hunting paintings, the study could have been in a British country home. An area to one side held a leather chair, sofa, and coffee table arranged on an enormous Persian rug. The drapes on the window and French doors leading to a patio were damask curtains. Brian Randolph sat at an ebony, 17th-century desk like a monarch presiding over his dominion. He was perusing several sheets of paper.

Jonathan cleared his throat. "Good afternoon, Brian," he said. His voice sounded firm though husky. "You wanted to see me about something?"

Randolph looked up and started to rise but thought better of it. He sat back stiffly, swept his few strands of blond hair over his nearly bald pate, and resumed his imperious position. "Evening, Jonathan. Don't bother to sit down. This shouldn't take long." His voice was flat and distant.

Noting the cold greeting, Jonathan's smile slipped from his face and the knot in his gut tightened.

Yet Randolph seemed hesitant to get started. His eyes darted among the papers strewn on his desk. Finally, took a deep breath and sighed. "You understand, a man of my position and status must take measures to protect his family, he said.

"Yes, of course, Brian."

"Would you then also agree it is my duty as the loving father of my only daughter to protect her from liars, cheats, and con artists who are bent on using my family's name, influence, and money to improve their social standing?"

"Of course, Brian, I agree wholeheartedly, and if this is Priscilla we are talking about, I totally understand and would do the same," Jonathan agreed. "But what does that have to do with me? Why did you ask me to come here?"

Randolph's face darkened in anger. "Don't act so naive around me, young man. Your little charade is over," he spat. "You're an impostor." He swept his hand over the papers as his voice rose. "My information is unimpeachable and comes from the highest sources. You are either a scoundrel of the worst sort or an idiot, a naive Hillbilly, as Muffy has suggested. In either case, I must protect Priscilla from your kind. If she hadn't pleaded on your behalf, I would have turned this over to the authorities already."

Jonathan stood dumbfounded. Then he shook his head and said, "Please, Brian, with all due respect, you must be confusing me with someone else. I don't understand what you are saying: Me, a liar, a con artist? That's not who I am. I love your daughter with all my heart, and asking her to marry me had nothing to do with her social status or money."

Randolph scrutinized him and said, less vehemently. "Well, Son, if you are still in the dark about this, then what I am about to tell you will come as a shock. Following your little head bashing with Colonel Burdock at the Club the other night, where I might point out, you displayed a total lack of political candor, the Colonel took it upon himself to do a more detailed background check than usual."

Jonathan started to flare up, but Randolph held up his hand. "It is his responsibility to investigate all membership applicants thoroughly. Not to his surprise, yours turned up full of holes. The largest one calls into question your legitimacy. Lieutenant Michael J. Curtis, of the 134th Air Refueling Wing at McGhee-Tyson Air National Guard, was killed on maneuvers and is buried in the Knoxville National Cemetery, as you claim. But he is not your father."

Jonathan gasped. His knees started to give out and he quickly grabbed hold of the front of the desk to steady himself. He tried to speak with resolve, "Brian, I assure you, the Colonel is lying. My mother, my father…there is no question of my legitimacy. I have a birth certificate to prove it. It is a legal document." He started to tick off additional evidence on his fingers. "I have a photo album of my father in his uniform, holding me when I was an infant. I have a scrapbook full of my father's accomplishments. My mother told me stories of his exploits when they were dating. The preacher at my Pentecostal church back home in Lafollette talked with me, on many occasions, about how my father expressed his love for my mother. He married them in that very church and then Christened me. Those are not lies."

"Not lies, you say? Why should I believe you, rather than Colonel Burdock, a highly decorated military officer, a patriot, and a man I have known for years?

Jonathan was about to interrupt again when Brian picked up a FAX document from the table. It had an official-looking seal and several initials on the cover page.

"This is a report from the NSA." He laid it in front of Jonathan and tapped it with his fingertips. "As I told you, Jonathan, my information is unimpeachable and comes from the highest sources, in this case, the best investigative agency on the face of the Earth."

Jonathan was stunned. "You had me investigated by the NSA?!"

Randolph nodded. "Colonel Burdock did. You messed with the wrong fellow, Son. And, in a way, I guess I should be grateful."

"The Colonel has the clearance to obtain information from the NSA for a mere membership application to a country club? That's preposterous. I don't believe it!"

Sneering dismissively, Randolph said, "As far as I'm concerned, the Colonel was wise to question your heritage, Jonathan. He told me, 'He's too dark to be of English descent, Brian. My guess is there's a you-know-what in the woodshed.'" While I don't necessarily share his view, considering all that's come out so far, who knows what else you've been hiding? I won't get into why Colonel Burdock has top clearance, but, yes, he does."

He opened the NSA document to its first page and read out loud, "Michael J. Curtis, born in Murfreesboro, Tennessee, worked as a C.P.A. for an accounting firm in Nashville. He was a loving father to his children, and a faithful husband to his wife who, I might add, are still living in Murfreesboro. He reported to work daily, spent weekends gardening in his backyard, and went to church every Sunday. On vacations, he took his family to a cottage he owned on a nearby lake. There are no gaps in his history to suggest a second family, no mention of a common-law wife, or even an incidental 'romp in the hay.' When he died, he left a trust, a life insurance policy, and his military benefits to his wife and two surviving children. There is no reference to your mother or you in this file."

Brian cast an accusing stare at Jonathan. "Did you or your mother ever receive any of these benefits?"

Jonathan's eyes burned with anger, but he made no rebuttal.

"Just as I thought." Priscilla's father pursed his lips in disdain. "Do you even know how he died? Lieutenant Michael J. Curtis received a citation for bravery after a fatal crash over the Bahamas on a routine training mission in October of 1988. His aircraft experienced a sudden loss of altitude and control due to wind shear and –"

Jonathan interrupted, "It happened on October 18, 1988. Michael Jonathan Curtis risked his life attempting to stabilize the equipment. He was successful but suffered fatal injuries. What you have there is a copy. I keep my father's original citation framed over my bedside. My mom and I went to the Knoxville National Cemetery where he is buried many times to place flowers on his grave. I am named after him, Jonathan Michael Curtis."

Randolph gave him a dubious glance.

Pacing back and forth in front of the desk, Jonathan worked himself up. "The Colonel is lying. I don't know why he would fabricate this stuff and deprive me of the only father I've ever known," He became increasingly incensed. "This is outrageous, Brian. You have known me for over a year, and to credit these ludicrous accusations and not first check them out with me does not speak well of you. I thought you were a fair man. Obviously, I was mistaken."

The accusation hit home and Randolph cast his eyes on the papers lying on his desk as if to find answers there. When he looked up, his voice had a more conciliatory tone. "I was upset on first hearing this news, principally for the grief it would cause my daughter. I didn't want to believe the evidence the Colonel brought me. I figured there must be some mistake. But the more I read, the more credible it became, and the angrier I got that you would try to pull something like this on my family."

"Then allow me to clear it up!"

Randolph examined the young man standing before him for some time before he relented. "Very well, I will give you one week. Despite what you may think, I consider myself a fair man."

Relief spread over Jonathan's face. "Thank you, Brian," he said earnestly. "I won't disappoint you, and that's a promise. Now before I go, I'd like to see Pricilla."

Stiffening, Randolph clenched his jaw and said, "I don't think so, not until this matter is cleared up or settled. If you can't produce evidence exonerating yourself, I cannot let you marry my daughter and the engagement will be called off. Muffy is devastated over this. She has flown to a spa in New York for the week to recover. You should thank God she's not here to deliver this message herself. I cannot fathom the embarrassment she and my daughter might have to endure if you cannot come up with proof positive."

Stung by his unkindness, Jonathan said contemptuously, "You will have your proof, Brian. But I won't forget how little it took to shake your confidence in me. You say your wife and Priscilla would be embarrassed by this? Not coming to my defense is what's embarrassing."

Randolph rose, slamming the NSA document down on his desk. "Priscilla has no say in this. She will do as she is told. And, unless you can satisfy me otherwise, I can assure you that your future will not have my daughter by your side. I forbid it!" He went to the French doors and stared at the dark sky. Then he turned and said, "I think we're done here. I'll see that William escorts you out."

Recovering his voice, Jonathan answered sharply, "That won't be necessary. I know my way."

He walked from the study as if in a trance. Somehow, he ended up outside, climbed on his Harley, and drove off, the angry roar of the engine echoing his fury. The ghostly silhouettes of trees flashed past him in the darkness, like looming sentinels bearing witness to his humiliation. His mind swirling, Jonathan felt deeply hurt. He couldn't make any sense of what had happened. Why would the Colonel hate him so much to frame him? Where did these documents come from? And what if there was a kernel of truth to the accusations.... "Oh God, let it not be true!" he shouted into the air rushing past him.

At some point, the ringtone on his cell phone went off. Jonathan slowed the bike, dug the phone out of his pocket, and glanced at the screen. It was Priscilla. He pulled over to the side of the road and parked on the grassy strip next to a drainage ditch. Balancing the idling bike with his long legs, he answered.

"Jonathan?" The voice at the other end was tentative.

"Pricilla! Where are you? Are you okay?"

"In my room." She sounded like she'd been crying. "Oh honey, I'm so upset. What is going on? I don't know what to believe. Tell me it isn't true."

"Of course, it isn't true. It's all lies to discredit me. You must believe me. You warned me not to tangle with the Colonel, but I had no idea he was such a vindictive bastard. He made it all up. It's pure slander. You believe me, don't you?"

"I do. I want to. But all this stuff, an NSA report! You know I believe in you. But what if the Colonel is right? Oh... I can't imagine what our babies would look like. What would all my friends say."

She was becoming hysterical, letting her mind gallop away with her. Jonathan recognized the signs. "It is all fabrications," he said in a calmer voice. "Priscilla, honey, I love you so much. We will get past this. I have proof. Everything will be alright. Trust me. Remember all the plans we made? All the love we promised to share? We'll have all that and more."

"Oh, Jonathan, I sure hope so."

He could tell she was still uncertain, but at least she sounded more reassured.

"Listen, honey, I need to go and figure this out," he said. "I'll call you tomorrow. I love you."

"I love you, too, Jonathan."

He broke the connection and resumed his ride, deeply troubled. It hadn't escaped him that Priscilla had referred to the racist slur of the Colonel's. He just hoped she'd be strong enough to resist her parents' attempt to brainwash her and turn her against him.

As he rode on, tears welled up in his eyes. He felt alone, confused, and dejected.

Chapter 6

THE BREEZY BABE

At the Tarpon Springs Marina, *The Breezy Babe* tugged at her moorings, dancing in the erratic gusts of early morning winds. Loose sails flapped idly as soft waves lapped against her ivory hull. The skies were clear. The weather report called for 12 to 15 knot northwesterly wind, with only a light chop.

Despite several cups of coffee, Jonathan felt groggy as he swabbed the deck of his sailboat. The last thing he wanted today was an outing with Big Jack's daughter and to play the gracious host. He had been up all night, alternating between fits of panic and righteous fury at how Pricilla's father treated him. He had sorted through drawers and boxes, gathering everything that provided evidence of his heritage—his birth certificate, passport, family photo albums, and newspaper articles. He even discovered a heartfelt letter his father had written him when he was still a baby. A Google search did turn up one conflicting article about another Curtis family in Tennessee, but he felt certain he would find a reasonable explanation with a little more probing.

On his way to the marina, he tried to reach Priscilla and left several messages with the good news. As he passed the hospital, he was pleased that all the Gypsy Vardos had vanished—Big Jack had kept his word. Now he would have to keep his.

By the time Jonathan arrived at the dock and got on his boat, there was still no answer from Priscilla. Anxious and frustrated, he left her a message. "Hey, Babe, it's me again. I really want to hear from you. I'll be out sailing all day. I've got my phone with me. Give me a ring. Love you."

Having done all he could, Jonathan resolved to let it go and make the best of the day. He wrung out his mop, leaned on the handle, and looked around his boat. "What a showgirl you are, all decked out," he said with pride. "You're by far the prettiest boat in the harbor."

From the dock behind him, a brash voice boomed, "Hey, knucklehead, talkin' to your boat again like she was a real person?"

Wheeling around, Jonathan saw a tall, dark-haired man grinning up at him. It was his best friend, Jimmy Pappas. His thick, muscular body was beginning to show a bit of a paunch around the middle, the result of all the beer he'd been drinking.

"Yeah, you crude pervert," Jonathan shot back. "As if you've never put the moves on *The Shiny Penny*, straddling her transom, patting down her engines, polishing her chrome—pure, Triple X erotica, not fit for the eyes of children. Made me feel like a voyeur."

Jimmy chuckled. "Okay, okay, guilty as charged." He leaped nimbly onto the boat's deck landing on both feet and embraced Jonathan in a bear hug. But when he stepped back and caught sight of his friend's long face, his expression turned serious. "Okay, what's up?" he asked.

Jonathan's first impulse was to unburden himself, but there was not enough time this morning. It would only spoil their sailing trip, so he remained silent.

Jimmy got the message. "Okay, later," he said, smiling. "Well, it looks like a good day for sailing, and I'm gonna make sure it's a great one." He reached into his gym bag and pulled out a liquor bottle wrapped in a brown paper bag.

Jonathan tore off the wrapper. "The Macallan 18," he exclaimed, his eyes brightening. It was his favorite Scotch, but he rarely bought it for himself because of its exorbitant cost. "Thanks, Jim. But, it's too –"

"Forget about it. Nothing's too good for my buddy. I've been saving it for your wedding day, but now that's a year away. This way I get to drink it with you." When he saw Jonathan start to get a little mushy, he quickly went on, "So, I'll get our dive gear out of my locker. What'd ya think, a one or two tank dive today?"

"I think one will be enough. Mostly, I just want to sail."

"Sounds good to me."

As he turned to go, Jonathan held up his hand. "Oh, Jim, there's another thing. I don't think it'll mess up our plans, but we're going to have two passengers sailing with us today. Female."

Jimmy's face lit up as if he had just won the lottery. "Don't tell me—two buxom blondes from the Tampa Bay Bucs cheerleading squad in hot pink string bikinis?"

Jonathan chuckled. "No, nothing like that. It's more like a babysitting job. A favor for one of my patients. It's a long story, but basically, he wants his daughter out of his hair for the day."

"A babysitting job. You mean a kid?"

"No. She's a twenty-four-year-old Gypsy girl who's with her tribe camping out in the state park on Lake Tarpon."

"Now you're talking. Wow, a wild, exotic Gypsy babe!"

"Hold on, Jimmy. I seriously doubt she's an exotic beauty," Jonathan said. "Her daddy's tried to get her married off twice and can't seem to make that happen, and he's a Gypsy King. She may be butt ugly for all I know, but I owe him a big favor. Besides, he travels with two, gun-toting goons, so you be nice, or we'll both end up wearing concrete shoes at the bottom of the Anclote River."

Jimmy gave him an odd glance. Then he raised his arms in humorous surrender. "Anything you say, Old Buddy. But at some point, you're going to tell me what you've gotten yourself into, and what that long face was all about." He held Jonathan's gaze for a second, then climbed back on the dock.

As Jonathan went below to do a final check on the engine, he had second thoughts about not confiding in his best friend. He hoped there would be an opportunity to make it up to him later.

They had been best buddies since college. Both had gone to Duke and met in a freshmen math class. Despite their different backgrounds—Jimmy's family belonged to the Greek sponge divers who originally settled in Tarpon Springs, while Jonathan came from the foothills of the Appalachian Mountains—they quickly discovered that they were smarter than most people gave them credit. As a result, they shared a wry view of the world and a mocking sense of humor. Jimmy, the "silver-tongued" BMOC, was more worldly than Jonathan and got a kick out of introducing his naïve, "hillbilly" friend to the wilder side of Durham, using him as a wingman in his relentless pursuit of coeds. After the winter break, they rented a small apartment off campus and their friendship deepened. They made an odd pair—the Greek Adonis exposing the Tennessee "country bumpkin" to new adventures, while Jonathan provided some character and maturity to Jimmy's adolescent chasing after women.

They kept close after college, too. While Jimmy pursued a law degree, Jonathan became a doctor. Over summer breaks, they took hunting and fishing trips together. When Jimmy married his high school sweetheart shortly after law school graduation, Jonathan was the best man at the wedding. His introduction to Tarpon Springs included boating, fishing, scuba diving, and a rip-roaring night on the town for the stag party. Jonathan was intrigued and, during subsequent visits, fell in love with the place. He completed his residency in Durham and hung out his shingle in Tarpon Springs. And here they were.

Jonathan gazed around the galley of *The Breezy Babe*, pleased that the mahogany woodwork was shining and everything looked ship-shape. He primed the Volvo engine and pushed the starter button. He always hated the rattling sound it made warming up. The galley shook for a few seconds before the motor smoothed out.

When Jonathan heard the clanking of scuba tanks above him, he turned the engine off and headed upstairs to help Jimmy stash their gear.

Jonathan was about to lend him a hand when he heard car wheels screeching. He looked up as a black Wiley Jeep turned from the road and careened into the parking lot, stopping at the edge of the main dock.

The blinding sunlight reflecting off its windshield caused Jonathan to squint, and he pulled down the Ray Bans sitting on his forehead. As his vision cleared, he saw a young woman climb out of the passenger seat, carrying a white paper shopping bag. She was dressed modestly in a bright red Paisley cover-up and wore a candy red straw sun hat. Shuffling across the dock's wooden planks in leather sandals, she walked toward the boat. Her features were pretty in a conventional way, with a button nose and dark eyes. Her sallow skin made her look older, more mature than Jonathan had expected.

"Isha?" he asked as she stood before him.

She never had a chance to answer.

"Holy shit!" Jimmy exclaimed next to him, staring google-eyed at the Jeep. "I'm thinking of becoming a professional babysitter," he gasped.

When Jonathan followed his gaze, he saw a bronze leg extending from the door to the ground, with a gold anklet shimmering in the sun. The young woman getting out of the Jeep was stunning. As she walked confidently down the pier, tiny silver bells adorning each gold sandal tinkled with each step. She wore a blue Paisley sarong tied low at her left hip, and as she advanced, the slit revealed long, shapely legs. Her hair, black as coal, was pulled back in a ponytail and held in place by a gold ring. A large gold cross dangled in the fold between her breasts, supported only by a tiny, powder blue bikini top. She ignored the gauntlet of men staring at her. Her mirrored, wrap-around sunglasses and the small pout on her lips gave her an aloof, unapproachable look. She had a sailing jacket in one hand and a large woven beach bag slung over her shoulder. When she stopped at the edge of the dock by the boat and removed her sunglasses, her eyes were dark as obsidian.

Jonathan stood there, breathless, staring at the most gorgeous woman he had ever seen. Two thoughts crossed his mind: Isha was definitely Big Jack's daughter and her marital status had nothing to do with her looks.

She looked at each of the men with a hint of mockery and asked, "Which of you is the famous Doctor Curtis?"

Jonathan was tongue-tied. Jimmy, never at a loss for words, was dumbstruck as well and pointed his finger in the direction of his friend. The young woman took her time studying Jonathan, letting her eyes roam from head to toe.

Jonathan had never felt so objectified before in his life. Irritated, he found his voice. "I am Dr. Curtis," he said coldly. "And this is my friend, James Pappas."

"Jimmy," his companion interjected, grinning.

Ignoring him, the young woman addressed Jonathan, "I am Isha. My father likes you." When he didn't respond, she continued, "First of all, let me apologize if we're causing you any inconvenience. This outing is all Big Jack's doing. I am grateful you have invited us to join you on your day off, Dr. Curtis." Her voice was soft, her accent somewhere between Eastern European and American. "By the way, this is my friend Katarina. Katarina speaks very little English and I speak very little Romanian, but we have grown to be good friends." She reached out to wrap Katarina's arm around hers and continued, "She is new to the States. My father asked that she accompany us."

When Jonathan looked at her, Katarina lowered her gaze. A rose-colored blush appeared on her face and neck.

Realizing he had acted rudely Jonathan attempted a more cordial greeting. "Please call me Jonathan." Turning to Isha, he added, "No matter why you're here today, you are welcome."

He extended his hand to assist Katarina. She accepted with a smile and stepped onto the boat.

Before he could help Isha, she threw her jacket over her shoulder and stepped aboard the Breezy Babe, balancing on the narrow gunwale like a seasoned mariner. "Katarina and I will not be a problem for you. We'll find a nice place to lie down on the bow and stay out of your way," she said. "If you need our assistance, just ask. We have both spent time aboard ships and are excellent sailors."

"I bet," Jonathan mumbled, miffed and cowed by her confidence.

Isha glanced around. "Nice boat. A Pearson 27, smooth lines, fast, comfortable," she said. Glancing at the sky she continued, "It should be good weather. Jonathan, Jimmy, plan to enjoy the sail as if we were not aboard."

She stepped onto the deck, ignoring Jimmy as he craned his neck to catch a more revealing view of her voluptuous breasts. "Call if you need us," she said, then placed her mirrored sunglasses back on and signaled Katarina to follow her to the bow.

Jimmy's eyes widened. "Isha, Katarina," he called after them. "Ah...there's plenty of room back here in the cockpit with me and Jonathan. Maybe join us for some coffee. Get to know each other better. It'll be a long sail to the reef."

Katarina gave him a questioning look, but Isha laughed. A whirlwind of hand gestures, some English phrases, and a smattering of a language Jonathan assumed was Romanian passed between them.

Then Katarina laughed, too. "You married, Jimmy," she said, pointing to the wedding band on his left hand. She held up her ring finger. "Me, too."

But Jimmy didn't leave it. "Hey, I may be married but I'm not dead yet," he countered.

Isha smirked, grabbed Katarina by the hand, and moved to the bow deck where they unrolled towels and lay down.

Jonathan had an epiphany. Katrina had come along as a chaperone. Big Jack wasn't going to bring dishonor to his daughter by letting her spend a day alone with two horny young men, least of all two Gadjos. Some of Isha's confidence surely was put on. He felt much better.

After Jimmy untied the mooring ropes, Jonathan motored *The Breezy Babe* lazily out of the harbor past Anclote Key. They rigged her sails for easy handling so that all maneuvers could be managed from the cockpit. As a steady twelve-knot wind pressed hard against the mainsail, the men leaned back relaxing in the stern while the sun warmed their faces. The wind held steady and the sea was smooth for the trip to their favorite reef about two hours offshore. With Jimmy keeping an eye on the GPS coordinates and weather reports, Jonathan nodded off for a while.

When he came to, Jimmy greeted him with a cup of coffee. "Rise and shine, Sleeping Beauty," he said, grinning.

"How long have I been out," Jonathan asked groggily.

"About an hour or so. We're almost there."

Sipping the steaming coffee, he felt like something brushed his neck, but when he glanced toward the bow, he only saw Isha adjusting her bikini and rolling over on her back.

His questioning look toward Jimmy was met with a helpless shrug. "I tried to be social, but nothing doing," he admitted sheepishly. "I can't believe I'm losing my touch."

Suddenly, the wind shifted, jerking and tilting the boat as the sails came about. Jonathan worried for his passengers but relaxed when he saw Isha and Katarina hunch down, allowing the jib to rush past them overhead.

Before long, they reached the reef and made anchor. Isha and Katrina sat up and watched as the men got the scuba equipment out and prepared to dive. Jimmy went first. He sat on the gunwale, keeled over backward, hit the water with a big splash, and quickly submerged. The two women looked over the side after him, exchanged a burst of hand gestures, and lay back down on the deck.

Jonathan leaned forward on one knee and watched the bubbles surface from where Jimmy swam forty feet below. It was peaceful on deck but too quiet. His thoughts turned to Priscilla and her father, and a surge of anger washed over him.

He felt a prickling at his neck again and heard a soft sound emanating from the bow. As the wind shifted again, he realized Isha had changed her position, sitting up to reposition her towel. At that moment, Jonathan spotted a pod of porpoises on the port side, skimming the rolling waves and chasing a large school of flying fish. As the sea churned with turbulence, a flock of pelicans rose to circle, preparing to join the feast.

"Hey, Isha, Katarina, look."

Startled, Katarina sat bolt upright. Isha turned toward him with a curious pout on her lips. Jonathan caught the glare from her mirrored glasses as she looked straight at him. "What is it?" she said.

He pointed. "Over there!"

The porpoises circled the silvery fish like a Wild-West round-up. Under attack, the silvery fish burst from the waves into the air by the hundreds, taking flight by fluttering their little wing-like fins. After a hundred yards or so, they dropped back into the water, and the pelicans, circling above, dove head-first and crashed into the waves in hot pursuit.

Isha and Katarina watched spellbound with their arms tightly wrapped around their knees. As they witnessed Mother Nature's bounty and breathtaking display of transcendent beauty in the struggle for existence, Jonathan felt the beginnings of a connection among them.

As the flurry of activity subsided and the sea calmed, Isha took off her sunglasses and looked at Jonathan. For an instant, her face betrayed a sense of uncertainty and wonder. "Thanks," she said, her voice mellow, conveying the same sense of wonder Jonathan felt.

Jonathan acknowledged her with a cool nod and a simple "You're welcome." Then he returned to monitoring Jimmy's bubbles, keeping his satisfied smile to himself.

A while later, Jimmy resurfaced.

"Any luck?" Jonathan asked. as Jimmy swam to the rear ladder and climbed aboard.

"Nothing but a bunch of snails, sponges, and small reef fish," Jimmy complained, throwing his fins over the side.

Jonathan grabbed the top of his scuba tank to assist him over the transom. His friend rarely came up empty-handed.

Removing his gear and wriggling out of his wet suit, Jimmy said, "I hope you have better luck. Maybe try going south from the anchor. I fished the whole drop-off to the North. Nothing there."

Jonathan strapped on his air tank, shoved in his mouthpiece, sat on the gunwale, gave Jimmy a thumbs up, and picked up a spear gun. Then he pulled his mask over his face and flipped backward into the water.

He swam to the ocean floor using the anchor line as a guide. The silence of the deep with only the rhythmic sound of his breath, the hissing of his regulator, and the bubbles that rose to the surface relaxed him. He was always amazed at how different the ocean looked below the surface—a world of beautiful, multi-hued magic and mystery. Fan Coral in a collage of bright reds, yellows, and purples waved at him, nudged by undersea currents as if welcoming his arrival. Massive Brain Coral rose along the crystal, sandy bottom. Iridescent Blue Angelfish played within their crevices. Jonathan swam over a bright, white Star Coral mound before plunging another five feet to the ocean floor. There, Spiny Lobsters and crabs scurried about the sandy bottom, sensing a potential threat from a large predator. Lazy conch and other snails crawled across the surface less hurriedly.

The best fishing was usually along the lip of the drop-off where groupers and red snappers hid in search of smaller reef fish. A curious eel poked its head out of its hole but quickly retracted as Jonathan approached the ledge. Swimming along the south ridge as Jimmy had advised, he focused on any unusual movement, a flurry of sand from the flicker of a large fin or the scurry of a school of small fish as they avoided being eaten by a predator.

Usually, this reef teemed with large fish, but today there was no such luck. After coming up empty for nearly twenty-five minutes, Jonathan realized he had only another five minutes of air. He pulled himself under a shelf and focused through the crevices when he felt a tug on his leg. Something large grabbed him and then let go. Chilling thoughts of a Tiger shark flashed through his mind. In a desperate panic, he spun around to face his foe and instead saw the vision of a mermaid in the oval of his face mask.

It took him a moment to realize that it was Isha, free-diving with only her goggles and fins. Forty feet below the surface, she swam as easily as a fish! Her long, black hair moved about her head with the changing ripples of ocean currents.

Jonathan's instantaneous relief gave way to curiosity and amazement. What was she doing here? And how could she stay down so long, so deep, on only one breath of air?'

Paddling backward, Isha motioned him to follow. She swam along the bottom of the ocean floor, graceful as a dolphin. Jonathan trailed close behind until she stopped short of a large cluster of Star Coral. Pointing to a center crevice, she nodded with her head, then moved her hands two feet apart and pointed again to the opening. Jonathan signaled back that he understood and received a thumbs-up. As he approached the crevice, Isha waved and headed to the surface.

Soon after, Jonathan emerged near *The Breezy Babe*, with a thirty-five-pound black grouper in tow.

Jimmy congratulated him, "Great catch!"

"All because of Isha," Jonathan said.

They gazed toward the bow where Isha stood like a maritime goddess, beads of water on her back sparkling like diamonds in the sunlight against her tawny skin. She dried herself off and settled back down on her towel. As Jonathan stowed his dive gear, he filled Jimmy in on what had happened at the reef below. Then he took four sub sandwiches and bottles of beer from the cooler and called to the bow of the boat, "Isha, Katarina—Jimmy and I are going to have a bite to eat. Care to join us?"

Isha turned to Katarina, made an eating gesture with her hand and mouth, and received an eager nod. "Sure, thanks. We were getting a little hungry," she called over her shoulder. As she and Katarina got up, gathered their bags, and scooted around the sail shrouds, the men moved up on deck to join them.

Sharing the meal, the atmosphere among them became cozy. Isha no longer pouted, Katarina's blush diminished, Jonathan enjoyed himself, and Jimmy regained his confidence.

"So, how come you two are so comfortable sailing?" Jimmy asked. "And you, Isha, free-diving? I've never known anyone, man or woman, who could hang forty feet down for over two minutes."

"I've spent many days on the water, Jimmy—the Florida coast, the Caribbean, the Mediterranean, diving in the Greek Isles, Hawaii, The Great Barrier Reef. Katarina's father in Romania is a fisherman on the Black Sea. She has spent countless days on the water."

Jimmy almost choked on his sandwich. He stared wide-eyed at the two women. Just as mystified, Jonathan said, "Australia, the

Greek Isles? Isha, you've been there? I got the idea you lived with your father, traveling in a caravan from state park to state park."

Isha burst out laughing. "You must lead a very sheltered life, Jonathan," she mocked.

Holding up his hands in surrender, Jonathan grinned good-naturedly.

"How did you find that grouper?" Jimmy asked, running interference. "It's the largest we've ever caught spearfishing."

"It was by accident. I was down there looking for lunch."

"With only your bare hands?" Jimmy queried doubtfully.

"Yes, some small shellfish or a lobster, anything like that."

"Well, did you find something?" Jonathan asked.

"Yes, of course," Isha replied.

Taken aback, Jonathan said, "And, what was it?"

"I found this Quiznos sandwich and Heineken beer," she replied straight-faced before the corners of her mouth turned up humorously.

Jimmy and Jonathan laughed. Katarina gave a puzzled look, not understanding a word, then smiled.

"I did find two conches," Isha continued. "We were going to have them for lunch, but then you asked us to join you. I still have them. Would you guys like to share?"

Jonathan and Jimmy both nodded, their interest piqued. This was something they had only witnessed the dive guides do in the Bahamas.

"I will need a strong, heavy knife and a cutting board. I don't want to scar this beautiful boat of yours!" Isha said.

Jimmy immediately reached for his diving knife, while Jonathan headed to the galley to retrieve a small wooden cutting board. Isha pulled two conches and a fresh lime from her bag and handed them to Katarina. Then they followed Jonathan into the cockpit. The men watched over Katarina's shoulders as she popped a small hole in each conch with the blunt end of Jimmy's knife. Then she removed the meat, sliced it into bite-size pieces, and squeezed lime juice over it.

Isha took one and offered it to Jonathan. "This is what I usually eat on trips like this."

He put it into his mouth, never taking his eyes off her. "Delicious!"

As she held his gaze, her expression of apprehension and wonderment returned. Then, she laughed and they both looked away at the same time.

Meanwhile, Katrina had given Jimmy a taste. "Mmmm," he said. "This calls for some Scotch."

"Yes, it does," Jonathan agreed, grateful for the interruption. Moving to the hatchway, he added, "Let's wait on The Macallan, Jim. I've got a great bottle of fifteen-year-old Dewars in the galley. Glasses, Isha?"

She shook her head. "We both like it straight from the bottle."

When Jonathan returned Dewars in hand, Katarina's eyes widened. "Mmmm, whisky good!" she said, smiling.

Jonathan uncorked the bottle with a pop and offered it to Isha who took a swig. "Whoa," she exclaimed, her eyes watering, and passed it to Katrina. Wiping the neck, Katarina tossed down a good-sized belt, turned her thumb up, and repeated, "Mmmm, whisky good!"

The four lounged with their backs against the cool, smooth fiberglass as they passed the bottle around. Isha shared that Katarina was married to a young man who still lived in Romania. Her husband was the cousin of a prominent member of their tribe and would be coming to America to reunite with her as soon as his papers were in order. Jonathan shared funny stories from the ER, and Jimmy told naughty tales from their college years, earning indulgent chuckles from the two women.

With their bellies full of sandwiches, beer, Scotch, and conch, Jonathan and Jimmy cleaned up and packed their diving gear away. Isha and Katrina remained in the cockpit.

At some point, Jonathan noticed that the sun had begun its westerly descent in the Gulf. "Time to head home," he said with regret.

The women pitched in, helping him and Jimmy prepare *The Breezy Babe* for her return trip. When they were done, Jimmy and Katrina went to the bow to sit and enjoy the view. The air was still warm and dry. Puffy white clouds floated low above them, their underbellies starting to reflect a rich golden glow. When Jimmy brought out a joint and dangled it before Katrina, she smiled and nodded. He lit it and they started to pass it back and forth.

Jonathan at the helm pointed at them and looked at Isha questioningly. She shook her head, declining.

"Can I steer for a while?" she asked.

"Sure," Jonathan said.

He stepped aside and Isha took over the tiller, handling *The Breezy Babe* like a veteran sailor. She appeared at ease keeping an eye on the wind direction, speed, and the boat's bearing.

Impressed and reassured, Jonathan sat back and relaxed, yielding to his pleasant buzz. He contemplated Isha, illuminated by the late afternoon sun. How different from Priscilla she was—intriguing, mysterious, and sophisticated, yet wild as the wind and fearless as an eagle. Part of him envied her. She had been raised by a loving father. He had never known his own. Was that why she possessed such uninhibited freedom?

Isha felt his steady gaze upon her, probing for answers. She had some questions of her own. Throughout the day she had been observing Jonathan with interest and growing curiosity. Although her father had described him as shy and somewhat withdrawn, he was anything but. He had not wilted under her teasing, nor fawned over her goo-goo-eyed, like so many other men who found her attractive. Her Gypsy intuition told her that there was something solid beneath his charming exterior, something that others sensed as well. In just a few days, Jonathan had become a celebrity among her people. Her aunts Kizzy and Bicca were wild about him; her father seemed to adore him; and Pinky, who made a point of hating every Gadjo he met, had told her he thought Dr. Curtis was "a pretty OK guy."

The young doctor certainly deserved a closer look, and she decided to complete her errand. "I have something for you," she said.

Jonathan steadied the tiller while she went to the bow to dig in her bag. She returned with a folded piece of paper and handed it to him with a quick, penetrating glance. Then she took over the helm again.

As Jonathan gave her a puzzled look, a gust of wind pushed the boat sideways, requiring all of Isha's attention.

Holding on to the gunwale, Jonathan steadied himself. He unfolded the paper. The handwriting on it was in small, carefully shaped letters. As he deciphered the note, he sobered up in an instant. A vise-like tension squeezed his forehead like a metal band tightening.

The note read, "You must come and see me as soon as possible! Tatyana."

Chapter 7

TATYANA

The throaty rumble of Jonathan's Harley-Davidson Fat Boy rounded Curlew Road heading east out of Tarpon Springs. Accelerating his bike through the curves, Jonathan's mind raced. He hadn't heard from Priscilla all day and was sick with worry over the possibility of losing her. He considered turning around and riding back to her home in Palma Verde in the hope of seeing her and showing her all the memorabilia he'd found of his father, rather than heeding the call of a Gypsy fortune teller con artist. But Tatyana's note had conveyed a sense of urgency. It was less than an hour since *The Breezy Babe* had motored into the harbor. Isha and Katrina thanked him, got into the Jeep, and returned to camp. Jimmy, noticing Jonathan's agitation, had volunteered to wash down and moor the boat, and sent Jonathan on his way.

The sun was setting when he pulled into Tatyana's campsite among the pines. The Gypsy woman sat beside her multi-colored table with her back to him. With the sound of Jonathan's motorcycle coming to a stop, she rose and turned. The last sun rays glistened on her brightly colored dress and turned her hair into a fiery halo. For a moment she looked to Jonathan like an otherworldly spirit. Then Mugs barked and came running to sniff his crotch, wagging his tail so his whole backside shook, and restored the world to its ordinary reality.

Jonathan petted Mugs and removed his helmet.

Tatyana waved and called to him. "Dr. Curtis, so good of you to come. Please, take a seat."

He waved back hesitantly. "I got here as soon as I could. What has happened that you wanted to see me tonight?"

"Your timing is perfect," she said, fixing him with an evaluating gaze. "You look well-tanned and glowing from a day in the sun. I trust you had a good time with Isha and Katrina."

Embarrassed, Jonathan stammered, "Uh…well…yes,"

Tatyana's eyes crinkled as she smiled knowingly. "I did want to talk to you, but before we do, I sense you have something on your mind you are struggling with. You can talk to me about it."

Jonathan's face paled. He stood still.

"Or not." Tatyana continued. "Maybe just join Mugs and me for a cocktail and quiet reflection. It's Happy Hour here at the camp—for the women. Their menfolk are up and about, taking care of business in the area. I always like to take a break around this time of day. It's so peaceful to see the sun sink beneath the trees and turn the clouds from puffy white to coral red, listen to the forest animals settle in for the night, and watch the stars come out."

Jonathan frowned. Tatyana's note sounded serious, and now she acted as if she didn't have a care in the world.

"Sometimes stripping the busyness away can reveal our inner essence," Tatyana mused. She motioned with her head for him to join her. "Come, have a seat at my table. We can enjoy such things together. Can I get you a cocktail? A vodka, scotch, or a glass of wine?"

Reluctantly, Jonathan joined her. "Scotch on the rocks sounds good," he said, sitting.

Tatyana went into her Vardo. While she was gone, Jonathan looked around the campsite. Nothing had changed since he and Priscilla visited. Mugs surprised him, though, by curling up quietly at his feet. His soft, brown eyes peered at him with a look of affection. He reached up with his wet nose and nuzzled Jonathan's hand.

Tatyana soon returned and handed Jonathan a glass of Scotch. But before taking her seat at the table, she circled him like a she-wolf protecting her young, taking in his scent. Jonathan was taken aback by Tatyana's strange behavior, crouching down and sniffing him from different angles. "Odd," he mused, feeling for a moment as if his inner being had been laid bare, but he quickly shrugged it off as some harmless Gypsy ritual.

Finally, Tatyana sat across from him, raised her glass in a silent toast, and drank her Vodka tonic.

For the remainder of the sunset, she and Jonathan sat quietly while sipping their drinks and breathing in the soft, sweet air. The Scotch was decent, and Jonathan felt himself relax. He was about to start sharing the turmoil of his past two days when he remembered why he had come. He finished his drink and asked, "So why am I here, Tatyana?"

She scrutinized him until he became uncomfortable and said, "The day you visited me with Priscilla, I saw a sensitive, powerful man standing before me. Led only by his intellect, he was a bundle of nerves with an overburdened conscience, compelled by what he should do rather than what was in his heart. I predicted that your future would be full of struggles and anguish if you continued along that path. I still believe that is true. But now, you have an opportunity to change that course. It does mean facing the truth about yourself—who you are. If you do that, I'm also certain you will soon discover the truth about your father."

Her last statement blind-sided Jonathan like a sucker punch. He sat there stunned, at a loss for words. Finally, he managed, "How...? What do you know about my father?"

"Nothing...yet. But based on sharing your vision of the other world, my intuition told me that his identity is of utmost importance for your life," she said calmly.

As the darkness of night closed in around them with foreboding silence, Jonathan straightened and said softly, "You also told me that the cat is real and very close. What did you mean by that?"

Tatyana's expression grew serious. "That is what I wanted to talk to you about this evening. I felt his hot breath on the back of my neck, as well. There is evil lurking about. You must keep your guard up."

Jonathan felt a shiver run down his spine. Was he being conned again? He gave Tatyana a bewildered look and said, "I had the same disturbing nightmare as a child, sometimes for several nights in a row. I thought I left that terror far behind me.

Tatyana probed gently, "Did you have other dreams and visions as a child?"

Jonathan's eyes darted around the campsite and the surrounding woods. "Yes," he finally admitted. "They are vague memories now, but I know that some of them were related to the future. Most peculiar were the dreams that did come true."

"Most peculiar were the dreams that did come true," Tatyana echoed cryptically. Then, as if she'd reached a decision, she said with mounting excitement, "Jonathan, this is what we will do. There is something about your dream we must know. In our journey the other night, I heard a voice calling to you, "Stay away, it's too dangerous!" We must discover who that was and what he or she meant."

Jonathan felt a wave of exhaustion come over him. He shook his head. "Tatyana, not tonight. I have too much on my mind..."

Tatyana reached out and grasped his arm fiercely. Jonathan felt her fingers digging into his skin like the talons of a powerful bird, channeling its strength into him. Her eyes were pitch-black and piercing, brooking no refusal, and her voice sounded like an ancient sybil proclaiming an irrefutable truth. "Jonathan, this barrier has been opened—for you. A spirit from the other side has reawakened those childhood nightmares for a reason. I know you want an answer to this riddle as much as I do, but believe me when I say, 'This door may be open for only a short while.'"

Jonathan stared back for only a moment. Then he straightened and nodded his assent.

Tatyana lit the red candle sitting in the center of the table. Jonathan wondered if she planned for this outcome all along. She got up and retrieved sprigs of dried sage wrapped into a tight bundle, lit one end, snuffed the flames out in a dish, and wafted the pungent smoke in the air and around his body. Then she took a small bit of the charred sage ash and drew a long line across Jonathan's forehead.

When Jonathan wrinkled his brow, she said, "Just clearing the air of unwanted spirits. The smudge is so I can recognize your spirit body in the other world."

Jonathan's brow furrowed more deeply.

Tatyana smiled and said, "Don't worry about it. Just do as I say."

Jonathan nodded in acknowledgment.

As she sat next to him, she said firmly, "Close your eyes."

As Jonathan followed her order, he heard the thumping sounds of drums beating from somewhere near the center of the woods.

"The nightly ritual of drumming around the tribal fire circle has begun," Tatyana whispered in his ear. "Focus on their beat."

The percussive rhythms rose, echoing among the yellow pines and sable palms, creating a mesmerizing pulse. Jonathan felt the throbbing move inside him, as he became one with the beat. He felt his body quiver. In his mind's eye, he and Tatyana dematerialized into a million particles of fluorescent slivers and dust that whirled into space. Jonathan's spirit led with Tatyana's following close behind, connected to his consciousness only by the mark of burnt sage ash on his forehead.

Suddenly, all the flecks and fragments coalesced, and he found himself back among the smoke and distant lightning strikes overlooking the meadow where hundreds of men, women, and children lay impaled on wooden stakes, moaning in agony. Their blood ran toward the bottom of the valley forming a river of dark red.

The cries pleading for death pierced Jonathan deeply. "I have failed them," he lamented in a heart-rending voice.

He heard Tatyana next to him say, "You are not alone and no longer a child. Look at yourself. You have grown into a man and I am here with you.... And there is someone else."

"There is no one else... It's dark."

"There is someone."

He glanced to his left and saw a knight in battle armor carrying a broadsword caked with dried blood. For a moment Jonathan thought the iron-clad figure had caused the carnage, but when the man turned to him, his features were distorted in a grimace of agony. Jonathan noticed that he was wearing a golden brooch designed in an unusual shape, but he couldn't make out what it was.

Jonathan wanted to get a closer look when he heard voices calling him, "'Come now. We need you, now."

In an instant, the particles of his ethereal body fused and he found himself sitting back at the table under the pines. Tatyana was holding his hand. She seemed to be in a trance, her eyes closed. Untangling himself from her grip, Jonathan heard sounds of splintering wood, metal being pounded, and glass breaking by the other Gypsy caravans. Without thinking, he rose and sprinted toward the loudest noise.

When he reached the edge of the drum circle, he saw women and children running amok, panicking, screaming. They were pursued by four young men dressed in army boots and cut-off fatigues, wielding baseball bats. Their shaven heads glistened in the light of the flickering torches surrounding the encampment.

One of them ran at an older woman who was shielding a child behind her and shouted, "Get the hell out of our city, Gypsy whore!"

When she didn't move, frozen in fright, he hammered the bat against the wagon next to her, denting the metal. She flinched and crumpled to the ground.

Another goon demolished the wooden stool and chairs and flung pieces into the fire pit, launching flaming sticks of wood high into the air. He tossed the rest about with no concern that they might hit someone.

From the corner of his eyes, Jonathan spotted Isha amidst the chaos. She was jabbing with a broom at one of the goons. He swatted at her, breaking the handle in two, and advanced on her, his bat raised above his head. Without hesitation, Jonathan bounded across the compound. Everything slowed down around him, but he continued moving at top speed. Deflecting the bat coming down, he let it glance off his shoulder. Then, he punched the man in the face, shattering his nose. The young thug howled and fell to the ground. As Jonathan stomped on the side of his foot, breaking his ankle, he noticed a tattoo on his right forearm.

The shrieks of pain caught the attention of the others. Seeing their companion writhing on the ground, two skinheads advanced on Jonathan from either side with their bats held ready. Before they could launch their attack, Jonathan kicked the one on his right between the legs and, as he bent over in agony, brought his elbow crashing down on his neck. The other thug dropped his bat, pulled out a knife, and came at Jonathan swinging it back and forth. Jonathan easily avoided his swipes. When the frustrated ruffian lunged at him, Jonathan sidestepped the thrust and grabbed his arm. He wrenched the knife from his assailant's hand and flung it away. Then he broke the man's arm at the elbow over his knee.

"Jonathan, look out!"

He heard Isha's terrified voice just as a wooden bat slammed across his shoulders with a loud crack. His body shook from the impact, but he felt no pain. Turning, he confronted the twisted face of a young, unshaven goon. He also had a tattoo on his raised right forearm. Before he could bring down the bat again, Jonathan barreled into his chest, driving him against a wagon. The impact made him drop the bat, and he came at Jonathan with fists flying. To Jonathan, he was still moving in slow motion, so it was child's play to duck his onslaught and trip him. As he went down, Jonathan gave him a blow to the head with his fist and left him twitching on the ground. Straddling him from behind, Jonathan twisted an ear and pulled up his head.

"Better get out of here and take your friends to the hospital or you won't leave here alive," he growled.

He let the man get up and limp to his companions.

Supporting each other, they beat a hasty retreat, hobbling into the woods. Soon Jonathan heard the roar of a souped-up V8 truck engine and the sound of tires churning up the shell road as it sped away.

As he turned back to the camp, his body and mind gave out like a battery going dead, and everything went dark.

* * *

When Jonathan came to, his head ached. He felt a tickling sensation on the side of his neck. It moved up onto his cheek and crawled across his face to perch on his nose. Opening his eyes, he dimly saw a pair of long feelers and two gray, lusterless orbs—the visage of a monster. He instinctively raised his hand to brush the critter from his face only to rake his sore knuckles across a metal surface. The eyes and feelers disappeared, scurrying across his shirt. When he lifted his head, he realized it was a palmetto bug. As his groggy vision cleared, he could make out piping running overhead and a round cross piece connected to wheels on either side. He was below the undercarriage of a large motor vehicle. The ground beneath his back felt damp and sandy. The rectangle between the ground and the chassis was bright, like early morning light.

"Where am I?" he wondered and crawled toward the daylight.

From above his head, he heard Isha calling, "Jonathan." She called again, "Jonathan, are you all right?"

"Isha, that you?"

"Yes, I heard you moving about."

"Where the heck am I?"

"You're under my dad's motor coach. Tatyana and I felt it best to leave you there after last night. Come on out, over here. Crawl toward my voice." She sounded closer.

Jonathan shimmied his way past the wheelbase of the right front tire and emerged next to the steps to the side entrance. As he stood, working the kinks out of his cramped muscles, Isha appeared, looking at him with searching eyes. She was wearing a long Tampa Bay Bucs nightshirt. Jonathan gulped. Her nipples were visible, rigid from the coolness of the morning.

"How are you feeling?" she said with a concerned voice.

"Okay, I think, although I've been better."

"Thank goodness you were here last night, Jonathan. The way you took care of those skinheads was amazing! I believe they were the same gang that attacked my father at J-Wags. Thank you for saving us."

In an instant, it all came back to him—Tatyana, the drums, the knight in armor with the strange insignia pinned to his chest, the attack on the camp. He remembered the goon with his bat raised over Isha's head and springing into action to protect her. He saw himself move as if in a dream.

Isha interrupted his reverie. "When did you learn to fight like that?"

Jonathan wrinkled his forehead. 'What?'

"You never told me you knew martial arts. Most guys brag about such things. You look big and strong, but you can really fight."

Jonathan shook his head. "Except for a few scuffles in school when I was young, I've never been in a fight."

She looked at him in disbelief. "Well, tell that to the four goons from last night. Look, I've been around fights before, and I've never seen anything like it. Tatyana thanks you, too. She said she has to check some things out and will be in touch when she knows more. She called you her 'knight in shining armor.' She was joking, perhaps?"

Jonathan looked around. The camping area had been cleaned and swept, and there was no sign of a scuffle. "I don't know, Isha," he said. "The way I see it, I took some kind of acid trip and woke up under your motor home with a cockroach crawling on my nose."

Isha scrutinized him as if he were putting her on. "Then how do you explain this?" she asked. Leading Jonathan to a large live oak tree at the edge of last night's campfire area, she pointed to the handle of an army knife buried to the hilt in the trunk. "None of us, including the strongest guys, could make it budge. Pinky even tried to pry it out with a crowbar!"

Jonathan tugged at the knife. It was firmly embedded like it was part of the tree. He shrugged his shoulders. "I don't know. Looks like someone drove it in with a sledgehammer."

"It wasn't a sledgehammer," Isha said. "It's the knife you took from one of the skinheads and flung away. I saw it as it shot from your hand as if fired from a cannon and lodged here!"

Thoroughly bewildered, Jonathan yanked at the knife once more with no more success than before. He extended his arms in a gesture of helplessness. "I have no idea, Isha. Please believe me."

Seeing him so perplexed and vulnerable, she gave him a re-assuring smile. "Okay, I do. Why don't you come to the motor coach? There's coffee. You're probably hungry from all that exertion. I'll make us breakfast."

Jonathan nodded gratefully. Realizing how tired he still felt, he muttered, "Love some," and followed her inside.

Chapter 8

THE WIZARD

Colonel Burdock was in a foul mood. Dressed in khaki pants and a striped shirt, he paced around his office like a caged panther. "Imbeciles!" he snarled and ran his hand through his short-cropped hair for the umpteenth time.

Mazy watched from the doorway with her head tilted in concern.

Burdock had gotten little sleep after receiving an urgent telephone call from the leader of the recruits. In a whiny, self-pitying voice, Carter had reported on their disastrous efforts to raise Cain at the Gypsy camp. Burdock had spent much of the night getting them medical care off the books from an old army friend, a retired military surgeon in Clearwater. The last thing he wanted was for his sorry crew to go to a hospital for treatment. Their injuries were serious enough to get the police involved, risking exposure of the organization. The Wizard would read him the riot act if that happened.

The Colonel had had enough difficulties dealing with the altercation that the same incompetent quartet had caused at a local bar a few days earlier. When the sheriff of Tarpon Springs notified him about the incident—at least the morons had the presence of mind to give his name as their contact—he was able to contain the damage. The sheriff was a personal friend, and they both agreed a combination of too much youthful testosterone and alcohol was no reason to bother the boys any further. After all, they had only meant to scare the Gypsies into leaving town, which the sheriff decided would be best for everyone. Nevertheless, he reminded the Colonel that his job was maintaining peace and order and he did not want any more trouble.

Burdock stopped pacing and scowled at the gallery of photographs on his wall. They showed happier days when the troops he commanded were seasoned professionals, not a bunch of stumble-bum amateurs he was trying to whip into shape for the cause.

But what irritated him most was that the reason for all the mayhem was none other than Dr. Jonathan Curtis. Herbert had recognized him in the flickering torchlight before the doctor had kicked him in the balls and delivered a brutal chop to his neck that sent him flailing to the ground. And Scott had heard the Gypsy bitch cry out, "Jonathan," before he managed to hit his adversary in the back with his bat. It should have been a crippling blow, but Scott ended up in the dirt instead and Jonathan's wallop gave him a concussion. With the single blow of a fist!

At least the doctor had revealed his true colors, sneaking around at the Gypsy camp. "Wouldn't be surprised if he was one of them," Burdock snarled.

He was glad he had sniffed him out at Brian Randolph's party and saved his friend from throwing away his daughter on an imposter with a questionable pedigree. He would have to look further into Dr. Curtis and his past. There was nothing in his record to suggest any of the fighting skills he possessed, even if he did ambush his men when they were too drunk to know what they were doing.

"He's a devious bastard hiding plenty more, I'm sure of it, Mazy," he addressed his dog. "We're going to get that son-of-a-bitch and make him pay, one way or another!"

Mazy barked in response and wagged her tail, earning her a smile from her master.

"That's right," Burdock grumbled.

Calming allowed him to think clearly. He sat at his mahogany desk and jotted down notes about how to best convey the news to the Wizard. He would have to choose his words carefully.

* * *

Thirty miles southwest of Salzburg, Austria lay the *Salzkammergut*, a region of scenic Alpine mountains, lakes, and deep salt mines. The area has been a favorite of vacationers, sightseers, hikers, and people who visit the famous underground caves, some dating as far back as the Middle Ages.

In a secluded valley far from the popular tourist spots, along a forsaken, rural road, was a metal gate marked with "No Trespass" signs. From there, a serpentine dirt path wound upward through a dense forest until it reached a chalet overlooking a gorge. Rarely did any vacationers stumble upon the entrance, much less the country lodge; and the few that did, found themselves quickly surrounded by a squad of blond-haired, muscular men in uniforms carrying assault rifles. The guards were intimidating yet polite. After questioning the intruders, they escorted them to the gate and sent them on their way with the impression that the owner was a wealthy recluse, an eccentric odd duck who valued his privacy above all else.

Had these unwelcome visitors managed to glimpse the chalet or, even less likely, set foot inside it, everything from the rustic furniture to the cozy atmosphere would have confirmed that notion. They wouldn't have had the slightest idea what the place really was—the headquarters of a secret, international movement and a laboratory for all kinds of genetic experiments whose primary purpose was to keep the owner alive.

A secret doorway in the kitchen accessed an elevator that went down a deep mine shaft to the facility hidden in an ancient cave. The walls shielding the interior were five feet thick and of the most advanced building materials. Lined with lead and Kevlar, they could withstand the most technologically advanced weapons. With two years of living supplies, including oxygen, the facility was impervious to attack—an impenetrable command center.

Inside, stainless-steel partitions and clear doors and windows, made of the same acrylic used in aircraft windshields, created a labyrinth of rooms. They contained computers for data processing and science labs with the most up-to-date biological and chemical research equipment. Communication with the outside world occurred via underground, fiberoptic cables connected to encrypted satellite hookups above ground. The place was a warren of busy male and female technicians, researchers, and medical personnel. Most were also blond-haired and blue-eyed.

One unusual area was a nursery for infants and toddlers, overseen by several bustling nurses. There were at least forty children.

But the most active area was a large, central room with a king-sized, state-of-the-art hospital bed. In it lay a tall man with withered, yellowish skin. His face had a wax-like pallor and a long scar extended from his right jaw down his neck. His thin lips were pressed together and his eyes were closed. A host of tubes, IV lines and surgically implanted, indwelling ports connected him to the most up-to-date medical equipment.

Everyone called him "The Wizard"—although no one knew why—and he was 125 years old.

He lay there deep in thought, finishing his daily treatment, a cocktail of stem cells, harvested from the children, growth hormone, testosterone, and other pharmaceuticals. It would allow him several hours of physical mobility and the strength to communicate with his leadership cadre to monitor the most recent developments across the globe. His cause was nothing if not grandiose. He meant to cleanse mankind—he abhorred the more inclusive term "humankind"—of all inferior, diseased, or impaired gene pools on the planet, paving the way for a superior race of intelligent, physically fit beings, perfect specimens, beautiful in every way.

An early disciple of Adolf Hitler, he had been 25 when he read Mein Kampf and, by the time "The Führer" rose to power in 1933, he was a true believer. He was especially enamored of Hitler's racial theories. The defeat of the Third Reich, though devastating, had made him only more determined to succeed in the cause. He would not make his predecessor's mistakes. Hitler had been too impatient, and reckless. Fighting a war on two fronts, against the Western powers and Russia, overextended and exhausted the regime's resources. Instead, the Wizard had proceeded as patiently as a spider spinning its web. All he needed was more time.

But time is what he didn't have.

Twenty-first century, Anti-Aging medicine and innovative surgeries to replace worn-out organs and joints had extended his life, thus far. His team of doctors took full advantage of every new technology available. No expense was spared. Just the stem cells harvested from the umbilical cord blood of newborn babies cost a fortune. However, even with his huge financial investment and the world's medical knowledge at their fingertips, his doctors could not, as yet, promise him more than a few years. He desperately desired immortality. He wanted to see his dream of a master race dominating the world come to fruition.

A breakthrough touted to keep him alive and in a more youthful body for another hundred years was on the horizon! Genetic researchers at the Max Plank Institute for Biology of Aging in Cologne, Germany had demonstrated how to slow down, or even reverse the genetic clock, doubling the lifespan of rodents. Not only did the older rodents in the study live longer, but they also took on the health, vigor, and memory of younger ones. According to the most prominent scientists, it was only a matter of time before this technology would be available to humans.

But the Wizard didn't have the time to wait for them. He had his doctors extrapolate on the rodent studies, pioneering a new technology never before used in humans. In a process called parabiosis, they connected his circulatory system for an extended length of time to the circulatory system of healthy babies and toddlers raised in his nurseries. The fact that it sometimes cost them their lives didn't bother him. Sacrifices had to be made for the cause!

A series of beeps marked the end of treatment, and the Wizard opened his eyes. He looked around at the members of his medical team. The doctors and nurses relaxed when he took a deep breath and nodded with satisfaction. They were secretly pleased that he kept a serious expression. When he smiled, his face turned into a skeletal grimace that sent shudders down their spines.

Two orderlies, dressed in identical, sterile white uniforms, helped him sit up and supported him as he got out of bed, to make sure he could stand on his own.

"I'm all right," he rasped in German, looking in disgust at the wheelchair they had brought, just in case. He spit out the words like a snake and pushed the wheelchair to the side.

Bolstered by Titanium joints, the Wizard hobbled toward the door to his communication center, trailing an array of mobile monitoring devices. He felt reasonably fit for the moment, although the sense of his heart being squeezed in a vice and shortness of breath were still with him. He entered a room with subdued lighting, designed to be easy on his eyes. There were banks of computers, scanners, telephones, and other messaging equipment. The cave, which held a constant cool temperature and humidity, made a perfect environment for the vast processors needed to support his worldwide communication systems. One area by a large desk was outfitted with an ergonomic chair designed expressly for his use. He settled in and got ready for his international phone calls.

Everything he did was orchestrated to eliminate randomness and minimize chance occurrence. With his fingers in every major political organization, terrorist group, and national and mercenary militia, he had amassed an impressive track record of success. He gloated over his organization's new-found prosperity, fueled by the paranoia of wealthy donors worried by the turbulence resulting from globalization and the projections of the results of over-breeding inferior human stock in Asia, Africa, and South America. Money poured in from everywhere and he began to sense the momentum of his crusade building. Unlike his predecessor, whose attempt at world domination through military force failed miserably, the Wizard planned to assume worldwide control through a gradual build-up of personnel and technology, and carefully timed regime changes, until his movement reached critical mass.

A computer screen on his desk flickered to life, interrupting the Wizard's reverie. He knew it meant an incoming call from one of his people, who had been on hold for three minutes. Knowing the Wizard's insistence on punctuality, his contacts called in ahead of their scheduled time, preferring to wait rather than be a second late and suffer his wrath.

A young aide cleared his throat and held out a headset to him. "Colonel Burdock, Sir."

As the Wizard put on the headset, he thought about the Colonel. He was one of the first recruits to the cause in the American military, and his contacts had proven invaluable. Although he tended to be long-winded and couldn't see the bigger picture, he was a loyal follower, and the Wizard gave him some leeway. He didn't want to alienate Burdock and have him complain to the many people he knew.

So, he listened patiently as the Colonel listed his meager accomplishments for the month—an uptick in recruitment with many newcomers from a military or police background. The Wizard was about to interrupt to move the conversation along when the Colonel mentioned two unusual altercations. Something piqued the

Wizard's interest, a vague intuition, especially after hearing about the second incident at the Gypsy camp.

"Do you have any intel about this doctor—any martial arts or special ops training," he asked in English with a thick German accent.

Burdock's voice sounded as clear as if he sat next to him. "No, Sir, on all accounts. I'm baffled by the whole thing myself."

"So, am I to understand that a non-combatant with no fighting experience took out four of your well-trained soldiers in less than thirty seconds and with minimal damage to himself?"

"My guess is these boys had been drinking a little too much and this Dr. Curtis got the drop on them."

The Wizard started to feel an itch in his memory. He had witnessed such an encounter himself as a young officer in the S.S., assigned to exterminate Gypsies and Jews in Romania. They had been chasing a man through a forest in the dark of night. He was called der Schwarze Mischling, "the black mongrel," because he would not come out and fight like a man in the light of day. But he single-handedly had thwarted a number of their nighttime operations. Once, they managed to corner him, but he got away, putting up an almost superhuman fight, killing several of his pursuers. The Wizard fingered the scar on his neck, a painful memento from when the man slashed him with a hunting knife.

Barely hiding the excitement in his voice, he said, "Do you know anything about this man at all, Colonel?"

Burdock's voice resonated with eagerness. "Quite a lot. He lied about his personal history in an attempt to marry into a prominent, wealthy family in Tampa. Fortunately, the girl's father asked me to look into his background. When I made inquiries about the heritage of the doctor, an NSA search revealed that he was posing as the son of a fallen military hero when he was actually born in the backwoods of the Appalachian Mountains to a poor single, mother. Luckily, I managed to expose the bastard in time and my friend was able to call off the wedding."

"Backwoods?" the Wizard asked.

"Yes, in Tennessee."

The Wizard's heart beat faster. Too many coincidences. Could it be that the boy was still alive? Nearly thirty years ago, he had sent a kill team into the mountains of East Tennessee to eliminate a pregnant woman and her husband who had fled from Europe and belonged to a deviant bloodline. In those days, the only way to deal with one of these freaks of nature was to eradicate them from the face of the Earth. But now, with the development of cloning, genetic recombinants, and nanotechnology, it might be possible to take advantage of this situation and help him in his quest for immortality.

"Listen to me very carefully, Colonel," the Wizard said. "I want you to call off your witch-hunt. Go back to your friend and tell him that you made a terrible mistake, that the good doctor is exactly who he claims to be."

"But, but…"

Hearing Burdock sputter at the other end of the line, The Wizard's voice became hard as steel. "This is an order, Colonel. There are circumstances at play here that directly affect the cause, our cause."

Burdock gasped, "But what—"

"You will be informed when you need to know more," the Wizard promised. "For now, bring Doctor Curtis closer to the fold. Get friendly, apologize and make up with him, get to know him, whatever it takes. I don't have to tell you that this operation must be carried out with utmost discretion and secrecy. That is an order!"

Burdock immediately responded, "Yessir!"

The Wizard smiled, his hazel blue eyes sparkling with excitement. "And another thing, Colonel. Get me a sample of the doctor's blood, enough for a DNA test."

There was a silence at the other end.

"Did you hear me, Colonel?" the Wizard asked, his voice hissing like a pit viper.

"Yes, Wizard, but it may be difficult without arousing suspicion."

The reptilian face turned predatory. "You'll figure it out. I trust your abilities," he said, throwing Burdock a bone.

"Yessir."

"Good," the Wizard said, grinning. As he closed the connection, he imagined the Colonel clicking his heels and saluting.

Chapter 9

REPRIEVE

By the time Jonathan reached the hospital after breakfast at the Gypsy camp, he had missed patient rounds. In the ER, Hawkins met him with a sneer of contempt, which he ignored. Fortunately, all incoming cases were routine, allowing him to catch up on lab results, discharge orders, and consultations.

When he entered Big Jack's room, the Gypsy King was alone. "Good news, Big Jack!" Jonathan said with an upbeat tone of voice. "I just got off the phone with Dr. Harris. He says your heart cath went smooth as could be. You have very little heart damage and only needed two stents. Your blood pressure is down, and your rhythm is stable." After listening to his chest with a stethoscope, he squeezed Jack's shoulder. "Tomorrow morning, we'll take you off oxygen, get you out of bed, and see how you handle normal activity."

Big Jack gave him a lopsided grin. "Doctor Curtis, you'll never know just how good that sounds. You know I put on a good act, but to tell you the truth, I've been worried for a while now. You've taken a great load off my mind. I am in your debt—in more ways than one."

Jonathan gave him a puzzled look. "What do you mean?"

"I had a visit from Tatyana this morning. She told me all about what happened last night at the camp," Big Jack said. "Isha called me. She is grateful, too. I told her to take you to dinner tonight— my treat."

Blushing, Jonathan said, "I don't know about that, Big Jack. I'm engaged to be married. Does she know this?"

"Oh no, no." Big Jack patted his arm. "Please don't take this the wrong way, Dr. Curtis. I'm not proposing a date; simply a thank you for helping us out of a tight spot last night." He chuckled. "I know my daughter all too well. She is stubborn and has never shown an interest in the Gadjo. About your engagement, I figure I'd leave that detail up to you."

"Yes, of course, and don't take this the wrong way either," Jonathan said, scratching his forehead. "I am grateful for the offer of the dinner, but I'm uncertain of my plans for tonight."

"Hmm." Jack's calculating look turned into an expansive smile. "Let me see if I can make this easy for you. If at the end of the day you're free, let me treat you to dinner. Isha will be here anyway. I'm sure she won't mind. After hanging around this stuffy old hospital room all day, she'll be grateful for a change of scenery. If you're tied up, then that's the way it is. You can take a rain check. How about that, eh?"

"Okay..." Jonathan acquiesced. "I'll be back making rounds about 5:00. I should know something by then."

The rest of the day he was distracted. The thought of spending an evening with the intriguing young Gypsy woman caused his heart to beat faster.

When he returned to Big Jack's room later that afternoon, Isha sat at her father's side. She wore sandals, a green, calico print peasant skirt, a revealing cream-colored blouse, and hand-crafted jewelry on her arms and around her neck. Her dark pupils glistened when she saw him. For a moment, their eyes locked.

It lasted just long enough for Big Jack to take note. "Well, I'll be," he muttered to himself. With a big grin, he continued expansively, "Then it's settled. Go have fun."

He shooed them out the door, giving them no chance to object.

In the hallway, Jonathan and Isha tried to decide where to go for the evening, acting casual. But something had changed since this morning. The carefree goodwill from earlier in the day when Jonathan, exhausted from his nighttime battle, had welcomed Isha's ministrations to help him regain his strength was gone, replaced by an uneasiness and undercurrent of sexual tension. They looked like two awkward teenagers, realizing they were attracted to each other.

Finally, Jonathan suggested the Sponge Docks for dinner. The historic area along the river boasted some of the best Greek restaurants in Tarpon Springs. Isha would drive her Jeep since she wasn't wearing the right clothing for a motorcycle ride. After Jonathan finished making rounds—in about 15 minutes—they agreed to meet at the front entrance to the hospital.

Jonathan watched as Isha walked down the long corridor, then turned to the nurse's station to make notes on Big Jack's chart.

* * *

When Isha rounded a corner of the hallway, she nearly collided with a young woman. The pretty blonde was dressed in a white Oscar de la Renta pantsuit. Every hair on her head was in its proper place.

"Impressive," was Isha's first thought as she took her measure. But then the back of her neck prickled. She sensed the familiar judgment and dismissal, the air of superiority bred of arrogance, ignorance, and fear.

Priscilla briefly noted the exotic beauty of the young woman facing her but focused on her obvious lack of breeding and culture. "A Gypsy, no doubt, from that disgusting little rat hole of a camp at Lake Tarpon," she thought. "That dated hairstyle, revealing dress, and gaudy jewelry belongs in a Halloween party." Priscilla shuddered. She would not be caught dead wearing such garb.

The air was rife with tension. The two women moved past one another observing the laws of Physics, where two objects of equal force repelled each other like two powerful magnets. Neither looked back but walked on with determination.

Pricilla's pace quickened as she neared the nurse's station where a doctor stood with his back to her. "Jonathan," she cried out.

He turned, surprised and his face lit up with a broad smile. "Priscilla!"

"Oh Jonathan, I have the best news!" she burst out. "I just couldn't stay away!" She rushed into his arms and they embraced fiercely. Priscilla pulled back for a kiss, crushing her lips against his.

The cardiac nurse next to him tried to make herself invisible and moved away, busying herself with a nearby computer.

"The best news is that you are here, now, in my arms," Jonathan said, laughing. "It's so good to see you. I didn't hear from you. I couldn't reach you. I've got the proof, the proof your daddy asked for. I –"

Priscilla put her hand over his mouth. "Shhh. Shhh. Listen. You don't have to prove anything. Colonel Burdock called Daddy this morning and told him it was all a big mistake."

Jonathan pulled her hand away. "What?"

"Is there somewhere we can talk in private? I want to tell you the whole story. Oh, I am so happy, Jonathan. I've missed you so."

Becoming aware that everyone in the vicinity was staring at them, Jonathan guided Priscilla to the nearest nurses' break station. He locked the door and smothered her with kisses.

After the heat of their reunion had cooled, Priscilla explained, "Colonel Burdock is very sorry for causing such a big mess. He invited you, me, and my parents to dinner at the club tomorrow night. He wants to make a formal apology. Your membership in the club has been accepted. And of course, the engagement is back on. Isn't it great?"

Jonathan hesitated. "I am flabbergasted." He gave Priscilla a lecherous grin, pulled close, and pressed himself against her.

It was not a subtle gesture, and Priscilla responded in kind. "Mmm," she cooed and thrust her hips against him. "My car's outside and your apartment is just down the street. Are you thinking what I'm thinking?"

His mind was racing. He most certainly had the same thoughts, but Isha was waiting for him at the front entrance. "I have some unfinished business to attend to first," he said with a husky voice. "Meet me at the rear entrance of the hospital. I'll be there in ten minutes."

Priscilla kissed her finger and touched it to his lips before sashaying from the room.

Jonathan followed her out and headed in the opposite direction. When he was out of her sight, he made a run for the front entrance.

* * *

Isha waited by her Jeep as Jonathan came through the entrance doors. She started to smile until she saw his hangdog expression.

When he came up to her, he said, "I'm sorry, Isha, but something's come up—an emergency. I don't know how long it will take." He scratched his head. "We better do this another night. I was so looking forward to it."

He should have known better than to lie to a Gypsy. Perhaps another woman would have believed his excuse, but Isha saw right through him.

"An emergency," she echoed, noting his dilated eyes and the beads of perspiration on his brow.

"Yes, an emergency," he repeated, unable to look at her directly.

Isha cocked her head. "Very well, Jonathan, I'm disappointed, too, but I understand."

He mouthed "Thank you" and hustled back to the entrance, disappearing through the large glass double doors.

Looking after him, Isha narrowed her eyes and murmured, "Let's see what kind of emergency that might be."

On a hunch, she drove her Jeep to the side parking lot and waited between two minivans. It wasn't long before she spotted a white Mercedes sports car with the top down, heading toward the exit. The haughty blonde with the neatly coiffed hair was driving. Jonathan sat in the passenger seat with his arm draped over her shoulders. They seemed to be having fun.

For an instant, Isah felt hurt. Then she became furious. "The lying, conniving bastard!" she shouted. Driving off in a huff, she vowed not to speak to Jonathan ever again, regardless of what Tatyana or her father said. You couldn't trust men, especially if they were Gadjos.

* * *

As soon as Jonathan and Priscilla entered his apartment, they tore each other's clothes off. Then they indulged in a flesh feast that lasted for several courses. Thoroughly sated at last, they lay next to each other between the sheets of the bed, staring at the ceiling fan gyrating overhead.

Jonathan felt better than he had in days. The nightmare was over. Everything with Priscilla was back on track. He couldn't help but wonder about the Colonel whose blunder had nearly cost them their happiness. Was that issue resolved for good? He rolled onto his side, rested his head on his arm, and looked at Priscilla.

When she turned toward him, sleepily, he said, "Promise me, darling, that we will never let anything like that separate us again."

She smiled with her eyes closed and said, "I promise." Then she felt for his free hand and guided it under the sheet to her breast. As he cupped and squeezed lightly, she purred, "Mmm." She continued in the same sultry voice, "You know, Jonathan, I have a little favor to ask of you."

"Anything, darling."

"It may seem like an odd request, but I'd like a small sample of your blood."

Jonathan stopped fondling her breast. "We don't need that test until right before the wedding," he said.

"It's not for VD, silly. Daddy wants it for a DNA test."

Taken aback, Jonathan withdrew his hand and sat up. "What is this about? The Colonel said it was all a big mistake. Now your daddy wants a DNA test? It doesn't make sense."

Priscilla grasped his hand again. "What's the big deal? I mean, it's just a little test," she pleaded. "Just do it for me." She looked up at him with her baby-blue eyes, pleading. Something gnawed at the back of his brain. "Let me think about it."

"Of course, darling." She pulled him to her, nuzzled his ear, and whispered, "If you don't want to, I'll tell Daddy. It won't make a difference to us."

Jonathan yielded to her reluctantly, then with increasing pleasure and enthusiasm.

Chapter 10

AUNT AGNES
AND THE MIDNIGHT VISITOR

After kissing Priscilla goodnight and watching her drive off, Jonathan went back inside his apartment to look at the pictures of his parents and read all the documents again. Something wasn't right. Priscilla's revelations about the Colonel admitting his mistake and her father requesting a DNA test left him as confused as ever. It didn't help that Tatyana's voice kept echoing in his head, "I'm certain you will soon learn the truth about your father."

Only one person could throw light on this situation—Aunt Agnes, his remaining living relative. However, Jonathan was reluctant to call her because he felt guilty about how little effort he had made to stay in touch with her. The last time they had spoken at length was five years ago when she came to his medical school graduation. It was a gracious gesture on her part, and he had repaid it by virtually abandoning her. How would she react when he called her out of the blue? But "desperate times called for desperate measures," he thought as he punched her number into his cell phone.

To his surprise, as soon as Aunt Agnes heard his voice, she responded with all the warmth and care he remembered. When he mentioned he was traveling her way and wanted to stop by for a visit, she sounded pleased.

"It's so good to hear from you, Johnny," she said. "Why, I haven't seen you in a coon's age. Please come and stay the night. I have a spare bedroom, you know. It's not much, but you're welcome to it. I'll make that 'melt-in-your-mouth' apple pie you've always loved."

"Wonderful," Jonathan said. "Can't wait to see you and catch up."

His next call was to Jimmy Pappas. "I know this is spur-of-the-moment, but would you go on a trip to Tennessee with me? I want to leave right away. It's important."

His best friend didn't hesitate. "I'm game," he said. "But you have to tell me what this is about. All of it!"

When Jonathan picked him up in the rental car, Jimmy volunteered to drive the first leg from Tarpon Springs to Atlanta. Along the way, Jonathan filled him in on all that had happened—the visits to the gypsy camp, Tatyana's predictions, the questions regarding his parentage, and his reconciliation with Priscilla. When Jimmy heard about the afternoon of passionate sex. he let out a whoop of joy. But when Jonathan told him about Colonel Burdock's surprising retraction and Priscilla's father's insistence on a DNA report, he was just as baffled.

"It's a good thing we're taking this trip," he insisted. "You've got to put these questions about your past to rest!"

They drove through Atlanta, with Jonathan at the steering wheel, at sunrise. Passing the bright orange and white Varsity sign just off I-75, pleasant memories crossed his mind of the first time he had seen this famous icon. His mother had taken him to the big city for his birthday and lunch at the largest hot dog stand in the world. While only a modest adventure by most people's standards, it had been a monumental occasion for him and reminded him of his mother's caring nature.

From the outskirts of Atlanta, Jonathan headed to the high mountain roads. He turned off the air-conditioner, rolled down the windows, and inhaled deeply as he felt the cool, crisp air rush past his face, a welcome relief from the sultry summer heat of Florida.

He looked over at Jimmy, slumped in the passenger seat. His friend shifted his weight, pulled up his jacket around his neck, and went back to sleep. A smile crossed Jonathan's face. It was good to have someone he could count on in his court.

Far from the heavily trafficked Interstate on mountain roads known only to locals, Jonathan made excellent time.

They reached Knoxville early in the morning and stopped at the National Cemetery. Jonathan wanted to pay his respects to his father. Standing before the simple grave marker, he felt saddened that he had never gotten to know him. He said a prayer, hoping his father would forgive him for the questions he was going to ask his aunt. After all this time, it felt like a betrayal.

Half an hour later they arrived in Lafollette. Jonathan caught Jimmy looking around with a quizzical expression on his face. This was his first visit to Jonathan's hometown and he was visibly surprised by the unpretentious, small white houses, the oak-canopied yards, and the quiet, deserted streets. It was a far cry from his Greek community in Tarpon Springs, where every home was painted in bright colors, and the neighborhood was noisy and bustling with people in the morning hours.

They made another stop in the parking lot of a small Pentecostal church. In the cemetery out back, many grave sites predated the Civil War and were overgrown with weeds and thick Rhododendron bushes. In a well-tended section, Jonathan found his mother's gravestone, guarded by two alabaster angels. Maintained by his mother's sister, Aunt Agnes, it looked as new as the day she'd been buried.

Staring at the grave surrounded by blooming Lilies of the Valley, Jonathan had second thoughts about his mission. He hoped his mother would understand and bowed his head, thanking her for the love she had given him.

It was close to 10 o'clock when they drove the remaining few blocks up the road, to a simple, white-frame house with blue window shutters. Jonathan parked in the driveway, got out, and walked up the path, lined by a flower bed of yellow and gold day lilies. He knocked on the screen, but there was no answer except the yapping of a small dog. As Jonathan opened the door, a black and white mutt came out wagging her tail. She sniffed him and rolled over on her back, wiggling back and forth over his shoes.

"What a good little guard dog you are, Ella," Jonathan praised her. He reached down and rubbed her belly. She nuzzled his hand, got up, and began bouncing around. "Okay, Okay, I'm glad you recognize me."

Ella sniffed at Jim, but her greeting was not as effusive.

Inside, the house was just as Jonathan remembered it. Old, unmatching furniture filled the parlor, living room, and dining room, including a blue vinyl recliner he had jumped on as a child. Through the window screens, he could feel cool mountain air drifting lazily into the house, mixing with a familiar, musty odor.

He called out, "Aunt Agnes," but received no answer.

In the kitchen, the intoxicating aroma of apples and cinnamon met them. Under a cheesecloth on the window sill sat one of Aunt Agnes' delicious apple pies.

Poking his head out the screened-in back porch, Jonathan yelled louder, "Aunt Agnes!"

From the maze of flowering shrubs and plants in the garden came a muffled reply. "Johnny, I'm out back pickin' us some fresh 'maters for breakfast."

Jonathan peered through the dark brown mesh but didn't see anyone. His view was obscured by dense, purple, and pink clematis which spread along the back porch screen. White and blue hydrangeas grew above the eves cascading over one another.

Finally, a spry, middle-aged woman rose beyond the rose bushes in the backyard and waved. She was wearing a short-sleeved white cotton shirt and blue jeans. A floppy straw hat shaded her thin face.

Jonathan burst out the screen door and ran up the slope toward her with Jimmy close behind.

She welcomed him with outstretched arms. "Johnny, Johnny! You're such a sight for sore eyes! Come on out and give your old aunt a hug."

Given Jonathan's huge frame, Agnes nearly disappeared into his arms. "Oh, Aunt Agnes, it's so good to see you, too."

Close to his belly, her next words were muffled. "Johnny, I swear it seems like you just keep getting bigger or I'm shrinking, or both. Why, I remember when I could cradle your little body in my two arms." Stepping back and grasping both his arms, she continued, "I was so glad to get your call. Driving all night. You must be bushed."

"Not really. Jimmy and I shared the driving." Jonathan gestured to his friend. "You remember Jimmy Pappas, my roommate back in college? You guys met at my medical school graduation."

Aunt Agnes removed her work gloves. "Never forget a handsome man like you," she said, grinning. "Good to see you again, Jimmy."

"Nice to see you again, too, Aunt Agnes," Jimmy replied, looking around her backyard. "Never saw such a beautiful garden."

"Oh poo!" Agnes blushed. "I mean, thank you, Jimmy. It's a blessing and a curse, this green thumb of mine. So many weeds and such."

Jimmy chuckled.

Agnes started to walk back toward the house. "Why don't we go to the back porch, grab a seat, relax, and have some coffee and pie," she said. "I'd love to hear what's been happening with you."

Jonathan frowned. "There's a lot of stuff goin' on, Aunt Agnes. Things we need to talk about."

Stepping onto the porch, she gave him a knowing look and said, "You get out the plates and silverware, the good kind—you know where they are—while I brew us some coffee."

While Jonathan retrieved china cups and dessert plates with pink flowers around the edges from a cupboard in the living room, Aunt Agnes puttered around in the kitchen. Soon the aroma of coffee wafted inside the house, and before long she returned carrying a tray. She set it on the small cane table and served coffee and generous slices of her 'melt-in-your-mouth' apple pie.

Like a small sentry on duty, Ella sat at their feet looking up with soft brown, begging eyes in anticipation of crumbs falling from the table.

The pie was heavenly. Even Jimmy, a lifelong connoisseur of Greek pastry, smacked his lips with pleasure and quickly said yes when Aunt Agnes offered him a second slice. All the while, she kept up light conversation, telling stories about the locals—Lafollette was a small community where everyone knew everything about everyone else's business and gossiping was a favorite pastime. Aunt Agnes had plenty of it, rivaling the headlines of tabloids at the check-out counters of the grocery store. She knew Jonathan had little interest in women's tittle-tattle, but she could tell he was tense and upset and needed to settle down.

Eventually, Agnes pretended to run out of stories. She leaned back in her chair and, with a sweet smile, said, "So there's lots of stuff happening, Johnny. Tell me about it."

Jonathan stared darkly ahead and sighed. "I don't know where to begin."

"Sometimes it's best just to start somewhere," Agnes said kindly. "You know. I practically raised you since you were a baby, and I know all your little fidgets and stutters. I can tell that there's somethin' goin' on." She reached out to touch his hand. "Tell me, Johnny."

The air left his chest like a balloon deflating. "Things seem to be falling apart, Aunt Agnes. My engagement nearly ended when my future father-in-law had my background investigated."

The words flowed once there was a crack in the dam, and Jonathan unburdened himself. As he rambled on, Aunt Agnes nodded to keep him going until his narrative had run its course. She exchanged occasional glances with Jimmy for confirmation and became increasingly tense.

When Jonathan was finished, she looked at him and said, "I was afraid this day would come, even though I prayed it never would." She glanced up at the ceiling. "Oh, how I wish Nell were still with us. She could tell it better than me." She sighed and continued, "The man you thought was your father is not your father, and Nell is not your mother."

Instantly, the color drained from Jonathan's face. Jimmy reached out and put a steadying hand on his shoulder.

Agnes got up and went inside the house leaving Jonathan sitting in his chair like a stone statue. She returned with a bottle of whiskey and three glasses. "I think we could all use a drink."

She poured for everyone and, without waiting for the others, downed her glass with one swallow and gave herself a refill. Jonathan followed her example and held out his glass. She topped it up while Jimmy sipped his bourbon carefully.

Then, she sat back down and said, "You were adopted when you were about one year old. Nell never wanted you to know about it, and for good reasons. She tried to make everything seem as if you were her own."

Jonathan frowned. "But, what about my birth certificate and all the stories mom told about me as an infant?"

"Your mother convinced Reverend Billy at Faith's Tabernacle, to falsify a marriage document and inveigled ol' Doc Tinsley, the physician she worked for, to make out a birth certificate," Agnes explained. A brief smile crossed her face. "Hell, she had so much dirt on each of 'em, neither could refuse. Reverend Billy brought the matter to a session at the church. The deacons prayed about it, passed snakes, and figured if God was good with it, they were too."

Jonathan shook his head in disbelief, "The church agreed and stuck to it? All of the congregation? I grew up with my whole life a lie and everybody knew it?"

"Well, not many knew the real story, and they weren't about to talk to outsiders. A lot of them quickly forgot. Then, ol' Doc Tinsley died and took that secret to his grave."

"But my father holding me in his arms, his medals and Certificate of Honor, his gravesite. Those are all real. I've treasured them my whole life."

"Unfortunately, those things are also lies," Aunt Agnes said sadly. "I'm so sorry, Johnny. It breaks my heart to tell you this. But you must believe me, Nell and I loved you as our own." Agnes took another sip and continued, "How Nell figured all that out still befuddles me. The first month we had you, she hid you from everyone. We lived in the old family home back then, and we both doted on you. You were the most precious gift to us. About that time, an obituary showed up in the paper: 'Lieutenant Michael Jonathan Curtis killed during maneuvers. The highly decorated veteran will be buried in Old Grey National Cemetery in Knoxville.' Nell figured he would make a perfect father for you, someone to look up to and give you an honest name. She invented the whole romance and wedding, lied to everyone, and then had Reverend Billy swear to it. Since Curtis was her given last name, Nell considered it to be a God-send, and she was so headstrong about it, no one dared to challenge her."

Agnes leaned in closer. "The day of the funeral, she drove to Knoxville and signed in as a visitor. While everyone was at the graveside, she stole all the memorabilia she could carry from the vestibule. When she got home, she put together an album, placing photos of Michael Curtis next to pictures of herself, our family, and you. There were several photographs of him holding a baby, but it's not you. Nell reckoned a baby wrapped in blankets, held close to the lieutenant's chest would look like any other. If you go back to your album, you'll notice that there are never pictures of Nell and Michael together, nor anyone else you would know. As for the wedding album, your mother claimed it was stolen. Also a lie."

Jimmy, who had kept quiet, gasped and shook his head.

Agnes kept her focus on Jonathan. "As you grew up, we kept up the illusion—all the trips to your father's grave in Knoxville. As you know, Nell loved you with all her heart, and I did too." She stopped, and silence descended on the back porch, interrupted only by birds chirping outside.

Finally, Jonathan said, "I don't recall anything from my early days. What was I like?"

Agnes' eyes took on a distant look. "At first, we were amazed at how fast you grew and developed. At one and a half, you walked and ran around the yard but you also could swing a bat, kick a ball, and play like any four- or five-year-old. At two, you began reading. Neither Nell nor I knew how you learned. I was proud of you, but Nell worried about you playing with the other kids. You stuck out. 'Different,' Nell called it, and she was fearful of people prying into her business."

"When you were four, we bought you your first bicycle. Do you remember that red Roadster with training wheels and every-thing? Why, it wasn't two days and you took those wheels off, and before long, you were doing tricks with it in the front yard and on the street in front of the house."

She chuckled, "It wouldn't be unusual for most kids to ride a bike at that age, but you were standing on the handlebars and rid-ing on one wheel down the driveway. Neighbors began gathering 'round to watch. Heck, you were just playing like any other kid. You had no idea how unusual that was. But your mother knew better. She took your bike away and didn't give it back to you until you were much older."

Tears welled up in Agnes' eyes. She slowly shook her head and gazed up at Jonathan. "You were special in so many ways. And look at you now, a handsome young man and a doctor!"

Jonathan swallowed and said bitterly, "I can't believe you deceived me all these years, Aunt Agnes. My whole life, a lie! How could you? Why?"

"Oh, Johnny, dear Johnny. Please don't believe that. Your life has not been a lie. Yes, there was the lie about your natural father and mother. But you were precious to us. We loved you in every way. We were a real family. That is not a lie."

"Then who are my real parents?"

Agnes looked to the ceiling again, as if seeking guidance. Then she sighed and lowered her voice. "Okay, I will tell you why I've kept this a secret until now. Your mother and I were told that the revelation of your true identity was a matter of life or death!"

Taken aback, Jonathan cleared the tears from his eyes and looked intently at his aunt.

Taking a deep breath, Agnes said, "Lordy, I remember the first time I set eyes on you as clear as day. It was a cool spring night. Nell and I were playing cards on the back porch of our old homestead. It got to be, my guess, around midnight. I'm sure we were the only ones with lights on. Suddenly, there was a loud rap on the screen door. It sent a chill down my back. We peered out into the night and saw a young woman holding a wad of blankets close to her bosom. 'Please, please,' she cried. 'Can you help me? I'm being chased by evil men. They're going to kill me! You are my last hope to save my baby.'"

"Nell rushed to open the screen door and bid the poor woman to come inside. She sat down at the living room table, trembling in the darkness. Nell pulled the curtains and locked all the doors before turning on the lights. Then we could see her more clearly. Her skin was sallow and smudged with dirt. Her eyes were sunk deep into the sockets of her head and darkened beneath. Poor thing, she was half starved to death. So, I fetched her a glass of milk and a slice of apple pie. When I returned from the kitchen, she had rearranged the blankets to reveal a baby—you—sleeping like a little cherub in her arms. Nell and I looked at your ruby-red lips, your little nose a-flaring with every breath, your chubby little cheeks, and we felt an immediate connection."

Agnes looked up at Jonathan, her face conveying the anxiety and danger of that moment. "The woman, your natural mother, gulped the food down like a ravenous animal. After consuming two glasses of milk and two more slices of pie, she told us what had happened to her."

"She and her husband had been on the run for months, ever since you were born. The men that were hunting them wanted to kill you. She and her husband had been living safely in the mountains with a tribe of Cherokees when they were discovered. There had been a fight and the assassins murdered her husband and some of the Cherokees. Their bravery had allowed her to escape with you. She'd been running and hiding in the forest with you for three days, keeping ahead of her pursuers. She trusted no one, feared the police and the sheriff, and was at the end of her rope. She begged us to take you in and raise you as our own. She also warned us never to reveal your true identity. To do so, she claimed, would ensure your death."

"She got more and more agitated until Nell said, 'I'll take him.'"

Agnes' eyes widened. "It was an impulsive decision. She didn't need to think about it. She had always dreamed of having a child, but she and I being spinsters 'n all, it was never going to happen the natural way. So, right on the spot she agreed to adopt you, promised to raise you as your mother, and swore to protect you from evil."

"Your real mother was so thankful. For a few minutes more, she sat in the chair weeping a flood of agony, holding her baby for the last time. Then, she kissed you and placed you in Nell's arms. 'His name is Luka, my precious baby boy,' she whispered. Then she stared Nell straight in the eyes and said, 'Never call him that again.' She gave us instructions on how to take care of you. The reason you were so healthy-looking is that she had been breastfeeding you. She alerted Nell that you would be hungry when you awoke and that you were such a loud crier it would be advisable to have a bottle of warm milk on hand. As she reached to take one last look at you, the blankets came loose and a gold brooch fell from the swaddling and hit the floor with a clunk. Your mother carefully picked it up and handed it to Nell. 'This is his only inheritance.' she told us. 'It has been passed down through my family since medieval times.'

"She leaned forward with a fierce, haunted look, as if she meant to etch your face in her mind, and turned to us. 'I'll try to get as far away as I can to divert attention from your place,' she said. Then she left without another word. The door slammed behind her, and we never heard from her again."

Jonathan leaned back, feeling overwhelmed. Jimmy looked at him with compassion.

Agnes took Jonathan's hand, "Please don't hold it against us. Nell and I, we did it as a promise to your mother and for your protection. I figure it's been long enough, and you wanting answers, I guess there's no harm in revealing the truth now."

Jonathan sat in silence, reflecting on all he had heard. His poor mother and father were killed, protecting his life. Aunt Agnes and Nell perpetrating a lie as a promise to his grieving mother and to assure his safety.

"Did my mother tell you her name? My father's name?" he finally said. When Agnes shook her head, he asked, "But why? Why was I being hunted?"

"We never found out," Agnes said regretfully. Then her eyes brightened. "By the next morning, Nell was already planning how to legitimize your birth. The first thing she did was to get rid of any evidence of your past. She burned your blankets and buried the brooch in the garden out back. That same day, while Nell went to K-mart to buy some baby things, I dug it up and hid it in a secret compartment of that old Empire dresser of mine. It's stayed there until now."

She got up, went to the cupboard, and pushed something in the back. A secret drawer opened in the front paneling. Reaching inside, she retrieved a dirt-stained cloth. She handed it to Jonathan. He unwrapped it and gasped. It was the brooch from his visions, made of solid gold and shaped like a dragon biting its tail. A lock of golden hair was tightly wrapped and held to its back by the clasp.

"What is it, Johnny?" Agnes asked.

"Nothing," Jonathan quickly recovered. "Seeing something from my real mother is a shock. What was she like?"

"Unfortunately, there's not much more to tell, Johnny. She was only with us for half an hour." Agnes' eyes darted back and forth as she searched her mind. "Let me see. She was tall and her face was kind. She spoke haltingly, with an odd accent. She was dark-skinned with coal-black hair and eyes like yours and wore her hair tied up. We thought she might be one of the Indians." Agnes hesitated for a moment, then gave a jolt, as if startled. "I remember one other thing. It was the fragrance of her perfume. When I asked her about it, she told me she wore it as protection against evil. Of course, on hearing that, Nell gave a huff, knowing it was only by the Grace of our Lord and Savior, Jesus Christ, that one could be delivered from evil, but I smiled at her on hearing it, thinking it was kinda sweet."

Jonathan was wide-eyed. "The fragrance, Aunt Agnes. What was it?"

"I remember that too, Johnny. Your mother told us it was frankincense."

Aunt Agnes appeared as if a burden had lifted off her shoulders. "I always dreaded this day coming. I never knew how you might take it. Now that it's over, now that you know, I feel relieved. That part of me can rest in peace. I hope you can forgive two old maids who loved and raised you as their own and understand why we couldn't tell you about your true parents. I pray this has helped you, so you can find peace in knowing the truth."

Jonathan stood up and wrapped her in his arms. "Thank you, Aunt Agnes."

* * *

On the way home, Jimmy drove the rental out of the mountains, heading south to Florida with Jonathan in the passenger seat. Despite Aunt Agnes' invitation to spend the night, they left soon after brunch. Jonathan had his dinner to attend.

He'd said goodbye to Ella and kissed his aunt. She'd stared at him fondly and put up a good front, growing misty-eyed only at the end when he took her in his arms once more and kissed her cheek. The way she waved after them made Jonathan realize that she figured it was the last time she would see him, and it made him sad.

But he didn't sit with those feelings for long. He had too much to think about. While the visit had confirmed his worst fears, it had raised more questions than it answered. Who were his biological parents? Why were they in hiding? Who chased after them, wanting to kill him as a baby? Did Burdock and Randolph know more than they let on? And the brooch. Why did his mother leave it for him? Tatyana seemed to know more about it! Could he trust her to tell him the truth?

At some point, Jimmy asked, "Want to talk about it?"

"Yeah," Jonathan said, welcoming the interruption. "It was tough news, but, in some way, I feel relieved. There were things about my childhood that never made sense, things my mom always told me not to be so concerned about. Like not having an extended family, my dad's relatives—no cousins, aunts, uncles. Eventually, I quit asking, but I never quit thinking about it."

They talked some more, as Jonathan kept fingering the ancient heirloom absentmindedly. At some point, he laid his head back on the seat and closed his eyes, but sleep refused to come. What to tell Priscilla, her parents, and Colonel Burdock? Should he keep silent, accept the Colonel's apology, and act as if nothing had happened? It didn't feel right to enter into a marriage with a lie.

He kept trying to figure out what to say to them, but the words felt hollow and unconvincing. Exhausted, he finally gave up with a sigh and nodded off to sleep.

Jim gave him an empathetic glance and drove on, humming to himself.

Chapter 11

OF THOROUGHBREDS AND MUSTANGS

It was nearing dusk when Jonathan pulled his Harley into the side parking lot of The Palma Verde Country Club. Jimmy had dropped him off at his apartment in Tarpon Springs less than an hour before. With just enough time for a quick shower, he had thrown on a pair of blue jeans, a powder blue open-collar dress shirt, and the only blazer he owned. Glancing in the mirror, he'd noted the scruffy, two-day beard and shrugged it off. No time for a shave.

As he bounded up the portico staircase at the side entrance, he removed his helmet and straightened as best he could. He took a deep breath and entered the thick, Castilian wood doorway into the spacious garden atrium courtyard. Rounding the water fountain, he passed a little statue. The lawn jockey was hunched over. Its black face had exaggerated features—large red lips, and a flat bulbous nose—like a caricature. Oddly, he hadn't noticed it on his first visit. Perhaps it had been hidden from view behind the throng of party guests.

Priscilla sat on a stool at the outdoor bar sipping a wine cooler. She turned as he arrived, hopped off the stool, and rushed into his arms. "Jonathan," she cried out jubilantly.

His grin broadened as they embraced for a passionate kiss. When she pulled away and looked into his eyes with her baby blues, he melted. For a moment, he forgot his worries.

Priscilla babbled happily, "Oh, Baby, it's so good to see you. Isn't this just wonderful? I am so happy!" Then she noticed his troubled expression. "Jonathan, are you okay?" She reached out to take his hand. "Nervous about this evening, Honey? Oh, don't be silly. Daddy is totally over it. And, the Colonel is ready to eat crow. You'll have no problem with either of them, I promise."

She gave him a coquettish smile, then took him by the hand and led him into a private dining room overlooking the golf course.

The sun setting behind the tall cypress trees cast a golden glow over the lavish dinner arrangement. From the table in the middle of the spacious room, the Colonel and Priscilla's father and mother looked up at him expectantly. The men stood and shook his hand, wearing pleasant smiles.

No one said anything while three waiters served the meal, starting with a tossed salad of greens, carrot shavings, grape tomatoes, and feta cheese. Jonathan realized that they were all African Americans, wearing short, white dinner jackets and white gloves. One of them offered him pepper with a subservient tone of voice, as if he didn't want to intrude. The main course was a marbled steak, large enough to feed two people, and a baked potato slathered with sour cream and chives.

As they were eating, Muffy kept up a stream of inconsequential conversation about her favorite football teams and how well she played golf during the afternoon. The Colonel and Priscilla's father chimed in from time to time, feigning interest.

Watching their performances evoked a welter of conflicting emotions in Jonathan. While he felt anxious, he still harbored considerable anger from his previous meeting with Brian Randolph. He found Colonel Burdock's efforts to involve him in the conversation laughable—to think they had anything in common because they'd been raised by single mothers when their fathers were killed serving in the military. Muffy's idle chatter bored him. The only redeeming feature was Priscilla's presence—beautiful Priscilla, looking at him with adoring eyes.

As Jonathan continued to nibble on his steak, Colonel Burdock rose and cleared his throat loudly. Muffy and Brian turned expectantly toward him.

Priscilla shot Jonathan a glance of relief and mouthed, "Finally."

"Brian, Muffy, Priscilla," the Colonel began dramatically. "It is a rare event that I stand before anyone, much less my good friends, and admit I was wrong. But I must do so tonight." He turned to Jonathan. "I owe this young doctor, who sits here before us, an apology. A computer glitch misled me, but it was my fault that I jumped to conclusions too quickly. For that, I am sincerely sorry." He lowered his head, as if ready to accept his punishment.

Brian rose to his feet and exclaimed, "Here, here. Water under the bridge!" Muffy beamed and Priscilla nodded in agreement.

As the two men were about to sit back down, Jonathan held up his hand. "Excuse me, Colonel, please hold your apologies until you hear what I have to say."

With his grand gesture rejected, Burdock frowned. Then he smiled and shrugged his shoulders. "The floor is yours, young man."

Priscilla peered up at her beau with a surprised look. "Jonathan, what's going on?"

Jonathan rose from his chair and took a deep breath. His heart beat so loudly that he worried everyone would notice how nervous he was. But when he made eye contact with the others at the table, he saw only puzzled expressions. He singled out Priscilla's parents. "Brian, Muffy," he began, "I am passionately in love with your daughter. Since the day I met her, I have dreamed of spending the rest of my life with her and having a family. While I might not be equal to her in social standing, you have been generous and received me as one of your own."

He hesitated for a moment before continuing.

"However, the last time we spoke, Brian, I left your office hurt and angry. Because Colonel Burdock questioned my paternity, I suddenly wasn't good enough for your daughter. Now that the Colonel has admitted his mistake, I'm back in your good graces. It seems like shaky ground on which to build a future. I hope that you can accept me for the man I am and for my love for Priscilla and not judge me by some arbitrary color of my skin or the socio-economic status of my parents. So, my question to everyone here tonight is, 'How little would it take for me to be out of your favor again?'"

He let the question hang in the air, glancing expectantly around the table.

When Brian spoke, his voice was expansive. "Why of course, Son. We accept you as our own."

Muffy quickly agreed. "Oh Jonathan, we all love you and are so proud of you."

Priscilla looked up at him mystified. "Of course, I love you, Jonathan. You know that. For better or worse. Isn't that what marriage is all about? But why this inquisition? Tonight's supposed to be a celebration."

Only Colonel Burdock leaned back in his chair with a calculating expression, as if he expected worse to come.

Jonathan looked around the table again and nodded. "Then what I have to tell you next shouldn't change anything." He took another deep breath. "While trying to find proof of my heritage, I also ran into some discrepancies. They brought to mind lifelong questions about my childhood. Last night, I drove to my hometown in Tennessee in hopes that my Aunt Agnes, my only living relative, could clear things up for me. Well, she did…."

Jonathan looked at Priscilla and laid a gentle hand on her shoulder. "It seems my father, the military hero, was not my father after all. And, my mother is not my mother. I was adopted."

"What?" Priscilla cried out. "I…I don't understand!"

In broad strokes Jonathan outlined what he discovered—his true father's murder, his mother's perilous flight through the mountains to save his life, and his aunt and adoptive mother taking him in. He had to stop several times when his feelings nearly overwhelmed him, but he soldiered on. When he was finished, he sat down and waited.

An ominous silence filled the room.

Finally, Colonel Burdock spoke up. "Interesting revelation, Young Man," he said. Then he turned to Brian Randolph. "I don't see how this news has to change the wedding plans. In fact, I have to give Doctor Curtis credit. A lesser man could have kept this information a secret. To come to us tonight with the truth speaks to his good character. So, I have to agree with Jonathan. By now, no matter his heritage, he has earned our respect. Surely this fine young man, handsome and blessed with an intellect bar none, would make an ideal husband for your daughter."

Jonathan couldn't believe his ears. Colonel Burdock was the last man he expected to rally to his cause.

But Brian Pennington Randolph, III was livid. He shot back. "Easy for you to say, Burdock. You don't have a daughter's future to protect. I can't believe you, of all people, would defend such a story. I had just gotten over the fact that my little girl was engaged to some hillbilly from the wrong side of the tracks. Now I have to contend with an even worse scenario: his parents on the run like common criminals. From whom? The law? What's next?"

He glared at Jonathan. "I don't know if love plays any part in it at all, Young Man." His tone was harsh and his eyes blazing with hatred. "Depending on who or what you are, you marrying my daughter could be seen as an abomination in the eyes of God. The Bible spells it out clearly. An unholy mixing of races is in defiance of God's law. Intellect and good looks aside, you can't breed a mustang to a thoroughbred and expect to birth a thoroughbred. It's against the laws of nature and the command of God!"

The Colonel quickly interceded. "But Brian, at present no one knows where Jonathan came from. Wouldn't you like to know? Run a DNA test to find out his background?" Jonathan looked around the table. Priscilla was crying silently, her eyes fixed on her hands held stiffly together. Muffy and Brian scowled at him, as if he were the Devil reincarnated. Colonel Burdock evaluated him with a strange smile. There was only one person in the room Jonathan needed to hear from. He turned to her and pleaded, "Priscilla, Honey, talk to me."

Priscilla raised her tear-stained eyes from her tightly held fists. "Oh Jonathan, this is all such terrible news," she said, her voice ragged.

Unsure of how she meant it, Jonathan asked, "Last night, you asked me to get a DNA sample. Was that your daddy's idea or..." He hesitated. "Why did you want it?"

Priscilla wiped the tears from her eyes. "I love you, baby. But it's even more important now that we know your background. It's for our protection."

"Our protection?" Jonathan echoed.

"Yes, can't you see?" She searched his face. "I mean, what would people say? What would they say if they were born...well, you know?"

The implications of her words struck Jonathan like a blow. He felt his knees grow weak but caught himself. He would not buckle before these hypocritical paragons of virtue and self-righteousness. He felt a searing pain in his chest and gave Priscilla a look of anguish and disappointment. Then he took in a deep breath and let the air out slowly, nodding his head. Just as calmly as saying goodnight, he said. "Let me make this easy on all of us. I'm calling off the engagement. I can't join a family of bigots." With that, he turned and walked out the door.

He barely heard the flurry of remarks that followed in his wake—Brian Randolph sneering, "Good riddance," Muffy huffing, "Well, I never!" and Priscilla sobbing, "Oh, Jonathan, how could you do this to me?" He did register Colonel Burdock muttering, "Crap! This whole thing sure turned to shit!" and thought, I couldn't have said it better myself!

Chapter 12

GYPSY CAMPFIRE

After leaving Palma Verde Country Club, Jonathan drove his Harley toward the Gypsy camp by Lake Tarpon, but before he reached the entrance to the state park, he accelerated and kept going like a man possessed. The wind whipping against his face did nothing to cool the burning anger he felt over Priscilla's betrayal. How could he have been so blind not to see the truth earlier—that she was cut from the same cloth as her smug, racist parents? He had shown them who he really was and had left with his head held high. But for all his bravado, his world had collapsed, and he felt like a lost soul.

Racing aimlessly into the night provided little relief. Soon the anger became an ache in his chest, and he decided to turn back and head toward the camp. Perhaps Tatyana had answers for him. If she could shine even a sliver of light on his origins, the evening might not end in complete disaster.

When Jonathan reached her campsite, the surrounding woods were as dark as a witches' midnight. Coming to a stop, he turned off the motor and pushed his kickstand down. As he removed his helmet, he heard a dog bark. It was Mugs. The scraggly little mutt came running up, tail wagging, to sniff his hand.

Tatyana was eating dinner at the outdoor table, to the soft yellow glow of a kerosene lamp. Her cat Clementine lay sprawled to one side. The Persian barely raised her white, powder-puffed head, gave him an indifferent look, and then went back to sleep.

"Dr. Curtis. So nice of you to come and visit," Tatyana called to him and motioned him to join her.

Jonathan was momentarily mystified—how could she know it was him?

As if reading his mind, Tatyana said, smiling, "The sound of your Harley preceded you. But I've been expecting you." "Oh, how so?" Jonathan asked as he pulled up a chair.

"The last time we met—the journey, the armored warrior, the tussle around the campfire. Maybe you don't remember. It ended so abruptly. I figured you would have questions," Tatyana said. "By the way, I never got to thank you for helping us with those goons."

Jonathan nodded soberly. "The whole thing seems like a nightmare. I have no idea what got into me. Does that kind of thing happen often around here?"

Tatyana rested her gaze on him. "I can see you are here for a different reason tonight. What's on your mind?" She held up a hand with a smile. "No abracadabra. Again, your face gives you away, Doctor."

Jonathan chuckled sardonically. "I'm only now getting used to the idea that you can see right through me. The foretelling about my father the other night...you knew, didn't you?" He looked into the darkness, then back at her. "About my mother, too?"

Smiling knowingly, Tatyana said, "Just as I told Priscilla, the day the two of you came to me for a reading. I make no promises or guarantees, certainly not about the future, but there are things I know, and not just what I pick up from the people who come to see me."

Jonathan's stare hardened. "About Priscilla—I called off the engagement," he said. "But you knew that was going to happen as well, didn't you?"

"I'm always sorry to hear of love lost," she said, "but you didn't need a fortune teller to predict that outcome. However, you didn't come here tonight to talk about that either, did you?"

Jonathan shook his head. "No. I need to ask for your help. It's about my true parents and a piece of jewelry my mother left for me."

He reached into the front pocket of his blazer. When he pulled out the golden brooch, Tatyana gasped. Surprised by her reaction, Jonathan asked, "What do you know about this?"

But Tatyana did not answer. She took it from him, folded her hands around it, and brought it to her heart. She lowered her head for some time, as if listening to an inner voice. Then, she opened her eyes and stared at him.

It seemed to Jonathan that she'd visited another place far away, amazed and troubled by what she'd seen.

When she spoke, there was urgency in her voice. "Please, go on. You must tell me everything!"

As Jonathan related what he'd learned from his aunt about the night his mother took refuge with her and Nell, Tatyana leaned toward him, her gaze intense and searching. Upon hearing of his father's murder, her face sank to her chest. When she raised her head, there were tears in her eyes. In the silence under the forest canopy, they grieved together. From the darkness, a whippoorwill called, answered by another, and a dog barked in the distance.

Finally, Tatyana said, "Oh Jonathan, what a tragic story." She returned the brooch to him and wiped the tears from her cheeks. Then she reached across the table and grasped his hand in hers.

To Jonathan, it felt like the gentle, welcoming hands of a long-lost relative, but then Tatyana's hold tightened.

"So many things are beginning to fall into place," she said, looking deep into his eyes. "As for me giving you answers, this is one of those times I can't. You will need to find them on your own. There is a way, however, if you are willing to undergo another test."

Jonathan wanted to withdraw, but Tatyana held his hand with an iron grip. "Jonathan, if you could find your spiritual truth and accept your heritage without pain, I would be more than happy.

But this is the only way." She gave him a brief sympathetic look. Then, her face grew serious again and her voice took on a conjuring quality. "I believe that the warrior you have seen in your visions is one of your relatives. He has a message for you, but it is up to you whether or not to accept it."

When Tatyana looked at Jonathan, he seemed far away, staring into the darkness. She released his hands and pulled back, startling him. The metallic charms from the bracelet on her wrist clinked, causing Jonathan to awaken from his daze.

"What's this?" he asked. "I saw one just like it on Isha's wrist the other day."

Tatyana lifted her arm from the table. "It was a gift from Big Jack from when we were in Italy. He had it made—one for Isha and one for me. It's solid Titanium and loaded with magical powers." She twirled her wrist, and the charms danced and shimmered in the lantern glow.

Jonathan looked at them with undisguised interest. "Magical powers, you say?"

"Yes, very," Tatyana said, surprised at his reaction. "You noticed it on Isha the other day?"

Jonathan blushed and quickly said, "Yes. Is she here?"

"No, she took a group of teenagers to the mall." With a cunning look, she said casually, "I think I should give you a simple test. I know she would be quite pleased if you passed it."

A glimmer of hope and desire crossed Jonathan's face, but he was still apprehensive. "What kind of test is it?"

It's called a Kris. You drink a brew I will make and it will induce a vision that will take you further on your journey."

Jonathan mulled it over. His two other experiences with Tatyana had been disturbing but also exhilarating, and he had felt no ill aftereffects. Surely, he would come through this challenge with all his faculties intact as well. If it provided answers, it would be worth the risk.

"All right, I will do it," he said with resolve.

Her eyes glistening, Tatyana gave him another intent look and rose from the table. "Then I must get things ready. Excuse me for a little while, Jonathan. Mugs and Clementine will keep you company and make sure you're safe here by yourself," she said smiling humorously. Then she strode toward the Gypsy encampment.

She appeared taller and more determined than before. Jonathan wondered what Gypsy hocus-pocus he had agreed to this time. Then an image of Isha came into his mind. The thought of pleasing her made him happy. It was the first moment of joy he experienced all day, and it surprised him. He had just said his final goodbyes to Priscilla, yet he already felt like she belonged to another life of his, a past he hardly recognized anymore.

Mugs brushed up to his leg. Jonathan bent down and rubbed him under his chin. The little mutt closed his eyes in pleasure and licked Jonathan's hand. Clementine continued to sleep on the tabletop.

Drumming sounds started in the camp, just like the night of the fight.

Tatyana returned, looking solemn and mysterious. "Are you ready, Jonathan?" she asked. When he nodded, she beckoned. "Then come with me to the campfire."

Jonathan was bewildered. "I didn't realize this was going to be a public event."

"Yes, a Kris is a tribal ritual," Tatyana explained. "Everyone here is waiting for you."

She led him through the forest to a circle of RVs, the same place where the goons had attacked the Gypsies only two nights before.

The coaches were pulled into a large circle around a blazing campfire. Women sat in wooden and aluminum folding chairs chatting and laughing. Young children ran around, some poking sticks into the fire, others skipping and playing with hula-hoops. Still, others were juggling and performing carnival acts. The younger boys beat on drums, while teenage girls gyrated before them, challenging them in a mock belly dance. The light from the fire extended beyond the Vardos into the forest and created a glowing dome high under the crowns of the tall pines and oak trees above.

When Tatyana and Jonathan entered the circle, the drumming stopped, all chatter ceased, and every head turned toward them. Jonathan recognized Kizzy and her friends from the hospital. They glanced at him in wonderment and guarded concern. But when they noticed him looking in their direction, they waved to him, smiled, and nodded encouragingly.

Like an unruly horde, the younger children came running from all directions to greet Tatyana. She held out her hands to them and spoke in a stern voice, "Shhh, children, mind your manners." Then she turned to the crowd and announced, "We have a special guest with us tonight." She motioned to Jonathan, "Some of you know Dr. Jonathan Curtis already. He has graced us with his company to undergo a Kris. He is a Gadjo, no doubt, but welcomed by myself and under the protection of Big Jack." She chuckled. "So, no cons tonight, ladies."

Boisterous laughter greeted her announcement. Tatyana turned to Jonathan, and said, smiling. "It is an inside Gypsy joke. Take no offense. Everyone will now welcome you."

There followed a concord of warm greetings; "Welcome, Dr. Curtis. Thank you for helping us with those thugs. We have heard so much about you. Good things. And, thank you for saving our king. Please, come join us. Please, take a seat at our campfire."

Tatyana gestured to Kizzy, who got up and disappeared behind a Vardos. Then, she led Jonathan to a folding chair inside the circle in full view of everyone. She remained standing by his side as the others took their seats. When they had settled down, Kizzy returned, carrying a tray with a fancy goblet decorated with elaborate, silver swirls. She attempted walking ceremoniously, as if bearing a sacred vessel. Jonathan could see she was trying to appear dignified for the occasion, but her colorful scarves, spangles, and swaying hips defeated her efforts.

Tatyana whispered in Jonathan's ear, "It is a special tea, seldom brewed, only for men; and then only for the most special of guests."

As Kizzy entered the circle, the others started to chant, "*Pi-Vortemo, Pi-Vortimo, Pi-Vortimo.*

"It means 'drink of purity,'" Tatyana explained.

She took the goblet from Kizzy's tray, raised it high for everyone to see, and handed it to Jonathan. It had a pleasant, herbal smell he recognized as anise and ginger. But when he took the first sip, he gagged at the bitter-sweet taste and the burning sensation in his throat. He coughed and grabbed his chest. His eyes widened. The sharp, aromatic essence filled his nostrils and lungs, opening them as no drug ever had. He heard chuckling and tittering from around the circle.

Tatyana grinned. "The first sip always catches men off guard," she said. "Drink up. It is good to set out on a new path in life."

Jonathan took another sip. Tatyana was right. The second one was easier. By the time he had drained the goblet, a warm feeling had invaded his whole body. He gave the goblet back to Kizzy who returned to her seat.

Then, the children led Tatyana to a chair nearer to the center of the circle, where the light of the fire brightened her face. With eager, shining faces, they called out, "*A-paramitsha, a-paramitsha,*" and kneeled or sat cross-legged on the grass around her.

She stared into their expectant faces. When she stopped smiling, a hush fell over the entire circle. Only the crackling of the oak logs burning in the fire could be heard.

Tatyana's eyes rolled to the back of her head, showing only the whites. As she returned to normal, she seemed to have changed to an older woman, an ancient Sybil. When she began to speak, her voice was deep and breathy as if it came from another time.

"The tales say we were many in the beginning, and we came from a land that was destroyed long ago. We were and still are a happy people and we have many friends.

"One day, as we were celebrating, a man came to our camp and, as was usual, we invited him in. This, my children, was a mistake and it came to be our curse. The man was a powerful necromancer who wanted us to serve him. We refused. We love life, we told him. Why then would we cheat death and serve chaos?

"In a rage, he cursed us, saying that we would forever wander the Earth as outcasts, never to settle in any land. Then he disappeared, and we laughed. But the next day, our land was destroyed by enemy invaders and many of us died.

"The survivors ran seeking safety and refuge. But wherever we went, it was always the same. We were shut out. Finally, we fled and regrouped on a mountain. Gathering in a circle, we drew knives, cut our arms, and shed blood on the earth. We vowed to preserve nature, serve the spirit world, and protect the land. When the last drop had soaked into the ground, a strange feeling came over us. The land seemed to embrace us. We heard a voice like the swirling wind telling us that we would be cursed to wander, yes, but we would be able to adopt like-minded humans into our tribe. Having spilled our blood to safeguard the earth, we now could curse those who would cause our deaths.

"My children—Aleandro Kalderasha has equipped us well for our journey. He has assured us that in time of need, the gift of his seed, the Great One, the Zor-Tracheban, will come to our aid and protect us. That is his promise. That is our destiny."

As Tatyana finished, she sat in silence until her face recovered its normal features. The children slowly stood and returned to the sides of their mothers.

When she sat next to Jonathan, he nodded, "I got it, a *paramit-sha*, a children's story."

"You are correct, a children's story," she said. "But, within those fables are instructions handed down by our ancestors that have guided Gypsy clans for generations, encouraging us in times of oppression. They describe our history and culture, giving us a sense of belonging and purpose."

"Who is Aleandro Kalderasha?" Jonathan asked

Tatyana took a deep breath. "One of our most famous heroes, but not a hero in the sense you might understand. He wins over his enemies through cunning and wit. Charms and spells are his weapons. His heroism is more in line with the Roma way. His opponents, or *doshman* as they are called in our language, are generally evil creatures symbolizing horrors like unhappiness, hunger, poor health, and bad luck—the scourges of our people. It is prophesized that when all seems lost, the seed of Aleandro will rise to appear before us. We call this legendary hero, The Zor-Tracheban. His name means 'strength' and 'truth.'"

While Tatyana spoke, the air came alive with the magical sound of drum beats. Softly, rising from a slow, mellow beat, their resonance filled the circle, flowing outward to blend with the atmosphere of the nighttime forest. Jonathan listened intently, overcome by a strange sensation. Not only could he hear and feel their rhythm, but he could experience it in different shades of colors.

Close to his ear, Tatyana said, "We drum to reconnect to the rhythm of life, Jonathan. We recall it as our mother's heartbeat. We drum as a group to represent our rhythm while remaining in a relationship with someone of a different rhythm. Drumming creates understanding without the restraints of a common language. Through drumming, we believe the energy of chaos can be transformed into harmony."

When the beat slowed, Tatyana leaned even closer and whispered, "Watch closely now."

As Jonathan turned his attention back to the fire, the colors of the flames became more vivid and bright, framed in mosaic patterns, as in a kaleidoscope. He shook his head to clear his vision. "Too much to drink?" he first thought. "But I haven't had any alcohol." He leaned back in his chair and took a few deep breaths. "What is happening to me?"

Peering through a gap in the tall pines into space, he felt like a veil had lifted from his eyes. The star-filled heavens and the beauty of patterns and textures melted into one. A deep purple sky housed an infinity of crystal galaxies, with billions of stars, each revolving in concentric discs around their black holes.

"Beautiful," Jonathan murmured, looking at Tatyana to see if she noticed the same phenomenon too.

The steady cadence of the drums seemed to resonate with the flickering of the firelight, beckoning him to rise from his chair and join the dance of the flames. He felt himself being drawn into the blaze. The physical world around him began to disintegrate. The stack of burning logs and embers began to wobble. Faces and bodies around the circle turned to liquid in the fire's reflection—rippling, shifting, melting. Jonathan stared into the flames again as images of a hundred hands burst forth, hot from the depths of the earth, pulsating and reaching for him to join them.

A dark cloud like a mantle of evil started to cloak everything, extinguishing the light. Jonathan sensed the tiger prowling nearby in the darkness, whetting its claws, scratching, growling. Terrified, he reached for the hands he could no longer see. His fingers touched them but he was unable to grab hold of them. Desperate, he cried out.

Then, he saw the knight from the field of slaughtered bodies, rising like a ghost. The golden brooch on his chain mail shone brightly, banishing the darkness and shadows. Beckoning to Jonathan, he said urgently, "Come, come with me. It is time. Come now."

Far away, Jonathan heard Tatyana's voice supporting him, "Go, Jonathan. It is time. Go now."

Mysteriously, he became part of another fire circle hundreds of years in the past. Great logs were stacked before Jonathan, rising to the height of a small building, with flames raging 40 feet into the air. The acrid smoke of burning timbers roused him to the new reality. Rugged men with untrimmed beards and mustaches surrounded him. Long black locks of curly hair hung down to their shoulders. He realized they were soldiers on the night before a battle, drinking and carousing, as if it were their last time on Earth.

Jonathan and the knight stood side by side, watching the scene. "Who are you?" he finally asked his companion.

"I am Lucian," the knight answered. "Tomorrow I will battle with the army of the Great Saladin. I will fight to avenge the vicious killing of my wife and the massacre of my tribe, tortured and impaled at the hands of Vlad, the Prince of Moldovia, the one they call Dracula. I will kill him and plant his head high above the battlefield for all to see."

He looked into the distance, and Jonathan could see the fire burning in his eyes, revealing the rage and anger in his heart. But when he turned to Jonathan, his expression was serene. "You will have your own battles to fight," he said. "Be proud and strong, and trust that you have the power to protect your people against the Order of Evil."

The knight grasped him by the arm, a powerful energy emanating from him. For a moment Jonathan became one with him and saw the universe through his eyes. It was so strange and otherworldly that he shied away from the feeling.

Then, the mystical line between the present and the past wavered. The fabric of time-space shifted, transporting Jonathan back to the Gypsy fire circle. As the effect of the hallucinogenic wore off,

Jonathan found himself wandering amid the folded chairs spinning around in circles. Even more embarrassingly, as the cherub faces of the Gypsy women and children came back into view, he realized he was at the center of a celebration.

Laughing, clapping, cheering, the Gypsies chanted aloud, "*Tah-ves bac-ta-loh*!—Welcome to the tribe, Doctor Curtis."

Jonathan looked around in confusion, as if caught between two improbable worlds.

Like a shadowy apparition, Tatyana's face appeared. It kept moving around his body and coming in and out of view.

"What's...what's happening? What's all the chanting and clapping about?" Jonathan stammered.

Tatyana quieted his trembling body and said, "Come over here."

As the chanting and clapping diminished and the clan of Gypsies dispersed to their Vardos, she led him to one of the folding chairs and helped him sit down. "You passed the test, and we're welcoming you into the tribe," she said triumphantly.

Jonathan grabbed at his head. He felt feverish and hungover, as if awakening from a drunken bender.

Tatyana offered him a glass of water. "Here, drink this. It will help"

"I think I've had enough of your brews," he protested.

She smiled. "It's water so you can rehydrate."

Jonathan looked at her dubiously but took a tentative sip. It felt cold and soothing on his tongue. He drank more in ever bigger gulps until the glass was empty. As he put it on the table, he said softly, "I saw the knight again. He was wearing the golden brooch."

Tatyana became very still, but her face was glowing. "The Zor-Tracheban."

"He talked about avenging himself on someone called Vlad, or Dracul, and the Order of Evil and my mission. I don't understand any of it."

"You will," she answered.

"But none of it makes any sense. *Pi Vortemo*—what does that mean? And why all this pomp and circumstance with everyone watching?"

Tatyana gazed at him for some time. Then she said, "Let me explain, Jonathan. What you achieved here is a great thing. Few are granted the privilege. The Kris is a test of true character. *Pi Vortimo* means 'a drink of purity.' We do not administer it lightly, and not everyone passes. You were judged pure of heart and more! The Zor-Tracheban spoke to you! That is highly unusual."

Jonathan frowned. "What happens to those who don't pass?"

The smile left Tatyana's face. She looked down and hesitated, then reached a decision. "Now that you are one of us, I might as well tell you," she said. "The Kris will kill those who come to us with impure intentions. If you had not passed the test of purity, you would have died."

Jonathan felt like a glass of cold water had been splashed into his face and he instantly sobered up. "What? I could have died! How could you do this to me, put me in mortal danger?!"

"I was ninety-five percent sure you'd make it," Tatyana said matter-of-factly. "As a doctor, you know that all medical procedures involve some risk."

"Yes, but we tell the patient ahead of time. We let them decide. You drugged me under false pretenses." His eyes flashed with fury. "You didn't do this for me, you did it for your own purposes. You Gypsies are all alike, schemers, scammers, swindlers!"

"Jonathan."

Tatyana reached for his hand, but he reared back.

Jumping up from the chair, he shouted, "No! No more! I'm done with you!" He stumbled toward Tatyana's Vardo, mumbling about "Voodoo magic" in a sarcastic voice, and disappeared into the darkness.

* * *

Tatyana watched dispassionately as he left. She had expected Jonathan to react vehemently upon hearing the truth. He was right, of course—she had tricked him. But if she had been honest with him earlier, he would never have consented to the Kris. Confirming his role and purpose in their lives had been worth the risk, even if it meant he rejected her.

She heard the engine of the motorcycle roar to life and, after some revving, the sound of Jonathan driving away. It upset her, but only for a moment. She would find a way to bring him back and return him to his true path.

Chapter 13

AMBUSHED

Jonathan was in no condition to ride his motorcycle. The lack of sleep and emotional events of the past 48 hours had taken their toll, and he still felt groggy from the aftereffects of the Kris. But he needed to get home and catch some sleep before going to work early the next morning.

As dull as his brain felt, thoughts and images ran through his mind—Priscilla, Isha, Tatyana, the mysterious knight, the golden brooch. Jonathan considered himself a man of reason and science who believed in empirical evidence, but he was beginning to question his sanity. His encounter with the warrior had felt so real. Could it be that it was just the power of hypnotic suggestion while he was under the influence of a hallucinogen Tatyana had tricked him into taking? Could he have fallen prey to an elaborate Gypsy con?

But the brooch was real, a concrete object and the key to finding out who his parents were and why they had been murdered.

Distracted by these musings, Jonathan failed to notice a black Humvee waiting by the side of the road outside the park gate. By the time it pulled out to follow him, he had a good head start, but with its V-8 turbo diesel engine, the Hummer had no difficulty closing the gap.

Glancing in his rearview mirror, Jonathan noticed two bright headlights approaching, coming up fast behind him. It was too dark for him to see the occupants. "Someone else is in a hurry," he thought.

He slowed and pulled to the side to let the automobile pass. But before he could react, the Humvee closed in on his rear tire and sideswiped him off the pavement onto the sandy shoulder. Desperate to keep control of the slewing motorbike, Jonathan vaulted over a drainage ditch. Instinctively, he looked for a soft place to land on the other side of the culvert, but it was too late. He hit the embankment at thirty miles per hour, and his Harley flipped, throwing him head-first over the handlebars into a thicket of Palmetto bushes.

The motorbike came tumbling behind in a cloud of dust and landed just short of his head. Jonathan lay there for a moment, his breath knocked out of him. When he finally struggled to his feet, groaning, he felt sore but nothing seemed broken. As he raised himself, the Humvee's high-powered searchlight centered on his body.

Squinting, Jonathan could make out four human shapes approaching. They all wore armless military surplus jackets, blue jeans, and boots. One of them limped, his ankle encased in a walking cast, another had his arm in a sling. The other two had bruises on their faces. It was the four goons who had attacked the Gypsy compound. The tops of their shaved heads glistened in the light from the Humvee.

The leader, a bearded young man, sneered and said, "We meet again, Doctor. This time we won't let you sucker punch us."

As they fanned out to surround him, Jonathan felt anger surge inside him. After all he'd been through, now this! Once again, he started to experience the scene in slow motion and felt ready to attack, but he never got the chance. One of the thugs tasered him.

Zap! Jonathan felt excruciating pain and his body convulsed. He crashed to the ground, shaking, before becoming rigid and losing all motor functions. His vision faded momentarily to darkness. He felt a hard boot in his side and a crack as if his ribs were breaking

Another kick, which lifted his body off the ground, sent a jolt of pain through his entire body. Jonathan wanted to fight back, but he lay helpless in the sand, unable to move. He heard one of the goons say, "Okay, guys, enough. The Colonel said to hurt him, not to kill him. Let's collect the blood sample we came for and get out of here before we get any visitors." Jonathan recognized the voice as the same that had spoken before.

"Roger that. Hold his arm for me," said another thug with a higher-pitched voice.

One of the men grabbed Jonathan's right arm, stretched it out, and pulled up his jacket sleeve, exposing his antecubital vein, while the other reached into his pocket and pulled out a venipuncture needle and syringe. Jonathan could make out the dragon tattoo on his forearm.

"Hope all that paramedic training was good for something," the man said, as he rubbed an alcohol swab over the crease in Jonathan's arm. "Flunked out anyway," he added with a chuckle.

The others joined him in cynical laughter.

As the man lined up the syringe to take the blood sample, there was a loud blast, like a cannon being fired. The explosive sound reverberated throughout the woods, echoing off the sabal palms and palmettos.

BOOM! Another explosion. Jonathan felt his arm being released and fall limp to his side. Looking up, he saw his attackers with their hands held high in the air like frozen statues. Another floodlight was aimed at them.

By the side of the road, away from the bright beam, stood a stocky man. He called out to Jonathan's attackers with a gravelly voice, "That's right! You boys can't see me, but I can see you clear as day. Right now all you scumbags are looking straight down the hurtin' end of my little Betsy. She's a large bore, loaded with dou-ble-aught buckshot, and, make no mistake, I'm not afraid to use

her. There's one in here for each of you and two more for my pleasure, and it's my call, high or low, where you get it. If you don't die
on the first or second shot, you'd be wishing you were dead."

The man strode forward into the light holding a sawed-off
shotgun firmly to his cheek. Jonathan recognized his medical colleague, Dr. Miller. Most likely, he'd been heading home from the
bars in Tampa's Ybor City.

"If you boys want to keep breathin' one more second, you'll
drop the taser and your sissy fighting sticks and step away from my
buddy. Do as I say! Drop 'em!" he ordered.

Jonathan heard the clattering sounds of the thugs complying.

"Now, you've got exactly thirty seconds to get back in your car
and get the hell out of here."

The skinheads needed no additional encouragement. They
bolted like scared rabbits, jumping across the ditch and hurling
themselves into their Humvee. With the engine revved to full
torque, they screeched away laying a patch of rubber.

Jonathan hadn't felt such relief since he'd learned he passed his
medical board exams.

If Dr. Miller had been thirty years younger or sixty pounds
lighter, he might have hurried to rescue his friend. But with his belly bulging on both sides of his belt buckle, he tottered to the edge
of the ditch, squatted on all fours, let himself fall in, and rolled over
to the other side. Climbing up the embankment, he breathed hard
and approached Jonathan. He knelt by his side, took his pulse,
checked his pupils with the light from his cell phone, and felt for
any broken bones.

"Just lay here, Curtis," he said, "You're gonna be all right. I
know you can't talk right now, but it looks like you just got some
scrapes and bruises."

Dr. Miller remained at Jonathan's side until the taser's effect
wore off.

Finally, Jonathan turned his head up and muttered, "Damn, that hurt! What'd you do, Joe?"

Joe laughed. "I didn't do anything except save your skinny ass. Not that I would expect a thank you." He held up the taser. "I think this is what put your lights out."

By this time, Jonathan's mind was clearing and his muscles were responding again. He wrinkled his forehead. "A Humvee ran me off the road. Who was it? What happened?"

"I was going to ask you the same question. Do you know these guys? Are you in some kind of trouble?"

"I was in a fight a couple of nights ago and did some damage," Jonathan said, holding out his hand. "I don't remember much of it, but I think it was the same skinheads out for revenge"

As Joe helped him sit up and dust off the sand and debris that soiled his clothing, he chuckled. "Sounds like some of the escapades of my youth. Just sit here for a minute, Curtis, and get your bearings."

Jonathan grimaced. "Did you get a good look at them?"

"It was too dark to make 'em out exactly. I'd say all were in their early twenties, skinheads with tattoos and piercings everywhere. There were four of them—a regular bunch of miscreants."

"The tattoos, can you describe them?"

"Oh, some daggers on their necks and shoulders, and some skulls and dragons on their forearm. You know, the regular crap those scumbags decorate themselves with."

Jonathan groaned. "Yeah, that's them. The ones I fought a couple of nights ago."

Joe tilted his head. "I did recognize one of 'em, though. Known him since he was a little fella. Nice kid, used to be, anyway, from a good family. Heard he'd gotten in with the wrong crowd. I know his father quite well. Want me to give him a call? I got their license number."

Jonathan raised an eyebrow, "You remembered a license number through all that mess, Joe! I have to hand it to you."

Joe chortled. "I know I'm just a ridge runner from Kentucky, but you don't have to be a Phi-Beta Kappa to remember the letters FU-AK47."

Jonathan laughed so hard he had to clutch his sore ribs. When he recovered, he said, "Well, that will make it easy to identify them when I call the cops on them."

Scratching his head, Joe said, "That might not be such a good idea, Jonathan. Some of the local police may be in cahoots with that gang of white supremacists. They'll hush it up, and claim they didn't get anywhere in their investigation. I think it's better if we keep this between ourselves for now."

Seeing Joe's worried expression, Jonathan thought about all that had been going on. The old doctor knew the area much better than he did, and it made sense to take him seriously.

"Okay, let's do that. Mum's the word."

Joe stood back, relieved, and gave Jonathan another quick once-over. "You think we ought to call an ambulance or the paramedics?"

"Naw," Jonathan said with a strained grin. "I'm feeling all right now. What's the ER gonna do anyway? Call you to see me? You've already checked me out."

Joe chortled and asked, "Need a hand up?"

"I think I got it, Joe," Jonathan said. He pulled his knees to his chest, grimacing painfully, and attempted to stand, but faltered. He moaned. "On second thought, maybe I could use a little help."

When he finally stood, he shook his arms and legs and checked to see if all his parts worked. "Well, looks like I'm okay. Now let's see if that Harley still runs."

Much to his surprise, his motorbike still worked. It looked scuffed, and the rearview mirror had broken off, but nothing important was damaged. After Jonathan wheeled it to the road, it started right away.

Dr. Miller looked at him doubtfully. "Sure you can ride after what happened?"

Jonathan nodded with confidence.

"Okay then," Joe said. "But I'm going to follow you home."

"All right," Jonathan agreed. "By the way, thanks for saving my ass."

Once he got on the Harley and headed home, he kept the speed low until he felt confident handling the bike. He tried to concentrate on the ride, but at some point, a puzzling thought came to mind: Why did the goons want a sample of his blood? What possible use would they have for it? And then he remembered that one of his assailants had said something about "the Colonel." Did he mean Colonel Burdock? Was Burdock behind this?

Chapter 14

YURI

Hunched over a computer in his Alpine lair, the Wizard closed the video link with Colonel Burdock, removed his headset, and spat out a string of profanities. Had he not been so frail physically, he would have swept the coffee cup and plate with his favorite Danish off the table.

These idiotic Americans, so overconfident and arrogant, so full of easy promises, yet unable to perform even the simplest task and deliver a blood sample from the doctor for genetic analysis. He gave an order to Burdock and the colonel sent inexperienced boys on the mission. Imbecile!

Well, he would not waste any more time on an incompetent sycophant, no matter how committed to the cause. Time to bring in a professional he could trust to get the job done. He called up a database of his available agents on the East Coast of the United States. Squinting at the screen, he ran his skeletal finger down the list and considered his options. There were several choices, but one possessed the unique talents to handle this matter. Using him was tricky and could even be considered overkill, but this assignment was too important to leave to amateurs.

If this Dr. Curtis proved to be the One—and the Wizard increasingly believed he would—it was more than likely that he possessed some of the super genes of his grandfather. With them and the doctor's sperm, the Wizard could fix his decrepit, useless shell of a body and become all but immortal in a more youthful, genetically superior physique. His scientists would see to that.

He noticed the anxious faces of his assistants monitoring him from outside the soundproof glass walls. Glaring at them until they turned away, he put his headset back on. Then he clicked on the screen, automatically calling the telephone number of the name of the man he had chosen to carry out the assignment.

* * *

Deep inside an old bathhouse on a seedy backstreet of Coney Island was the home of a fight club known to insiders as XO. Catering to a select clientele—wealthy men and women with a taste for bloodsport—the contests in the heavily secured backroom made MMA bouts look like schoolyard scuffles. The competitors fought with no holds barred, including attacks below the belt, scratching, eye-gouging, and head-butting until one combatant was dead or could no longer get off the floor. Referees in the fighting cage only determined if a fighter was too damaged to continue. The events allowed admittance by invitation only. Ticket prices were exorbitant, betting extravagant, and winning purses for the surviving gladiators, especially repeat contestants, would make most other highly compensated professional athletes cringe with envy.

That morning training sessions were underway. Sparring mats, punching bags, and weightlifting equipment surrounded the fixed metal cage in the middle of the room, and the acrid stench of sweat and testosterone filled the air. Most participants—wiry, muscular young men with tattoos on their arms and shoulders—were hopefuls for regular MMA careers, sweating and grunting to master the necessary skills. Usually, the strain of the young trainee's voices and sounds of feet and fists striking flesh and bone echoed off the metal rafters in a cacophony of pain.

But not today. Everyone was watching the central mat where two fully armored opponents with large wooden clubs stalked a single man. He was wearing only gym shorts and no headgear or padding. With his large, glistening, muscular frame, he looked like a bronze statue by Rodin. His blond hair was cut short, accentu-ating his chiseled face, high cheekbones, snub nose, and green-ish-blue eyes suggesting Slavic origins.

The two men circled the goliath cautiously. Then, as if by pre-arranged agreement, they lunged forward from opposite sides, striking out with their clubs.

The man in the middle did not bother to parry but absorbed the blows to his body by tightening his muscles, causing the clubs to bounce off him like drumsticks. Bellowing with laughter, he shouted at the men, "Is that all you've got? You hit like girls!"

Stung, one of the youngsters ran at him, the club raised above his head, while shouting at the top of his voice. Before he could bring it down, the giant stepped toward him, inside the swing, rendering him helpless, and fisted him on the nose, not enough to draw blood but with enough force to send him staggering back. Then he ducked under the swing of the second young man who had rushed him from behind. Lowering himself to the ground with an unexpected nimbleness, he swept his attacker's feet out from un-der him. The young man landed on the mat with a thud and groan.

The big man stood quickly, prepared to face the other young-ster who had recovered enough to come at him again.

Just then an older man with a bald head burst through the door and shouted in a Russian accent, "Victor, you have a call." For all his boldness, he appeared nervous, having broken the cardinal rule never to interrupt a training session. But the voice at the other end of the line telling him to convey the message had frightened him even more. So, he added in his defense, "Some guy calls himself the Wizard."

Victor hardly glanced in his direction. He bowed to the young men with his hands steepled before him. The two young men bowed back, visibly relieved to be let off the hook so easily by their teacher. They looked after him in awe as he left the room.

Victor, also known as V, was a legend in the underground fight world, having survived four bouts in the cage of death virtually unharmed. While it was an honor to spar with him, few escaped his training sessions without a tattoo of painful bruises. Had they known his background, they would have considered themselves lucky to be alive.

In his former life, V was Captain Yuri Zuroff, the pride of Spetsnaz, the elite of the Russian Special Forces that could strike fear into the hearts of most military opponents. His exploits behind enemy lines were legendary.

But, for all his accomplishments, Yuri was a wild card, a psychopath with a deep-seated need for blood and torture. He could have been a mass murderer or serial killer, had he not found a more legitimate way to channel his obsessions.

An orphan who had been in and out of institutions since an early age, young Yuri was fourteen and wandering the streets of Kharkiv, a small town in Ukraine, when he joined the Russian Mafia. His bosses soon learned that he had a knack for killing and took pleasure in inflicting violence and pain on others. When he was arrested by the police, after a psychiatric evaluation, the authorities quickly recognized Yuri's unique talents. At the time, Russia was in the midst of the second Chechen War and they were happy to use a man like him.

Spetsnaz trained him to be an assassin and interrogator, honing his skills in torture and the use of weapons, including knives, sniper rifles, automatic assault guns, and explosives. Although he had no formal education, he was blessed with a superior intellect and finished training at the head of his class. In the conflict with Chechnya, he reveled in missions with a near-zero chance of survival, which allowed him to exercise his darker urges.

But when the war ended Yuri no longer had an outlet for his compulsions. He became temperamental and got into fights that left several of his fellow soldiers crippled. After another psych evaluation, in which he assaulted the female interrogator who asked a question he didn't like, his Army superiors concluded that he was an uncontrollable psychopath and dismissed him. The Russian Mafia took him back for a while, but his predilections turned embarrassing for them as well, and he became an exile in his own country. When he went abroad, even the most hard-core terrorist group shunned him, and Yuri found himself, once again, on the streets.

Fortunate for him, the Wizard, who kept tabs on all kinds of people who could be useful to the Order, heard of Yuri and invited him to join the cause. When they met and talked—the only time they saw each other face-to-face—Yuri was impressed. He recognized an older, kindred spirit, as ruthless and intelligent as himself, who looked down on most other members of the human race and hated anyone he considered inferior. They included women, people with darker-than-lily-white skin, and whoever held religious beliefs.

Yuri pledged his loyalty to the man. He was pleased with the cover the Wizard provided him in the Russian émigré community in New York City. It never occurred to him that some of the off-the-books assignments of the Wizard were conceived to allow him to exercise his special needs. As far as he was concerned, he had found as close a home as he'd ever had in the Order.

So, he was eager and excited when he picked up the phone in the club's administrative office and identified himself. He felt a frisson tingle his body as soon as he heard the familiar voice saying, "Hello, Yuri, this is the Wizard. I am in need of your special talents."

Chapter 15

ORLANDO

When Jonathan got to the hospital the next morning, there was enough time before rounds to stop by Radiology for X-rays of his ribs and spine. He was relieved that the results confirmed his diagnosis. He had no fractures. The nurses eyed his scrapes and bruises with surprise, fascination, and sympathy. But Hawkins scoffed with undisguised sarcasm, "Another night of carousing, Dr. Curtis? Hope you're enjoying the local bar life."

After Jonathan got a cup of coffee in the lunch room, he made his patient rounds. He kept Big Jack for last.

The Gypsy King was alone in his room. When he saw Jonathan, his eyes sparkled, then narrowed. "What happened to you, Doc? You look all beat up."

"I was ambushed by four goons last night," Jonathan said matter-of-factly and pulled out his stethoscope to listen to Jack's chest.

"I'm sorry to hear that," Jack said, shaking his head. But you're OK, right, Doc? When Jonathan nodded, he continued, "I wouldn't call the cops, though. They can be your worst enemy. Do you want me to tell Pinky to visit your attackers and tell them to leave you alone? He can be very persuasive."

"No, don't trouble yourself on my account," Jonathan said. "It was just a minor scrape."

He finished listening to Jack's heart and lungs and put his stethoscope on a side table. Leafing through the lab report, he said, "Your heart seems to be functioning well off oxygen, and all your other vitals are back to normal. We can discharge you today, but you must take better care of yourself or you'll be back in no time."

A big grin spread over Big Jack's face. "That is just great, Doc. I can't thank you enough!"

"Just doing my job.," Jonathan said, keeping a professional demeanor. "I'm glad you're well again."

Big Jack gave him a speculative glance and said, "Listen, Doc, I heard about what happened at the camp last night and I'll tell you straight: that wasn't right. If I'd been there I wouldn't have allowed it. We Romani don't always do things by the book, but Tatyana crossed a line making you do the Kris without your consent. I'm going to give her a piece of my mind about that when I see her." His voice became more intimate. "The good news is you passed. Now you're one of us!"

Jonathan's eyes flashed and all the pent-up frustration poured out. "Let me tell you something, Big Jack. Ever since you and your tribe blew into town, I've had nothing but trouble. I've gotten into two fights, broken up with my fiancée, and had your people take advantage of me at every turn. I didn't ask for any of that!"

Scratching his head, Jack said, "You're right. I'm sorry you were drawn into this mess. We Gypsies are used to it—intolerance has plagued us throughout our history. But it's not your fight. Why don't you come by when I get back to the camp, and we'll have a real celebration. I'm sure Tatyana will be really sorry. And my daughter will be glad to see you, too."

At the mention of Isha, Jonathan caught his breath. But then he stiffened and said firmly, "I'm done with all that."

Big Jack assumed a hang-dog expression. "I'm sorry you feel that way, Doc. I was just beginning to like you. You sure we can't let bygones be bygones?"

A sense of weariness swept over Jonathan. "No. It's time for my life to get back to normal."

Jack contemplated him for a moment. Then he said, "In that case, I thank you again for all you've done for me and my family."

Jonathan relented. It wasn't the man's fault. "You take care of yourself, Big Jack—eat, drink, and smoke in moderation. Make an appointment to see me at my office in a couple of days. And good luck."

Big Jack tipped his hand to the side of his temple as if he were wearing a hat and smiled in acknowledgment.

Jonathan turned away and picked up his stethoscope. He didn't notice the crafty look Big Jack gave him as he left the room.

* * *

Later that morning, as Jonathan was leaving for his private practice, he witnessed Big Jack departing the hospital. It was quite an exodus with an entourage befitting an emperor. As Kizzy rolled Big Jack down the hallway in a wheelchair, other patients, volunteers, orderlies, and medical staff waved after him, calling out "Goodbye, Big Jack. Godspeed." The Gypsie King had made a lot of friends during his stay, Jonathan had to admit. He couldn't help but admire his charm and charisma. Watching Pinky assist Big Jack into the passenger seat of an antique Cadillac convertible at the hospital entrance, he noted that neither Tatyana nor Isha were among the throng of well-wishers.

While riding his Harley to his office, Jonathan hoped it would be an easy afternoon. It wasn't. The patients who showed up had routine ailments, but the business side of private practice threatened to drive him mad. There were lost lab reports, Medicare disputes over his charges, and HMOs denying benefits claims. Lynne Carrington rescheduled some appointments to grant Jonathan an early end of the day for which he was grateful. However, just as he was about to go home, Mrs. Sakellaridis phoned, anxious to "see the doctor right away"—something about her stomach again.

Lynne fielded the call for him. "Probably just some gas, Dear, like the last time," she said and scheduled her for an early appointment the next morning.

Jonathan mouthed "Thank you" and walked out the backdoor. The heat from the mid-afternoon sun radiated from the asphalt. Rounding the corner to get to his bike, he stopped short. The parking lot was empty except for Isha leaning posed like a model against the side of her Jeep. Her jet-black hair was pulled back into a high ponytail and held in place by a crimson-red scrunchie. She was wearing distressed denim shorts with a white ribbed crop top, and her gaze was both challenging and inviting.

Startled but glad to see her, Jonathan exclaimed, "Isha, what the heck? What are you doing here? You're the last person on earth I expected to run into." Then, he drew back, suspicious. "Did Big Jack put you up to this? Or was it Tatyana?"

Isha's eyes sparkled with humor. "Both. My father thought you needed cheering up, and Tatyana has answers for some of your questions." Her expression darkened momentarily and she gave him a searching look. Then, she continued with a pixie-like grin, "I think you're going to be surprised. I know I was... floored really!"

"About the Kris? The acid trip? What?"

"Yes, about the Kris and..."—she shrugged her shoulders—"some antique brooch."

Jonathan felt his skin prickle but tried to keep a casual demeanor. "Oh? There's more to the Kris than Tatyana told me last night?"

Isha nodded mischievously. "It's a long story that requires a rather lengthy explanation. If you're interested, I can tell you on our way to Orlando."

Taken aback, Jonathan wrinkled his forehead. "Orlando? That's at least an hour-and-a-half drive from here. Why in the world would we need to go to Orlando?"

"Because of the brooch, Jonathan." She handed him a piece of paper with a telephone number. "Tatyana gave me the contact info for a friend who might know something about it. He's there now. I just called him half an hour ago. He picked up the phone, but hung up as soon as I mentioned her name." Her eyes brightened. "But hey, we're losing valuable time. If we're going, we've got to leave now. I can fill you in on everything on the way."

Jonathan scratched his neck to give himself time to think. Despite his resolve to leave all things Gypsy behind, he was intrigued. It could be just another wild goose chase, but it might be fun. Isha seemed to bear him no ill will over his "emergency" excuse from the other day. "Oh, what the heck, why not?" he said. "Let's do it!"

He got in the passenger seat, buckled up, and looked around. The interior of Isha's ragtop Willys Jeep was not what Jonathan had expected. She had replaced the utilitarian seats with lush, low-back Recaro bucket seats and fitted the dashboard with a modern four-instrument cluster, rectangular digital display, and a navigation system. When they began the drive, it soon became clear that there had been changes under the hood as well. The antique-looking vehicle ran like an Indi car, with power steering, disc brakes, a fuel-injected engine, and a 5-speed, manual transmission with overdrive. Isha handled her "tricked-out" roadster as aggressively as a professional racecar driver, overtaking slower cars with daredevil maneuvers. On several occasions, Jonathan wanted to jump on the brake before she slowed down or got too close to the vehicle in front of her.

By the time they connected to I-4 in Tampa and headed east toward Orlando, Jonathan was wound up tight. Finally, as they settled into the traffic flow and Isha drove with less bravado, he relaxed.

Glancing at her at the steering wheel and breathing in her scent, he could not deny feeling attracted to her. If he was honest with himself, it was the main reason he'd agreed to the trip to Orlando.

"So," he said. "Tell me about the Kris."

"So," Isha echoed him and took a deep breath. "As Tatyana told you last night, it is a ritual test to determine if you are pure of heart. But, there's more, much more. I needed to check it out with my father before I told you about it."

Jonathan frowned. "I hope it's good news."

Isha grinned shyly. "Promise me you won't say anything until I finish." She waited until he nodded Yes and said, "You see, the Kris is usually given to a Gadjo only if he wishes to marry a Gypsy girl. If he survives, he is, by all intent and purposes, Romani. It is the only way, by our law, that he can marry into our tribe.

Jonathan's breath exploded from his lungs. "What?"

Afraid to look at him directly, Isha focused on the road. "I can understand that you're angry about it. I was livid, too, when Tatyana told me what she'd done. I really chewed her out."

"Why would you do that?"

Flushing, Isha peeked at Jonathan and said, "As a little girl, when I first heard about the Kris, I used to fantasize that a prince would come to my father, the Gypsy King, asking for my hand in marriage. He would risk death to win me, his true love. It was just childish make-believe but later on, when my father introduced me to men who were suitable marriage prospects, there was nothing special about any of them. I am a Gypsy princess, Jonathan, and maybe I'm just spoiled, but I wanted more."

"Oh boy," Jonathan muttered, cringing.

"Jonathan...listen," Isha urged. "Don't go south on me." Getting no response, she bumped her elbow against his shoulder. "I thought the Kris was about us, too, that Tatyana and my father were trying to play matchmakers, but that wasn't their intent at all. As I told you before, everyone in our clan adores you, and Tatyana knew almost for certain you would pass the test. And here we are."

"So what was her reason for rolling the dice with my life?" Jonathan asked.

Isha shrugged. "She wouldn't tell me."

"Figures."

Trying to lighten the mood, Isha chuckled and said, "So, you are now a Gypsy with no strings attached. You're under no obligation to marry anyone."

But Jonathan didn't bite. "It's a lot to think about," he mumbled in a tight voice.

They each settled back in silence, taking refuge in the hum of the Jeep's off-road tires on the pavement.

Isha sat forward tapping the steering wheel with her fingers and searching for something to say. Finally, she reached out and gently touched a deep scrape on Jonathan's forearm, she said, "Daddy told me about your encounter with the skinheads last night. He said he hated that you were being drawn into our troubles." When Jonathan glanced at the welts indifferently, she pressed on, "Be honest with me. The brawl with those thugs at the camp the other night wasn't your first time, was it? Were you in many fights as a kid?"

Jonathan touched his forehead, as if trying to ward off a headache. "No. Not really...well, once," he acknowledged. "It's kind of embarrassing. It was in the sixth grade and we were playing flag football in the schoolyard against the eighth-grade boys. They were bigger and stronger and ran all over us. Their quarterback was the loud bullying type and encouraged his teammates to beat up on our guys. It made me mad. I played linebacker on our team and started rushing through the offense to pull the flag off this guy every time the ball was snapped and..." He stopped, his eyes darting around the Jeep like he was reliving the moment.

"Yes, and...?" Isha prompted.

"He pointed his finger at me and sneered, 'You come at me again, and I'm taking you down'. On the next snap, I busted through the line, knocking down two linemen. As I closed in on him, he threw the ball on the ground, clenched his fists, and lit into me. He threw the first punch, but I ducked and put him on the ground and pummeled him, until one of the teachers grabbed me and pulled me off."

"What happened after that? Did you get into trouble?"

"No, two teachers witnessed the whole thing and reported that the quarterback started the fight. But"—Jonathan's voice started to tremble—"the boy was hospitalized with a broken jaw and multiple bruises and contusions." He took a deep breath before continuing, "Although there were no repercussions at school, my mom got word of it. She wasn't as understanding as the principal and forbade me to play any more contact sports. Here I was, the biggest guy in class, and I couldn't play football or basketball."

Isha kept her voice neutral. "I can't help but wonder, Jonathan. Deep down, did you like it a—that power to hurt, to inflict pain? I only ask because your voice was shaking as you told me the story."

Jonathan was surprised. "No, it was quite the opposite. It scared me that I could injure someone so badly. After that, I avoided any altercation, even if it meant appearing passive or cowardly. The last thing I wanted to be was a bully."

Putting her hand on his arm, Isha said, "Sounds like you were just standing up for yourself and protecting your teammates that time. However, that doesn't explain your amazing strength; it only makes it more curious and mysfying." As she returned to tapping the steering wheel with her fingers, the charms on her bracelet jingled.

Jonathan pointed at it, seeking to steer the conversation toward safer ground. "I saw Tatyana wearing a bracelet just like it last night."

"Oh, this." Isha lifted her hand. "Daddy gave it to me when I turned thirteen. It was made in Milano, Italy.

She playfully twirled her wrist allowing the charms to swing about. "It's solid Titanium and loaded with magical powers."

Jonathan nodded. "That's exactly what Tatyana said. What does that mean?"

"Mmmm...hard to explain. But Daddy told me never to take it off. I even wear it to bed."

Jonathan grinned. "You mean to bed—to sleep?"

Isha pretended to be offended. "Maybe that's none of your business, Doctor. And, you're doing a terrible job of trying to change the subject."

She focused her eyes on the road. "Tatyana mentioned that you broke off your engagement just yesterday. You never told me you were engaged. I would have thought –" She narrowed her gaze. "Let me get right to what's bugging me: Was she the emergency you had the other night when you stood me up at the entrance to the hospital? I was sitting in the parking lot when you two drove away in a white Mercedes sports car."

Jonathan paled, then turned three shades of red. "I, uh, uh... well," he stammered.

Isha continued mercilessly. "I was really looking forward to going out with you that night, Jonathan. But I was hurt and angry that you lied to me." She looked at him. "Why did you?"

Jonathan sat still as a petrified log. For a moment he considered that his best option might be to jump out of the car. Then he said, "I was embarrassed, although not as embarrassed as I feel right now. I'm sorry."

As quickly as she had angered, Isha calmed. Her voice softened. "Okay, just don't lie to me again."

"I promise I won't."

They drove in silence for a while. Then Isha said, "So you broke off your engagement with Priscilla last night. How are you feeling about that?"

Surprised that Isha knew her name, Jonathan hesitated. Then he said, "I thought I was head over heels in love with her, not to mention her family's standing in the community and the doors it would open for my career. And maybe I was, but it blinded me to certain attitudes she and her family had. Once that became clear, I had no choice but to leave. To tell the truth, it's like a burden has been lifted from my shoulders and I'm a free man."

Isha nodded, feeling her body relax. Although she gave him a sympathetic look, inwardly she smiled. It was what she had hoped he would say.

Chapter 16

THE COMPOUND

When Yuri Zuroff's plane landed at the Tampa airport, he picked up a rental car and wasted no time starting the hour-and-a-half drive north to the Hunt Club, the Order's Florida headquarters near Crystal River. His mission was straightforward: Subdue a local doctor and obtain a sample of his blood in a secretive manner with no collateral damage.

On the surface, his mission sounded uncomplicated, but Yuri could not help but wonder. The Order had flown him to Florida in first-class accommodations on the first available flight and at combat-level pay. Why did the Wizard order him, a top-ranked agent in the organization, to subdue and take blood from a practically unknown civilian? Why arrange for a nuclear missile to do the job that required a pop-gun? Yuri shrugged. It was not his job to question. He only hoped he'd get the opportunity to satisfy his personal needs along the way.

He drove fast and arrived at his destination in just over an hour and a half. After turning off the main road into an area of dense Florida forest, he rode on a sandy dirt road surrounded by sable palms, tall yellow pines, and vast carpets of saw palmetto. He passed several "No Trespassing" signs until he came to a 10-foot high, chain-link closed gate. The tall fence to either side was topped with rolled razor wire, giving the impression of a heavily secured prison facility, rather than a sportsman's club. A young man in camouflage battle fatigues stood guard. As Yuri lowered his car window, he heard the sounds of gunfire farther inside the compound—high-powered rifles and automatic weapons. Recruits practicing, he imagined.

The guard with chestnut hair and a sunburned face seemed young enough to be in high school, but he cast a penetrating look at the passport Yuri presented for identification. His hazel eyes flicked back and forth between Yuri's picture and face several times. Then, he said, "Colonel Burdock is waiting at the lodge up ahead, Sir," saluted smartly, unlocked the gate, and opened it wide enough for Yuri to drive inside.

Ahead, the single road soon divided into several sand tracks. Yuri kept on the widest, which turned into a shell-covered drive that led to six one-story Florida camp cottages with metal roofs, a tall, concrete-block building, and a larger house made of dark cedar wood, the Hunt Club lodge. Hummers, Jeeps, and motorcycles were parked alongside. Docked on the river were several high-speed boats of different sizes and colors. In the distance loomed the two ominous-looking stacks of the decommissioned Crystal River Nuclear Power Plant.

As Yuri pulled into an open spot and got out of the car, two men in battle fatigues appeared on the porch. No doubt the guard at the gate had called ahead. Yuri recognized Colonel Frank Burdock from a photograph he'd found online while preparing for his mission. He seemed trim and in good physical shape for a man in his 70s, and his ramrod-stiff stance was meant to intimidate. The other man was in his late thirties and showed a similar military bearing.

The Colonel let Yuri approach before greeting him with a smile and professional handshake. "Pleasure to meet you, Captain." He turned to the man by his side and said, "This is Lieutenant Vince Stryker, my second-in-command. He will show you around the compound. When you are done, come and see me for a briefing."

Yuri nodded and saluted smartly, "With pleasure, Colonel."

Although eager to start the hunt for Jonathan, Yuri decided to play nice for now and act as if he respected the chain of command. He could tell that although he was outwardly gracious, Burdock seethed from anger and embarrassment. He would have too, if the Wizard had questioned his competence. But he needed the locals' knowledge of the area to make his work easier, so he allowed the older man to save face. Time would tell if Yuri needed to assert who was really in charge. If it came to that, he would take considerable pleasure in showing the arrogant American how things stood.

So, he followed Stryker to one of the military hummers, got in on the passenger side, and contained his impulse to wave flippantly as they drove off.

* * *

Burdock, looking after them, kept his composure but his gut churned with anger. He hated to be upstaged by a captain, a foreigner no less. But he was also wary because of what he knew of Yuri Zuroff's military life. As soon as he'd gotten off the phone with the Wizard, he had done his research. What he found was impressive and troubling, both for what it said and didn't say.

Considered dangerous and highly intelligent, Yuri was an elite soldier. The Spetsnaz training had turned him into a killing machine in various forms of hand-to-hand combat and with weapons from handguns to sniper rifles to explosives. He had distinguished himself in Chechnya and during the invasion of the Crimea, surviving several "suicide" missions.

While it wasn't clear why the Russian military dismissed him, it didn't take a genius to read between the lines. Yuri was an anti-authoritarian loner who took pleasure in violence, torture, and killing. Also missing from his file was how the Wizard had recruited him and managed to exercise control over a psychopath who had no natural outlet for his murderous skills and violent needs in peacetime.

Returning to his office in the lodge, Burdock was suspicious and leery. He had spent several years building his para-military organization and was not about to sacrifice it to an unpredictable newcomer. He already had his hands full managing the male egos of his younger cadets, and the last thing he needed was for them to adopt a loose cannon, like Yuri, as a role model. He would have to keep a close eye on the man.

But the Colonel was also a realist. If Yuri could deliver Dr. Jonathan Curtis, it would be one less headache for himself. So, he would offer him what support he needed—within reason—and bide his time.

* * *

As Lieutenant Stryker drove Yuri around the camp, they soon discovered that they had many things in common, including elite military training and surviving dangerous missions. While Yuri had cut his teeth in combat against the Chechen death squads, Stryker, a Navy SEAL, had been a sniper in Afghanistan, targeting the Taliban. But as that conflict cooled down, he was reassigned to teach a Cadet SEAL training team on San Clemente Island infiltration and assassination techniques, including underwater warfare and demolition.

Stryker soon grew tired of the routine. He missed the excitement of battle and the thrill of killing, both at a distance and in close combat. Then, he met Colonel Burdock and found that becoming part of a larger mission gave him a new purpose. He didn't even mind teaching the raw recruits, who were eager but mostly ignorant crackers, as far as he was concerned.

Stryker had read some of the Intel on Captain Zuroff, but his take was different. Both he and Yuri were soldiers of fortune, who would never fit comfortably into regular society. If that meant that ordinary citizens, military leaders, and politicians considered him a sociopath, so be it. They were happy to benefit from his work which kept them safe, but rather than showering them with medals for their service, they were quick to point fingers and prosecute men like him for war crimes, when word about their actions leaked out. Stryker regarded Yuri as a legend among mercenaries and considered it an honor to show him around.

Yuri was surprised how easily he and Stryker saw eye to eye and found evidence of the lieutenant's competent hand in every corner of the compound. The initial impression suggested a simple sportsman's club, but the reality beneath the façade told a different story.

The compound's boat dock looked like a resort marina in a secluded bay, with quick, direct access to the Gulf of Mexico. Four sleek, off-shore motorboats bobbed lazily in their berths. A 60-foot Hatteras motor yacht swayed in a separate slip. Expensive, but nothing out of the ordinary.

Stryker pointed out the vessels' special features as he inched the Hummer past them. The racing boats had high-powered twin engines, high-tech guidance systems, and mounts for machine guns and missile launchers. "The Hatteras is not as harmless as she looks either," he said proudly. "She's outfitted with similar topside weaponry and two underwater launch torpedoes!"

From the harbor, they drove to the largest utilitarian building, a two-story metal warehouse, painted in basic Army khaki with a corrugated steel roof. Inside, the absence of air conditioning seemed designed to give amateur hunters a "roughing it" experience in a jungle-like atmosphere. But Yuri knew better: the temperature and humidity were perfect for the rigors of training 'initiates' to tolerate extremes of body heat, exhaustion, and dehydration.

Spread across the concrete floor were sparring mats and weight-training equipment. A dozen healthy young men strained at various activities and machines. Dressed in military combat attire, they all bore the tattoo inked on his right forearm, too—the insignia of The Order of the Dragon. Their grunts, together with the direct commands of their superiors, echoed off the metal rafters.

But the real jewel of the compound lay in a secret section behind the rear wall. Yuri had never seen such a large stockpile of high-tech munitions in a non-military compound—pistols and rifles, MK Grenade machine guns, 60mm Mortar launchers, and M72 Light Anti-Armor Weapons. Off to one side, encased in a walk-in bomb-proof safe was a supply of explosives—C4, TNT, HMX—enough to blow up a small city.

As they returned to the Hummer outside, Yuri said, "I'm impressed, lieutenant, but puzzled. You obviously know what you're doing. Dealing with a civilian would be a walk in the park for you. What am I missing here?"

Stryker considered how to answer. He had concerns about his superior but wasn't ready to share them with a stranger. "Colonel Burdock wanted to use the assignment as a training mission for some of our recent recruits. The first time they were not as ready as we anticipated and got blindsided. The second time was just bad luck. They had him, but then a redneck friend of the doctor's showed up with a shotgun."

Yuri noted Stryker's initial hesitation but decided not to pursue it. Instead, he focused on the mission. "I want to know everything you've got on this Dr. Curtis, and I want to recon where he lives and works, and how he spends his free time," he said. Leering like a hungry wolf he added, "And then, we'll find the right time and place to pay him a visit."

Chapter 17

ANTIQUITIES ROMANI
AND THE LORE KEEPER

It was late in the afternoon when Isha pulled her Jeep into the small parking lot on the eastern outskirts of Orlando. It had been hard to find, located on a back street next to an old industrial district, where paint chips peeled off the metal and stucco exteriors of the factory sheds and hangars.

Jonathan looked up from the Google map app on his cell phone. "This is the address," he said, puzzled by the dilapidated appearance of the small antique shop in front of them.

Time, weather, and sun had taken their toll on the old, two-story building. Green algae and mold rot had attacked most of its yellow pine siding, which had been painted in a bright lime-white a long time ago. The cedar shake roof was covered in rotting pine needles. Air plants and grass sprouted from the cracks and wide fissures, as if Mother Nature was preparing the old structure to be absorbed back into the tropical Florida jungle.

Anyone driving by who gave it a passing glance would miss the small, faded white sign, "Antiquities Romani," above the front door, and think it was abandoned.

Isha eased her Jeep across a rusted railway track and parked next to an old, pale yellow Land Rover, the only other car in the lot. She and Jonathan got out and looked around. The shop appeared vacant despite the "OPEN" sign hanging inside the window pane of the front door. But as they looked more closely, they caught the faint glimmer of a lit light fixture inside. The dirt and spider webs clinging to the windows had obscured their visibility from afar.

When Isha pushed the doorbell, a chime rang inside, but there was no sign of life. She pressed again. Still no answer.

Jonathan shrugged. "No one's here. Let's just go!"

"When we've come this far?"

"It's probably locked."

"Then, we'll unlock it." She twisted a crucifix charm on her bracelet and it transformed into a lock pick. "Told you this is full of Gypsy magic," she said grinning.

Jonathan raised his eyebrows. "Break in?"

Isha smirked. "The sign says Open." She turned the knob, gave a push, and the old door creaked inward. "See," she grinned.

When they stepped inside, a rush of heavy, stale air met them, replete with the dank and musky smell of mildew. Dust was every-where as though the place had not been cleaned for ages.

They looked around in wonder. The large single room looked like an eclectic museum, with steel-frame industrial shelving along the walls, crammed with books, magazines, and cartons overflow-ing with trinkets. There were tables with more boxes containing rocks, necklaces, charms, and baubles. A wide wooden staircase ascended on one to a mezzanine.

Jonathan called, and then shouted, "Hello!" No answer.

Curiosity got the better of him, and he went to one of the shelves. The books stacked there looked old and uncared for. Their worn leather covers had titles embossed in rune-like characters. He picked up two and held them to the light. When he blew on them, a wreath of dust rose, causing him to sneeze.

He called to Isha, "Check these out. Can you read any of this?"

When she came over and had a look, her mouth crinkled at the corners. "They're written in old Romani," she said. "One is about sorcerers and spells. The other is entitled *A Book of Charms and Changelings*. There are more over here on dragons and curses. Want me to buy one for you?"

As Jonathan gave her a sardonic grin, he noticed a palm-sized, metallic rock lying on the floor by her feet. He picked it up. It was heavy for its size and sparkled like a jewel in the light.

A loud, husky Rottweiler-like cough issued from the mezzanine.

Startled, they looked up. An alien-looking creature stared down at them over the edge of an old oak desk. His eyes were the size of saucers and his nose was bulbous. The rest of his face was hidden by long, gray, curly hair and a shaggy gray beard. As Jonathan peered closer, he could see that the size of his eyes, looking like great dark marbles, was a distortion caused by the thick jeweler's glasses he wore over his head.

"Put that down!" the gnome ordered in a thin nasal voice with a heavy foreign accent. "That's 'Cat Silver' you're holding, and only women may pick it up. Put it down, now!"

Jonathan carefully placed the rock back on the floor, but the man's demeanor irritated him. "Is there anything I can touch in this mausoleum?" he asked derisively.

"It doesn't matter!" the man barked. "I've decided not to sell anything to you, anyway."

Realizing that the meeting had gotten off on the wrong foot, Isha said, "You must be Motshan, the one they call the Lore-Keeper. I rang you earlier today."

The man gave her a cursory glance. "It's established who I am, but just who do you think you are to come into my place mocking me?"

"My name is Isha. I am the daughter of Big Jack Lee. We are camping with our tribe in Tarpon Springs. Tatyana told us to come here, that you might be able to help us."

Before the man could answer, Jonathan reached into his pocket, pulled out the brooch, and held it up for the Lore-Keeper to see. "I meant no offense. This is what I wanted to ask you about." When Motshan squinted at the glinting object, he added quickly, "It bears the emblem of a dragon biting its tail. There's a lock of golden hair wrapped inside the pin."

His words produced an unruly racket. The roll-top desk rattled and paraphernalia scattered across the floor as Motshan bolted upright and tore off his magnifying glass. "The symbol of the Order of the Dragon?" he shouted in a booming, agitated voice. "A lock of hair, you say? Don't move!"

Jonathan pocketed the brooch and waited. The man who came down the stairs was surprisingly vigorous with no gnome-like qualities, and Jonathan realized that his earlier incarnation had been an act. He greeted Isha cordially, with the respect befitting a Gypsy princess, and asked after her father and Tatyana. When Jonathan introduced himself, he shook his hand and invited them into his inner sanctum.

The area was roughly the same size and, unlike the other side of the mezzanine, clean and tidy. On one side was a small apartment with a sofa, a small table, and a kitchenette with a stove, a refrigerator, a microwave, and an Espresso coffee machine. Through a doorway, Jonathan could glimpse a brass bed. The other side held the real treasures of his shop, items of finer quality than out front. The books were better cared for. Many bound leather tomes were neatly embossed with gold or silver lettering and cover designs. Some of the more curious pieces were composed of ivory and inlaid with jewels and precious metals.

Noticing Jonathan's inquisitive glances, Motshan said, "Most of these articles are talismans used for divination, to help predict the future or contact the spirit world. But please, won't you sit down? Do you like Espresso?"

When Jonathan and Isha nodded, Motshan went to the kitchenette and bustled about. A look passed between them as they sat down, and they used the opportunity to observe their host. He wore a burgundy red T-shirt and Khaki pants. His wrinkled skin was the color of tanned leather and his short, rotund body was slightly stooped over, he moved with surprising ease for a man in his late seventies.

To keep the conversation going, Isha asked, "Why would a famous Romani lore keeper confine yourself to a house in a large city?"

"I tired of the travels as I grew older and never had a place to store all my important possessions," Mosthan replied. "You see, Isha, I am somewhat of an introvert. There is a wonderful Romani tribe here in Orlando. They've taken me in, provided me with this space, and helped me out. I have no family and yearned for a quiet spot where I could spend the rest of my years being useful to my people, surrounded by 'my babies'. These collectibles are my family, my friends, my children."

Isha smiled sympathetically as Mosthan served them two small coffee cups. Suddenly, he looked stricken and said, "What a terrible host I am. Is there anything else I can get for you two? I don't have much, perhaps a plate of cheese, some sardines, and crackers? Vodka?"

Jonathan turned to Isha who gave a subtle shake of her head. Although he was hungry, he said, "No thank you, Motshan. The Espresso's plenty. We're just here looking for answers, but we appreciate the offer."

As he joined them at the table, Motshan's eyes widened. "Yes, yes, the brooch. May I see it?"

When Jonathan placed the brooch before him, a flurry of emotions crossed his face—awe, joy, fear, and fascination. His hand trembled as he picked it up to examine its workmanship. He turned it over several times, ran his finger over its surface, and brought it closer to his eyes, peering at it through his jeweler's glasses.

Then he gazed at Isha and Jonathan with a wondrous expression. Suddenly, he rose from his chair and without a word left the room. When he returned, he carried a large, well-worn, leather-bound book. The title on the cover was imprinted in faded gold letters of an obscure language.

"Antiquities of Eastern Europe," Isha read as the lore keeper laid the book before them, earning her a curious glance from Jonathan.

Motshan nodded with a smile, "Yes, Isha. You have been schooled well,"

He thumbed through a few pages until he came to an illustration. It was a full-size drawing of a brooch that looked identical to the piece on the table.

A jolt pierced Jonathan as he compared the two.

"An exciting find, and extremely rare—one of only four such pieces were made," Motshan said almost reverently. "If it is authentic, this is the golden broach that went missing nearly five hundred years ago in the Kingdom of Walachia."

He turned to Jonathan, his eyes black and penetrating like a hunting falcon. "Before we go further, Dr. Curtis, I would like to know how the brooch came to be in your possession."

The question threw Jonathan for a loop. It was simple enough, but the answer, at least what he had learned, was problematic. His face turned red and he found himself at a loss for words.

At the same moment, Isha felt a tightness in her chest, followed by the sudden opening of a channel between them. When she reached out and took Jonathan's hand, the spark between them felt like an explosion that reached into her heart, forging a connection she had never experienced with anyone else before. She sensed his confusion and anguish and felt an overwhelming impulse to protect him. As Jonathan remained sitting next to her, tongue-tied, she interceded. "My friend is new to our Gypsy ways, Motshan, having just undergone a Kris. But Tatyana vouches for him. Otherwise, she would not have sent us here with my father's blessing. Will you tell us what you can do before we try to answer your questions?"

Motshan cast her a dubious look but acquiesced. "Very well."

But before he could say anything more, Jonathan spoke up. The connection with Isha cleared his mind and gave him confidence. "I must apologize, Motshan. I found out only two days ago that I was adopted as an infant. My real mother and father were murdered trying to protect me. Before she was killed, my mother gave this brooch to the people who adopted me as my only inheritance. She said it had been passed down in my family since Medieval times and was the key to my true identity. She insisted no one talk about it because that would put me in mortal danger!"

Motshan looked stunned.

Isha, whose eyes were misting, spoke with a quivering voice. "I had no idea, Jonathan. I can't imagine how devastating that must be for you."

Jonathan gave her a grateful look. Then he started to relate what he knew of his mother's plight. It felt good to unburden himself, and he found that he could tell the story without getting overwhelmed emotionally.

Isha listened with rapt attention, beginning to understand that Jonathan may have been Romani all along and that Tatyana, although she hadn't known for sure, had certainly sensed the possibility. The story affected her deeply.

Motshan's eyes kept darting about as if searching for clues within the tale. He leaned back in his chair, twirling his beard with forefinger and thumb. His only comments were an occasional mumbled "Ah-ha" or "Mmm-huh."

When Jonathan finished, a silence settled over the room.

Finally, Motshan nodded and said, "Well, that is quite a tale! Let me see if I can shed some additional light on your story." His eyes gleamed as though instantly transported to another time and place. He looked at them secretively. "No doubt you have heard of Dracula?"

"Of course," Isha answered, startled. "A vampire. One of the undead. A monster."

"A fictitious character," Jonathan said, dismissively, reverting to his rational, scientific self.

"Yes, fictitious, but based on history." Motshan lowered his voice. "His enemies knew him as Vlad the Impaler. Ironically, he came from a family of religious crusaders. The Pope bestowed the Order of the Dragon on them for their service to the church. But the real Dracula, like his demented father, was no saint."

Mosthan's expression turned morbid. "Impalement was the cruelest torture of the time. The live bodies of defeated enemies were run through with a wooden stake, raising them in the air to writhe and wail as they suffered an agonizing death. Most, pierced through their vital organs, died quickly. However, Dracula devised an even crueler torture. Pushing the blunt end of the spike through his victim's rectum, the stick worked its way slowly up the body, leaving the poor souls crying out in pain for hours on end."

Jonathan shuddered as the visions of the slaughtered and impaled bodies on the ancient meadow came back with almost physical force. Seeing his distress, Isha grasped his hand and gave him a reassuring squeeze.

"What does all that have to do with the brooch?" Jonathan asked with urgency. "You said something about the Order of the Dragon. What did you mean?"

Ignoring his impatience, Motshan continued, "Let me tell you about Dracula and his half-brother, who is also well-known in Gypsy lore. That may reveal the significance of this piece of gold."

And he began to relate the story of Vasilissa tricking her husband by sneaking her newborn son out of the castle and giving him to a Gypsy woman. But Motshan went further, recounting the story of the only other time she saw him when he was grown and needed her help again.

CASTLE OF DRACULA
WALLACHIA
1458 AD

Vasilissa paced feverishly in her castle chambers. Not since she first discovered she was pregnant with Vlad Dracul's child, two decades earlier, had she been so desperate. Back then, she had found a way to trick him and save her newborn son from his monstrous plans. Now the child had grown into a man and returned, only to be imprisoned by his half-brother, Dracula. A stirring frenzy had reawakened within her the instinctive need to protect her own again. How she wished Cejorn and Ioana were still alive. But her faithful servants were no longer among the living. She would have to rely on her wiles.

With a shudder, she recalled that horrific time when Vlad had become suspicious and imprisoned her and her handmaidens, threatening them with torture and death. He didn't believe their claim that the child had been a stillborn baby girl. When he asked about the missing golden brooch with the dragon symbol, she told him she placed it alongside the dead child to help her on her journey to Heaven, as was her Moldovian custom. Because of her steadfast insistence that she was telling the truth and her father's angry letters about her treatment, threatening terrible retribution if even a hair on his daughter's head was harmed, Vlad had finally released them from prison.

After that terrifying experience, Vasilissa vowed not to bear Vlad another child. But she could not refuse him his conjugal rights, and although she took precautions taught her by her midwife, she became pregnant again. Fortunately, this time the child was a girl. Frustrated that he had failed to add another male heir to his royal lineage, Vlad believed her incapable of bearing a male child and turned to other women for pleasure and procreation. Vasilissa felt relieved when he died from an infected wound incurred in battle.

When his son, Dracula, ascended the throne, he refused to grant Vasilissa's request to return to her father's home in Moldovia with her daughter Ingrid. Instead, he installed her as the honored queen mother. While he paid little attention to his half-sister, he planned to marry her off when she came of age to cement a politically important alliance. Dracula also expanded Vlad's experiments to create a superior race, cheat death, and live forever. But while he brought the finest alchemists to the castle, all his efforts to achieve immortality came to naught. Whenever another trial failed, he became furious and unleashed his anger on innocent people. He hunted and killed any strangers found on his lands, including Turks, Jews, and Gypsies, fulfilling his mad bloodlust by torturing and murdering them. It pained Vasilissa to watch him become a demented, sadistic ruler, like his father.

Recently, however, his reign of terror had reached its limits. A Gypsy band led by a warrior, a giant with golden hair and the features of a Viking, resisted Dracula at every turn. Soldiers who encountered this Goliath in combat swore that he possessed the power of a hundred men. Wielding a mace and sword the size of tree trunks, he rode through battle unshielded, as if guarded by magic. Arrows and lances did not affect him. He seemed invincible. His name was Lucien, and he wore a golden brooch with the insignia of the Order of the Dragon on his armor.

The first time Vasilissa heard about him, her heart skipped a beat. Was it possible? Could this warrior be her son? She listened to the tales soldiers returning from battle shared about him with excitement and prayed for his success and well-being.

Although Dracula scoffed at the reports, he was shrewd enough to worry about his reputation as the ruler of his kingdom. When the men he sent after Lucien and his band of Gypsies suffered defeat after defeat, and several attempts to assassinate him failed as well, Dracula decided to change his approach. He sent a courier carrying the white flag of truce to Lucien, inviting him to come to the castle to negotiate and sign a treaty making peace between them. He swore a holy oath guaranteeing Lucien's safety. No harm would come to him while he was a guest at the castle.

Wishing to end the bloody war between his clan and Dracula's army and trusting in the king's vow, Lucien sent a favorable reply.

Two days later, accompanied by six of his most trusted guards, he appeared at the castle gate and announced himself ready to negotiate peace.

Dracula put on a spectacular show, involving everyone at the court. Banners with the Order of the Dragon symbol were hung from the walls and rafters, illuminated by large candles and torches. Soldiers, decked out in their best parade uniforms stood at attention. Vasilissa could barely contain her excitement at the opportunity to lay eyes on Lucien. She and Ingrid sat near Dracula's throne as everyone waited for the warrior and his entourage.

All murmuring and conversation ceased when Lucien entered the great hall. Even Dracula stared in awe at the man who dwarfed everyone around him. Given his formidable size and reputation, Dracula's soldiers cautiously gave way, clearing a large circle for him in the middle of the room.

Lucien looked around the royal hall without fear. Vasilissa was taken by his penetrating, blue eyes and almost gentle expression, more curious than fierce. Nothing in his features suggested he was the offspring of Vlad except his dark, tanned skin. If anything, he looked like her father. She saw the golden brooch pinned to his tunic, but her eyes were no longer strong enough to make out the emblem from a distance. She wished he would come closer.

Dracula rose and descended from his throne extending his hands in a gesture of welcome. But as he advanced to greet the giant who had given him so much trouble, a mad flicker danced in his eyes.

Surprised, Lucien halted at the edge of the carpet and stood in wait. He seemed fascinated by the golden brooch on his enemy's tunic, bearing the same image of a dragon eating its tail as his own

If Dracula took notice of their identical emblems that matched the banners in the room, he gave no indication. He smiled and gave a small hand sign. In an instant, the stone slab where Lucien stood dropped away. Vasilissa gasped in horror as he lurched at the edge for a moment, then plunged into the opening and disappeared. His men were stunned. By the time they recovered and reached for their weapons, the King's soldiers surrounded them and butchered them.

Vasilissa watched in dismay as Dracula severed their heads himself and kicked them through the opening in the floor. "I will honor my oath," he shouted into the prison cell below. "No harm shall come to you, but you will be my prisoner for the rest of your life!" He cackled with laughter. "I will exterminate every last member of your clan and there is nothing you can do about it. You will beg me to kill you when I bring their remains."

Back in her chamber, Vasilissa did her best to comfort Ingrid who had burst into tears as she witnessed the ambush of Lucien and his men. Ingrid had never seen bloodshed up close and it had shaken her to the core. "Is there anything we can do to help that poor man?" she asked, once she had calmed.

"I don't know," Vasilissa admitted, feeling desperate. Surely, Lucien was her son; but even if he wasn't, she couldn't leave him helpless in Dracula's clutches.

Just then, the whinnying of horses echoed in the inner ward yard below. Vasilissa rushed to the window. Dracula and his cavalry were preparing to depart. Normally, he would have taken pleasure in taunting and tormenting his prisoner further, but he wanted to complete his plan—to annihilate Lucien's clan. The Gypsies had been a thorn in his side. He meant to make an example of them so frightful that no one would ever dare rebel against him again. Leaving only a small contingent of soldiers behind to guard the castle, he rode through the gate ahead of his troops.

Watching them disappear in a cloud of dust, Vasilissa made a plan of her own. She went to Ingrid and took her by the shoulders. "Do you want to save Lucien?" When the girl nodded eagerly, she continued, "You must trust me. Have our maidservants prepare a meal for us and bring it here."

While her daughter did her bidding, she went to the fireplace and touched a hidden lever. Then she pulled the tapestry next to it away from the wall, revealing a small, secret compartment, now open, filled with jewels and bottles. She selected a dark green vial and hid it in a pocket of her gown.

Soon Ingrid returned, followed by servants carrying two trenchers with meat, cheese bread, and a flagon of wine. They put them on the table, curtsied, and withdrew, shutting the wooden door behind them.

As Vasilissa uncorked the vial and poured the contents into the pitcher, she cautioned her daughter, "You must never speak to anyone of this. Now follow me."

They took the backstairs to the dungeon below, making sure no one saw them. As they descended into the bowels of the castle, the air became dank and heavy and smelled of blood and urine. At the prison cells, dimly lit by two flickering torches set in wall sconces, they met two soldiers who sat at an oak table. Dracula had posted two of his most trusted men to stand guard. When they saw Vasilissa and Ingrid, they jumped to their feet.

"Your Highness," the older soldier gasped. "You shouldn't be here. This is no place for you and the Princess."

"We wanted to see the prisoner up close," Vasilissa said innocently, acting like a nosy maid. "We didn't get a good look at him before. Things happened so quickly in the throne room."

"We brought you some food, in case you haven't eaten," Ingrid joined in sweetly, placing the trenchers on the table. She filled two pewter cups with wine. "This is for you to enjoy."

A look passed between the guards. They cast longing glances at the food and wine. "I suppose, it's all right," said the older soldier. "But be careful. He is a dangerous, evil creature."

They moved aside, letting the two women approach the iron bars that ran floor to ceiling. Inside the cell, Lucien lay on a pile of straw. He looked up at them, surprised. He seemed younger and more vulnerable than when he first arrived. Vasilissa nearly fainted, overcome by his resemblance to her father. She put her hands against the wall behind her for support. When she had recovered, she said, "What is your name, young warrior?"

Sensing a kindness in her, he said, "Lucien, Your Highness. Please, my wife, my infant son. I fear for them without me by their side to protect them. I beg of you, do not let harm come to them. Kill me instead. I believe you are honorable. I appeal to your compassion. Spare my family, my clan."

"Your clan?" Vasilissa asked in a hushed voice.

"My group of travelers means no harm to you or yours. We are a peace-loving people and fight only when attacked."

Vasilissa continued to stare at him. Up close, she could make out the familiar emblem of a dragon biting its tail on the pin anchored to his sash. She recognized the Gypsy craftsmanship and her heart beat faster. It was hers. She was sure of it.

"How did you come by this brooch?"

"My mother, Anuska de Taulere, gave it to me, Your Highness."

Vasilissa never knew the name of the Gypsy girl, but she was sure Lucien was her son! There was no doubt in her mind.

"Mother." Ingrid tugged at her gown and pointed to the guards who, unable to resist tasting the wine, were hunched over the table, sound asleep.

Vasilissa snatched the keys to the cell hanging from a hook in the wall. The rusted lock creaked as she opened the cell door. She went inside, unafraid. "Come. We don't have much time," she said. "You must follow me. We will show you a passage to escape to safety."

Overwhelmed with gratitude, Lucien clutched the folds of her gown and kissed it. "Thank you, Your Highness, and your daughter."

Vasilissa took one of the torches and ushered him past the snoring guards into the lower labyrinth of the castle, with Ingrid bringing up the rear. Lucien had to duck whenever they passed through another doorway in the tunnels. When they arrived at the hidden side door in the castle wall, the same Ioana had used to rescue Lucien as a baby, they halted. Vasilissa pointed to the door. "This leads to the outside. Go and help your people."

But Lucien stopped her. "Why are you doing this for me?" As Vasilissa wavered, unsure of what to say, he confronted her, "You are my real mother, aren't you?"

When Vasilissa gasped, he continued, "I was told about the adoption—that my natural mother loved me so much she gave me up, for me to have a better life than she could offer. I have often wondered if I would ever meet you."

"I wish it were under better circumstances," Vasilissa said. "This is Ingrid, your sister."

They looked at one another dumbfounded and overcome by emotion. Although each had a thousand questions, there was no time for answers.

Instead, Lucien kissed the hands of his sister and his mother and said, "I will never forget you, and I will make you a promise: This brooch will be passed to my son and to the first grandson who follows, so that my bloodline will remember the story of your selfless love."

Tears brimming in her eyes, Vasilissa nodded. "Thank you, my son. But you must go now. Your family's survival depends on you."

Lucien lifted the heavy crossbeam from the iron door like a toothpick. As it swung open, the afternoon sun made the brooch sparkle. He looked at his mother and sister once more, as if he meant to etch their images in his brain. Then, he stepped outside, descended the steeply sloped meadow, and bolted into the nearby forest.

Ingrid called after him, "Godspeed, Brother."

As they went back through the warren of tunnels, Vasilissa said, "Go upstairs now. I will come anon and answer all of your questions."

She returned to the prison cell, arriving just as the guards were starting to wake up, still woozy from the drug. When they realized Lucien was gone, the blood drained from their faces.

Stepping into the flickering light, Vasilissa looked like an ancient witch and they gasped terrified. "I see you're frightened, and you should be. I am too," she said. "I could hardly believe my eyes when several three-headed snakes slithered through the bars and wrapped themselves around the sleeping prisoner. After they devoured him, they left through the holes in the wall. There was nothing left of him. It was horrible."

The two soldiers looked bewildered.

Vasilissa continued with compelling force. "If you wish to survive, that is what you must say. It is the only way, your only chance.

And you must not mention me or the Princess. We were never here. If you mention either of us, Dracula will never believe your story. Do you understand?"

The two men nodded as if awakening from a dream. Vasilissa made them tell her what happened in their own words. Then she left, confident that their fear would convince Dracula, a superstitious man, that something otherworldly had caused Lucien's disappearance. Even if he didn't believe the tale, his brooding about it would buy her son much-needed time. When the truth came out, and it was bound to happen when Lucien reappeared, she would have to figure out how to protect her daughter. For now, her son was safe and that was all that mattered.

Chapter 18

LUCIAN'S LEGACY

Isha looked at Motshan in wide-eyed wonder, like a child spellbound by a fairy tale. Jonathan seemed preoccupied, however. He rubbed his forehead as if trying to keep a headache at bay. The implications of Lucian being his ancestor threatened to overwhelm him. He was relieved to hear Isha ask, "What happened to Vasilissa and Ingrid?" and was surprised when Motshan laughed.

Seeing their befuddled expressions, the Gypsy lore keeper explained, "I laugh because the outcome was so mundane. You'd think someone as paranoid as Dracula would be suspicious, but he bought the story the guards told him, hook, line, and sinker. There are no accounts of him looking for Lucian, or going berserk like Vlad twenty years earlier, searching for the lost baby. There also are historical mentions of Vasilissa and her daughter some years after this event, indicating that they suffered no dire consequences."

"What about Lucian?" Jonathan's voice sounded hoarse.

Motshan turned several pages in the book until he came to a drawing of a warrior in the uniform of a Turkish Janissary. Seeing Jonathan blanch, he asked, "You have seen this image before?"

Although the picture shook him—the soldier looked just like the men he'd seen with the knight during his vision at the Kris—Jonathan tried to make light of it. "Maybe. It reminds me of something I saw in a history book once. Please go on."

Giving him a calculating look, Motshan resumed his tale. "After Lucian escaped into the forest and managed to steal a horse from a nearby farm, he rode at breakneck speed to the Gypsy camp, but it was too late. As he neared, he saw dark clouds of smoke rising and when he crested the hill, he came upon a field of carnage. While he had been locked in his cell, Dracula and his army had butchered everyone they could find—men, women, and children. Some had been hacked to pieces, and most were impaled on the high hill, above the burning ruins of their meager encampment. A few were still alive, moaning and writhing in agony. The earth ran red with their blood."

Jonathan gasped in anguish.

Startled, Motshan paused, uncertain why Jonathan was so upset. He would have expected Isha to respond that way, but a trained physician? He pretended regret, "Dr. Curtis, I apologize for the grisly details. It is a gruesome story, I agree."

Jonathan shook his head. "No. No. That's not it at all." He noticed Isha's eyes narrow and glance away.

Isha felt his agony—a dark, deep pain from his past. Something assailed her consciousness, something she wanted to understand. A chill ran down her spine, but she turned to Motshan and said, "It's all right. Go on."

The lore keeper shrugged and continued. "Lucian desperately searched among the dead and dismembered bodies. He found his mother, Anuska, and wife, Kalisha, impaled on stakes. They were dead. A great howl of fury and grief erupted from his mouth. Then, he took their bodies down. But he could not find the remains of his six-month-old son, Brishan. As he picked through the mangled carcasses of his friends, putting the still-suffering souls out of their misery, his heart froze. He had heard rumors that Dracula and his army cannibalized the flesh of their victims, especially tender young children.

Then he remembered the plan he and Kalisha had made when the raids on their camp began and prayed that she had time to carry it out. He hurried into the forest where a waterfall flowed from a rocky outcropping into a small pond. Lucian's feet quickened as he neared the gushing sound. In a cavern, concealed behind the cascading water, he found his baby son wrapped in a blanket, safe, crying for his mother's breast. Lucian wished Kalisha had stayed with him, but she had rushed back to help defend her people.

By the time he carried his child back, a few Gypsies were at the camp. They had managed to survive the slaughter by hiding in the forest too. That night, with their help, Lucian erected a large funeral pyre and burned the remains of his mother, wife, friends, and other members of the tribe. With every loved one they consigned to the flames, his rage grew into a searing passion to exact vengeance."

"Did he?" Jonathan asked in a low voice.

"Yes," Motshan replied eagerly. "Lucian joined the army of the Ottoman ruler, Sultan Murad II. Two years later in a valley in Southern Bulgaria, he fought in a battle against Dracula's forces and got his revenge. There is an account of the battle, written by an Ottoman scribe." He rose from the table with enthusiasm and disappeared. Within seconds, he returned carrying another leather-bound manuscript. "Yes, here it is," he said as he laid it on the table, turned the pages, and began to scan the writing. "It has a somewhat mythic quality. I'll summarize."

"Eyewitnesses reported that he rushed into battle on his steed, a golden brooch pinned to his armor, crying the name of his beloved wife Kalisha. His attack was so fierce that it astonished even seasoned veterans. Foot soldiers scattered as he cut a swath through the mounted knights sent against him, swatting them away with his mace like insects. At the top of the hill, with his sword raised, Lucian rode after Dracula who was fleeing on his horse. He cornered his half-brother and cut off his head with one blow. Some accounts say that lightning struck and thunder rolled at that very instant, and Dracula's soul entered the gates of hell. When Lucian mounted the bloody head on a pike and waved it high above the battlefield, Dracula's soldiers lost heart and ran away. The army of the sultan chased after them and killed every man caught."

Motshan had become so excited telling the story that he'd risen from his chair and paced around the room. Breathing heavily, he looked triumphantly and said, "So you see, my young friends, if your little piece of jewelry is what I think it is, Lucian wore it into the battle that day."

Isha stared at him in amazement. "Did Dracula and Lucian know they were half-brothers?"

"I don't think Dracula did. Lucian must have, after meeting Vasilissa. An ironic twist of fate, wouldn't you say?"

But Isha went on undeterred, "What became of the Gypsy boy, Brishan?"

"Lucian raised his son to be a warrior like himself. They joined another Gypsy tribe and became defenders of their people. Together they proved invincible and both remained true to Lucian's promise to Vasilissa."

"Such superhuman strength seems out of the ordinary," Jonathan ventured.

Motshan's eyes twinkled. "No doubt, some witnesses exaggerated and embellished their stories. But there is another wrinkle to this tale. It was rumored Lucian's wife, Kalisha, was the direct descendant of a well-known Gypsy hero of ours, Aleandro Kalderasha."

Isha's eyes lit up. "And, Aleandro Kalderasha has equipped us well for our journey. He has promised us, in our time of need during our quest for purity, the gift of his seed, The Great One, the Zor–Tracheban. Tatyana has told us that story, time and time again."

Jonathan blinked and turned to Motshan. "Those are just children's stories. But you've said what you've been telling us is based on history. Is any of it real? Is the brooch authentic? Are Vasilissa, Lucian, and Brashian my ancestors?"

Isha gave a nod expressing her approval to the question. "Your ancestors, Jonathan. Yes," she mumbled under her breath.

Motshan nodded, "The stories I have told you are real." He put a finger to his nose. "However, there is only way to know if the brooch and the lock of hair are authentic, and that is not within my purview or expertise. But I know someone who can help us, a professor at the University of Sofia in Romania. Dr. Serban Kevenko is an expert on these matters, as well as on the Order of the Dragon." His look became crafty. "He'd have to have the brooch himself, as well as a sample of your blood. I can take care of that for you if you like."

An involuntary shudder ran down Jonathan's back. The goons that attacked him had tried to collect his blood as well. Why was everyone after it? Could there be a connection? He felt confined in the small room and wanted to get out. But he remained courteous and said, "There is one thing I don't understand. Why did both Dracula and Lucian adopt the symbol of the Order of the Dragon for their cause?"

"That is one of those curiosities of history, like black and white magic, two sides of the same coin, and it happened accidentally," Motshan said, smiling. "The Pope in Rome bestowed the order on Vlad and his family because of his ruthless fighting against the Turkish infidels. Vlad had four golden brooches made with the emblem, one for himself and the others for each of his sons, including the one he anticipated having with Vasilissa. It was the queen who found a Gypsy goldsmith to do it."

"That must be how she got to know Anuska and trusted her with her baby," Isha said.

Motshan nodded and became pensive. "I don't think you realize, Dr. Curtis, what you have stumbled upon—a battle between good and evil that has been raging for centuries. I'm sure Isha knows all about it. If not, then certainly, Tatyana. It is part of our heritage." His expression became calculating. "Would you like me to pursue testing the brooch?"

Glancing at Isha, Jonathan said, "Thank you, Motshan, but I'm not sure I'm ready to do that yet. You've given me a lot to consider today. Let me mull it over and get back to you on that."

The lore keeper did his best to hide his disappointment, but his manner cooled considerably. "Of course, Dr. Curtis. I am at your disposal should you need me. Is there anything else I can do for you today?"

Jonathan shook his head. "You have been very kind." He rose from his chair. "But we should go. I need to get back to the hospital tonight."

Motshan turned to Isha. "Give my regards to Tatyana and your father," he said. "And take good care, both of you."

He accompanied them to the front of the shop. After they exited, he locked the door and flipped the sign to "Closed." He continued to watch them through the window as they got into the Jeep and drove off, barely able to contain his excitement. Then he scurried upstairs, picked up his cell phone, and made a fateful call.

Because it was quite late in Romania, Dr. Kevenko did not pick up, so Motshan left a voicemail, "Call me when you can, Serban. You won't believe it, but I think I just saw the long-lost brooch of Vasilissa Dracul."

Chapter 19

ASSAULTED

Jonathan and Isha hurried back to Tarpon Springs. They spent much of the ride in silence, lost in their thoughts. At first, Jonathan was quite overwhelmed by all the new information. He tried to sort it out scientifically making mental lists on how to check out the brooch and hair to verify their authenticity. From time to time, he glanced at Isha. He wished he knew what she was thinking, but she looked intent as she focused on the road.

For her part, she sifted through the Gypsy lore she knew so well and tried to relate it to what she had learned. Tatyana obviously sent her on this errand with Jonathan as much for her own sake as his. Isha would have plenty of questions for her and hoped she would be more forthcoming now. Knowing that Priscilla was no longer in the picture changed things, too. Finding out more about Jonathan and his history made him even more attractive. Unlike Jonathan, she trusted her intuition and feelings.

It was still light when they reached the parking lot where Jonathan had left his motorbike, but his office was closed by then. They looked at each other uncertainly, not wishing to break the bond that had developed between them.

"Well," Jonathan finally ventured. "This has been quite a day. Thank Tatyana for me. I'm glad she put us in contact with her friend."

Isha nodded. "I will." She tilted her head coyly. "You know, you still owe me that dinner my father promised. How about tomorrow night?"

Jonathan's heart leaped in his chest. "I'd love to," he said. "Where would you like to go?"

"I leave that to you. You know this area better than me. Pick someplace fun."

He pretended to think. "I have office hours until five tomorrow. Shall I pick you up afterward at the camp?"

"On your Harley?" She pouted with mock-disappointment. "That doesn't sound very romantic."

"I thought you liked adventure," Jonathan teased back.

"I do, but it will muss up my hair. Why don't I come by here and pick you up?"

Jonathan said, nonchalantly. "Okay. See you then." But he got out of the Jeep feeling ready to dance on air. The fact that she glanced back and smiled, as she drove away, made him feel even better.

He got on his motorbike and rode to his apartment, where he microwaved a taco for dinner and called Jimmy. He caught him up on what had happened with Priscilla and asked his advice for the most romantic restaurant in Tarpon Springs.

"Why do you want to know that? Who are you taking there?" Jimmy asked, perplexed.

"Isha."

"Wow! You don't waste much time. What has gotten into you?" Jimmy exclaimed. Before Jonathan could answer, he continued, "But good for you. If I weren't a happily married man, I'd ask her out myself."

"Actually, she asked me."

"This is getting better and better," Jimmy said, astonished. "I will want a blow-by-blow account of your evening with her, you hear?!"

Jonathan had to endure more good-natured ribbing before Jimmy gave him the name of a small restaurant on Athens Street in the Sponge Dock District.

Next, Jonathan called one of his mentors at Duke University. Dr. Martin Wade was an expert in genetics. Jonathan caught him at home just after dinner. He asked after his family—his wife and three children—but skipped the small talk and quickly moved on to the purpose of his call.

When he explained what he needed, Dr. Wade said, "You know, you can't tell age or gender from hair alone. You need part of the roots from which to extract DNA."

Hiding his disappointment, Jonathan said, "I'd be grateful if you'd try and tell me as much as you can from what you discover." He added, "And please, keep mum about this, in case anyone asks."

There was a slight pause on the other end of the line. Then Dr. Wade said in a wary voice, "This is all rather mysterious, Jonathan. What have you gotten yourself into?"

"You have no idea and, frankly, neither do I."

"Are you in trouble?"

Jonathan couldn't help but laugh. "Not yet," he said. "Depending on what you find, maybe. But at least it will clear up some important questions."

"I'll do my best," Dr. Wade promised.

"Thank you, Marty," Jonathan said. "I really appreciate it."

After hanging up he examined the hair from the brooch and discovered that it hadn't been cut off but had a slight thickening at the ends. He became more hopeful.

* * *

He slept surprisingly well and arrived at his office early the next morning feeling excited and looking forward to the day and evening. So many new possibilities were dawning in his life.

As he started to pack the FedEx box for Dr. Wade, placing the labeled plastic bags containing hair samples from his head and the brooch, the office phone rang. Jonathan let it go to the answering service. The phone rang again and then remained quiet.

By the time Jonathan finished packing the box and filling out the shipping label, Lynne arrived, carrying two cups of coffee. "You're in early, Dr. Curtis," she said, surprised.

"Yes, I want you to have this package picked up right away," he replied.

Before she could answer, the phone rang again. Lynnee walked to the reception desk and picked up. She listened for a moment and then held it out to him. "It's the hospital for you. Dr. Clark."

Puzzled, Jonathan took the receiver. The voice at the other end of the line sounded harried. "I've been trying to reach you all morning, but you aren't picking up your cell phone."

Cradling the receiver, Jonathan retrieved his mobile phone from his bag and looked at the display. Sure enough, there were several missed calls, all from the hospital. Checking the side, he realized he'd had silenced it.

"Sorry about that, Clark. What's up?"

"I've been dealing with a patient who showed up early this morning, in really bad shape—broken ribs, collapsed lung, ruptured spleen," his colleague said nervously. "His name is Manfred Lee. I've managed to stabilize him and put in a chest tube and a Foley catheter. His brother brought him in. Says he was attacked. According to him, you're his personal physician."

Jonathan choked on his coffee. Recovering, he said, "I don't know anyone by that name."

"He doesn't look like a patient of yours, but Hawkins swears his brother is telling the truth. I'm calling you because I've got to run in a couple of minutes. If it's true, I'm dumping this whole mess on you."

Jonathan sighed, "OK. Before you go, can you call Dr. Miller and have Hawkins contact the OR? I'll be there as quickly as possible. And, Clark, thanks for staying on like that."

* * *

By the time Jonathan arrived at the ER, a group of Gypsies milled around the hospital lobby entrance. They converged on him but kept a respectful distance.

When he got inside, Hawkins gave him a disdainful look and said, "Here we go again!"

Jonathan ignored her and asked for a status report.

"Dr. Miller is attending—and he wasn't out all night," she said. "He'll give you the details."

She directed him to the cubicle where a flurry of nurses hovered over a large man lying semi-conscious in the bed. Jonathan recognized him immediately. It was Pinky. His brother Carl was standing in a corner, wringing his hands.

When he saw Jonathan, relief spread over his face. "You saved Big Jack, Doc," he said. "Only you can help Pinky. Is he gonna be okay?"

Confidently, Jonathan said, "Of course, Pinky's going to make it, Carl. I've called in a good surgeon, a friend of mine." He stepped closer. "What happened to him?"

"I'm not sure. He was on the lookout at the camp, walking the perimeter. We heard a cry and the sounds of a fight. By the time we got there, the attackers were gone and Pinky was lying on the ground, bleeding and barely conscious. He was hurting like a son-of-a-bitch. We carried him to Tatyana, but she took one look at him and said we had to bring him to the hospital, so we rushed here."

His concern gave way to anger. "They must have ambushed him, the cowards, clocked him from behind. Otherwise, he could have handled those punks." He looked at the gurney, where two nurses were putting up the side rails preparing to wheel it to the OR, and sighed. "I just wish I'd been there to help, covered his back like always."

Jonathan put his hand on Carl's shoulder, "No time to be second-guessing yourself. We'll take good care of your brother. Now, if you'll excuse me…"

He hurried to the OR and found Dr. Miller in the X-ray viewing room, examining Pinky's CT scan. He squinted, adjusting to the dimness of the narrow corridor, lined with fluorescent viewing boxes.

Without taking his eyes from the X-rays, Dr. Miller said, "Cracked spleen and pneumothorax. Bruised kidneys, but no serious damage. A friend of yours?"

Jonathan replied in a strained voice, "One of the Gypsies."

Dr. Miller tut-tutted. "He took one heck of a beating. Must have been a small army that attacked him. Wouldn't want to meet up with the guys who did this without old Betsy by my side. Does this have anything to do with those hoodlums we tangled with the other day?"

Jonathan kept his eyes straight. What Dr. Miller suggested was probably true, but this went beyond harassment, escalating to violence. Pinky would be okay, but his injuries indicated an increased threat. Jonathan feared what might be coming next.

Dr. Miller continued to scan the films, but he could tell Jonathan was torn—this was more than a routine ER patient for him. "Want to scrub in?" he asked.

Jonathan nodded, almost relieved.

Although the surgery took three hours, it went without a hitch. Despite his late-night outings, Dr. Miller was a fine surgeon, and Jonathan was happy to assist. Only Pinky's spleen had to be removed. Immediately after the internal bleeding stopped, Dr. Diamandis, a local ENT, wired his broken jaw.

Afterward, Jonathan cleaned up and returned to the reception area. Sitting at the desk, Hawkins looked exasperated, confronting a contingent of Gypsies. Big Jack and his daughter had arrived as well. Isha had her arm around a distraught woman she introduced as Pinky's wife, Kizzy Lee. Jonathan recognized her from earlier visits.

When the others saw Jonathan, they surged forward. He raised one hand and called out, "The surgery went well. Pinky is doing fine.

He'll be here for a day or so, but there is nothing to worry about. You can come back tomorrow and see him. For now, he needs rest."

People started to hug each other in relief and celebrate, but no one looked ready to go home. Jonathan approached Big Jack and said in a soft voice, "Can you take them outside? The hospital will call the cops if they don't leave, and they only listen to you."

A look of rage crossed Jack's face as he glanced around, but he realized Jonathan was right and brought himself under control. He nodded and gestured to Carl for help.

Meanwhile, Jonathan took Isha and Kizzy to the ICU. Pinky was lying in bed, still unconscious. Kizzy let out a cry, rushed to his side, and was about to throw herself on him when Jonathan caught up to her and grabbed her from behind. Holding her closely, he reassured her, "Pinky's fine, doing great. But he needs rest—no disturbance."

A look of understanding passed between him and Isha as a nurse brought two chairs and set them near Pinky's bed. Jonathan ushered Kizzy into one and Isha sat in the other. She took Kizzy's hand and stroked it gently, murmuring comforting words.

Catching Jonathan's eye, Isha made a regretful face—their evening plans would have to be rescheduled.

Jonathan nodded and left, feeling vexed. This is not how he imagined the day would turn out.

But it wasn't over yet.

On the way to the coffee station, Mrs. Jackson, the ICU charge nurse, intercepted him and said, "Sorry to bother you, Dr. Curtis, but there's an officer outside who wants to question you regarding Mr. Lee's condition."

Surprised, Jonathan rubbed his hands over his eyes. "A policeman? Mr. Lee?" He sighed. "All right."

He recognized the policeman waiting for him in the hallway. He and Officer McGillicuddy had encountered each other before under similar circumstances—follow-up investigations after local bar fights. Officer Mac, as his friends called him, was generally pleasant, if a little thick-headed.

Mac stood practically at attention and held a clipboard wedged under his arm. When he saw Jonathan, he relaxed and grinned. "Thanks for meeting me on such short notice, Doc. I'm investigating a charge of aggravated assault regarding an incident occurring in the state park last night."

Jonathan let out a sigh of relief. "I'm glad someone's looking into what's happening around here." Noticing beads of sweat on Mac's brow and patches of dampness bleeding through his neatly pressed shirt, he motioned to an empty waiting room on the other side of the hallway and said, "Why don't we get out of this chaos to where we can talk privately."

Mac smiled gratefully. "Good idea. I've been on the beat all day. It'd be nice to get a load off and chill in air-conditioning."

As the two sat, he took out a pen, crossed his legs, and turned to a blank sheet of paper on his clipboard.

"Do you know who attacked Mr. Lee?" Jonathan asked curiously.

Mac looked at him in surprise. "Dr. Curtis, Mr. Lee is the perpetrator under investigation. Commissioner Higgins filed charges of aggravated assault and battery this morning after his son came home with a black eye."

Jonathan was taken aback. "What? That is preposterous. Pinky was attacked in the middle of the night, unprovoked, by a gang of punks. He is lying unconscious in the ICU."

Putting up his hands in appeasement, Mac said, "Jeremy has witnesses. He and his friends claim they were minding their business when Mr. Lee attacked them." He flipped through the pages on his clipboard, "Yes, here. He and Roy Collins claim it was the same large man who attacked them in J-Wags. Luckily, Jeremy, who has been taking karate, was able to get in a couple of defensive licks and run before Mr. Lee could hurt them again."

With barely contained fury, Jonathan said, "This is ridiculous! Those *boys* you mention are grown men in their twenties and troublemakers, Mac. I believe they are the same ones who ran me off the road a few days ago and knocked me out with a taser. If Dr. Miller hadn't driven past and come to my rescue, I would have been in the same shape Pinky is in now." Jonathan caught his breath. "They almost killed him. He was hanging on by a prayer when he was brought to the ER this morning. He underwent three hours of surgery, which included removing his spleen!"

Mac looked uncomfortable. "Look, I am truly sorry for Mr. Lee's condition, but what's he to expect, running around Tarpon Springs causing trouble, threatening the safety of our law-abiding citizens? Jeremy's dad is a prominent attorney in town and plays golf with my chief. Those boys are solid citizens, Dr. Curtis. I can speak for Jeremy. Maybe he's a little wild, but weren't we all at that age? As for those Gypsies, I wouldn't trust any of 'em as far as I could throw them, and you shouldn't either. Crimes have been up in the area since they moved into the park. Reports of theft and vandalism—up."

Jonathan's voice became brittle. "So, let me get this straight. All these crimes that occurred around town, the Gypsies did them?"

"All of them are trouble. Pinky Lee and Carl Lee list their occupations as bodyguards. They and their king, Big Jack, live in million-dollar-plus Prevost Coaches. I've seen them in the park. You think they make that kind of money playing penny-ante poker games at the clubs we have around here? Trust me, they're up to no good. This whole town would be better off if they left. I'd lay down an ordinance against 'em if I could, but then some fancy lawyer from the ACLU, or other dipshit organization like it, would ask for an injunction to protect that trash."

"Mac, I won't have you talking about the Gypsies that way. It's certainly not in keeping with the ethics you've been sworn to uphold."

Stung, Mac's voice rose in irritation, "Look, Dr. Curtis, you play this game long enough, and you'll soon see who's on your side. And right now, I'm not so sure about you. Never pegged you for a 'Gypsy Lover.'"

Jonathan knew things had gone too far. With his hands trembling in anger, he relied on an old trick. He drew out his iPhone and claimed he had an emergency. When Mac asked him to sign the statement, he ignored him and stormed passed him through the ICU doors. It took several seconds for his breathing to settle.

He looked in on Pinky who was still unconscious. Big Jack and Carl had joined Kizzy and Isha. Jonathan decided not to interrupt and withdrew to get a cup of coffee.

* * *

Late that afternoon, Jonathan ran into Joe Miller sitting alone in the doctor's lounge. When he told him of his encounter with Officer Mac, the old surgeon said, "Jeremy Higgins. I recognized him right off the bat. He was one of the punks who forced you off the road the other day. Used to be a good kid, but lately, he's been hangin' around with the wrong crowd. I can't believe his father's defending him like that. It's disappointing. But I wouldn't want to take him on. Tom Higgins is a powerful man around town He's chairman of the city commission, a friend of the mayor and police chief, and has many judges in Hillsborough and Pinellas County in his back pocket."

"So, I should just let it go," Jonathan asked exasperated.

Joe shook his head slowly, "Listen, Johnny Boy, I'm not tellin' you it's right, it's how things are. My advice: keep as far from those Gypsies as possible. They're likely to screw up everything around town, then pull up and leave one night, never to be heard from again."

Jonathan's look would have turned a less weathered man to stone. But Joe only sighed. "This has become personal with you," he said.

Finding himself at the end of his rope, Jonathan hesitated and then decided to recount all he had witnessed between the Gypsies and the locals. After all, both he and Joe Miller were country boys, fundamentally decent and fair.

After listening carefully, Joe took a deep breath. "Okay, if you are going to fight, you'll need outside help. Someone big enough to take on the county and city government, and all their courts," he said. "My advice, call the Southern Poverty Law Center in Montgomery, Alabama. They're a powerful, non-profit civil rights organization with nationwide reach and visibility. I saw them in action back in Kentucky, handling a case of threats and violence against black churches from the Ku Klux Klan. Their lawyers are experienced in such matters and have ties to the FBI."

Jonathan considered his friend's counsel, which echoed Big Jack's warning not to involve the local officials. He thanked Joe, went to a private cubicle in the doctor's lounge, and took out his cell phone. "Might as well strike while the iron is in the fire," he thought, searched for a number, and made the call.

The woman who picked up on the other end had a smooth Alabama drawl. "Southern Poverty Law Center. This is Audrey. How may I help you?"

Although his cubicle was soundproof, Jonathan lowered his voice and asked for legal advice regarding hate crimes against a family of Gypsies in Southwest Florida. After a short explanation, Audrey transferred him to the organization's investigation department, promising a retired New York City Police homicide detective would talk to him.

A confident, cigarette-raspy voice picked up the line, "Detective Dave Lindsay, here."

Jonathan described what he had experienced and seen over the past week in great detail, and shared his fears that matters would escalate.

"Do you have any evidence these crimes are connected to any organized hate groups like the Ku Klux Klan, Dr. Curtis?" the detective asked. "Do the perpetrators have any distinctive markings, armbands, or tattoos?"

"Yes," Jonathan confided. "The attackers had identical tattoos on their forearms, a circular snake or dragon biting its tail." His face flushed as he remembered the brooches with the same symbol he had seen in his visions with Tatyana.

"Dr. Curtis, are you still there?"

"Yes, sorry. I'm here at the hospital and got distracted."

"Our organization deals with all sorts of hate groups," the detective said matter-of-factly. "That tattoo has become associated with white supremacists and Neo-Nazis. Sounds like you and those Gypsies have stepped smack in the middle of a hornet's nest."

Jonathan's mind kept racing. "These young men don't seem like Ku Klux Klan types. One of them comes from a good family. His father is a well-respected lawyer in town."

The detective chuckled, but there was no humor in his voice when he said, "Actually, that's pretty typical of most of those groups nowadays. Their members are more sophisticated than the Klanners. Many have college degrees. Their leaders are usually older, sometimes ex-cons or ex-military. But the bulk of their members are in their twenties and thirties."

"But, how do they recruit them?" Jonathan asked, trying to focus on the present. "I don't see any banners posted along the roadside, 'Sign up here for hate classes.'"

"It's quite covert," the detective explained. "Much of it happens online, in chatrooms and on the dark web. Many of these kids come from upper-middle-class families. But they have one thing in common: something amiss at home – a lack of parental supervision, abuse, divorce." He continued, "Most of these kids are not bad or even racist going in. That comes later when they're bonafide members. As they become immersed in the gangs, they commit crimes, starting with robbery, drugs, and vandalism and progressing to beatings and rape. Before long, the violence escalates to bombing a synagogue or mosque, or even murder."

Jonathan shook his head. "I had no idea."

"Yes," Detective Lindsay said. He cleared his throat. "I need to make a few calls. Expect to hear from me in a couple of days. In the meantime, you best stay out of their way. Watch your back and please pass the warning on to your friends."

"I will," Jonathan assured him.

Clicking off his phone, his mind in disarray, he leaned back, hands clasped behind his head. He felt anything but reassured himself. This was worse than he'd thought.

Chapter 20

THE ALLEY CAT

Yuri sat holed up in the back of a white Chevy van parked among old, broken-down skiffs in an Orlando boatyard. The afternoon sun cast lengthening shadows on the ground, but his view of the front door of Antiquities Romani about a quarter of a mile away remained unobstructed. He had adapted one of the van's fixed rear windows to slide down, allowing him to easily surveil the area. So far, he'd seen no signs of life.

There was no breeze and the small open roof vent did nothing to circulate the air inside. During Yuri's two-hour vigil, the temperature within the cab had soared and sweat soaked his shirt, but he didn't mind. His training had made him impervious to extreme heat or cold. He kept looking through the telescope on his SVU Russian sniper rifle, his eyes alert, like a tiger stalking its prey.

Yuri was still annoyed because of the phone call from Europe early in the day. The Wizard had sounded harried. Wheezing and coughing, he had reprimanded Yuri for letting things get out of hand at the Gypsy campground with Burdock's clumsy trainees. "You're jeopardizing the mission by drawing attention to yourself," he scolded.

Keeping quiet, Yuri endured the dressing down, waiting to hear the real reason for the urgency. He found out soon enough. The Wizard had received information from a professor in Romania about a visit Dr. Curtis had paid an old Gypsy in Orlando. He had brought along the golden brooch of Vasilissa Dracul and claimed it belonged to him.

Convinced that the doctor was a carrier of Aryan genes of a master race of super-warriors, the Wizard ordered a change in plans. With rising excitement, he said, "DNA identification is no longer needed. I want you to locate the brooch, capture Dr. Curtis alive, and bring both to me. Burdock can facilitate travel arrangements. But first, go to Orlando and silence the old Gypsy, and before you do, find out who else knows about this. Eliminate them as well. I don't care what methods you use. Just make sure no trace of this information is left behind."

If the Wizard had left it at that, Yuri would be happy. The thought of applying his special methods of persuasion quickened his pulse.

But then, the Wizard issued another order: "Under no circumstances engage in direct contact or physical combat with Dr. Curtis when you take him. Consider him extremely dangerous at close quarters." When Yuri didn't respond immediately, he barked with steel in his voice, "We can't risk any foul-ups. Do I make myself clear?"

Clenching his teeth, Yuri answered, "I know what I must do."

"Good," the Wizard said and broke the connection.

Yuri shifted his weight in irritation, keeping his eyes on the Gypsy's shop. He didn't mind the changes in his mission. He was used to a shifting battlefield, although exfiltrating the doctor to Austria would take some doing. He hoped Burdock had better resources to get it done than his inept recruits at the compound. If he didn't, Yuri would have to improvise. He didn't mind that. What rankled him was the Wizard trying to tell him how to do his job, micromanaging the doctor's kidnapping.

His superiors in the Russian army had always let him call his own shots, and he liked it that way. But then, after Chechnya, he'd gotten into scrapes with other soldiers, and they'd ordered him to report for a psychiatric evaluation by that bitch, Major Nika Belev-ich. Although she had pulled her hair back severely and looked like a ferret, she was surprisingly attractive.

At first, things went okay. She had shown Yuri a series of oddly shaped, black inkblots and asked him to tell her the first thing that came to his mind. He had played along until the card that remind-ed him of an alley cat.

"Why is that?" the bitch had asked. "Tell me more."

He made a mistake and told her about roaming the streets of Kharkiv and entertaining himself by observing the creatures of the night. "The alley cat sits patiently in wait for a mouse. Then, when the time comes, he pounces. But he doesn't kill, not im-mediately. Rather than crunching his victim's larynx, as he could easily do, he tosses the mouse into the air, bats it down, and lets it run. Smelling its fear and terror, he repeats the process, playing with his victim. The alley cat wants to enjoy himself and extends the fun as long as possible. When the mouse is dead, the party's over, and he eats it."

Dr. Belevich fell silent, startled by his intensity. Her eyes nar-rowed and she said, "And you identify with the alley cat?"

Yuri glared at her, unblinking. "Not really. Look, any real man would know what I'm talking about. It's no different than the hunt for a woman. When a man's eyes focus on the object of desire, noth-ing can stand in his way of having her. He stalks her and romances her. Why? For one reason only—to have sex with her! When that time comes, he will attempt to sustain the height of arousal for as long as possible. After he climaxes, he's done with her." His eyes bore into hers. "No doubt you've had that experience, Doctor?"

"You're sick," she spat at him.

He'd erupted from his chair, backhanded her, and flung her to the floor, ready to tear off her clothes. What he hadn't count-ed on was that others were monitoring the session by video and immediately sent in a team of soldiers, who pulled him off the frantic woman and locked him in a prison cell. His discharge from the army soon followed.

For a moment, the memory of his humiliation engulfed Yuri, and only a movement at the parking lot brought him back to the present.

A pale yellow-colored Land Rover pulled up to the front of the store. Yuri was instantly alert. Training the telescope on the shop, he watched as a short, older man with a mane of gray hair got out and hobbled onto the porch. It had to be Mosthan, the lore keeper. Yuri's hunch was confirmed when the gypsy looked around, suspiciously, before unlocking the door and heading inside.

Yuri leaned back, disappointed. He had hoped for someone more challenging. Still, he would have his fun. After he extracted all the information, he would continue until the Gypsy scum begged Yuri to kill him. But, like the alley cat, Yuri would toy with him, prolonging his agony for as long as possible.

With his eyes glistening with anticipation and a feral grin on his lips, Yuri exited the van and crept across the parking lot.

Chapter 21

SPONGE DOCKS

The following afternoon, Jonathan closed his office and walked outside to the porch. He felt exhausted, yet his mind was abuzz from the events of the last several days. It had been a busy time, making rounds and trying to see all the patients whose appointments he'd canceled the day before. At least Pinky was out of danger, although it would be some time before he fully recovered. Moved from the ICU and doused with painkillers, he was enjoying the attention of the string of visitors from the Gypsy camp that trekked through his private room all day long.

Jonathan looked forward to a quiet evening of recovery by himself but, to his surprise, Isha was again waiting for him in the parking lot. She had pulled up her Jeep next to the building and was leaning against the side of his Harley, a small backpack at her feet and a helmet in her hand. She was dressed in a scarlet halter top and black cotton leggings and had tied her hair in a long ponytail with a bright yellow scarf. As soon as he walked out, her eyes lit up.

For a moment, Jonathan looked puzzled. "Isha....is everything alright?" he asked.

Isha smiled coquettishly and said, "Yeah. Everyone is healthy as can be, thanks to you." Her dark eyes flashed. "So, I decided to collect on that dinner you promised me." She gestured in the direction of the bike. "I came prepared for an adventure. Did you come up with a suitable restaurant?"

His feeling of tiredness vanished. Loving her free-wheeling spirit, Jonathan put on his helmet, unlocked his Harley, straddled

it, and pushed the starter button. Over the engine's roar, he shouted, "Hop on."

Isha swung her leg over the bike, wrapped her hands around
Jonathan, and pulled her body close to his. A magnetic pulse surged
between them and they recoiled from each other in surprise. Quickly regaining her composure, Isha drew close to Jonathan again, as
he engaged the clutch and spun out onto the highway.

While only a short jaunt to the Sponge Docks, this was the
most sensuous motorcycle ride Jonathan had ever experienced. Her
arms tightly wrapped around his waist and breasts pressed against
his back, Isha molded her body against his. Whenever the wind
coiled around his back, her long ponytail whipped gently across
his neck, stroking him like the tail of a soft kitten. Jonathan was
almost disappointed when they reached their destination.

Tarpon Spring's Sponge Docks, reminiscent of a seaside village
in Greece, was a favorite spot for tourists and locals alike. Restaurants and cafes served traditional Greek cuisine and fresh seafood
on both sides of Dodecanese Blvd, the main thoroughfare along
the Anclote River. Boutiques sold everything from real sponges to
imported merchandise and souvenirs. Behind the waterside shops
and eateries, large, barnacle-covered shrimp boats lined the docks.

Jonathan maneuvered his motorcycle along the street, stopping
for people who stepped off the crowded sidewalk, jaywalking, and
for children who broke loose from their parents and ran in front
of oncoming traffic. He found a free parking spot just off the road
and pulled in. He and Isha dismounted and began walking down
the street with the rest of the tourists.

Even among the colorful crowd, they were a striking couple:
Jonathan, tall and muscular, walking beside Isha whose dark exotic
features and sexy outfit attracted the attention of passers-by.

"Hey, Doc, that your girlfriend?" an elderly Greek man called
out and waved as the couple passed his booth, with a large white

sign, "The Nicholas III," swaying above it. Jonathan waved back good-naturedly at the grinning fisherman, whose white teeth contrasted sharply with his darkly tanned and furrowed face.

"Nic Bilirakis is there every day from just after sunup until dusk, selling tickets for his family business," Jonathan told Isha. "Every two hours, his sons take their boat out into the harbor. They've fitted it with a glass bottom and treat their passengers to an authentic, hard-hat sponge diving experience, recreating a scene from the early 1900s when sponge diving was the leading industry of Tarpon Springs."

As they continued, others recognized Jonathan. Most just waved or smiled, nodding their heads in acknowledgment. A few said, "Hey, Doc" or "Doc-tor-a Curtis, good evening." Jonathan returned their greetings cordially.

"You're quite the local hero," Isha whispered, smiling.

"I didn't expect to be running a gauntlet," he whispered back.

When they turned off Dodecanese Blvd and headed up the hill to lose the crowds and stares, Jonathan finally relaxed. They walked up Athens Street, past small, one-story shops, until they came to Paul's Restaurant, across the street from Mama's Greek Cuisine. The small hole-in-the-wall eatery was Jonathan's favorite—he was glad Jimmy had reminded him of it. With no fanfare or bright lights to mark its red doorway, the place had the reputation of being the best Greek seafood restaurant in Tarpon Springs.

Inside, the atmosphere was intimate, and the aroma tantalizing. Small, four-top tables with captain's chairs, some arranged for larger parties, were positioned around the room. A long, solid teakwood bar, which appeared to be over a hundred years old, ran along one wall. Dark, square wooden support posts subdivided the space and mounted fish displays covered the walls.

Helena, a pert, high school-aged waitress, and Paul's granddaughter, told them to sit anywhere. They saw only one other couple in the whole place. Jonathan chose a table next to the window, and they both ordered a glass of Retsina. Through a doorway, Jonathan could hear Paul banging and clanking cooking utensils in the kitchen.

For a few moments, he and Isha lapsed into an awkward silence, finding and avoiding each other's eyes, trying to deny the erotic tension between them. Jonathan thought he noticed a faint blush on her olive skin. He wished he knew what to make of this enticing woman, so worldly and sophisticated on the one hand, yet also genuine and fierce in her independence.

Isha caught him looking searchingly at her and saw him blush. She felt torn. Ever since the sailing trip, she was aware of her physical attraction to Jonathan but emotionally troubled by his peculiar make-up, the mixture of power, compassion, and mystery. His superhuman feat of strength amazed and frightened her. Nor did she know what to make of Tatyana's comment, "He is something special. There is a spirit locked inside him."

As if reading her mind, he said, "We know so little about each other, yet..." He left the remainder of the sentence hanging in mid-air.

Isha smiled at the obvious gambit to open up the conversation without committing himself. "Now that you are one of us, I guess it's okay to let you in on some things about my people and me. But only if you answer some questions, too," she said

"Fair enough, I'll start," Jonathan agreed. Two questions had lingered in his mind. "Your dad, he's a charming man. If he had stayed in the hospital any longer, he'd be running it. But, all that gold jewelry, traveling in million-dollar coaches, playing at penny-ante card games all night. It doesn't add up...." He locked eyes with her. "And then there's you—worldly, sophisticated, interesting, smart, attractive, and...." He looked away.

Isha blushed and said, "Single."

"Yes. That doesn't add up either."

Isha nodded. "Okay," she said, her gaze at him unblinking. "My dad was raised on the streets of New Jersey. His parents were straight off the boat from Slovakia. That part of my family was, the lot of them, gamblers, crooks, and con artists, and they taught my dad the trade. By the time he was sixteen, he dealt blackjack in Atlantic City. Soon he was playing high-stakes poker games in New Jersey and Manhattan. He could count ten decks of cards at a time and became known as Black Jack. After his parents died, Daddy moved in with Aunt Zelda, Pinky, and Carl's mother. His cousins began running security for him. As Dad's fame rose, he became wealthy by Gypsy standards and the breadwinner for his entire family. About that time, Kizzy, Bicca, and my mother, Maria, arrived on the scene. All the boys agreed to arranged marriages."

Isha's face saddened. "My mother died shortly after I was born. According to Aunt Kizzy, who cared for me during her illness, her death almost killed Daddy. He took to the road, lived hard, and became an even greater risk taker. By the time I was a teen, I went along on his gambling trips all around the world. I've been almost everywhere, Jonathan, seeing the world—or at least every casino."

Isha smiled wistfully as she continued to talk about her travels and all she learned in Las Vegas, The Bahamas, Monte Carlo, Macao, on cruise liners, and in private games with high rollers; and meeting Arab oil sheiks, sports legends, hedge fund billionaires, and professional gamblers. While she had plenty of adventures and fun in their company—many pursued her—she also became aware of their less appealing qualities—ruthless competitiveness, narcissism, and disdain for the rest of humanity, and her people in particular.

"Daddy eventually made so much money, he lost his appetite for glitz and glitter," she said. "That's when he decided to join Tatyana's little tribe." She sighed. "As for me, I was tired and disgusted by the whole show of wealth and privilege. It put me off men for some time. "I went along with him to see what a 'normal' life would be like."

"Although Dad still gambles almost every night, nowadays it's just for fun. But he's grown accustomed to the freedom of traveling 'under the radar' and likes it that way. That little fiasco in the bar Monday afternoon was unusual. Nowadays he doesn't like to draw attention to himself that way. I think he just got fed up with those brats."

Isha began rotating her glass on the table. "But, enough about me. Tell me about your childhood, Jonathan."

Inwardly Jonathan relaxed, feeling closer to Isha than ever with Priscilla. He told her what it was like to grow up in the Tennessee mountains as a country kid. Fishing for bass in the Spring, hunting in the Fall, church picnics on Sunday afternoons, bonfire parties on Saturday nights, drinking beer with the guys at the rock quarry on Friday nights. The feeling of freedom on his first motorcycle, an old clunker. Never really fitting in with his schoolmates, no matter how hard he tried; not playing sports to avoid any physical altercations, afraid he might hurt someone. How becoming a doctor had almost been like an antidote. He'd found the ability to help people deeply gratifying and stopped worrying about his past…until now.

Talking to someone who truly listened felt like a welcome opportunity to themselves. They were so lost in conversation that neither noticed the waitress coming by twice to take their orders. Their fingers touched and intertwined, and they stared at each other across the table, like two soul mates. When they finally returned to reality, they ordered—Isha shrimp and Jonathan octopus. Both were delicious.

They continued to talk and, after the second glass of wine, and another, began laughing, joking, and having fun. Jonathan shared amusing stories about some of his most trying patients. Isha retaliated with tales of Big Jack, who was known as a hustler's hustler, easily conning his biggest marks. For a while, they forgot about all the strange happenings and mysteries surrounding them and just had a good time.

Isha, who prided herself on her self-control, became giddy. "Dancing. I want to go dancing, Jonathan," she said as they paid the bill and got up from the table. Heading outside, she leaned her head against his shoulder, looked up with a coy smile, and repeated, "I want to go dancing."

"All right," Jonathan offered with a twinkle in his eyes. "I recommend Greek dancing…because that's all they've got here in Tarpon Springs. But I must warn you," he cautioned her. "You may be taking your life in your hands. I have two left feet."

"We'll see," she said, wrinkling her nose at him.

Jonathan enjoyed being seduced by the feminine charms of his companion. With Isha, he felt an awakening of his spirit: something male and virile and exciting. He grabbed her hand and led her up the street. "Follow me to Zorba's, my fancy dancer."

Consumed with each other, oblivious to their surroundings, they didn't notice the tall man lurking in the shadows of a doorway across the street. Yuri, disguised as a homeless derelict, slowly followed them.

If Paul's was the most authentic Greek restaurant in town, Zorba's was the best Greek nightclub. A large, gaudy gold sign hung above the red entrance doorway. Capitalized bold-faced letters spelled out the name, surrounded by three hundred antique-style light bulbs. The sign was so old that elderly Greeks living in the town remember it being this way when they were young.

Standing inside the doorway, George Baros, the owner, immediately recognized Jonathan and greeted him like a long-lost friend. "Doc-tor-a Curtis," he said, beaming. "*Kalosórisma*—Welcome. Please come in. Let me show you to a table."

Contemporary Laïká music, performed by musicians on vintage bouzouki instruments, blared from the stage on one side of a solid parquet dance floor. Isha's face brightened in response to the vibrant atmosphere and rhythmic beat as George led her and Jonathan to a small round table, just to the side of a brass railing overlooking the dance floor. Like all the other tables, it had a glowing candle in the middle and the flickering flame reflected sparkles off Isha's face.

George asked, "Some Ouzo, Doc-tor-a Curtis? And for the lady?" He raised his eyebrow. "She's your girl, eh? First drink on the house. For both."

Nodding eagerly, Isha wiggled in her seat, anxious to be on the dance floor.

Jonathan turned to George. He started, "Thank you for the offer, but she's not –" When Isha poked him in the ribs, Jonathan glared at her curiously and continued, "Oh, never mind. Two ouzos! Thank you, Mr. Baros."

While they waited, Isha smiled sweetly at Jonathan. As soon as a waiter placed the anise-flavored liquor before them, she grasped the shot glass, raised it to her lips, and downed it in one gulp. Then, she popped up from her seat and held out her hands to Jonathan. "Dancing, Jonathan. I want to dance with you."

He downed his ouzo and let her lead him to the dance floor. He prayed that the liquor would help his dancing. Fortunately, the music carried a strong beat so he could move his feet in easy steps. Swaying from side to side, he focused on Isha.

Moving her hips to the rhythm of the music, she raised her hands overhead and untied her scarf, letting her hair fall over her shoulders.

Jonathan's heart beat double time as she circled him. Her dark, glistening eyes searched his face as she placed her scarf around his neck and drew him closer. Her body swayed to the beat until her breasts grazed his chest. Isha turned and danced with her back to him, then twirled and allowed her scent to envelop him. It smelled of sweet coconut and something else, a strangely familiar essence that, mysteriously, reminded him of soft, pleasant dreams from his past.

When the music ended, Isha slowly withdrew her scarf from around his neck, and Jonathan felt momentarily bolted to the floor. "Oh, dear God, one more ouzo, and surely I'll have no moral fiber left," he thought.

The band leader came to the microphone and said something in Greek, met by rousing applause and cheers. Jonathan didn't understand but noticed all the men taking their seats, leaving only women on the dance floor. He wanted to return to their table too. However, when he tried to coax Isha into joining him, she pulled away. "I want to dance," she begged.

A large circle of Greek women formed at the center of the floor, and the musicians started to play. Jonathan recognized the tune as a popular, traditional folk dance, the Mantili Kalamatiano. A middle-aged woman wearing a red lace shawl held out a white table napkin to a pretty, young woman with a white lace shawl demurely draped over her head. The older woman led her to the middle of the circle and amid clapping and dancing, promenaded her proudly. Then, with both holding onto the napkin, they rejoined the circle. The rest of the women danced steadily to the music, six steps to the right and six steps in place. The pageant was classic and fun to watch.

Isha, wishing to have fun, invited herself into the circle to the dismay of the other women. Suddenly, an object flew through the air, barely missing Isha's head, and landed on the dance floor with a thud. It was a shoe. Jonathan looked and saw an older woman, all dressed in black, rise from her table, scowling. She shook her fist and yelled a Greek insult across the room.

Isha was too enthralled with dancing to notice.

Abruptly, George Baros appeared by Jonathan's table, looking alarmed. "Doc-tor-a Curtis, Doc-tor. Please, you must do something quickly. Your girlfriend…she's stirring up a hornet's nest. There will be a wedding in two days, and this dance honors the mother of the bride—for family and friends only! Mrs. Argyros has just shouted her objections. She's the family matriarch, and it won't be long before all the women follow her lead. You must do something or there'll be a riot!"

Jonathan rose and took in the situation—Isha lost in the music; men chuckling, enjoying the spectacle; other women casting angry looks and shaking their fists from the sidelines; several reaching down to unbuckle their shoes. He dashed to the dance floor and tugged at Isha. "Come, it's time to leave."

But Isha loosened his grip and tried to rejoin the circle. "I want to dance, Jonathan. I'm having fun."

He pulled again, harder, and escorted Isha to the front door. As soon as they were outside, she broke away and ran into the street. Like a wild mustang set free, she reared up, then twirled with her arms out. Jonathan quickly caught up to her, anxiously glancing up and down the street. Fortunately, there was no traffic. He placed his hand around her waist and pulled her to him. She wrapped her arms around him and buried her head in his chest.

Peering up at him, her dark Roma eyes caught the light of a street lamp. "That's not fair," she complained. "I like dancing, Jonathan. I like dancing with you. Come, let's dance by ourselves."

A sudden cacophony of female Greek voices drew their attention. Women poured out of Zorba's with shoes held high in their hands—the swarm of hornets Mr. Baros had predicted. They started to run down the street in bare feet, shouting profanities.

Jonathan alerted Isha, "Let's get out of here before they shoe us to death."

Together, they bolted down the hill as fast as their legs carried them. By the time they reached Dodecanese Blvd, the angry mob of Greek women had drawn a crowd of curious onlookers who filled the narrow Athens Street shoulder to shoulder, stopping their onrush.

Caught in the throng, Yuri towered head and shoulders above the others. He had been waiting in a side shop, hoping to waylay Isha and Jonathan on the quiet, empty street when they came out of Zorba's. Although he tried to shuffle people aside, he couldn't move quickly enough without attracting the attention of the policemen gathered on the corner of the intersection. Trapped among the Greek women and amused onlookers, he watched impotently as his quarry made their get-a-way on Jonathan's Harley.

Chapter 22

SUNSET BEACH

When they were at a safe distance from the Sponge Docks, Jonathan slowed his bike and called to Isha over his shoulder, "Now, where would you like to go?"

"The beach. Swimming," she yelled close to his ear.

"Swimming? Did you bring a bathing suit? I don't have one."

Isha reached into her side bag and pulled out a pair of over-sized swimming trunks. "Got you covered," she shouted above the roar of the Harley and waved them over Jonathan's shoulder. They flapped like a banner in the wind. "Stole them from Daddy's dresser. It's the Gypsy way, you know. My guess is they'll be kind of big on you and they're a bright purple. I heard that's the style nowadays, big and purple."

Jonathan laughed. "Baggy, you mean. Baggy and purple? Where did you hear that was in style? South Beach?"

When they reached the beach park entrance, Jonathan drove by and decelerated. "It's closed at night, but I know another way in," he said. He found a narrow dirt path into a thickly wooded area and made their way to the beach. A secluded picnic shelter occupied a spot where the vegetation gave way to glistening white sand.

Isha slid off the back and removed her helmet. Jonathan lowered the kickstand and looked up. He fantasized about untying the back of her scarlet halter top and placing his hands along her waist to feel the rounded smoothness of her hips, barely hidden under tight, cotton leggings.

Isha stowed her tote bag in the gazebo and disrobed, revealing a black bikini. She fought hard not to laugh when Jonathan stepped from behind the pavilion wearing her father's baggy, bright purple swim shorts. Although he had pulled the drawstring as tight as possible, the trunks still slid to his hips, ballooning around him with the hem of the legs falling well below his knees. As they walked to a spot on the beach beside a grassy knoll of sea oats, Isha's lips remained puckered in a merry smirk.

Terns at the water's edge bobbed their beaks into the sand, searching for food. A cluster of seagulls broke as a wave rolled in, sparkling in the moonlight. For a moment, they took in the dreamy atmosphere scene. Then, they collected driftwood and built a small fire inside the dunes. "It will take about half an hour for the flames to die down," Isha said. "A good place to warm up later."

They walked hand in hand down to the Gulf and into the water. It was warm and refreshing. Soon they were frolicking like children in the crashing waves, enjoying the pull and tug of the surf as it splashed around their bodies. Together, they dove head-first into the swells. As the waves curled over their heads, they glided back with the returning surge, laughing, splashing one another, and floating on the counter currents.

After a while, they returned to the fire to dry off. Isha lit a joint, took a toke, and passed it to Jonathan. He took a puff and, holding his breath, gave it back to her.

Off to the west, towering cumulus clouds were building. Isha lay down in the sand and pointed toward the largest. Lit from behind by the moon, its edges had a silver glow. "Look, Jonathan, over there, the big one," she said, pointing. "It looks like a mountain, covered in snow. We could ski from the top over that big bulge, and then down and dive right into the water." She drew an imaginary route in the air with her finger. "Would you come with me, holding hands on the way down?"

"That's the oddest thing to think about," Jonathan mused. But he decided to play along. "Sounds great, Isha, but how do we get there?"

"We imagine ourselves there, and then we will be...but I like lying here on the sand with you, too."

When Jonathan, lost in thought, didn't respond, she passed him the remains of the joint. He took it absentmindedly and brought it to his lips.

As he inhaled, Isha teased, "Tatyana told me you said you were 'smitten' with me."

Jonathan choked and coughed, a cloud of smoke pouring from his mouth and nostrils.

Isha's smile became a mischievous grin. "I looked up the word just to be sure: 'Charmed, enamored, infatuated, taken with.'" Her dark eyes lowered. Her voice softened. "Are you smitten with me, Jonathan?"

Jonathan blushed and, in a throaty whisper, said. "May I show you something?"

Isha nodded, "What is it?"

Jonathan leaned over to kiss her. The waves crashed on the sand and rocks. His lips brushed hers. She lifted her chin with her lips slightly parted.

At that moment, lightning flashed across the black horizon and a clap of thunder shook the sky. Jonathan drew back. He looked up. The threatening clouds were closer, almost looming overhead. "Should we go back?" he asked

Despite the growing darkness, Isha's face was aglow. "We don't have to go anywhere," she said. "The park is closed. We're all alone. Besides, I've always loved thunderstorms."

Jonathan slipped his arm around her. She rested her head against his shoulder and relaxed into him. Wrapping Isha in his arms, he held her tightly. This time, their lips met firmly. The kiss had a different kind of passion, something vibrant and alive. Jonathan felt her tongue against his. He was acutely conscious of her body responding and breathed deeply as her fingers moved lower. When he slid his hand down her back, she sighed and tilted her pelvis into his, allowing him to cup her buttocks. Impulsively, she sat up, slipped off her top, and lay back down. Jonathan could see her breasts, round and firm, with nipples erect, stimulated by the fresh sea breeze. He gently caressed them. With quickened breath, they each sought the touch of flesh, warm and soft and yielding. She kissed his navel and his ribs and tugged at the string of his suit.

Another clap of thunder exploded overhead, instantly followed by rain pouring down on them. Isha wiped the water from her eyes and began to giggle. Peering down at her, Jonathan felt his excitement return. They both looked toward the shelter, having the same thought, and got up.

Laughing and wet, they held hands as they ran past the doused fire toward the safety of the picnic shelter. Around them, the storm reached its climax as thunder crashed followed by lightning flashes in short order. Water poured off all four sides of the gazebo in cascades. Gradually, the lightning strikes diminished and the thunderclaps sounded like distant cymbals. The air was cool, and a wet wind swept under the eaves. Shivering, Jonathan and Isha each grabbed a dry towel from her bag. Seeing her tremble uncontrollably, he said, "Some dry clothes?"

"Yes," she responded but made no move to get any.

Their eyes met. Without shame or hesitation, Isha dropped her towel. She wanted him with every nerve of her body. Jonathan released his towel, too, and advanced on her, his manhood erect and his eyes devouring her.

Jonathan came just close enough so that his penis touched her lower belly as her breasts made contact with his chest. The sensation of her skin against his was like fire, and they smelled each other's heated scent. Aglow with passion, he cradled her face in his hands and tilted her lips to his. It was a hungry kiss this time, tasting and exploring each other.

Jonathan cupped Isha's buttocks with his hands and lifted her to his waist. She wrapped her legs around him. Her buttocks flared and her pelvis opened as he lowered her slowly onto his erection. Without relinquishing contact, he laid her on the wooden table, and they moved together in a deep rhythmic rocking, each of his feverish thrusts bringing them closer to the moment of release. When that moment arrived, both shuddered and cried out in ecstasy. Then, spent in the hot sweat of fulfillment, their breaths quieting, Jonathan used his last bit of strength to lift Isha from the table and carry her to the pallet of towels. He laid her down across them on the cool concrete and joined her.

Holding each other, they were quiet for a while, watching the distant lighting make jagged patterns across the dark sky and listening to the thunder booming ever farther away. Then, as the rain continued to pelt down, they made love a second time, this time unhurried, soft, and loving. When they finished, Jonathan wrapped his arms around Isha.

Sometime later—it was hard to know how much time had passed—he rose to look beyond the shelter. The rain had become a gentle mist. Tree frogs began to sound their melodic chirps, singing to one another. Above them, the night sky had cleared. Soft moonlight and a myriad of twinkling stars illuminated the beach.

Jonathan gazed at Isha looking at him in the soft light. "This was everything I ever dreamed it would be," he said.

After softly caressing and gently kissing one another, they got up and dressed for the ride home. As they were about to get on the motorcycle, Jonathan asked, "What about your father?"

Isha rolled her eyes humorously. "I'm a big girl now," she teased. "And, well, you're not engaged, and you're not Gadjo. I think Daddy will be fine with it. There are some things we might not want to mention. But…"—she grinned and mimicked a roundhouse punch across his jaw - "You'll have to watch your back around Pinky, though, as soon as he's better."

Jonathan chuckled. "I'll take my chances with Pinky. Do you know why?"

Isha tilted her head but didn't say anything.

He took a step toward her. "Because I am truly smitten with you." When she looked surprised, he quickly added, "You don't have to say anything back. That's not why I said it."

Isha closed the distance between them. Rising on tiptoes, she wrapped her arms around his neck, placed a finger to his lips, and whispered in a husky voice, "Shhh." She looked at Jonathan with lambent eyes. "What I haven't told you is that night you stood me up, I returned to camp and spent two hours crying to Tatyana about how I had finally found the man I am drawn to, and he's a lying jerk." She buried her head against his chest and sighed deeply. "Oh, Jonathan, I'm smitten with you too."

As soon as she had spoken, she knew there was more to it. In some mystical way, the man she first ignored had become as important in her life as air. The moonlight shimmered and the stars blinked, as if to remind her what she had just admitted to herself. She had fallen in love for the very first time.

Chapter 23

DNA

Yuri had spent a frustrating evening. Losing Jonathan and Isha at the Sponge Docks was a rookie mistake. He should have put a GPS tracker on the doctor's motorbike, as he had done on the Jeep, the sailboat, and the motorboat anchored in the harbor. He had driven to the doctor's apartment building and parked in the shadows but with a good view of the entrance door, hoping Jonathan would return there at some point. But he had been disappointed.

Yuri considered that they might ride back to the clinic, but the parking lot would be too open for him to make a surreptitious approach. So, he had to watch helplessly on his tracker software as the girl took off in her Jeep around 5 a.m. and drove to the Gypsy camp. And still Jonathan didn't return to his apartment.

When Yuri drove past the clinic after it opened, the Harley was parked by the side of the building. He decided now was as good a time as any to check out the apartment and look for the golden brooch. On the way there, he considered his options. After three days, he'd had only a few glimpses of the doctor. A surveillance team might have made it easier to grab him, but the Wizard had specifically ordered as few eyes on the mission as possible.

Last night, as he sat at the outdoor bar across from Paul's, he'd had the opportunity to size up Jonathan. Although tall and well-proportioned, he didn't look all that formidable. Surely, he couldn't be as dangerous as the Wizard had warned. However, his girlfriend, with an oriental-sounding name, made his pulse quicken. The Gypsy in

Orlando had revealed that she accompanied the doctor on his quest for information about his heritage, which meant, per the Wizard's orders, that she had to be eliminated. Too bad, the old man's heart had given out so soon after telling Yuri everything he'd wanted to know. It had left his sadistic needs dissatisfied and unfulfilled. He would have to make up for it when the time came to eliminate the girl. He was looking forward to making her scream and beg for mercy before he snuffed out her life.

Yuri grunted with satisfaction as he pulled into an empty parking space near Jonathan's apartment. It was only a matter of time before he succeeded in cornering the good doctor alone. He got out a tool kit containing lockpicks and equipment to disable any alarm system inside, put on a workman's cap, and approached the building looking like an A/C serviceman.

* * *

Jonathan's day began with a busy morning office schedule. It didn't help that he had a raging headache. During his noon break, he sequestered himself behind the locked door of his office for a quick nap. With the blinds closed and the overhead lights off, he reclined in his chair and closed his eyes, thinking about the glorious night he'd had with Isha. When they got back to the parking lot, burning with the passion of their new romance, they found it difficult to part. They stood against Isha's Jeep, wrapped in a tight embrace for a long time before he let her go and watched her drive off.

He didn't realize he had dozed off until the shrill buzz of the intercom on the desk awoke him. His assistant Lynne's voice was apologetic: "I've waited as long as I could, but three of your afternoon patients are here. One of them is a walk-in. I tried to reschedule him, but he insists on seeing you today. Claims it's an emergency but won't say what. I've placed him in exam room three and taken his vitals." Before Jonathan could answer, she continued, "And there's a fax for you from Dr. Wade at Duke University."

That last piece of news made Jonathan sit up quickly. It could hold the keys to his past and future. "I'll be right there," he called out. Then he rose from his chair and took several deep breaths. Containing his excitement, he unlocked his office door and headed down the hallway. Much as he wanted to pore over the results of his blood work, it would have to wait until after his patients.

Outside exam room three, he grabbed the chart from the rack and glanced at the new patient information. Sex: "Male," Name: "Liam McLaren," Occupation: "blank," Complaint: "blank."

"Odd. What kind of emergency could it be?" he thought and went inside.

The man standing next to the examining table was in his mid-thirties, tall, wiry, red-haired, and unshaven, with steel gray eyes that observed Jonathan intently. He had a tattoo on his arm, the figure of a dragon biting its tail.

Instantly on his guard, Jonathan asked, "What can I do for you, Mr. McLaren?"

"Call me Liam, Doctor Curtis," the man said. "I've got a proposition for you." He pulled out his wallet. Flipping it open, he revealed an FBI badge. "We were contacted by the Southern Liberties Law Group and told that you were someone I should talk to."

Glancing at the tattoo, Jonathan felt bewildered and decided to stall for time. "This is not a good time for me right now. I have a full schedule of patients this afternoon."

Liam chewed his lip. "I understand, but this is a matter of some urgency, and my situation is, shall we say, constrained and precarious."

"Can't it wait till tomorrow or the next day?"

Liam gave Jonathan an evaluating glance and said, "I suppose so, Dr. Curtis. We want you to know that we've got our eyes on the group in question. Please avoid them so we can do our job. I'll be contacting you soon, someplace less busy."

Jonathan nodded, relieved. "Thank you. I will. And I'll write you a prescription for a muscle relaxant, so it won't raise eyebrows with my nurse when you check out at the front desk."

"I appreciate that. I'll be in touch."

Jonathan left puzzled. For the rest of the afternoon, his patients kept him busy. When he finished the last appointment and went to the reception desk., Lynnee handed him Dr. Wade's fax with a questioning look.

"Thank you, Lynnee," Jonathan said. "I'll look it over. You might as well go home. I'll lock up when I'm done here."

He ignored her curious stare and waited until she left. Then he went to his office and started to read the cover page:

Genetics Report

prepared at the request
of Dr. Jonathan Michael Curtis.

Specimens Received:

    1. Hair sample believed to be C.E. 1400s

    2. Buccal smear- Dr. Jonathan Curtis

    3. Whole blood—Dr. Jonathan Curtis

    4. Hair sample—Dr. Jonathan Curtis

Tests Requested:

    1. Hereditary Genetics—All specimens

    2. Accelerator Mass Spectrometry,

    Radio Carbon Dating—Specimen No. 1

As he was about to look at the next page, his cell phone rang. He looked at the ID screen, annoyed at the interruption. But when he saw that the call was from his best friend, he answered, "Hey, Jimmy. What's going on?"

"What's going on? I should be asking you that question." Jimmy sounded incensed. "George Baros called me this morning about a ruckus at his club last night involving Mrs. Argyros. Seems like you were there with a Gypsy girl who, from the description, sounds a lot like Isha. Naturally, I want to get your side of the story. Yesterday, Officer Mac, down at the courthouse, told me about an attack on Tom Higgins' kid by some Gypsy bodyguard; and you're somehow involved with that, too. So, I'm asking you…is everything all right?"

Jonathan smiled, his cheeks reddening. "There's been a lot going on, Jimmy. Mostly all good," he began. "I know I should have called you before now."

"Definitely," Jimmy cut in.

Jonathan scratched his head. "Can I get back to you later? I'm kind of in the middle of something, but we do need to sit down and talk. This is going to take some time. Could you meet me on Friday after work at J-Wags? We'll have some beers. Catch up."

"Okay. But you're buying!"

"Deal."

Jimmy chuckled and rang off.

Jonathan put the receiver down thoughtfully and returned to reading. He waded through a sea of charts, symbols, numbers, and algorithms that would look as incomprehensible as ancient Sanskrit to a non-scientist. The figures told an incredible story. Reading the accompanying report, which was more explicit, astonished Jonathan even more. He picked up the phone and made a long-distance call to Durham, North Carolina, to speak directly to Doctor Wade.

Chapter 24

REVELATIONS

When Jonathan arrived at the Gypsy camp later that afternoon, he found it all but deserted. A young woman hanging out laundry to dry by one of the Vardos told him Big Jack, Carl, Bicca, and Kizzy were at the hospital with Pinky.

Jonathan knew he was early. He had texted Isha earlier saying he was on his way over with news he wanted to share with her and Tatyana. She had texted back that she was teaching a group of children, and Tatyana was with a client., They would meet him as soon as they finished.

Sitting on one of the wooden benches in the picnic area, he leaned back and took in the spacious pine canopy overhead with the sweet aroma of wild hyacinth wafting in on a cool breeze. Except for the tropical fauna, it felt much like the peaceful surroundings he remembered growing up as a boy in the hills of Tennessee. But he was too wound up to enjoy the tranquility and ease.

When Jonathan caught sight of Isha coming around one of the RVs, his heartbeat quickened. He rose and was about to call her name when she saw him. They moved toward each other and, before they knew it, found themselves in each other's arms. Parting, they started to speak simultaneously and burst into laughter when they realized it.

"You first," Isha said. "You look like you're dying to tell me something."

Trying his best to put on a poker face, Jonathan wrinkled his forehead as if deep in thought. Well...," he drawled.

But he didn't fool Isha one bit. She cackled in delight. "Then realization dawned on her face. "You got your genetics test results! Didn't you?"

Before Jonathan could answer, they heard a Vardo door slam, followed by muffled female voices.

Isha's face brightened. "It's Tatyana. Her last reading of the day." She tugged at his arm.

As they made their way through the Australian pines, Jonathan followed close behind Isha. Nearing the rear of Tatyana's Vardo, Isha held up her hand and signaled him to slow down. Then she placed a finger to her lips, "Shhh..."

Tiptoeing closer, they heard an unfamiliar voice. "Thank you for selling me the last of your dear grandmother's prized candles," a woman said. "It means so much to me knowing that you care."

"Oh, that is so sweet," Tatyana replied. "I can feel my dear grandmother beaming down from above. All I ask is for you to care for it as she would have. Be sure to place it on your bedside table, and light it on the very first night of your honeymoon."

When Isha winked at Jonathan conspiratorially, he grinned, having heard similar words just a few days before.

With excitement in her voice, the woman said "Thank you, I promise." Soon a car door slammed, followed by an engine revving up, and tires crunching on the shell driveway.

Isha signaled Jonathan to come along. She moved with such nimble eagerness toward the front of the Vardo that he had to jog to keep up. Catching sight of the Gypsy sitting at her table, she called out, "Tatyana! Jonathan has a special announcement!"

Looking askance at Isha, she said, "A special announcement? Don't tell me you're..."

Isha blushed. "No, oh no. He hasn't told me what it is yet, but not that!"

Jonathan broke in, "Wait a minute. You're the fortune teller. You tell me what it is."

Tatyana snickered. "While it is true that I read fortunes and conjure spirits, Jonathan, I am not a TV quiz show host. I don't play *The Price Is Right*."

Jonathan rolled his eyes and continued to banter, "Well, oh Great Sorceress, break your routine for once and take a wild guess."

"Okay, smart-ass. You are going to propose to Isha."

Isha's eyes grew wide. "Tatyana!" she squealed. "Quit messing around."

Tatyana exploded into a deep-throated laugh. "Well, he asked for it. And time will tell." Relenting, she threw up her hands. "Okay, I surrender. Tell me. But do sit down!"

After Jonathan took his seat, he leaned toward Tatyana and said, "When Isha told me about the consequences of failing the *Pi-Vortimo*, she also told me that you knew, without reservation, I would pass the test." He brightened. "I just got off a video conference with a geneticist colleague, Dr. Wade at Duke University, who confirmed that, according to my DNA, my mother and father were both Romani. But you have known that all along. Haven't you?"

Tatyana gasped. "My Dear, from the first time I met you, I could feel a special purity within your spirit, almost as if we were connected on some cosmic level. But I don't profess to know everything. Please, tell me what else you found out."

Jonathan nodded as Isha and Tatyana pulled their chairs closer to the table. The bright afternoon sun filtered through the pine canopy, dappling their rapt faces. Hesitating briefly, he announced, "Dr. Wade said that the odds were a billion to one that the hair in the brooch belonged to my maternal great-grandmother. It's all but certain that I am a descendant of Vasilissa Dracul!"

As Tatyana listened, his words seemed to waken familiar spirits within her. Her glowing face told Jonathan he'd guessed correctly—she had known. Glancing at Isha's expression of wonderment and delight, he continued, "Dr. Wade brought up another finding that struck me as quite incredulous." He scratched his cheek. "Besides his studies in Comparative Primatology, Functional Genomics, and Biotransformation, he also researches Super Genes."

Both women looked at him, puzzled.

"These genes confer special abilities on those who carry them," Jonathan explained. "Elite athletes, gifted artists and musicians, people with photographic memory, and others who perform feats well beyond anything an ordinary person could achieve have them. Dr. Wade was amazed to find multiple such genes in the hair sample. Super genes are extremely rare. An individual who exhibits more than one is even rarer. But Vasilisa, amazingly, possessed several."

In his excitement, he missed Tatyana's changing expression. She closed her eyes and seemed to withdraw into herself.

"Any of these genes being passed down from one generation to the next is the exception rather than the rule. But when Dr. Wade checked my DNA samples, he was shocked to discover that I had Vasilissa's super-genes too!"

"He told me that it's hard to predict what they produce, but if they result in a special talent, it will flourish only if cultivated. Otherwise, it will remain hidden."

Jonathan stopped for a moment as a thought crossed his mind. "I wonder which of my parents gave them to me?" he said. "I wish I could have known them." He lowered his head sadly. "I have no recollection of my father whatsoever. And, all I have of my mother is the gold brooch and a memory of the scent of her frankincense." He looked at Tatyana. "Do you have anything more you can tell me about them, anything at all?"

To his surprise, Tatyana was weeping.

"Tatyana, are you all right?" Isha asked and reached out to clasp her hand across the table.

"Yes, I am all right," Tatyana answered, wiping her eyes. "The pieces of the puzzle are beginning to fall into place." She turned to Jonathan. "That day in the ER, when I met you caring for Kizzy, I knew. I could have told you earlier that you were one of us. But you needed scientific evidence to believe the truth." She reached out her other hand to grasp Jonathan's. "Perhaps I can shed some light on your history. Your mother's name was Yana, Yana Kucera, and your father's Pali. I met them, briefly. And, while I never knew your grandfather, stories of his bravery are often told around our campfires. All Romani know him as a hero. I owe him my life."

"You knew my mother and father?" Jonathan gasped. "Please, I must know everything. Just hearing their names is a blessing."

"I only met them once, Jonathan, but it was a time I shall never forget," Tatyana said. "I was a bright-eyed girl of seventeen, busy learning fortune teller arts from my mother and grandmother. Having lived only two years in the freedom of the New World, I had my whole life before me."

She closed her eyes, as if searching her memory, and continued, "Our tribe was camped just outside of Ocala in Alexander Springs. One afternoon, we learned your mother and father would attend our evening campfire. The entire caravan was abuzz with the excitement of meeting the daughter of one of our great heroes.

"That night, our leader first introduced your father. Pali was tall and statuesque—you have his physique. When Yana came into the bonfire circle and stood beside him, I was overwhelmed by her beauty—her coal-dark eyes, hair the color of midnight, and soft, inviting smile. There are times when you remind me of her."

When Jonathan gasped, Tatyana opened her eyes and gazed at him kindly before continuing. "Pali spoke first, proudly announcing that Yana was pregnant—with you!—to the cheers of the fireside circle. Even by the dim flickering light, I could see Yana blush. Her speech was short and simple, but at the same time inspiring and hopeful. Like most of us, she had come from the old country to escape oppression and seek a new start. She reminded us that, here, in America, we were free to pursue our culture and heritage without fear; but challenged us to be good citizens and respect the laws of our new country. She expressed grief that her mother had been killed in Romania because of such hatred and prayed that here, there would be an end to it. Then she stepped back into the crowd."

Tatyana smiled wistfully. "I was awestruck and too embarrassed to walk up and speak to her. I had so much gratitude for what her father had done for me. I wish I had said something. Instead, like a sylph in the night, I snuck over to the Vardo where she was sleeping, and left a bottle of my best frankincense outside the doorway, along with a note wishing her and her baby a safe journey. 'Wear this as a protective spirit against evil,' I wrote. The next morning, she and Pali were gone. They'd slipped away under the cover of darkness. I never saw them again."

Tatyana sighed with regret, "And that—was that."

Jonathan lifted his chin and looked into Tatyana's eyes. "I can't tell you how wonderful it is to have a living connection to my parents. Thank you. But you also spoke of my grandfather? Did you know him, as well?"

"Oh yes. But only from stories. He is well-known by all Gypsies. Tales of 'The Black Dog' are often told around our campfires."

At the mention of that name, Isha's eyes lit up. Her voice rose, "'The Black Dog.' You're saying Jonathan's grandfather was…" She bit her lower lip. "But that would mean…!" Her eyes darted to Jonathan. "Yes, that does explain a lot."

Tatyana turned to Isha and said in a quiet voice. "And, now, you are putting the puzzle together."

Then she faced Jonathan with a warm smile. "The stories about your grandfather may explain some of those genes your doctor friend spoke of. Your grandfather was a hero of the resistance mounted against the Nazis during World War II. Due to his bravery, thousands of Jews and hundreds of Gypsies were saved. Many, like myself, owe their lives to him."

Isha beamed. "Oh, Tatyana, please tell Jonathan about him. I could listen to the stories of his heroism anytime."

As Tatyana gathered herself, she looked from Jonathan to Isha and her lips became a thin line. When she resumed her narrative, her voice sounded clenched, trying to keep her emotions under wrap.

"Let's go back to World War II. When my father, Gregor, was eight years old, he became one of the many captives placed in a Nazi relocation center near Warsaw to be sent to the Auschwitz concentration camp for extermination. The day before, he had stood helplessly as his father and mother, my grandfather and grandmother, were burned alive in their Vardo. That night was the first time he saw Nicolae. At first, he was frightened because the Black Dog wore a Nazi uniform. He had put it on to gain access to the camp and free the fifty prisoners held there. When they reached a clearing in the forest and Nicolai changed into a leather flight jacket, my father saw just how imposing he was. Although he was not yet 18, he stood tall and commanding, surrounded by other partisans on horseback. According to my father, he looked like an otherworldly hero, a god among men."

His voice was surprisingly powerful as he addressed the survivors, 'You are free now and no longer have to live in fear. Join me or go your own way. It is your choice.'

Most, including my father, decided to join the Black Dog.

Tatyana's face took on a special glow as she told Jonathan, "Your grandfather saved my father, as well as thousands of others who would have been tortured and executed by Hitler's death squads. That is why I owe him my life. That is why I was so moved and awe-struck when I saw your mother in our camp that night. I only wish I'd had the courage to thank her for all her father had done."

Mesmerized by her story, Jonathan reached across the table and grasped Tatyana's hand. "But you did," he said fervidly. "You gave her the frankincense. It is the only memory I have of her. I thank you for that blessing." Eager to hear more, he asked, "Is there anything else you can tell me about my grandfather?"

Tatyana hesitated before continuing. "After the war ended, he continued to hunt and expose Nazis who escaped and went into hiding or came to America. "Your father thought he went to South America, perhaps Argentina or Brazil or Paraguay, to continue his pursuit of Nazi criminals who had settled there."

Just then, Tatyana's cell phone came to life. The ringtone was loud and penetrating, startling all of them. Tatyana looked at the screen in puzzlement. She almost silenced the call but thought better of it. "Let me take this," she said as she stood. "It's from Orlando…a friend."

She accepted the call, listened, and gasped. "My god," she exclaimed. "Where?" The color drained from her face. Finally, she whispered, "Yes…yes, I will…you too."

After she ended the call, she turned to Jonathan and Isha in shock. "It's Mosthan. He's been murdered."

"What!?" Jonathan jumped up. "What happened?"

Isha got up, too. But Tatyana waved them back. By the time she returned to them, she had herself back under control. Still, her voice betrayed a sense of urgency. "One of our people found his body at his shop. He was tortured before being shot and killed.

There were burn marks all over his body. Each of his fingers was cut off at the knuckle."

"But, but, why?" Isha stammered. "He was such a peace-loving man."

Tatyana sighed heavily. "I hoped to have this conversation later, but we have no time left. It is a matter of life and death—yours, mine, and possibly our whole tribe." She faced Jonathan, and her voice took on an urgent tone. "Whoever killed Motshan is searching for you. When Motshan was found, his hands had bled on an old manual of lithographs, its pages open to the golden brooch of Vlad Dracul. You are being hunted by the same evil men who belong to the organization that murdered your mother and father and tried their best to kill your grandfather. Now they seek you, his sole male descendant. I don't know the details of their plans, but they want to neutralize you one way or another."

Jonathan drew back and felt Isha tense beside him. "I don't understand," he said.

Tatyana spoke like an oracle, her voice disembodied, yet resonant. "A war between good and evil has been raging since the dawn of time. Your family became deeply entangled in it when your ancestor, Vlad Dracul, embraced the forces of night. His murderous schemes ended when another ancestor of yours, Lucien, beheaded Vlad's son Dracula, the Prince of Evil. They were half-brothers. But the battle has continued. And now you have been chosen to confront that enemy on behalf of the forces of light. That is your fate."

Jonathan shook his head in disbelief. "But you advised me to seek my true path. Now you present me with a purpose like I have no choice."

"Both paths are the same. Until now, you have lived so out of touch with your true nature it is hard for you to understand. But make no mistake, that way of life is over. Motshan's murderer will not stop.

The one who sent him will not stop until you settle it. Ignoring your destiny will have dire consequences for those you hold dear."

Jonathan got up and started to pace around the table. "Why can't I just live a normal life?" he complained. "I have no axe to grind with anyone. Why can't I refuse and let someone else do it?"

Tatyana responded with compassion, "No matter how reluctant you are or how much you try to hide from it, your fate will seek you out. Remember the prophecy of Aleandro?—He has promised us in a time of need and in our quest for purity, the gift of his seed, The Zor-Tracheban."

"But, The Zor-Tracheban is only a children's bedtime legend."

"Yes, the legend of The Zor-Tracheban is just that, stories told at fireside gatherings: some exaggerated, some sheer fantasy, but all with a kernel of truth. The fact remains you were born for a purpose, to stand as a beacon of light against the forces of darkness. And, make no mistake about it, they are on the rise. They are here."

Jonathan lowered his head and sighed. A heavy silence hung between them.

"I understand it is a great deal for you to take on," Tatyana said, smiling gently. "But surely you can't deny your gifts, DNA passed down through your bloodline, as Dr. Wade tried to tell you. From your Viking forefathers, you have inherited strength and power; from Vlad, a superior intellect, wisdom, and mastery of war and politics; from Aleandro Kalderasha, cunning and wit; and from your Gypsy ancestry, the gift of intuition, foretelling, and a relationship with the spirit world."

Jonathan stood spellbound. As if in a trance, he muttered, "All those weird visions…"

"Yes, they are there for your guidance. All of them; Vasilissa, Vlad, Lucien, Breshan, Aleandro, and many others."

"What about my mother and father?"

"Yes, them, too," Tatyana confirmed. "Especially your mother."

"My grandfather?"

"No, he is not among them."

"But, then, that would mean, he is..."

"Yes. He is present in the physical world."

Jonathan shook his head as if trying to ward off the onslaught of troubling information. Then he confronted her, "What did you mean by 'Especially your mother'?"

Tatyana gazed intently into his eyes. "Your mother had the gift of foretelling. She knew you would be born with the mind of a skeptic and require concrete proof before making decisions. But, as there is no time for debate, I give you this!"

Without warning, Tatyana reached out, gripped his hands, and placed them on the table, covering them with her own. Her eyes rolled back into her head revealing only the whites, and her voice took on an eerie resonance. "So that you will have your proof, your mother left you with a physical sign of this reality...your mother's sign, Jonathan."

Instinctively, he pulled back, but her fingers held him like a steel vise. "Trust in yourself, Jonathan. Trust in your feelings, not just your mind," she said.

Those were the last words Jonathan heard, because her body appeared to dissipate into a million particles of ash before his eyes. He was transported to a place he had not been before, yet it felt tangibly real. He was standing alone on a remote road covered in white sea shells. A bright Florida sun burned down onto a lush jungle of live oaks, dry palmetto, sable palm, and dense shrubbery.

Jonathan sensed that an urgent decision of life or death confronted him. Time was of the essence. What to do?

Guided by a premonition, he looked up. A cluster of cumulus clouds billowed in the distance, rising quickly to form an angry thunderhead that reached into the stratosphere. The clouds turned dark and pulsed with heat and energy. Jonathan could hear a rumbling growing with them, as electrical tendrils danced about their bellies. A bolt of lightning struck the ground nearby.

With the clap of thunder rolling in the sky, Jonathan knew his question had been answered and found himself back at the table. Isha and Tatyana eyed him with concern.

"I'm all right," he said firmly, as much to convince and reassure himself as them.

* * *

After the ride home to his apartment, Jonathan hardly slept. He tossed and turned in bed until morning. Motshan's murder, Tatyana's prophecy, his DNA results, and his ambiguous vision became a maelstrom of troubled thoughts, emotions, and unanswerable questions in his mind: Who is after me? How was it possible that my genes link me to the Zor-Tracheban? Why me? True, he had often fantasized about heroic deeds as a physician—saving lives by making unexpected diagnoses, and discovering a cure for various illnesses. But a hero with physical superpowers in an apocalyptic battle of good and evil, a savior of an entire people? It beggared belief!

Another thought kept gnawing at him. If the mystical inheritance from his ancestors was possible—and it was hard for him to doubt the scientific evidence—did he possess the negative qualities of Vlad, too? He thought about his irrational outbursts when he acted seemingly out of control. True, it had been against bullies and thugs to protect the vulnerable, but could he cause pain and damage to those he loved as well?

The next day, his morning shift at the hospital ER and afternoon appointments at the clinic brought no relief. Fortunately, none of the cases required special attention and Jonathan performed his tasks on autopilot without rousing suspicion among his patients, colleagues, and nurses.

He thought about calling Jimmy and getting his perspective but quickly rejected the idea. He could not imagine his friend being any less flummoxed than he was and needed more than his good-natured sarcasm and skepticism.

There was something even more pressing, something he had to disclose to Isha. Jonathan thought about inviting her for dinner. Then he had a better idea. Since he had the next day off, he would take her out on his boat. A leisurely day in the sun would do them both good. They needed private, undisturbed time together, away from the mounting chaos. He would call her when he got home.

A feeling of relief swept over him. He could handle this. Together, they would find a way forward.

* * *

Yuri smiled grimly as he listened in on Jonathan's phone call. Although the wiretap allowed him to hear only the doctor's side of the conversation, it generated a feeling of satisfaction in his gut. Yes, word had come from Orlando about Motshan's death, which meant that the Gypsies would beef up security at the camp and become more careful on their outings. But then Jonathan had invited his Gypsy girlfriend to meet him the next morning at the Anclote Marina for a day of boating to "just get away," and his excited exclamation "Great!" had made it clear she accepted.

Sitting in his car, Yuri rejoiced. This was what he had been waiting for. Tracking and tailing Jonathan on his motorcycle had not produced suitable possibilities for capturing him. Traffic had been too busy, and at the hospital ER and the Gypsy camp, the doctor had been surrounded by too many witnesses. Yuri had considered breaking into the apartment and subduing Jonathan while he was asleep, but the boat was a much better location—isolated and secluded. Besides, taking the doctor while he was with his attractive girlfriend provided a bonus: the ability to satisfy Yuri's sadistic desires.

As he drove off, he made his plan. It would require the assistance of another military-trained combatant, and Stryker from Colonel Burdock's compound was just the man. A slight bending of the Wizard's orders, of course, but it would be easier to beg for forgiveness than ask for permission. With the successful completion of the mission, any sensible man would agree that the end had justified the means.

Chapter 25

THE ISLAND PRINCESS

With a light thrust of her engines, the *Island Princess* made her way to open water through the narrow channel of Anclote Harbor. Jonathan stood at the helm. At the sea wall, shrimp boats were moored after delivering their nighttime haul to the warehouses. The early morning sun cast long shadows from their masts and bounced blinding rainbow reflections off the Princess' windshield. He squinted through the harsh glare to check the channel markers on either side of the boat.

As he stole a glance at Isha next to him, their eyes locked for a moment. Then, they looked away and returned to their separate thoughts.

The news of Pinky's assault and Motshan's murder had quickly spread throughout Gypsy camps in Florida from Miami to Tallahassee. Reigniting an old fear, it had fueled a paranoia many thought they'd left behind during their exodus from Europe to America—that they were the targets of hate crimes and oppression. Big Jack had put his tribe on high alert and hired a team of professional bodyguards that had arrived this morning. He even considered moving his group to North Carolina, but Tatyana had cautioned him against it, and he had heeded her advice to wait until the danger passed.

Jonathan and Isha had left with their blessing, eager to escape the chaos for a day on the water. Still, before they launched that morning, Isha had urged, "Please take Tatyana's prophecy seriously. Maybe we should have a bodyguard go with us."

While Jonathan was troubled by the recent events, he tried to calm Isha. "I understand your concerns," he said. "But let's take this boat ride together alone. I miss being with you like crazy."

Isha had yielded to his wishes but continued to feel apprehensive.

Just outside the No-Wake zone, Jonathan checked the GPS co-ordinates again. Then, he spun the wheel to the left and gunned the powerful twin outboard motors. The Island Princess surged forward. With her bow piercing the swells, the soft lapping of water against her hull turned to a thrashing spray, and the mellow purring of her engines morphed into a roaring mechanical growl, precluding any conversation.

They rode in silence until they reached their destination, a coral reef forty feet below the surface of the emerald sea. As Jonathan cut the engines, the boat started to slow and drift in the gentle breeze. He made his way to the bow and set anchor. The Island Princess swung to rest with a jerk, disturbing a flock of seagulls. For a moment, he watched the birds take flight circling in the sky. Then he returned to the cockpit.

Isha still looked worried. "What's to become of us, Jonathan?" she asked plaintively.

"By us, do you mean you and me?"

"No, I mean us…the Gypsies. I thought we left the bigots and haters behind us." Her eyes searched his face. "More than anything, I'm worried about you and Tatyana's prophecy that you are destined to be pitted against their evil."

Jonathan nodded and gave Isha a confident smile. "Quit your worrying about me. I can take care of myself. I know I'm in a war I didn't sign up for. Yet here I am. And I've realized that it's exactly where I want to be. Because I want to protect you. Because…." He placed his palms on her shoulders, his eyes glistening.

Isha's face flushed, her heart beating wildly in her chest. "Yes?" she whispered softly

Jonathan blurted out, "Because I've fallen in love with you, Isha."

A tear ran down her cheek. She grasped his hand, "Oh my Darling, you can't know how much I was hoping to hear those words.... I love you, too."

Jonathan leaned in. His lips met Isha's for a tender kiss. Amid soft murmurings, they exchanged loving hugs and touched each other gently. Jonathan caressed her hair. Isha brushed her lips against his neck.

The growing tension of their intertwined bodies moving together soon aroused more sensual feelings. Jonathan scooped Isha off her feet, cradled her in his arms, and carried her to the bow, where the seat cushions were spread out like a king-sized bed.

Their love-making was slow and affectionate, fulfilling their mutual desires. Afterward, Isha lay in quiet reflection, her body aglow. The breeze cooled the perspiration on her upper lip and chest.

Jonathan cuddled beside her and whispered, "I love you."

The words meant everything to Isha. For the first time, she was ready to give herself to a man, heart, body, and soul. "I love you too," she murmured as she snuggled closer.

Jonathan smiled and kissed her forehead. Then, he drifted off into sleep. Isha lay awake for the next thirty minutes, twisting the curls of his thick Gypsy hair and caressing his chest before pulling a large beach towel over them both and falling asleep herself.

When she awoke, the sun was higher overhead. She yawned, stretched out her arms, and rolled onto her belly. To her surprise, Jonathan stood on deck dressed in his neoprene wetsuit. His jet-black hair glistened in the bright light.

Jonathan raised his head and caught the glint of sunlight reflecting off Isha's charm bracelet. "Hey Sunshine, welcome back to the world," he said, grinning. "I didn't want to wake you. So, I decided to go down for a dip below and rustle us up something to eat." He pulled a scuba tank over his shoulders and took a couple of deep breaths through the regulator to clear his mouthpiece.

Isha pursed her lips and purred, "Okay, you go diving. But, hurry back; I miss you already." Smiling, she hugged her arms around a towel and flipped to her back. With her head suspended over the cushions, she teased Jonathan with her flawless breasts, her nipples erect from the soft sea breeze, and her black hair streaming around her face.

"I like the way you think—and look. So, hold that thought," he said, sitting on the gunnel and putting on his dive fins. Then he pulled a mask over his face and flipped backward, head-first into the water.

Isha sensed a flicker in the sunlight, which caused her to look up. Squinting, she saw something hovering high above like a seagull coasting on the wind currents. It must have momentarily blocked her view of the sun. "Not unusual for seabirds to be this far from shore," she thought. When she looked again, it had disappeared.

* * *

Two miles away in a yellow 35-foot Donzi, Lt. Vince Stryker put down the Cam Drone that had returned to his hands. He and Yuri Zuroff had used it to observe the *Island Princess*. When they saw Jonathan in scuba gear dive into the water and Isha look up, they pulled the drone back.

"Now is our best chance," Yuri said. "While the doctor is underwater, we go capture the Gypsy girl. Then we wait for him to come back up. With her as our prisoner, he will do whatever we ask."

"But what if she suspects something's up before we take her?" Stryker asked.

Yuri scoffed. "We'll tell her we're lost because our GPS went out and then ask for directions." He grinned. "Better yet, you ask her. That way she won't get suspicious because of my accent. You keep her occupied and when you bring the boat close, I'll leap across and subdue her."

Stryker scratched his head. So far, none of their efforts regarding Jonathan and the Gypsies had gone without a hitch. Still, it was as good a plan as any, so he said, "Tracking," using the military term for acknowledgment. He stashed the drone out of sight and took the helm. The engine roared to life, and the Donzi sped toward the *Island Princess*.

* * *

Below the water surface, Jonathan was in a state of euphoria; his fantasy of a life with Isha had become a reality. As cool undersea currents rippled past his face and hands, the sunlight created swirling patterns along the crystal-white sand. Jonathan twisted in a bath of bubbles, lay belly flat against the sand, and slid his spear gun under the ledge of a low-hanging coral shelf. He tried to clear his head. He would need to focus or he would return to Isha empty-handed.

Overhead, Jonathan heard the high-pitched blare of boat propellers approaching. It surprised him. Few divers knew the coordinates of this reef. It had to be Jimmy or another of his friends. He relaxed even though the whirling sound soon came from directly above him, and he could make out another boat pulling alongside the Island Princess.

Unexpectedly, he felt more than heard a whisper inside him, "*Save her.*"

It reminded him of the voices he sometimes heard before falling asleep, and he shook his head. But the voice repeated, this time more insistently, "*Save her!*"

Jonathan looked up again and felt jolted by an electric shock. The boat next to the *Island Princess* had the deep V-hull of an offshore racing craft. All his friends owned fishing and diving boats! The muscles of his neck and back tightened. Something was wrong.

He began to surface. Halfway up, he shrugged off his oxygen tank and tied it to the anchor line, allowing the regulator to flow freely, sending bubbles to the surface. Then, he swam to the stern of his boat and emerged to take a surreptitious look at what was happening.

A Donzi was bobbing near the *Island Princess*. Jonathan swam to the rear of the new boat and, carefully raising his head between the outboard motors, peered over the transom. A man was leaning over the gunwale near the bow, looking at the bubbles from his decoy scuba tank. He was muscular and had a machine gun by his side. "It should not be long now," He muttered with a foreign accent.

Another man, dressed in combat fatigues and holding a rifle, stood in the cockpit, guarding Isha. She sat slumped with her back against the helm. Her hands were bound with rope and her mouth was covered with duct tape. A trickle of blood ran from her hair down her temple. It looked like she'd been knocked unconscious. A surge of fury coursed through Jonathan.

Just then, Isha stirred.

"She's coming to, Yuri," the man called out.

In that instant, it became clear that Isha had been awake and only pretended to be out for the count. She sank her fingernails into the man's calf, tearing flesh like a wild animal and drawing blood.

Surprised, the man yelped in pain, then growled, "Feisty Bitch!" and shoved his foot forcibly into her abdomen.

Isha winced but held on to his leg, digging her fingernails deeper into his flesh.

The man grimaced. He raised his gun overhead to strike a blow to her head again, but before he could bring the butt down, there was a loud snap followed by a thud as the long shaft of a steel-pointed spear hit his chest. He looked down at himself with a macabre look of horror, took an unsteady step backward, and fell overboard.

Startled, Yuri glanced in the direction of the splash. "Stryker, what the...?" he called out. Then his body recoiled in recognition of trouble. Immediately, he crouched and his eyes darted toward the rear of the boat.

Jonathan ducked just in time as the man fired several short blasts from his machine gun in his direction.

"Fuck you, Curtis," he bellowed.

Taken aback that the man called him by name, Jonathan realized that this was not just a random act of piracy but a deliberate assault aimed at him. He reared out of the water and flung his scuba knife. The missile sped dead-center toward Yuri's heart but deflected off the rifle's handguard and barely nicked his hand before skittering across the deck.

Yuri aimed an ear-piercing barrage toward the rear of the outboards until his machine gun clicked on empty. As he quickly reloaded, the air became deathly silent. Then, noting suspicious ripples, he discharged another clip toward the *Island Princess*, strafing the boat from stern to bow.

Jonathan dove under the keel of his boat to escape the barrage. Surfacing on the other side, he saw that Yuri was aiming high. The goon didn't want to kill him. But without a weapon, Jonathan was defenseless and vulnerable. Scanning the horizon, he saw small crafts and formed an idea.

"Hey asshole," he called out. "See the boats to starboard. They'll alert the coastguard for sure. What are you going to do then?"

He was gratified to hear "Crap!" coming from the Donzi. The man had seen them, too.

But then he heard him shout, "I've got an ace in the hole here—your girlfriend."

When Jonathan peeked around the boat's edge, his heart skipped a beat. Yuri was holding Isha up with a knife to her throat. He planted a kiss on her cheek and shouted, "I know you're listening, so here are my terms. You come to my camp—alone—and we fight this out man-to-man. If you win, I'll let your girlfriend live. If you don't show, I'll make her my whore before I slit her throat."

For good measure, Yuri licked Isha's cheek, then threw her to the wooden floor.

Jonathan winced when she landed with a thud and moaned. Enraged, he yelled, "If you harm her, you're a dead man."

Yuri laughed and answered, "I'll be at The Crystal River Hunt Club, across the river from the old nuclear power plant. You're a clever guy. You'll figure out how to find it."

He fired up the Donzi and pushed the throttle. The boat shot forward with a roar, its wake rocking the Island Princess. He didn't look back.

Watching the Donzi depart, Jonathan's mind raced as he tried to put the pieces of the puzzle together. The man he'd killed had called the kidnapper Yuri, who had a distinctly Russian accent. Pinky had mentioned hearing a Russian voice from his assailant. Probably the same guy. Maybe he'd tortured and killed Mosthan. But why?

He pulled himself from the dive platform to the deck of the *Island Princess*. Crystal River was about 40 miles up the coast. He didn't know exactly where The Crystal River Hunt Club was located, but he'd find it.

Jonathan grimaced, as he attempted to push from his mind any images of what the Russian might do to Isha if he could not find her in time. He assessed the damage. The *Island Princess* was listing slightly to starboard. Thankfully, most of the bullet holes were above the water line, and he could hear the grinding valves of her bilge pump still operating.

When he pressed the ignition, the left Mercury engine fired up immediately. But the right motor, which had been in the direct line of fire, remained silent. "Two engines will get me there quicker,"

Jonathan thought, as he pushed the ignition of the right engine again. This time it turned over but stopped after only one revolution. Fortunately, with a third try, the injured motor sputtered puffs of blue smoke into the air but came to life.

Jonathan engaged the props and slowly increased RPM as the *Island Princess* inched forward. Slowly and steadily, she gained speed and the automatic bailing system began to pump the remaining water from her hull. Jonathan uttered a prayer of thanks and gunned the engines. When the motors responded, he turned the rudder toward Tarpon Springs.

Chapter 26

BLOODSPORT

Jonathan barely took time to tie up his boat at the docks of the Anclote Harbor Marina before he dashed to his motorcycle. His Harley sprayed a cloud of rocks and shells as he roared onto Route 19 and raced north to Crystal River. Speeding up the divided highway at 90 miles per hour, he paid little regard to the stop signs or red lights he encountered at the entrances of the retirement communities along the way. Fortunately, traffic was light and he could weave back and forth past other vehicles on the road.

Laser focused on rescuing Isha, he reviewed his options. Alerting the authorities did not seem like a good idea, considering his encounter with the local police after Pinky's ambush. Calling on Big Jack's bodyguards for help was a better choice, but they would take too long to join him. He would have to take on the Russian, and whatever backup he had, on his own and then improvise.

As the highway became more deserted, he called Jimmy on his cell phone. When his friend didn't pick up, he left a voicemail about what had happened. "Don't contact anyone, especially not the police, for the next three hours," Jonathan insisted. "If you haven't heard from me by then, send them to the Crystal River Hunt Club, but under no circumstances before. I trust you on this!" As an afterthought, he added, "If I make it out alive, I'll need to go into hiding. So, wish me luck. If I'm missing, don't worry."

Normally, the trip from Tarpon Springs to Crystal River took an hour, but Jonathan made it in less than half that time. He had been there many times with friends on scuba diving trips and was familiar with the river area.

He continued north until he came to West Power Line Street. Taking a hard left, he raced west along the railroad track until he saw the twin stacks of the nuclear power plant up ahead.

With his Harley at full throttle, the branches of trees lining the narrow road rushed past his face and felt like a windstorm. Through the thick forest, Jonathan looked for clues as to the whereabouts of The Hunt Club. Towering dark thunderclouds reached into the sky above, lightning crisscrossing their underbellies like the threads of a spiderweb. Suddenly, a searing lightning bolt flashed from one of the thunderheads and struck the ground deep in the forest to his right, followed by a deafening thunderclap. The scene was so similar to the vision at Tatyana's Vardo that the hairs on his neck stood on end.

Unnerved, he slowed and glanced in the direction of the lightning strike. He realized he had just raced past a narrow, sandy road whose entrance was partially hidden from view in the dense Florida jungle. Slamming on the brakes, he made a U-turn and headed down the path.

It looked like the right place. Tread marks of 4-wheel drive vehicles crisscrossed the white shell path. Soon after entering the thick forest, Jonathan saw bright red signs nailed to the Australian Pines and Live Oak trees: "No Trespassing" and "Beware! High-powered rifles."

Motoring along cautiously, he reached a tall entranceway, with a weathered sign hanging overhead that read "Crystal River Hunt Club." The wire mesh-covered gate stood wide open as if in invitation. A 10-foot high, chain-link fence topped with razor wire extended into the woods to either side. Jonathan ditched his motorcycle on the side of the road and proceeded on foot. The thick jungle continued for a while. As it widened, he saw buildings ahead and ducked into the forest, moving carefully from tree to tree.

A musty smell of decay and humidity surrounded him. Scratching an insect bite, he realized that his white tee shirt and yellow swim trunks lit up like a searchlight. He removed the shirt and smeared sand and mud over his skin and shorts. Then, he continued to sneak forward, parallel to the shell path.

Ahead, he could see a small cluster of one-story houses through the gaps in the trees. Covered with wooden shingles, they looked like old Florida fish camp cottages built on raised timbers, with porches and overhanging metal roofs. Moving closer, he noticed a tall barn-like structure made from concrete blocks. Streaming from one of the windows, he heard what sounded like country music playing on the radio. Otherwise, the place looked abandoned.

There was a heavy thud behind him. He had just enough time to turn and see a soldier in battle fatigues before he felt the sting of a taser high on his back. Instantly, his body seized.

His muscles went limp and he crashed to the ground. Lying there helplessly, he made out a grinning face above his head. As he tried to rise, a sharp blow struck him across his temple and the world went black.

* * *

When Jonathan came to, he felt groggy. A painful pulse stabbed in his right temple and a dull ache throbbed deep in his brain. Keeping his eyes closed, he became aware of obscure sounds and the stench of human sweat permeating the air. He kept quiet, with his head slumped to his chest. He wished he knew how much time had passed.

"Wake him up," a gruff voice barked, penetrating his consciousness.

Immediately, Jonathan felt a splash of water hit his face. He flinched and opened his eyes. Blinking, he looked around and realized he was inside the large barn. It appeared to be a workout gym, with a large, woven cane mat on the concrete floor before him. The windows were shuttered and overhead light illuminated the interior. Three young men stood awkwardly near him. They wore army fatigues and combat boots, with sidearms holstered at their hip.

In the haze of Jonathan's vision, a muscled figure came into focus, arms folded across his chest. It was the man from the boat who had kidnapped Isha. Anger surged through him. The ache in his head gripped him like a vicious vise.

The man chuckled. "Glad you're with us again, Dr. Curtis," he taunted. "We've been monitoring your arrival since you turned off the road. Florescent yellow swim trunks and crawling on the ground like a crab covered in mud. You made quite an entrance!"

"Where is Isha?" Jonathan said. His voice sounded raspy and guttural.

"Your Gypsy whore?" the man mocked. "She is quite a handful. I can't wait to tame her."

Jonathan reared up but found himself bound hand and foot to a metal chair with duct tape. "If you've done anything to her, I'll –"

"Allow me to introduce myself," the man said. "My name is Captain Yuri Zuroff. I am here on behalf of someone eager to make your acquaintance. Too bad he's overseas. We'll have to ship you there."

Jonathan looked at him bewildered. "I want to see Isha."

Yuri sighed. "Very well. Bring her," he ordered, then moved to a table and retrieved a cigarette from a pack. He lit up and leaned casually against a wall made of knotty pine, glancing at Jonathan like a jackal sizing up its prey before the kill.

The back door burst open, and two more young men entered with Isha. She wore a camo T-shirt over her black bikini. Her arms were bound behind her back and her mouth was covered with duct tape. Her beautiful hair was matted with blood. There was a bruise on her cheek.

When she saw Jonathan, she let out a muffled cry and jerked against the taller soldier. Her guard tightened his grip on her shoulder. Isha raised a leg and stamped her heels hard on the arch of his right foot.

This time, he flinched. Lifting her off the floor, he pressed a knife hard against her throat. As she went still, he shoved her roughly onto a metal chair and tied her legs to it with a piece of rope.

Yuri moved like a slithering snake to Isha's side and, in one quick motion, ripped the tape from her mouth.

Isha winced in pain, gasped for breath, and cried out, "Jonathan!"

Flexing his muscles against the duct tape shackles Jonathan shook his head wildly. His metal chair banged like a jackhammer against the concrete floor.

Yuri chuckled and sauntered to the middle of the room. "Well, now we're all here," he said haughtily.

Jonathan gritted his teeth and growled, "You'll never get away with this. I have friends. Isha has family. They'll be looking for us. People know who you are. If you hurt either of us, you'll spend the rest of your life behind bars." He took a deep breath. "At least let Isha go."

Yuri slapped his thighs and laughed uproariously. "Let the girl go? I'll never get away with it?" Then he turned serious. "Let me point something out to you, Doctor. You don't understand who's in charge here. You're the one that's tied to a chair. Besides, this is all your fault. You're the one who dragged your girlfriend into it." He leered at Isha. "A pity, too. I'd love to keep her around."

Jonathan's body erupted into violent motion, straining against the aluminum chair until it shook violently and skidded across the finished floor with an erratic screech.

As he stopped, one of the men mumbled to the young recruit next to him, loud enough for everyone to hear," Colonel Burdock will have all our asses when he finds out about this."

Jonathan was shocked. This was Frank Burdock's outfit? That's why some of the men looked familiar. They had run him off the road and attacked him—no doubt on Burdock's order. The Colonel may travel in elite, racist circles and have no integrity. Still, he would not want his hands dirtied. Aloud Jonathan said, "I'm sure Colonel Burdock would not agree with what you're doing here."

"Burdock?" Yuri said, irritated. "He'll fall in line. This order comes from the top, way above his pay grade."

The soft voice Jonathan had heard earlier, when under water, whispered to him, "*Provoke him!*"

Without thinking, he growled in perfect Russian slang, "Fuck you, too, Asshole," adding, "*Brave warrior you are, in front of a helpless man, wearing a gun and knife strapped to your hip. If I had my hands free, I'd kick your ass.*"

Taken aback, Yuri narrowed his eyes and replied in Russian, "*Well, that is unexpected.*" A smile spread over his face as he unbuckled his sidearm and put it on the table. "*Better? I wouldn't want this to be an unfair fight.*"

Turning to his men, he snapped, "Untie him." When they hesitated, exchanging uneasy glances, he barked again, "Untie him, I said!"

As Yuri pulled the camouflage shirt over his head, revealing his chiseled torso, he warned, "And, just in case you have any notion of running, Doctor, let me point out that there are only two doors out of here, both bolted. My men are armed, and you'll end up with a bullet in both legs." He moved to the center of the mat, cracking his neck and back with a stretch to either side. A cocky grin crossed his face as he took a relaxed stance and motioned Jonathan to approach. "Now, come on, Doctor. Let's see what you've got."

Jonathan remained still as he sized up his adversary with a sinking feeling. Yuri's muscular frame and battle scars attested to years of fighting in mortal combat and winning. His hands appeared like weapons of tempered steel. Whatever confidence Jonathan felt before melted away. But then the strange voice whispered to him again, "*Attack him!*"

Jonathan shook his head. Bolstered by the mysterious murmur, he loped across the mat and leaped to tackle Yuri. But before he could make contact, Yuri turned sideways and thrust a spear hand to Jonathan's throat, while landing a roundhouse kick to his torso.

The thrust only nudged Jonathan, but the heavy Army boot caught him squarely on the thigh. He spun horizontally in a disorienting gyration and landed on the concrete floor with a thud. Skidding over the finished surface, he slammed against the wall. With the breath knocked from his lungs, he lay against the baseboard, clutching at his throat and gasping for air.

Yuri released a deep belly laugh. Then he moved toward Isha, strutting like a cock of the walk and gloating. "Now you see who the real man is here?"

Isha glared at him with burning hatred and shouted, "Fuck you, Asshole." Then she drove her head back into the groin of the young man standing behind her, causing him to double over and expel a short burst of air. Straightening, his face clenched in pain, he put the knife back against her throat.

Witnessing her courage gave Jonathan the boost he needed. Gritting his teeth, he rose, first onto all fours, and then to his knees. Recovering his foothold, he kneaded his bruised thigh. Then he hurled himself across the mat to take another swipe at Yuri. But just as he reached him, Yuri dipped low and rolled hard into his legs. As Jonathan tripped over him and flew through the air, Yuri rose and slammed a fist into his kidney.

With an agonized groan, Jonathan skidded to the other side of the mat. Pain radiated throughout his body, and he lay on the floor as if paralyzed. Normally, such a blow from the Russian would have knocked out any battle-tested combatant for good. But an intense shock shot through Jonathan's temple as he struggled to regain his footing.

Yuri stood still and appraised his opponent again, more puzzled than surprised.

The incandescent lights strung along the rafters flickered. A bolt of lightning struck close by, followed by an ear-splitting clap of thunder. The walls of the barn shook like an earthquake.

Even Yuri jumped, startled, and glanced around the room. The others looked stunned and dumbfounded. Shrugging dismissively, he turned around and looked to see his opponent standing upright, as if nothing had happened.

Jonathan felt as if he were under a spell. Power surged through every muscle in his body. The air seemed to congeal around his opponent and time slowed. He observed Yuri more closely, evaluating him as a physician examining a patient. The scars on his body told of many traumatic injuries. His right knee edged slightly inward. "A medial collateral ligament repair," Jonathan supposed, "possibly a torn meniscus." The surgical scar over Yuri's left shoulder suggested the repair of a rotator cuff tear. His right arm hung lower from the clavicle than his left, which suggested an A.C. joint separation.

From orthopedic rotation during his residency, Jonathan knew that with such injuries joints never fully recover when they heal. Given the right blunt force trauma, they were subject to re-injury.

Gathering energy, he sprang across the mat again, this time outside Yuri's reach. With his long arm, he grabbed Yuri's foot. Although he managed to knock his adversary off balance, it was not enough. Yuri quickly countered by twisting cat-like in mid-air and came down hard, smashing his elbow into Jonathan's rib cage.

Jonathan grimaced with pain but held onto Yuri's ankle and yanked it sharply to the side. A loud crack echoed around the room. For a moment, Yuri faltered and reached down to check out the stability of his right knee.

It was just the time Jonathan needed. Rolling away, he sprang up and delivered a two-fisted blow to Yuri's right shoulder, feeling the crunch of cartilage under his hands.

The Russian winced and responded with an angry growl. Then he lunged at Jonathan with a flurry of martial arts moves, kicks, and punches delivered to the ribs, kidneys, and solar plexus.

As at the Gypsy camp battle, Jonathan saw them coming at him in slow motion while he responded with normal speed. He had plenty of time to read the subtle clues that broadcast his opponent's intentions. The muscles of Yuri's neck flexed a fraction of a second before he threw a punch; his abdominal obliques tightened an instant before he kicked. Anticipating and parrying or avoiding the attacks became easy for Jonathan. The blows that did reach him glanced off ineffectually.

Frustrated, Yuri started to swing wildly and take greater risks, giving Jonathan an opening. He slammed his open hand directly into Yuri's collarbone with a crushing blow.

Yuri bellowed in pain. This time he was hurt. The confident smirk vanished from his face, replaced by a grimace of crazed fury. He jumped forward, trying to throttle Jonathan in a bear hug. As they tumbled to the floor, he landed on top and tried to apply a choke hold. But Jonathan flexed his body and threw Yuri over his head. The Russian wheeled back quickly to grab Jonathan's head again.

He never got that chance. Jonathan grasped his arm and stood. Pinning Yuri's shoulder to the mat, he brought the weight of his body to bear and slammed into his opponent's back. Another brutal crack and what little remained of the ligament in Yuri's rotator cuff collapsed.

Yuri groaned, then screamed, "Get him off of me. Get him off me!"

Within seconds, the others came running to his rescue. The young man to Jonathan's right took a swipe at his head with a pistol. But, in a lightning-fast move, Jonathan repelled the attack with his arm, punched the man in the face, and swept his legs from under him. The gun spiraled to the floor.

As Jonathan stood to lunge at Yuri, he felt two stings in his naked back—the electric shock of the taser barbs. But this time, with all the adrenaline pumping through his body, they barely registered. The other two men threw themselves at Jonathan and tried to force him back down. As they took hold of him, he yanked up his arms and tossed them both into the air. They hit the metal rafters with a thud, fell hard to the concrete floor, and lay still.

The distraction gave Yuri time to recover. He grabbed the knife from Isha's panic-stricken guard and laid it against her neck. Pulling her head back, he exposed her throat and dented her skin, drawing blood. With a maniacal grin, he yelled across the room to Jonathan, "One more step and your girlfriend dies."

However, Yuri had underestimated Isha. As the last word left his mouth, she flung her fist up through his forearm, grabbed the knife, and twisted it from his partially disabled hand. Then she drove its blade deep into the calf of his already injured leg.

Yuri roared in pain. The knife was buried to the hilt, its pointed tip protruding on the other side of his calf. Blood seeped from the wound, spreading out along the pants leg of his fatigues. As he fell to his knees, he looked dumbfounded at the ropes that had bound Isha's wrists lying on the floor under her chair.

Simultaneously, the large burly soldier who stood at guard dropped his arms to his side and crumpled to the floor unconscious.

As Isha bent forward to untie her legs, she sensed further danger. Looking up, she saw Jonathan coming to assist her, while his first attacker was getting up. "Jonathan, watch out!" she yelled.

Glancing over his shoulder, Jonathan locked eyes with the young man. He had reclaimed his pistol and was raising it to aim at Jonathan's head.

At that same moment, Yuri, with superhuman fury, pulled the knife from his leg and rose to his feet. "Go to Hell," he growled.

As he flung the knife at Jonathan, a loud blast from the pistol rang through the rafters.

But time slowed for Jonathan again. Calculating the trajectories of the bullet and the knife blade a fraction of a second before impact, he ducked his head and lifted his hand. The bullet passed by harmlessly, and the knife deflected into the shoulder of the shooter. The young man screamed and collapsed on the floor.

Yuri looked at Jonathan bewildered: What he had just witnessed was impossible. "What kind of man are you?" he stammered.

He didn't have time to utter anything else. With a running start, Jonathan planted a foot into Yuri's chest. The Russian staggered backward, crashed onto the concrete, and lay there motionless.

With her feet untied, Isha reached out. She stood, shaking, as Jonathan steadied her with his arms around her shoulders. Together, they hobbled to the front entrance of the dojo, past the prostrate bodies of their captors.

The metal door was mortared into concrete blocks and bolted with a steel lock. But Jonathan rammed it with his shoulder, bursting through the frame as easily as a tank taking down a barricade.

By then, Isha had recovered and wrapped her arms around Jonathan. He felt her body tremble, her breath against his chest. "We're going to be okay," he reassured her. "How did you manage to get free?"

Isha jangled her bracelet. "Those idiots never took it. They didn't realize that one of the charms has a razor-sharp blade. Another is a tranquilizer dart."

From inside the barn, he heard mutterings of the young men coming to. "It won't be long until they regroup and come after us," he said. "We'll have to find a way to escape."

As they rounded the corner of the building, a man on the porch of the next building beckoned them from behind a wooden pillar. When he stepped into the open, arms away from his body and palms empty, Jonathan recognized him. It was Liam, the tall, redheaded FBI agent, who had visited his office only a few days earlier. He was dressed in fatigues like the others.

Hurrying, Jonathan and Isha met him halfway between the buildings. "They told me to watch the monitors at the command center and warn them if anyone else is coming," he said quickly. "We have very little time. Burdock is on his way here." He pulled a set of keys from his shirt pocket and thrust them at Jonathan. "They disabled your motorbike, but you can take mine. It's the BMW parked on the other side of the building."

When Jonathan grasped the keys, Liam reached into his holster. "And you'll need a gun, just in case." He handed Jonathan his Glock and made a face. "Before you go, you'll have to knock me out, so I don't blow my cover. You still have my phone number?"

Jonathan nodded.

"Good. If you need to reach me, don't call; text me. Now go quickly. They'll be after you soon."

Jonathan took a deep breath and said, "Thank you."

Then, without warning, he punched Liam in the temple and watched him crumble to the ground.

Chapter 27

PURSUIT

Colonel Burdock drove his Jeep hard on the jungle road toward the compound. A phone call from Liam sounding nearly hysterical had roused him. What was Yuri up to this time? Kidnapping a couple of tourists off a boat? The man was nothing but trouble. With his vehicle bouncing over the rutted roadway, Burdock had to pay attention to the trees on either side, so he almost missed the motorcycle zooming toward him at breakneck speed. He braked and pulled the Jeep to the side just in time to avoid a head-on collision with the BMW motorbike roaring past him.

It passed with such speed that Burdock didn't get a good look, although the rider, a big man, looked familiar. A young woman sat in the back with her arms wrapped around him and her long, dark hair fluttering in the wind. Burdock didn't recognize her either.

Bewildered, he came to a full stop and got out to look after them. Just as it dawned on him that the man was Dr. Jonathan Curtis, he heard the growl of another motorcycle being revved up. This time Burdock instantly recognized the rider fishtailing toward him—Yuri Zoroff.

Burdock stepped to the middle of the road and waved Yuri to stop, but the Russian did not slow down. As the Colonel jumped aside, the bike just missed him and Yuri whizzed by without the slightest acknowledgment, raising a cloud of sand and shell dust.

Furious, Burdock hopped back in his Jeep and, cursing, rode to the Hunt Club, where he wheeled into the parking lot with brakes screeching. The camp looked like a shit storm had blown through. The front of the brick building gaped wide open. Cement blocks and other debris were strewn about and the busted metal door lay on the ground. His men, some of them bleeding and limping, were sitting and standing around. They looked toward him with guilty, hangdog expressions.

The Colonel barked orders for them to gather around and report. It took him little time to conclude that Yuri had instigated the mother of all clusterfucks. For the next few minutes, he went on a tirade about observing protocol and the chain of command, laced with a string of profanities directed at the Russian renegade. He did not look forward to his conversation with the Wizard.

* * *

Car and truck horns blared as Jonathan weaved in and out of traffic on Highway 19, swerving around lines of slower-moving vehicles, passing through stoplights and intersections at blazing speed. The BMW, capable of speeds over 200 miles per hour, flew down the highway as if blasted from a rocket launcher.

Through the cacophony of honking, Isha was the first to hear the high-pitched whine of another sports bike approaching from behind. She glanced back and saw Yuri snaking through traffic and gaining on them. Her eyes widened and she punched Jonathan on the shoulder.

Jonathan glimpsed Yuri pursuing them on his motorcycle in the rear-view mirror and winced. His mind raced. This was sooner than expected. He immediately slowed down and swerved to the right, behind a large dump truck and out of Yuri's line of sight. But hearing the roar of the Kawasaki Ninja, he realized it would be only a few seconds before Yuri would be on them again. His machine had the same horsepower as his BMW but, with only one rider, it was more maneuverable and faster.

Then he and Isha got lucky. The car in front of Yuri veered to the side and clipped the rear fender of another vehicle. Braking hard, both cars swerved and stopped in a V-formation. Panicked drivers behind them tried and failed to stop in time. With tires squealing, the cars slammed into one another, jamming up the highway.

Yuri avoided the blockade by jumping the median strip. He deftly avoided the oncoming traffic and returned to the south-bound lane.

In his rear-view mirror, Jonathan saw Yuri on the Ninja flying through the air over the concrete divider. As he landed, he drew his gun and continued his pursuit. Jonathan nosed his motorcycle in front of another truck and slowed. As he moved to the truck's right, the BMW's chrome muffler scraped the raised, paved shoulder, sparks flying.

As the truck driver became aware of a motorcycle speeding up from behind and the rider aiming a pistol in his direction, he ducked his head and slowed. Jonathan adjusted his speed accordingly, causing Yuri to pass them by and move several lengths ahead.

Losing track of Jonathan and Isha, Yuri sped up. When he realized they were behind him, he wheeled around and headed back against the oncoming traffic. Noticing Jonathan and Isha helplessly pinned between the slow-moving truck and the curb, he took several shots across the truck's hood as he passed. The bullets missed their mark and ricocheted off the thick metal hood like firecrackers.

Yuri executed a one-eighty, causing bumper-to-bumper crashes of several cars, as he resumed his pursuit.

With no place to turn, Jonathan reached into the elastic waistband of his swim trunks and handed Isha Liam's 9mm Glock. No stranger to handguns, Isha aimed through the chaos but could not get a clear shot.

Just when it seemed like nothing could get any worse, a full-size Cadillac sedan stopped without warning on the highway directly ahead. The truck they used for cover locked its brakes but could not avoid a rear-end collision. The impact caused its front wheels to crush the Cadillac's trunk and shatter glass as it rolled over onto its side.

Jonathan had to stop dead on the highway, next to the high chain link fence that separated it from a side road. The snarl of wreckage ahead closed off that escape route. With no place to hide, they were sitting ducks. Seeing Isha training her pistol on him, Yuri pulled to a stop out of firing range. His face distorting in a jackal's grin, he popped a full magazine into his semi-automatic handgun.

His mind racing, Jonathan searched for a way out. He was about to despair when he heard the familiar voice whispering deep within, "*Trust yourself.*"

He blinked his eyes shut for a moment. When he opened them, he experienced a new reality and an intense awareness of his surroundings. Patterns and connections appeared along the highway as if projected on a 3-D Laser computer screen. Taking account of angular velocities, momentum, and vector forces at lightning speed, his brain identified several escape routes. The closest option was a pedestrian skywalk ahead, with concrete stairs rising steeply between the fence to a 20-foot-high pedestrian bridge. A narrow crosswalk traversed the entire width of the four-lane highway. Four school-aged youngsters leaned over the safety rail, high above the road, gawking at the chaotic wreckage below.

It seemed like an impossible climb and Jonathan was about to reject it when he heard the by-now-familiar voice from deep within, "*Trust yourself.*"

"Hold on, Baby," Jonathan called out to Isha. He turned the throttle full out, clicked his foot gear into first, and popped the clutch. Instantly, the engine responded, and the BMW surged forward, laying rubber across the pavement.

Isha gasped as she realized Jonathan was headed straight for a steep, concrete staircase to the crosswalk. She threw her gun to the side, put her arms around Jonathan's waist, and locked her hands.

Jonathan leaned back and the BMW's front wheels rose as it impacted the concrete steps. The rear tires grabbed and the bike bucked up the steps. It slowed near the top of the staircase but miraculously made it to the crosswalk. With his eyes focused across the narrow traverse, Jonathan bent forward and pushed the engine to its limits.

The BMW roared past the panicked school kids squeezed up against the railing.

Reaching over 100 miles per hour, Jonathan and Isha launched from the concrete ramp. They sailed over the chain-link highway fence and landed on the other side. Bouncing in the air several times, they held on before gaining traction on the hard, sandy ground and disappearing into a cloud of dust.

Hell-bent not to be outdone, Yuri holstered his pistol, lowered his head, and followed Jonathan's path. When he reached the top of the stairs, he clicked into second gear and started across the crosswalk. But he hadn't reckoned with the kids, who had climbed down from the railing and jumped right back up. Distracted, Yuri lost valuable seconds. Realizing that his Kawasaki didn't have the speed to make the jump, he laid the bike down on the crosswalk. His body quickly skidded to a stop, but his Ninja slid from between his legs, along the concrete surface, and shot off the edge as if fired from a cannon.

Smashing on the concrete slab below, the Kawasaki's frame burst apart, scattering parts like shrapnel from a hand grenade. Sparks flew in all directions as metal parts ground against cement.

Scraped and bruised, with chunks of skin flayed from his body, Yuri lay still for a few seconds and moaned. Then he crawled along the crosswalk and hobbled down the stairs. At the bottom. he pulled out his cell phone and headed for the safety of the nearby woods.

* * *

Colonel Burdock sat erect at the desk in his office at the compound, listening attentively on his SAT phone when Liam knocked on the door and entered the room. Burdock held up his hand, silencing him, and mouthed, "Not now!" He continued to listen and said, "Yes, Wizard. I understand. I appreciate your confidence in me. You can count on me."

After returning the handset to its cradle, he wheeled around and barked, "What?!"

"It's Yuri," said Liam. "He's lost the doctor and his girlfriend. Along the way, he caused enough car crashes on Route 19 to bring out the National Guard. He said he needed to be exfiltrated. His bike is totaled."

Burdock buried his head in his hands. Then he looked up and said, "That man is a one-man wrecking crew. He got Stryker killed and now this."

Liam looked at his feet, then ventured, "Sir?"

Burdock shook himself and made a decision. "Have him picked up," he said. "You lead a reconnaissance team and track down the doctor. He's not likely to contact the police, and he's not used to being on the run. There aren't many places he can hide."

Liam saluted and left.

The Colonel sighed and went to the cupboard to pour himself a glass of bourbon. The call with the Wizard had gone surprisingly well. He had heard the frustration in the old man's voice but received no recriminations or dressing down. The Wizard even acknowledged that Yuri might have gone over the edge. Although he still hadn't revealed why Dr. Curtis was so important to him, the quiet urgency in his voice had spoken volumes.

Burdock took a big swallow and felt the heat of the whiskey settle in his stomach.

Wiping the sweat from his forehead, he recalled the Wizard's final words, hissed like a snake, soft and sibilant, but cold as steel, "This is your last chance, Colonel. Do not fail me in this mission." Burdock knew that he would not get another opportunity.

Chapter 28

BLOOD MOON RISING

The calm sea of the Gulf of Mexico cast a spell of serenity. High above, jet trails floated lazily across the bright blue Florida sky. The late afternoon sun streamed across the deck of *The Shiny Penny*, Jimmy Pappas' 37-foot Contender, as she coursed through the offshore waters.

Onboard, the scene was anything but tranquil. Although in no immediate danger, Jonathan and Isha were still running scared. Like soldiers who found themselves alive after the adrenalin rush of battle had faded, they were more shaken now than before. At the harbor in Tarpon Springs, Jonathan had made a quick decision to commandeer his best friend's boat—he knew that Jimmy kept an extra key under the fire extinguisher—so they could make their escape. A sleek, white-and-yellow fishing vessel with high-powered outboard motors, she could exceed 70 miles an hour at full throttle.

Isha turned her face to the salty wind and squeezed the last droplets of blood from her jet-black hair. Now that her wounds had finally stopped bleeding, the bruises and contusions were more obvious. Her head throbbed as if a bell hammer banged inside it. She glanced toward Jonathan hoping to find some assurance. But his face looked stern and rigid, and she was more worried for him than herself. He had not spoken a word since they left Tarpon Springs.

"Hey, say something," she called out, trying to reach him above the roar of the engines.

But he remained rock silent, staring into the distance as if on autopilot.

Isha moved close and shook his arm, demanding his attention.

When he turned to her, his haunted look made her shiver. "What's wrong, Baby? Won't you please talk to me?" she pleaded.

Jonathan released a deep sigh and slowly shook his head. "I killed a man with my own hands…and left his body floating over the reef," he said in a low voice. "I could have harmed others. For all I know, I may have gotten Mosthan killed. And now, I've put your life in danger." He tightened his hand on the steering wheel. "I'm a doctor, dedicated to saving lives. I swore an oath to do no harm. It's not as if I'm a stranger to death. I've witnessed men and women die before, but never at my own hands. If this is the fate seeking me out, I want no part of it."

"They gave you no choice, Jonathan. It was either us or them."

Jonathan grimaced and continued to shake his head. "Less than two weeks ago, I had a medical practice with my future secure. Now I'm a murderer and on the run from assassins. I have no idea what's to become of us. And I don't even know why this is happening."

"You found out about your parents, that you are Romani. You met me, and we've fallen in love." Isha narrowed her eyes. "Are you saying, you regret that too?"

Startled, Jonathan looked at her. "Of course not. You and your family are the best thing that has ever happened to me!" His face sagged again. "But, Baby, what have we gotten ourselves into?"

Isha put her arm around his waist and held him tight. "Whatever it is, we'll figure it out together."

Jonathan hugged her and held her tightly against his body. As a familiar water tower came into view, he pulled back on the throttle, grabbed the steering wheel with both hands, and steadied his legs against the rolling sea. Then he made a sharp left turn to negotiate the shallow sandy shoals into Boca Grande Marina.

* * *

In the confines of his cave, the Wizard clicked off the satellite phone to disconnect his call with Colonel Burdock, and turned his chair to face a computer screen. He was churning inside, like a volcano ready to explode, but he forced himself to remain as calm as he had been during the phone call. At least Curtis was on the run which made him vulnerable, cut off from his friends and the Gypsy scum that protected him. It would have been better to kidnap and whisk him away quietly, but Yuri's underestimating the doctor had led to one debacle after another. He should have anticipated this course of events and never trusted a volatile operative whose ego would get in the way.

The Wizard slammed his feeble, bird-like hand on the laminated surface of the desk. There was a sharp crack but the jolt of pain he expected to shoot up his arm never came. Perhaps the treatment devised by his physicians was working. He was feeling better, younger, and more vigorous. He gritted his teeth and glanced at the medical team. They looked startled and worried. Good. Keep them on their toes. It was time to get to work.

He turned to an acne-faced technician and ordered, "I need you to locate a fishing boat off the west coast of Florida. The U.S. Coast Guard uses satellites to track possible drug traffickers and illegal immigration vessels."

As the young man sprang into action to hack into the government site, the Wizard commanded another of his minions, "Pull up any credit card activity on Dr. Jonathan Curtis, starting an hour ago and moving forward."

He smiled grimly as the man saluted and dashed to another computer terminal. Perhaps he did not need the doctor's supergenes after all, but he wanted them just in case. Always better to have two birds in the hand.

* * *

While their boat was being fueled, Jonathan and Isha found a private area at the end of a pier and made phone calls, using *The Shiny Penny's* Satphone. Jimmy Pappas still did not answer, so Jonathan left another message, that he and Isha had escaped, were safe for the present, and had borrowed his Contender to make a get-a-way.

Isha called her father and put him on speakerphone.

Big Jack picked up after only one ring. "Thank God!" he sputtered. "I've been worried sick. When I didn't hear from you, I sent Carl down to the dock, and he discovered your boat all shot to hell. Then, Tatyana told me things that made it worse. She is convinced that Jonathan's presence has roused a worldwide, evil organization that killed Motshan, his mother and father, and nearly murdered his grandfather..."

There were scuffling sounds in the background before Jack continued, "Jonathan, Tatyana is here right now, anxious to speak with you."

When Tatyana came on, she sounded relieved. "It's good to hear your voice, Jonathan. I'm glad you and Isha are safe." She continued urgently, "I know you have questions, and we need to talk, but not now. You must go into hiding right away. You are being hunted by evil of the worst kind. There isn't much time!"

"What should we do?" Jonathan asked.

"Follow Big Jack's guidance."

When Jack came back on, his instructions were short and to the point. "Head south to the bridge at Islamorada. We have friends there. I'll call you with the details shortly."

* * *

Inside the soundproof inner office in the Hunt Club, Colonel Burdock, Yuri, and Liam gathered around a Satphone and a computer screen. The Wizard's technician read off the coordinates and heading of Jonathan's vessel and gave them directions for hacking the U.S. Coast Guard site.

"Hmm, 400 gallons of fuel, food, and foul weather gear." Burdock muttered, "The doctor is making a run for the Caribbean or Mexico tonight."

He outlined a plan: wait until nightfall, then chase them down, disable the boat's outboard motors with an automatic weapon, sedate the passengers with a tranquilizer gun, capture the doctor, kill the Gypsy girl, and blow up any evidence. "Get the chopper ready, Liam," he ordered.

Liam saluted and left the office.

Like the Wizard, Burdock did his best to contain his rage. When Yuri returned to the compound, banged up from chasing after Dr. Curtis and his girlfriend, the Colonel had refrained from criticizing him in front of the men for going rogue. Nor had he complained to the Wizard during their call. That would come later. Now was not the time to deal with this arrogant inept egomaniac. All energy had to be directed toward capturing the doctor once and for all.

Burdock glanced at Yuri. Blood seeped through the bandage on his thigh where the Gypsy girl had plunged a knife, and the patches on his arm didn't cover all the raw-scoured areas. Yuri had refused any other dressing, preferring to bear the pain. Burdock admired his stoicism, but that's as far as it went. It was time to neutralize him, even if it did not sit well with the Russian. He took a deep breath and said, "I will lead this mission myself. With the plane's automated technology, we'll only need two men for the job. I've asked Liam to join me. You will stay here, relay us their position, and use the time to recuperate."

As expected, Yuri flared up immediately. "That is not acceptable. I'm perfectly fine. I can take care of this."

"That's not been the case so far!" Burdock shot back, trying to thwart any further argument. "I don't want to lose any more of my men."

Yuri stared daggers at him. "I have to finish this. It's become personal."

"That is exactly the problem, Yuri. It's clouding your judgment!" Burdock held up his hand to forestall any further argument. "Wizard's orders."

He held Yuri's fierce glare, hoping his gambit would work.

It did. Yuri, visibly deflated, walked to the corner of the room and flung himself into a chair, sulking.

When Liam returned and reported that the Black Hawk chopper was ready to go, Burdock was watching Jonathan's boat leave Boca Grande Marina and head south along the coastline.

* * *

Pushing *The Shiny Penny* at top speed, Jonathan covered the 160-mile distance to Islamorada in a little over two hours. He felt better having Big Jack on his side. The Gypsy King's resources continued to surprise him.

But then he received a text message from Liam: "They're tracking you!" and all his anxiety returned. Isha tried to reassure him, but when he brought the motorboat to a stop and pulled it up by the sea wall under the Islamorada bridge, he felt like his stomach was in a ringer again.

Two large, dark-skinned men, dressed in Bohemian Island style, signaled him to throw them the bow and stern lines.

When Jonathan climbed ashore, the larger of the two said, "I'm Django, and this is my friend Manfri. Big Jack called us and told us what to do." He pointed to a pile of equipment and provisions—extra gasoline canisters, food supplies, large rectagular storage lockcers, weapons, and a black gizmo that looked like a special GPS unit.

Tight-lipped, Jonathan nodded. They were stocking up for a long journey.

When Isha came out of the cabin and waved to them, Manfri grinned and, glancing at Jonathan, said, "Don't worry. We won't let any harm come to the daughter of our king." He jumped onto the boat deck to receive the gear from Django.

Surprised, Jonathan couldn't help but blush. He started to help Django and Manfri load the equipment into *The Shiny Penny*. It felt good to do physical work, and a sense of calm settled over him. Whatever he had to face, he didn't have to do it alone.

* * *

Colonel Burdock breathed more easily when the boat that the Coast Guard had been following was picked up again heading southwest toward the Yucatan Peninsula. With nautical charts in hand and a satchel of weapons slung over their shoulders, he and Liam walked down a remote jungle path to a large brush pile. Liam stood aside while Burdock reached inside the knothole of an oak tree and pushed a button. The two sides of the brush pile separated, revealing an airplane hangar and, on the helipad in front of it, a Sikorsky US-60 Black Hawk helicopter.

They climbed in the cockpit, and the Colonel went through the instrument check while Liam stored their gear in the rear cabin. Then, the two buckled up for take-off. But, as Burdock was about to press the ignition, his cell phone chimed. It was Yuri calling from the office. "The Wizard has some last-minute orders," he said.

Burdock looked annoyed, but exited the chopper,. Leaving his cell phone in the holder by the controls, he jogged back to his office. As he arrived, Yuri handed him the phone. But when he put the receiver to his ear, it was dead. Puzzled, he saw Yuri leave, slamming the steel door shut behind him. By the time the Colonel got there, it was bolted from the outside. When he tried the phone, he realized Yuri had removed the battery. All he could do was beat on the door with his fists and yell profanities.

* * *

When Yuri opened the door to the helicopter and hopped into the pilot seat, Liam was surprised to see him. Donning the headset, Yuri grinned and said, "Change of plans. The Wizard wants me to take charge of this mission while the Colonel figures out how to 'escort' the good doctor out of the country."

He started the engines, and the Black Hawk rose into the sky. The coastline of Crystal River came into view, and Yuri headed toward open water. He checked his instruments a second time before switching to jet mode.

Soon, they reached cruising speed. "Running smooth as silk," he said as he settled back into his seat. He was comfortable flying military helicopters in the dark and under all kinds of weather conditions. The Black Hawk was perfect for the job—Yuri had calculated the speed and course necessary to catch up to Dr. Curtis before he made landfall. Burdock had confided in him that this aircraft, stolen from MacDill Air Force Base in Tampa, had made many such trips to and from the Caribbean on drug runs. The money was used to finance the insurgent operation at the Hunt Club.

Yuri's grin became a predatory grimace. This time he would not give the doctor a chance.

* * *

As Jonathan and Isha were speeding south, the sky was aflame with streaks of red and orange from the rays of the setting sun. On the eastern horizon, a full moon had risen, dazzling and bright. Slowly, a blanket of clouds inching across the sky eclipsed its lower portion. With the last sunlight passing through the Earth's atmosphere, the heavens were transformed into a glistening tapestry of dark blood red.

Watching awe-struck, Isha whispered, "Blood moon rising."

Jonathan, at the helm, noticed her shiver. He put his arm around her waist and drew her close. "Better get windbreakers for both of us. It will be chilly and there's a lot of open water between us and our destination."

"I'm not cold, just worried," she said. "This isn't just Mother Nature showing off. Blood moon rising is a fabled phenomenon known to every Gypsy since the Middle Ages, signaling the opening of the realm between Earth and the spirit world of evil beings."

A week earlier, Jonathan would have scoffed at her explanation as more "Gypsy voodoo." But since then, he had experienced too many inexplicable occurrences not to take her seriously. Also, Liam's warning that they were being traced echoed in his mind. Who were these forces that could command the high-tech equipment only governments had at their disposal? He hoped Big Jack's hideaway was far enough off the grid to keep them safe.

The blood moon was beautiful but didn't last long. Soon, the clouds obscured it completely, surrounding them with darkness, and the starlight that peeked through cast a surreal luster on the water's surface. Far on the eastern horizon, heat lightning rumbled, as jagged bolts threaded their way through dark, puffy clouds, signaling an approaching storm—weather conditions that Jonathan welcomed as it would give them better cover. Exhaustion washed over him. It had been a long day. He caught himself nodding off. "Not to worry," he consoled himself, "The coordinates programmed into the GPS will keep the boat on track."

In the darkness, he heard whispers that swelled into a chorus of voices, emanations of evil coming at him from all sides. They mocked him with laughter, teasing banter, and sinister sneers: "You, a Savior? You are not man enough. A beacon of light against the darkness? We are an army of many, a host of multitudes, and you are but one single, puny mortal."

"Jonathan, Jonathan!"

As Isha shook him awake, it took a moment to realize where he was. He had fallen asleep after all.

"Listen!" There was panic in her voice.

Hearing the sound of an aircraft approaching from behind, he was instantly alert.

* * *

The Sikorsky helicopter swept low over the water, hidden from U.S. Air Defense detection. Following the GPS coordinates, its high-tech surveillance system picked up the signal of a small Contender heading southwest at 60 miles an hour before any visual sighting.

Liam's voice crackled on the intercom headphones, "We have 'em!"

Yuri answered, "Good going, Lieutenant. I'll turn off the turbos and try to slow the boat down. You get ready to disable the outboards."

Liam was anxious with anticipation. He worried that Jonathan had not received his warning text. Reviewing his options, all included getting aboard the Contender and taking Yuri out.

Shortly after beginning the flight, Yuri had shown his true colors. As they veered away from the coastline and headed into the Gulf of Mexico, Liam tried calling the compound and Yuri told him to stop.

Liam looked at him suspiciously and asked, "Why? With all due respect, Sir, what's going on?"

Yuri had turned to him with a cold sneer. "I started this mission, and I'm going to finish it. Like I said, a change of plans." He'd drawn his 9mm Sig Sauer from its holster, aimed it at Liam's head, and continued, "You have a problem with that order, Lieutenant? We can do this the easy way or the hard way. You decide."

Liam held up his hands, palms out, and calibrated his response. "No need to get your balls into an uproar, Captain. You don't have to point that gun at me. You're holding the stick, and I can't fly this chopper. I take you out, I go down anyway." He'd shrugged his shoulders. "A change of plans, like you said."

He'd breathed a silent sigh of relief when Yuri nodded with a perverse smile and holstered his weapon. It wasn't going to be easy neutralizing the Russian. Liam hoped he could count on Jonathan and Isha to help.

With the Contender's running lights in sight, Yuri slowed for a low-level fly-by. He wanted to see his prey squirm, realizing they had run out of luck.

* * *

When Jonathan heard the aircraft, he looked back, but it was too dark to see clearly. Next to him, Isha stiffened. "Face forward, and whatever you do, don't look at them directly," he said. "They may be using a facial recognition program."

There was a roar overhead, and Jonathan reached out to steady himself against the steering wheel. Isha gasped. Out of the corner of his eye, Jonathan caught a glimpse of a dark object flying past, like a prowling shadow silhouetted against the night sky.

It was gone in an instant, the sound of its engines fading. Isha sighed in relief, only to gasp as the aircraft turned 180 degrees and circled back toward them.

"Brace yourself," Jonathan said, reaching for the gun in the boat's center console.

* * *

As Yuri cruised past, he glanced at the Contender. From under the T-top, backlit by fluorescent running lights, he glimpsed Jonathan and Isha. Neither looked toward the helicopter. They both faced stubbornly forward as he shot by.

Yuri made a 180-degree turn and directed his spotlight onto the boat, fully expecting to see it slowing down. But the Contender kept going full throttle without a change in course or speed. Through the windshield, he could see the outlines of Jonathan and Isha standing at the helm and looking determined, seemingly unnerved. They had pulled the hoods of their storm gear over their heads.

"Fuck," Yuri muttered, frustrated. He had never encountered anyone, combat-trained or otherwise, with such resolve.

He made a tight turn and directed the Black Hawk's spotlight to the outboard motors. "We're coming too close to Mexican waters, Liam," he yelled. "No more time to screw around. I'll bring the chopper in close. You'll have to take your shot at sixty miles an hour."

Liam returned an affirmative nod. He tightened the gunner's harness around his waist, firmed up the grip on his M-16, and leaned out over the open door to aim at the motors. Dangling at the end of his harness, he squeezed the trigger but missed.

The helicopter bucked as Yuri turned the jet turbos back on and engaged the guidance system to the Delilah missiles. He glared wild-eyed down at the Contender, his face twisted with psychotic rage. "Let's see if this won't shake you up—assholes," he yelled out.

Liam fought hard to scramble back into the cockpit, but the immense torque of the turbos hurtled him full force into the passenger's seat, knocking the breath out of him. Immediately, he rebounded out the doorway again. Saved from falling overboard by the gunner's harness, he struggled back inside into his seat and buckled his seat belt, before all hell broke loose.

With a contemptuous sneer, Yuri bellowed, "Blow the head off that cockroach!" and pushed a red button.

Instantly, a Delilah missile launched from its pod in a flaming streak and raced toward *The Shiny Penny*.

Yuri banked the Black Hawk hard left, avoiding the blast, and took a last glance at the two passengers. Backlit by fluorescent running lights in the moist Caribbean air, they radiated a mysterious glow, as if surrounded by a halo.

There was a blinding flash.

With almost 400 gallons of fuel on board, the flaming inferno of *The Shiny Penny* lit up the night sky for miles around Fragments of burning metal and fiberglass rained down, only to be swallowed by the dark waters.

The Black Hawk was flung into a chaotic spiral. Yuri fought to keep it above the waves. Regaining control, he commenced a zigzag search across the wreckage, as close as he could get to the flames. An initial floodlight inspection revealed little remaining of *The Shiny Penny*. Not surprising, considering the catastrophic force of a Delilah missile. Only a couple of torn, blood-soaked life jackets, partial deck cushions, and shattered debris floated on the water's surface among patches of burning fuel. From his position above, Yuri could see sharks gathering below the wreckage.

Liam tried hard not to avert his eyes from the scene. He was angry with himself over his failure to help Jonathan and Isha. "The Wizard's going to have a lot to say about taking out his prized guinea pig," he said sarcastically.

Yuri's eyes shifted. "Fuck 'em all," he said with a cynical grin. "I've been in hot water before. Worse than this, and I'm still kicking!" A lump grew in Liam's chest as he looked down at the carnage, patches of burning fuel floating on the water's surface.

"Time to look for some verification," Yuri said.

Liam nodded. When serving in the military, he had followed similar orders on occasions involving the assassinations of top-level terrorist leaders, where the recovery of an identifiable body part, fingerprint, personal item, or DNA was essential to the completion of the mission. He scampered into the cabin, donned a skin-tight, aqua-blue Neptune shark suit, strapped on a scuba tank, and pulled on his swim fins. As Yuri kept the chopper close to the water surface, Liam exited and moved far out on the skids. Then he gave a "ready" nod.

"Positive I.D.," Yuri yelled above the engine noise before signaling to go ahead with a thumb-up.

Liam tightened his upper lip. Pulling the mask over his face, he leaned forward and leaped into the flaming waters twenty feet below. He landed with a splash and submerged quickly.

Yuri followed Liam's movement underwater by keeping his eyes glued to the searchlight. Even under the burning dark sea, the powerful Aqualite-S20 shone through to the surface.

When he lost Liam's light in the darkness, he waited. Time passed, enough for him to get worried. Then Liam surfaced on the far side of the flames and signaled the completion of his mission by flashing the light in Yuri's direction and waving an arm in the air.

Yuri guided the Black Hawk to where Liam floated. When it hovered over his position, water spraying in all directions, Yuri lowered a steel cable connected to a remote-controlled winch. Within minutes, Liam was back in the cabin, dripping wet, carrying what looked like a small suitcase. He removed his scuba tank, unzipped the wetsuit, and leaned over the passenger seat.

"Couldn't find much, mainly debris," he reported. "But then I spotted this first aid kit floating—they're pretty much indestructible. And guess what, this was snagged in one of the locks. He pulled something from his red, steel-meshed catch bag.

"Squinting in the dim cabin lights, Yuri asked, "What is it?"

Liam thrust his hand toward him.

Yuri flicked on his flood light, aimed it directly at the object, and chuckled. Curling his lip, he said, "Yeah, that'll do just fine!"

He waited until Liam was seated back in the cockpit and buckled up. Then he lifted the nose of the Black Hawk and headed North to Crystal River.

As they got underway, Liam examined his find more closely. In the dim red instrument lights of the cockpit and the soft white overheads, the silver-gray charm bracelet glinted the way it had shimmered against Isha's dark Romani skin.

Chapter 29

TORTOLA

Approaching Lettsome International Airport of Beef Island, Jimmy Pappas looked out the window of the InterCarribean Airways' island hopper at the nimbus clouds below. For the umpteenth time, he wondered if he was on a wild goose chase. It had been over a year since Jonathan and Isha had perished in an explosion in the Gulf of Mexico. The blast had turned Jimmy's boat into firewood, but that had been the least of his concerns. What had devastated him was the loss of his best friend.

Initially, Jimmy lived in a surreal daze. He listened to the messages Jonathan left on his phone repeatedly, trying to make sense of what had happened. The most cryptic was about leaving the golden booch for him in his lockbox at the marina. Jimmy retrieved it, but it offered no clues.

He also pursued the FBI and the Coast Guard for information. But while the motorcycle chase and shoot-out on U.S. 41 had made national television news—too many drivers had been affected to hush it up—the rest was quietly swept under the rug. Everyone was solicitous but none of the authorities shared credible intel. When the Coast Guard rendered its verdict, "Piracy at sea by unknown assailants," Jimmy angrily shook his head.

He tried to contact the Gypsies, hoping that they might be able to provide some answers. But when he drove to the campground, they had pulled up their Vardos and vanished.

A few weeks later, he attended the service in Jonathan's hometown of Lafollette, Tennessee. The closed casket funeral was more of a formality as few remains of Jonathan's and Isha's clothes were found, just enough for DNA identification. It was an intimate gathering, with Aunt Agnes and only a few of Jonathan's friends from his hometown and Tarpon Springs. Jimmy and five other buddies of Jonathan from Duke and medical school stood in as pallbearers.

For a while, Jimmy kept searching for clues regarding Jonathan's death and pestered various government officials. But his obsessive efforts bore no fruit and began to affect his legal practice and family life. Finally, his wife Tina tried to talk sense into him, and Jimmy agreed with her. Reluctantly, he gave up his quest hunt and resumed a normal existence.

But on the anniversary of his friend's death, he took out the bottle of 18-year-old Scotch from the desk in his office. He had given it to Jonathan on their last sailing trip, the day he had met Isha and Katarina. Jonathan returned it and asked Jimmy to save it for him until he got married. Jimmy managed to down a little less than half the Macallan before he passed out. His secretary found him the next morning, sprawled out over the files on his desk. She corked the bottle, put it back in the drawer, and woke Jimmy with a cup of black coffee and an aspirin for his headache.

After that unceremonious wake, Jimmy decided to put the whole thing behind him and forget all about it.

Until last week.

While he was looking over some real estate documents, his receptionist buzzed his intercom, sounding panicky. "Mr. Pappas, come here quickly," she sputtered. "There's a big, rough-looking man here demanding to speak to you. He says he has news of Dr. Curtis." She lowered her voice to a whisper, "Please come quick...I think he's carrying a gun in his back pocket!"

By then Jimmy was halfway to the door, his heart hammering in his chest. In the lobby, he encountered a large, dark-complexioned man whose casual stance exuded thinly disguised menace.

"I'm Pinky," he said. "My boss says for you to bring your bottle of Macallan's and deliver the gold brooch to Tortola in the British Virgin Islands." He held out a sealed envelope to Jimmy, who took it as if in a haze. "This is an incentive to do it quickly—the sooner, the better. And, don't talk to no-one 'bout this."

As he turned to leave, Jimmy called out to him, "What about Jonathan…" But the big man moved with surprising agility and exited the door without answering. By the time Jimmy had followed him outside, he was gone.

Walking past the stricken receptionist, Jimmy went to his office and ripped open the envelope. Inside was a packet of hundred-dollar bills—5,000 dollars' worth by his quick count. As he took out the half-empty whiskey bottle, questions flooded his mind. How did Pinky know about Jonathan's favorite Scotch? And the golden brooch his friend had left with him? Were these odd clues enough to go on a fool's errand? Wouldn't it be better to forget all about it?

As he held the bottle in his hand, curiosity got the better of him and he realized he had no choice. He called the head of the law firm and told him he needed to take off a few days because of a family emergency. Then he had his secretary book him a flight from Tampa to Puerto Rico with a connection to Tortola. The conversation with Tina that evening led to a heated argument, and their goodbyes in the morning were strained. Jimmy hoped the trip would be worth the friction it caused in his family.

The airplane dipping its wings to line up for landing on Beef Island, on the eastern side of Tortola, shook Jimmy out of his reverie. He felt his shoulders tense. What awaited him upon arrival? Would there be anyone to tell him what to do next?

The landing was bouncy, but clearing customs went smoothly. Jimmy pocketed his passport and headed to the airport exit doors carrying his briefcase and pulling a small roller bag behind him.

Outside, under the porte cochère, the humid heat assaulted him and he broke out into a sweat. He looked down the line of taxis parked at the curb, and to his surprise, a short, dark-featured fellow stood next to a rusted Checker Cab holding a makeshift, cardboard sign with "Jimmy Pappas" in squiggly letters.

As Jimmy walked toward him and waved, he perked up and smiled.

"I'm Ricco. Ricco Valentino," he said. "I've been told to pick you up and take you over to the other side of the island. Hop in." He took the suitcase—Jimmy held firmly onto his briefcase— tossed it in the rear seat, opened the front passenger door, and, with a slight bow, gestured for his passenger to get in.

Jimmy hesitated, but the old-fashioned, gentleman-like gesture reassured him, and he climbed inside, settling the briefcase on his lap. He looked for a seatbelt, but there was none.

For the first few minutes of the ride, neither man spoke. A warm wind whistled about the cab through the open windows. Jimmy welcomed the breeze and took this time to observe his cab driver. The man was handsome, although his round, naked belly hung out between a white sleeveless muscle shirt and beltless khakis, and his thinning black hair was pulled back tightly into a ponytail. Heavy gold chains hung around his neck, and he wore an oversized Bulgari gold watch on his wrist.

"He looks like a gangster," Jimmy thought and felt afraid. After they crossed the Queen Elizabeth Bridge to eastern Tortola and took the exit for Parham Town, he almost panicked.

"Got to get gas," Ricco said nonchalantly.

Jimmy relaxed when they pulled up to a station with two rusty pumps. But after Ricco had filled up, he drove around town, taking unexpected turns, and going around the block several times. He repeatedly glanced in his rearview mirror, putting Jimmy further on edge.

"Just making sure no one's following us," Ricco said, grinning.

Jimmy felt like he was in the middle of a spy caper.

Satisfied they were in the clear, Ricco drove back to Ridge Road, the main thoroughfare traversing the island. As they climbed the hills, heading west, he kept up a steady patter, pointing out various tourist attractions and historical details about the island. If he meant to relax his passenger, it didn't work. His driving had the opposite effect. The Checker cab was wider than most of the small island cars, and Ricco sped up the narrow two-lane road with one hand on the wheel, the other casually resting in the open window, swerving around tight turns and barely missing oncoming traffic.

Jimmy kept having to brace himself, his body gyrating back and forth. As they neared the top, the cab hurled through misty, low-hanging clouds and around several boulders to break into a clear panorama of blue seas and bright, lush green forests below. Ricco slowed down to let Jimmy enjoy the view.

"It's breathtaking," Jimmy acknowledged.

For the next few miles, they drove at a more leisurely pace. At some point, they reached an overlook with a view of a curving beach. A small armada of sail and motorboats were moored in the placid lagoon.

"That's Cane Garden Bay—our destination," Ricco said, pointing proudly to the inlet.

As they headed down toward the water, the cab's brakes, designed for city driving, squealed, making further conversation impossible.

Finally, the road leveled out, running along the curving bay.

A row of coconut palms interspersed with sea grape bushes rose oceanside. On the other side, colorful trees—firecracker-red Royal Poinsettias, purple Jacarandas, and yellow Golden Trumpets—lined the sidewalk. The rich scents of island flowers mingled in the air.

Just as Jimmy managed to clear his head after the terrifying descent, Ricco pulled off the road. The cab passed under a carved wooden sign—MYETT's GRILL—suspended from two poles over the driveway. Nailed to one of the posts was a piece of cardboard announcing "Closed for Private Party."

The taxi jolted to a halt in the white, shell-covered parking lot and Ricco announced, "We're here."

Jimmy blinked and said, "I'm not crashing a private party, Ricco. Maybe you should just let me out at the end of the road and —"

"Don't worry 'bout it." Ricco interrupted, "It's a great place to grab a drink and watch the sunset. Besides, I know the owner and his wife well." He gave his passenger a mischievous grin.

Shaking his head, Jimmy got out of the cab. Myett's Grill was a typical, one-story, adobe building. The exterior walls were painted a glossy turquoise. Strings of red chili pepper lights dangled from the branches of the trees that surrounded the house.

Ricco motioned with his hand. "I'll go ahead. You follow me," he said. "And don't forget the Macallan."

Jimmy almost choked in surprise. But he couldn't question Ricco because the cabdriver swiftly disappeared around the corner of the building. Jimmy retrieved the bottle of Scotch from his briefcase—he had bought a new one before making the trip—got out of the car and walked around to the beach side, passing an old motorbike leaning against the wall.

Turning the corner, he met an outdoor seating area in picture postcard surroundings. Less than a hundred feet away, the surf broke gently over sugar-white sand. A mild tropical breeze rustled the palm fronds overhead as squawking parrots darted from one tree branch to another. Near the water's edge, a steel drum band was tuning up for the evening. Ricco was nowhere in sight.

Attached to the rear of the bistro was a thatched roof gazebo with a simple bamboo counter and rattan bar stools. A young, pretty island woman with glowing, bronze skin and chubby cherub cheeks wiped the countertop. Her ample breasts nearly burst from a red flowered tank top. Her jet-black hair was long and styled into a tight rope weave, interlaced with caramel extensions and tipped by multicolored beads.

Becoming aware that Jimmy stared at her cleavage, the barmaid glanced up, then quickly looked away. Caught, Jimmy looked away as well.

A man sat at the bar with his broad back to him. His dark skin glistened in the sunlight that filtered through the palm fronds. He had long, dangling dreadlocks, sun-bleached to a ruddy orange at the ends. There was no one else. Apparently, the party hadn't started yet.

The Rastafarian turned to face Jimmy and said in a deep, angry voice, "Private party, Mon. Didn't yuh read da sign outside?"

He was a large man with sinewy muscular arms bulging from his sleeveless, white hemp vest. His beard was scraggly, thick, and long. His eyes burned into Jimmy's.

Wanting no trouble, Jimmy said, "The cab driver who brought me told me to come back here."

The young barmaid covered up a snicker with her hand.

"Cabby?" The Rastafarian questioned with a furrowed brow.

"Yeah, a short Italian fellow named Ricco. Says he knows the owner and his wife real well."

"What yuh be jokin' 'bout? Mi—dat's 'd owner," the man pointed to himself. "Mi, Kayo and dis be mi woman." He called over his shoulder. "Kymara, ya know dis mon, Ricco?"

Kymara shrugged with a pout of her lips. Then she moved from behind the bar, her eyes curious. Her pregnant belly was nearly bursting over her blue jean short shorts.

"Dis Ricco fella, drove yuh here, Mon?" Kayo chuckled. "You left your tings in his car?" A wide grin spread beneath his mustache.

"Holy Shit! My passport," Jimmy shouted. He patted his front pocket. "My wallet, too." He got up, overturning his chair. Flushing red, he scrambled to pick it up and set it by the table.

"Best be goin' wit' yuh, now," Kayo advised. When Jimmy grabbed the Macallan, he ordered, "Leave da bottle on da table, Mon."

Jimmy stuttered, "But, my..."

"Don't 'cha be stealin' mi tings. Dat a fi mi bottle, yuh be takin'."

Jimmy clutched the neck of the bottle tightly. "It's mine."

Kayo advanced threateningly and took a commanding stance.

All at once, things which Jimmy had noticed earlier, gelled in his mind. The pregnant Kymara wore a silver charm bracelet on her left wrist. The motorcycle parked to the side of the building was a Harley Davidson Fat Boy.

His legs buckled and he gasped. "Jonathan."

Jonathan broke into a big grin and tears welled in his eyes. Dropping the deep Jamaican Creole, Kayo said, "Jimmy, ya big fuck," and opened his arms wide.

They hugged each other in a tight embrace. Kymara joined them, completing the picture of a perfect reunion.

An angry look crossed Jimmy's face. He pushed back and uttered a sound somewhere between a cough and a sob, "Jonathan, I –"

Jonathan interrupted. "My name is Kayo Thompson now, Jimmy. I'm a doctor from Kingston, Jamaica, and this is my wife, Kymara. Jonathan and Isha died more than a year ago at sea."

A surge of fury rippled through Jimmy's body. His fingers curled into a fist. "How could you –"

Kayo raised up his hands in defense, "Hold on, Jimmy. I can see you're angry, but I can explain."

Jimmy glared at him. "Jonathan, Kayo—whatever! What the hell's going on? How could you pull such a stunt? I love you like a brother. I missed you, worried myself sick trying to figure out what happened to you, and grieved for you. I went to your funeral and now you stand before me like this. Tell me one good reason not to knock the crap out of you."

Kayo nodded, his eyes softening, "Look, Jimmy, I understand, but it's for Kymara's safety and mine, as well as your own. As for tricking you, we needed to test how well our disguises work. You're the first person from my former life to see me like this."

Kymara tentatively put her hand out to touch Jimmy's arm. "Please believe us. We didn't do it on a whim. We didn't have a choice."

Jimmy slowly unclenched his fists. "OK. The last time we spoke you had just broken up with Priscilla, and we were going to to meet at J-Wags. Then nothing but your crazy messages on my phone. What the hell happened?"

Over the next two hours, the two men sat alone at a table by the water's edge. Kayo told Jimmy about the search for his identity with Mosthan and his genetics professor, Mosthan's murder, Isha's abduction, his fight with Yuri at the compound, the shootout on Highway 41, and Liam, the FBI undercover agent who helped them escape.

Throughout the recitation, Jimmy remained skeptical. The idea of Jonathan being the target of an international terrorist organization seemed ludicrous.

"For reasons I don't fully understand, they wanted me for genetic experiments and Isha dead for simply knowing too much," Jonathan explained. "We had to escape. But where to? By ourselves, we had no chance to survive."

"Fortunately, Isha's father, Big Jack, came up with a scheme to fake our deaths and move us to a remote, safe location," he continued. "Two of Jack's friends in Islamorada rigged your Contender with a remote detonator and put various clues on board – clothes, blood smears for DNA matching on floating cushions, and passports in waterproof pouches. Then they sent it into the Gulf on autopilot with mannequins and dynamite timed to explode in

Mexican waters. We didn't expect Yuri to go haywire and shoot at the boat, but that worked out even better to cover our tracks. When *The Shiny Penny* met her fate, Isha and I were on another boat headed to Jack's private island in Turks and Cacaos." It was Isha's bracelet that convinced everyone we were dead. Liam turned it over to the authorities after Yuri went into hiding."

"For a short while, we lived on Jack's private island and considered staying there. But, when Jack learned the extent of the terrorist organization, we felt it safer to change our identities and move to Jamaica. Soon after arriving, we were married in a private ceremony on a mountaintop above Montego Bay. After living in Jamaica for a few months to cover our tracks, we settled in Tortola. Kymara is due to deliver a baby boy in the middle of next month. Surprisingly, we love our new life in the Islands."

Jimmy glanced around at the placid lagoon and said, tinged with sarcasm, "So, what's not to like?"

Kayo frowned, "We've both missed our family and friends dearly. It's been hard on us too, Jimmy." He raised his eyebrows. "To safeguard the FBI's ongoing covert operation, the details of Liam's findings were never reported to the public. That's why they stonewalled you." He sat back in his chair, "So, here we are."

Jimmy leaned back, too. "It's quite a story—a lot to take in."

Kayo nodded in understanding.

When they returned to the bistro, Ricco and another woman had joined Kymara at a table under the gazebo. Ricco pointed to the roller luggage and briefcase standing by the bar and shrugged as if he'd had nothing to do with them. Kymara formally introduced him as her father, Big Jack.

"No hard feelings?" Jack asked.

Jimmy decided to let it go. "You're quite the hustler, aren't you?" he said.

Jack grinned from ear to ear. "You have no idea."

The woman looked to be in her late fifties and wore a blousy, tie-dyed dress. "We've never met, but I've heard so much about you from Kayo," she said with a deep Slovakian accent. "My name is Tatyana."

Jimmy looked puzzled, unsure what to make of her.

"I am a shaman, a connection to the spirit world, a conduit to Kayo's ancestors," Tatyana explained." When Jimmy continued to look at her dubiously, she fixed her eyes on him and said, "Your wife will come around, especially if you bring her a necklace of conch pearls as a present."

"How do you know..." Jimmy asked, surprised.

Tatyana gave him a warm smile. "A Gypsy fortune teller's trick," she said and burst into cackling laughter. The others joined in.

Not sure they were not laughing at his expense, Jimmy frowned.

"Tatyana is my spiritual guide," Kayo assured him. "But she is also a dear friend and part of my new family. I am Romani after all. Without her help, Kymara and I would not be here today."

Jimmy nodded slowly but felt ill at ease.

As the night wore on, they shared the Macallan and enjoyed a savory feast of jerked chicken, rice, and tasty, exotic vegetables. After several slugs of the single-malt Scotch, Jimmy gradually loosened up.

At some point, he turned to Kayo and asked, "So what's the big deal with the brooch? Why didn't you just have Pinky pick it up and bring it here?"

Instantly, a pregnant silence filled the air. Kayo broke it, asking casually, "Would you have entrusted it to him?"

Jimmy chuckled. "Well, no."

Kayo grasped him by the shoulder. "Plus, I wanted to see you, you dope!"

Tatyana spoke up. "You have a role to play in all this, Jimmy. I'm not certain what it is, but I have a strong sense, and when I do, I'm never wrong."

Jimmy felt an anxious shudder travel down his spine. On impulse, he got up and went to his suitcase. He retrieved the golden brooch of Vasilissa and placed it formally in the middle of the table.

Tatyana gasped, her eyes becoming as large as saucers. "This little piece of jewelry, you and Jonathan picked up from Aunt Agnes, ties Kayo to his ancestral line," she said solemnly. "Beginning with the first Zor-Tracheban." She stopped when she saw Jimmy's forehead wrinkle with a look of concern.

Kymara glanced around the table at the other worried faces, picked up the brooch, and said, "Let's not get into it now. There'll be plenty of time for that later."

Catching her look, Kayo agreed. "Yes, let's celebrate our reunion. I'm happy you're all here and glad Kymara and I live in Tortola, safely removed from all that mess."

Jimmy raised his glass of Scotch and announced, "Here's to one of the worst and best days of my life."

Cheers and laughter echoed about the palm trees and continued late into the night.

Chapter 30

APOTHEOSIS

Jonathan awoke before dawn and sat bolt upright. This was the day. He had planned to get up before the others, but the empty bed beside him and the smell of coffee from the kitchen told him otherwise.

Jimmy had returned home a week earlier. Jonathan had enjoyed reconnecting with his best friend, but the visit also reminded him of his former life, enough to realize he missed it and that his disguise was merely a cover. He was not like an actor who relished playing a new role. Even after a year as Kayo, he felt like an imposter. Without meaning to, Jimmy had brought his deep-seated ambivalence to the surface.

And today he was to undergo a ritual with Vasilissa's brooch, another one of Tatyana's schemes to further entrap him in a fate not of his own making.

He pulled on his clothes and entered the kitchen. A chorus of "Good morning, Kayo," greeted him. They were waiting for him— Isha, Tatyana, and Big Jack.

Isha handed him a cup of coffee and looked at him with glistening eyes and he forgot all about his self-doubts. One look at her, her belly swollen with their baby, gave him the reassurance and purpose he needed. She and his child deserved his protection. Like the sacrifices his parents had made for him, he would do anything to keep them safe.

As he took a sip, Tatyana looked at him intently as if she understood his internal struggle, but there was no sympathy in her eyes.

"It is time, Luka," she said.

He nearly choked on his coffee. That was the name his mother had mentioned to Nell and Aunt Agnes—his given name, before Jonathan, before Kayo. Flustered, he said, "How do you know that name? And why do you call me that?"

The others looked at them, intrigued.

Tatyana ignored his question. "Are you ready?" she asked.

"I am," he said. "But I don't know if Isha should climb a mountain path in her condition.,"

"I'll be fine," she said.

Big Jack rubbed his hands together and said, "All right then." He handed Jonathan a shoulder bag with water bottles. He added, "Do us proud."

It was still dark outside when they all walked to the entrance of the jungle path that led into the hills a few hundred feet inland from the house. Big Jack waved after them as they embarked on their trek.

The morning air was pleasantly cool as they walked along the upward-sloping jungle trail in the pre-dawn twilight. Mockingbirds and turtledoves called out to warn their fellow birds of intruders.

Tatyana took the lead briskly, showing no signs of her age. Jonathan brought up the rear, watching Isha in front of him for signs of fatigue. Concentrating on her allowed him to keep from obsessing about what lay ahead. Tatyana had described the ritual he was about to undergo in general terms but he had no idea what to expect.

Soon they were covered in sweat and stopped several times to rest, surrounded by breadfruit trees, palms, cacao bushes, and wild orchids.

As daylight began to break over the horizon, bathing the ridgeline of the mountains in a mystical, golden glow, they arrived at a small, secluded clearing. Jonathan looked around. Lush vegetation crowded in on three sides, while an opening provided a view of the bay waters, its swells reflecting the dawn's light.

Isha braced her hips with her hands, then bent over. Breathing deeply, she said, "It is beautiful up here." She clasped Jonathna's hands in her own. "You'll do fine," she assured him.

He braced himself as Tatyana walked to the center of the clearing and took the golden brooch from a pocket in her dress. She squatted and laid it down on a large, flat stone. Then she gave Jonathan a penetrating stare and asked, "Are you ready?"

Jonathan nodded but felt anything but.

Turning the brooch over, Tatyana pointed to four slight indentations. "You must touch these points with your fingers while holding the lock of hair in your other hand," she said. Then she stepped back next to Isha.

As Jonathan reached out, he felt a shudder and drew back. He took a deep breath, removed the wispy, blond strands from the locket compartment. Holding them up in the air in one hand, he grasped the brooch with the other and lined up his fingers, feeling for the indentations on the back.

Then he took a deep breath, swallowed, and closed his hand.

Immediately, a surge of energy coiled around his arm and spread throughout his body like the flames of a fire exposed to oxygen. A powerful force flowed between the brooch and the lock of hair, like an electric current when a circuit closed.

Jonathan gasped, wide-eyed, as a kaleidoscope of images and people streamed through him: His mother and father smiling at him; Mosthan peering over his glasses; the warrior Lucian devastated by the massacre of his people and the night before going into battle; a blond-haired woman he knew was Vasilissa, and a long line of ancestors—olive-skinned men and women he didn't recognize but seemed familiar—beckoning to him.

A deafening thunderclap broke through the air. His body trembled like leaves on an oak tree. It felt like a volcanic eruption imploding as the images flowed together and became part of him. Their energies fed him, expanded his sense of being in the world, and enlarged his reach and understanding of the universe.

Luka-Jonathan-Kayo knew viscerally what he had resisted and denied for too long, knew it in his bones, his heart, and soul: He was the Zor-Tracheban, ready to take on the mantle of his calling.

Epilogue

WIZARDRY

Across the Atlantic Ocean, deep in the bowels of his lair in the Austrian Alps, the Wizard finished another round of treatment. As his medical assistants unhooked him from the tangle of intravenous tubes and monitoring devices, he dismissed his advisory staff. "Anyone who doesn't have to be here, get out!" he rasped.

The people who updated him on global events filed past him, many sneaking a second look before exiting the room. Over the past year, the Wizard had visibly de-aged before their disbelieving eyes. The hair on his head was thickening and returning to its original, yellow-blond color. The wrinkles of his skin were smoothing. He stood taller and could move about more freely.

Years of genetic research and billions of dollars had finally paid off. The Wizard's team had opened a major crack into the Holy Grail of genomics—the reversal of human aging!

His desire to live into the twenty-second century and beyond was becoming a reality. His dream of creating a new breed of superior human, who would be physically and mentally stronger than ordinary people, was within reach.

His advisors had just briefed him about the threat of global warming and overpopulation. They had questioned the benefit of technology to enable people to live more than 100 years beyond their normal age, when eight billion people living on the planet raised the specter of doing irreparable environmental damage.

The Wizard smiled grimly at their weak-minded, anxiety-driven projections. They didn't understand that a worldwide crisis would play into his hands. Frightened people were more malleable. Faced with impending doom, they'd happily agree to any way out. And he had just the plan—eugenics and extermination, first articulated as the Final Solution to the Jewish problem during the Third Reich. It was the inferior, non-Aryan races reproducing like cockroaches that were the problem. All they did was breed, consume, pollute, and defecate, adding little value to the world. They would have to be eliminated.

However, watching his staff shuffle from his room, he was not so sanguine about his prospects. The whole operation to capture Dr. Curtis had been a disaster. After blowing up Jonathan's boat with him and his girlfriend in it, Yuri had vanished; no doubt to avoid retribution for his impulsiveness and incompetence. The Wizard shook his head angrily. Had he known how crazy the Russian was, he would never have entrusted him with such an important task.

Burdock, to his surprise, had weathered the investigative fallout by cleaning up any trace of Jonathan's presence at his compound in Florida and shielding his cadre from the U.S. government agents that descended on the area like a swarm of locusts. A sneer curled at the edge of the Wizard's thin, drawn lips. It was a trivial victory in the face of the terrible loss of Jonathan Curtis and his stem cells.

When he'd first received the news of the debacle, the Wizard had refused to believe that Jonathan was dead. He had his teams go over satellite feeds of the area, hack into FBI and Coast Guard computers to retrieve the accident reports, and monitor the agencies with his infiltrated minions. But none of his efforts panned out. If any intel existed about the doctor's survival, his best computer geeks couldn't find it.

Still, the Wizard found it hard to accept that Jonathan was gone. It was a feeling he had, an occasional prickling at the base of his neck, a whisper in his rejuvenated bones. Although he no longer needed the doctor's superior genes to achieve longevity, he sensed that he would cross paths with him at some point in the future.

In the meantime, while he felt better than he had in many years, he didn't know how far he could trust his medical staff or how long his rejuvenation would last. He kept looking for ways to ensure the survival of his worldwide organization when he was gone. Several candidates showed some potential, but would they be ready in time?

To Be Continued

ACKNOWLEDGMENTS

What is true about *Gypsy Blood Moon*?

While I have changed the spelling of her name, Princess Vasilisa Maria of Moldavia is a historical figure. Her bloodline included Stephan the Great, a legendary warlord of Moldavia. The Medieval history of her husband, Vlad II Dracul, Wallachia's voivode (military governor and ruler) is well documented. He was a member of the Order of the Dragon, bestowed by the Catholic Pope to defenders of Christianity against the threat of Muslim armies. Princess Vasilisa lived in Vlad Dracul's castle for many years until she died in 1462.

Vlad's son Vlad III, also known as Vlad the Impaler, was crowned voivode after his father's violent death and also received the Order of the Dragon. Although considered a brutal despot by much of the world – like Ivan the Terrible, he earned his name because of the harrowing punishments he inflicted on his enemies – he was a hero in Romania. Much of Christian Europe supported his ruthless defense of Wallachia from Muslim attacks. Even Pope Pius II expressed admiration for his notoriously vicious military feats. He was killed in a battle against the forces of the Ottoman Empire in Bulgaria in 1479, purportedly by his half-brother. His severed head was paraded to Constantinople and placed in the hands of his enemy, Sultan Mehmed II.

The Order of the Dragon exists to this day.

Many of the stories and characters in ER of Tarpon Springs General Hospital (now, Ellis Memorial Hospital) are based on people I met there as a young GP/ER physician. I have combined aspects of various patients and staff and changed their names and appearances.

I also treated several Romani patients. Many of the Gypsie characters, including Tatyana, Big Jack, and his bodyguards, are based on Roma I encountered at the ER. In the process, I became fascinated with their culture. Much of the lore and legends in the book are based on my research. Any errors in representing their vibrant culture are my own.

There was a military "club" near Tarpon Springs, run by a group of retired servicemen who recruited high school boys. They taught them hand-to-hand fighting techniques, instructed them in the use of combat weaponry, and inculcated white supremacy beliefs. The son of a friend got involved for a while before the local police caught him when he participated in racial bullying at the local high school.

One of my favorite places to visit in Tarpon Springs was the Sponge Docks, where old Florida Greek culture thrived. I loved to stroll down Dodecanese Street, savoring the smells of Greek restaurants, markets, and bakeries. I based Jonathan's culinary excursion with Isha on Paul's, my favorite Greek restaurant, and Zorba's, my go-to spot to enjoy Greek music and Ouzo.

The Southern Poverty Law Center Group was founded in 1971 by two civil rights lawyers in Montgomery, Alabama. A powerful, non-profit civil rights organization, it is known for fighting legal cases against white supremacists and hate groups, as well as promoting tolerance education programs. As I was doing research for *Gypsy Blood Moon*, I called the center. The person who answered the phone was quite helpful and connected me with an officer, much like Detective Dave Lindsay in the book. I told him that I was writing a novel about white supremacist organizations, and he was generous with his time, answering all my questions.

The anti-aging techniques used by the Wizard's doctors are real.

As a board-certified, expert in regenerative medicine and, since the 1990s, a member of the American Academy of Anti-Aging Medicine (A4M), a world congress of doctors, scientists, and specialists, I am familiar with cutting-edge research for anti-aging therapies. The goal of the A4M is to slow down, stop, and/or reverse the aging process.

Over the last century, the average human lifespan increased from 45 to 80 years. This increase has been achieved through better access to nutrition and medical care, and by eliminating the more common infectious diseases. However, because of our greater longevity, we now face a rise in the degenerative diseases of aging: arthritis, cardiovascular diseases, Alzheimer's, cancer, etc. So, the goal now is to increase our lifespan and eliminate these diseases.

Researchers, scientists, and doctors around the world believe this is possible. But it will take a new way of thinking. I frequently read peer-reviewed articles about breakthroughs in reversing cellular aging. These findings are leading the way for new treatment options for age-related diseases with the goal of whole-body regeneration.

This is what the Wizard's doctors and technical staff are trying to do for him. They are pushing the edge of what is available in Anti-Aging Medicine today. They have at their fingertips everything available in the modern world to keep him alive and functioning: stem cells, joint replacement, intravenous therapies, growth hormones, polypeptides, SIR 2 gene stabilizers, SIRT 1-activating compounds, AMPK activating agents, mTOR inhibitors, STAC and NAD boosters, mitochondrial enhancers, etc.

The most ethically controversial method of anti-aging used by the Wizard is called heterochronic parabiosis. It involves conjoining the blood supply between two animals of different ages: in this case, the Wizard and the children in the nursery. The Wizard's cells and tissues are rejuvenated, and the young children undergo accelerated aging. While this method, to my knowledge, has never been used outside experimental labs with animals, I have employed it on the Wizard who has no scruples harming others in the pursuit of immortality.

What is not real is the breakthrough discovery mentioned in the book's epilogue. After years of genetic research, the Wizard's doctors have, through gene modification, discovered a therapy that reverses his physiological age. This is still the stuff of fantasy and fiction, although, who knows, by the time the sequel for this book appears, we may be close to attaining success.

This being my first novel, I soon realized that finishing it was a longer process than I had anticipated. Fortunately, I had a lot of help, and I wholeheartedly thank everyone who supported me along the way, specifically:

My wife **Sherry Watts**, for always supporting me and believing in my dreams. Also, thanks for the many grammar checks.

My editor and publisher, **Chris Angermann** of Bardolf & Company for streamlining the manuscript from its early stages to its present form and overseeing all aspects of getting it into print.

My cover illustrator, **Autumn Kerr** of Cultivate Place Creative, for providing a wonderful visual for the book.

My sister-in-law, **Connie Cruthirds** who is also a writer, for her encouragement.

Tamy Califano for hanging in there with me when this book was just a jumbled draft of scribbled handwriting on legal paper.

Margaret Pennington, **Bob Morris**, **Ferrell Marrs**, **Dr. Larry Baucom**, and **Walton Beacham** for reading early drafts and giving me their honest opinions.

Steve Tatone for suggesting ideas for what might be needed to bring this book to the screen.

Harvey Schonwald and **Susan Angermann** for reading the finished manuscript and offering feedback, copyediting, and encouragement.

Sarasota restaurants and eateries—**The Banyon Tree Grill, Rendez Vous**, **Origin Pizza**, **The Clever Cup**, and **Brine Grill**—for allowing me the space to get away by myself and dream and write.

Steven King for his wonderful book *On Writing*, which provides excellent advice to new novelists and gave me insight and inspiration to write *Gypsy Blood Moon*.

Dr. Stephen McConnell for helping me explore publishing options.

Southern Poverty Law Center for its willingness to give me a clearer understanding of organized hate groups.

Doctors **Ronald Klatz** and **Robert Goldman**, founders of the A4M, for inspiring me on my journey in Anti-Aging, Functional, and Integrative Medicine, and learning a new and better way to deliver medical care.

And finally, to you, my **Readers**, for allowing *Gypsy Blood Moon* to come to life someplace other than just my imagination.

A board-certified OB/GYN and expert in Regenerative Medicine, **Dan Watts, MD,** is an authority on the healing powers and potential dangers of genetic and stem cell research. He currently lives in Sarasota, Florida with his wife Sherry. They have two grown children and four beautiful grandchildren. Dr. Watts has coauthored two medical books and published many articles in magazines and journals. He enjoys playing with his grandchildren, hiking, camping, off-road biking, and good scotch after a long day's work. This is his first novel.